E.G. FOLEY

THE GRYPHON CHRONICLES, BOOK SEVEN:

THE DRAGON LORD

Books by E.G. Foley

The Gryphon Chronicles
The Lost Heir (The Gryphon Chronicles, Book One)
Jake & The Giant (The Gryphon Chronicles, Book Two)
The Dark Portal (The Gryphon Chronicles, Book Three)
The Gingerbread Wars (A Gryphon Chronicles Christmas)
Rise of Allies (The Gryphon Chronicles, Book Four)
Secrets of the Deep (The Gryphon Chronicles, Book Five)
The Black Fortress (The Gryphon Chronicles, Book Six)
The Dragon Lord (The Gryphon Chronicles, Book Seven)

50 States of Fear Series:
The Haunted Plantation (50 States of Fear: Alabama)
Bringing Home Bigfoot (50 States of Fear: Arkansas)
Leader of the Pack (50 States of Fear: Colorado)
The Dork and the Deathray (50 States of Fear: Alaska)

Credits & Copyright

Come not between the dragon and his wrath.

~Shakespeare

TABLE OF CONTENTS

PART III

PART IV

Author Note

Next Up!

About the Authors

PART I

PROLOGUE
The Usurper

Nathan, Lord Wyvern, rematerialized from a transport spell in the moonlit field outside the Black Fortress. As soon as his body had fully recomposed from the puff of black smoke he had briefly become, he turned around to take in the sight of his handiwork in the distance and smiled.

A quarter mile behind him, across the rolling hills of the English countryside, the Order's stronghold of Merlin Hall was a glorious smoking ruin.

Beneath the black October sky, towering flames consumed the great garden maze that hid their sacred yew trees at its center.

He laughed with satisfaction, then slid his wand into its leather sheath at his side. His plan to seize the throne from the sorcerer-king, old Zolond, was moving right along.

His attack on Merlin Hall had been brash, but this was a deed that would impress even the most skeptical tribes of the dark world.

It hadn't come easy. His body hurt all over from the six elvish arrows that had pierced him during the battle. Unnaturally tall and powerful of stature, he supposed he offered a large target.

He had pulled the arrows out and healed himself quickly, of course, but the flesh was tender, and though triumph pumped in his veins, he was still rather dazed from that last wand blast to the head at point-blank range.

Not that he'd dare to show weakness in front of his ruthless followers.

Nearby, his top three co-conspirators also arrived in human-sized billows of black smoke. Well, human-*ish*.

Beside him, the beautiful but deadly Red Queen, Viola Sangray, was still gnashing her fangs after the fight, distraught over the loss of some of her finest vampire courtiers.

General Archeron Raige, warrior extraordinaire, had been in his element throughout the battle, of course. Herculean of build and every bit as mad as the berserkers in his lineage, the soldier's camouflage face paint was smeared with sweat and his uniform was torn, but he had enjoyed himself immensely.

He laughed as soon as he reappeared and slapped Wyvern roughly on the back. "Smells like victory to me!"

Raige was in a rare good mood, clearly proud of having killed the Order's head wizard, elderly Balinor, with an expertly thrown magical knife in the back.

Wyvern had put the general in command of their gray-skinned, half-troll mercenary troops, some two hundred Noxu barbarians.

Raige had already sent the tusked fighters jogging back to the Black Fortress with their plunder from the palace, along with Wyvern's fearsome pet manticore.

Last, but by no means least, came Wyvern's future bride, Lady Fionnula Coralbroom, a mighty siren-enchantress from the depths of the Irish Sea. Her long, dark hair was a mess and her frilly gown was grass-stained from her wand duel against old Ramona Bradford, but they had won.

That was all that mattered.

And yet, as the first into battle and the last to leave, the four leaders of the night's violent festivities opted to land a short distance from the warlocks' moving castle, requiring a moment to regroup privately before going back inside to resume command of their minions.

Admittedly, the last few minutes of the fight had not been particularly...flattering.

Especially for Wyvern.

In fact, for a split second there near the end, he had believed he'd been truly captured by the enemy.

Immobilized in a dreaded Entangler's Net, Wyvern had experienced a rare moment of dread. He had a horror of being strapped down like that, unable to move a muscle.

Perhaps Fionnula realized that, for the moment she returned to solid form again, she turned to him and scanned his face with concern. "Are you all right?"

Wyvern bristled at her impertinence. "Of course I am. What kind of a question is that?"

She blinked at his cold monotone. "Nathan, you passed out from that wand strike—"

"No, I didn't," he warned.

Fionnula scoffed, failing to take the hint. "Yes, you did! You were out cold when I found—"

"I am the half-blood son of a demon, madam, lest you forget!" He lifted his chin, willing away the dizziness. "Nephilim warlocks do not *faint*."

"Ah." The sea-witch pursed her rosy lips and looked away. "Whatever you say, dear."

He harrumphed. "I was distracted, anyway. If *you* had done as I asked and killed Waldrick Everton when he escaped, then that insufferable Peter Quince could not have taken me by surprise."

"Oh, I'm sorry," Fionnula said sweetly, "I was busy dealing with *the Elder witch!* A far more dangerous opponent—"

"Quit squabbling, you two, please!" the Red Queen wrenched out. Wyvern growled, shook off his mild concussion, and ignored his feisty fiancée. "I lost four of my beloved followers tonight! By Dracul's chalice, I will destroy Janos! How dare he betray the Breed? Turn against his own maker?"

Wyvern kept his comments to himself, in no mood for typical vampire drama. His pride was still smarting over the fact that Fionnula was actually telling the truth: she had indeed saved him from the Entangler's Net that had nearly ruined his night.

Just one more reason to despise Sir Peter Quince.

It was he, the Order's second-in-command, who had thrown the charmed rope netting over Wyvern's head, capturing him for those few humiliating moments.

But he'd pay.

One day, Wyvern vowed, when all of this was over, when he had successfully overthrown Zolond and ruled the realms of evil as the new Dark Master, he would hunt down that irritatingly cheerful scholar-wizard and send his soul to the netherworld.

By the time Wyvern was done with him, there'd be nothing left of Peter Quince but his irksome tortoiseshell glasses.

For now, though, Wyvern had bigger problems to contend with. The huge chalk-outline man who'd been etched into the green hillside a thousand years ago—Aelfric, the so-called Long Man, ancient guardian of Merlin Hall—had rallied himself to fight back again.

Of course, there was little the Long Man could do. Wyvern had deliberately landed the massive Black Fortress atop his grassy chest, pinning him to the ground, where he belonged.

Aelfric struggled against its weight, kicking his legs as best he could and banging on the walls of the Black Fortress with chalky fists as big as stagecoaches, shaking the whole building.

The reverberating booms made Wyvern's head ring.

And if that wasn't enough, there was also the highly annoying fact that his chosen son and heir, Jake Everton, had managed to slip through his fingers *again*.

The lad had put on a most impressive show during the battle, flying up on his pet Gryphon to disable the guns of the Dark Druids' airship. *The Dream Wraith* had been raining down cannonballs on the palace until bold young Jakey-boy put a stop to all that.

Although the plucky thirteen-year-old had cut short the Dark Druids' air assault before escaping through a Lightrider portal with his friends, Wyvern couldn't help feeling proud of his future son.

Clearly, there was a reason the Horned One had picked him for the next Black Prince.

Once they got the wild lad under control, (which sometimes seemed a very big *if*), the young Lord Griffon would become Wyvern's heir apparent after he'd successfully seized the throne.

All in due time.

For now, it seemed that, along with Aelfric's temper tantrum, something was going on inside the Black Fortress.

Oh, what now? Wyvern thought with a frown.

Few things scared the Noxu, but the big, burly half-trolls suddenly began pouring out through the open drawbridge amid frightened grunts and panicked shouts.

Even Thanatos, his manticore, ran out of the Fortress, his lion mane bristling, his scorpion tail whipping about as it always did when something had disturbed the beast.

Then Wyvern heard roars from inside the great hall, and his eyes widened with startled recognition.

Oh, no...

"What was that?" Fionnula cried, turning to him in alarm.

Wyvern didn't answer, but narrowed his eyes and stared toward the castle. "They had better not hurt him," he muttered. Then he glanced at her. "I suggest you all stay back."

"Nathan?" Fionnula and the vampire queen exchanged a puzzled glance, but took his advice and hung back uncertainly.

Raige flashed a grin, however, catching on. "I'm going with you."

Wyvern immediately turned and pointed a warning finger in Raige's face. "You are not to draw your weapon on my dragon. Is that clear?"

"Aw." Disappointment flickered in the hulking warrior's eyes. "Well, if he gets out of the Fortress, can I help you hunt him? I haven't been on a dragon hunt in ages. Such sport! They make the most challenging..."

Raige's voice faded at Wyvern's icy stare.

"I am going to pretend I didn't hear that," the dragon lord replied, then stalked on, hurrying to save his pride and joy from harm at the hands of those Noxu brutes.

Ever since he was a boy, all dragons obeyed him, but some were special, and his Ruffed Orange Darter had grown close to his half-demon heart.

As Wyvern strode toward the open drawbridge, the manticore ran to meet him. He uttered a comforting word to the creature and commanded him to calm down.

He did not bother giving the Noxu mercenaries the same reassurance as they continued flowing out. They were now joined by the uniformed bridge crew who ran the castle-ship, along with the dozen white-coated scientists in charge of the absent Dark Master's experiments.

"Commander!" One of the navigational officers rushed toward him. Wyvern believed his name was Lantz. "Oh, thank the Horned One you're here, sir!"

Wyvern glowered at him. "You abandoned your post?"

"I-I-I'm sorry, sir! It's j-just that y-your dragon got out! The chalk man's raging upset him, and he chewed his way out of his stall! He couldn't escape through the carriage entrance in the back, s-so he came up through the stairwell, a-and now h-h-he's running amuck. He's eating people in there, sir!"

"Humph. Anyone important?"

"Er—no," the officer said abruptly. "Just a couple of Noxu so far, but—"

"And his fire collar. It's still on?"

"Y-yes, sir." The frightened navigator bobbed his head.

"Good. Then there's nothing to worry about. Pull yourself together and get back to your post!"

"Yes, sir," Lantz mumbled with a crestfallen look.

Raige arched a brow at the man, then followed as Wyvern marched into the vast great hall, where his naughty dragon had caused, well, a bit of a bloodbath, to be honest.

The Orange Ruffed Darter was still scarfing down bits of Noxu, gleefully tossing them up in the air and swallowing chunks of flesh amid growls of pleasure.

Wyvern winced to note the upper half of a gray half-troll corpse dangling from the round iron chandelier.

Tazaroc must've flung it there in his vicious delight at breaking free from his quarters.

Raige's smile faded at the bloody prospect of the escaped dragon, Wyvern noted with amusement.

Taz might seem rather docile and well-mannered when he was hitched to the flying chariot, but that was only because Wyvern kept him under expert control.

The fact was, left to his own devices, the Darter was wilder and more vicious than most people realized.

The general's hand came to rest uneasily atop the horse pistol by his side. "I thought you said he was tame."

"*Trained,* not *tamed,* Raige. No dragon is ever truly tamed. It's part of their charm. Don't worry. As long as that collar stays on and holds the ruff down, he can't breathe fire. It's only then I'd consider him really dangerous."

With that, Wyvern gave Raige an arrogant wink, then sauntered across the black granite flagstones toward his escaped pet.

Tazaroc crouched over his midnight snack, his brownish-orange wings spread out across the floor, ready to swat anyone away who tried to come between him and his catch.

Not that dead Noxu could taste very good. Wyvern grimaced and shook his head. The beast was even gulping down the half-troll's sweaty leather armor.

That had better not make him sick. Wyvern was a conscientious owner, but in the middle of his coup against Zolond, he did not have time right now for a visit with the draco-veterinarian.

Every hour counted, for no one could say how long the old, frail, complacent Dark Master would remain away on his much-needed holiday in the Balefire Mountains.

Unfortunately, Wyvern feared his pampered carriage dragon would be vomiting up Noxu limbs by dawn.

As a pedigreed Darter, Tazaroc was used to only the best dragon feed on the market—the very blend of dried meats and herbs recommended by the breeder. He preferred meals that tried to escape, of course, but that was not always practical.

Ah, but every now and then, Wyvern knew, a well-kept dragon had to taste fresh blood.

Make his own kill.

They loved the chase.

Wyvern would play with him sometimes in the castle's big, empty loading bay—throwing the dragon's giant version of dog toys and letting him fetch—but it was hardly the same.

He pressed his lips together with a rare flicker of guilt. *This is my fault.*

He'd been so preoccupied lately pursuing his ambitions to seize the Black Crown that it had been months since he'd taken Taz out for a proper hunt.

Darters in general were known to be a bit high-strung. They required exercise.

They were one of the smaller dragon species, standing about nine feet tall with all fours on the ground, with a long neck, golden eyes, and a twenty-foot wingspan. In every other respect, however, the Darters were the thoroughbred racehorses of the dragon world: fast and sleek, with elegant lines and high intelligence.

Temperamental...and expensive.

Rather like Fionnula, Wyvern mused as he walked cautiously toward his pet.

In any case, Wyvern had had Tazaroc trained for both saddle and harness, but even *he* took care to keep that fire collar *on.*

A physical restraint infused with magical inhibitors, the collar prevented the headstrong dragon from roasting his caretakers. Tazaroc would never harm *him,* of course. The clever beast knew his master, understood Wyvern's commands and always obeyed.

He didn't always like it, though.

"Tazaroc," Wyvern said firmly as he approached. "No!"

The Darter was gnawing on a Noxu leg, his tail twitching happily.

"You heard me."

The tail went still. The dragon looked askance at him, wickedness in his amber eye with its vertical-slitted, coal-black pupil.

"Bad dragon!" Wyvern said. "Put that down."

Of course, the words sounded different to the others cowering around the edges of the great hall, for they left Wyvern's lips in a language no one had ever taught him.

He'd been able to speak it for as long as he could remember, and the dragon knew perfectly well what he was saying.

Tazaroc hissed at the order.

"Don't give me that! It's time to go back to your stall. Tazaroc: Come!"

The Darter gave an unhappy growl, turning his sinuous body to face Wyvern, then pushed up with his front legs to a seated position, the brawny Noxu leg still clamped between his jaws.

It was all that was left of the half-troll.

Wyvern pointed at the floor, never mind that the creature towered over him. "Drop it. *Now*. Bad dragon! What did you do?"

Tazaroc shook his head no and hissed past his prize while his eyes burned with resentment.

"Put. That. *Down*."

Still, the dragon resisted. His tail thrashed, his hiss turned to a snarl, and the edges of the fancy flap of skin adorning his neck fluttered dangerously.

"Don't make me punish you." Wyvern reached for his wand.

At once, Tazaroc dropped the leg with a disappointed look, loosening his deadly jaws and letting it flump down onto the flagstones.

"You're a bad dragon! This is unacceptable behavior!"

Tazaroc hung his head and grumbled unhappily, small puffs of steam rising from his nostrils.

"Humph!" Wyvern scolded. "You're happy now, but you'll be sick by morning. Well, come along, then." Well aware that the dragon could easily take his arm off if he chose, Wyvern reached up boldly and grasped his dangerous pet by one of his short, back-facing horns.

Pulling the dragon's head lower, he began leading him away. "Come on, back to your stall. There's a good boy. Somebody clean up this mess!" he added over his shoulder to some onlookers as he headed for the wide stairwell down the corridor. "And let the ladies know it's safe to come in now."

"Commander?" Lantz, the navigational officer from outside, ventured after Wyvern, keeping a wary distance from Tazaroc. "Do you, er, have any orders for our next coordinates yet, sir?"

Wyvern paused halfway across the great hall, considering his options while Taz nuzzled him, nearly knocking him off his feet in an effort to get back into his good graces.

It was as close to an apology as a dragon ever came.

Wyvern patted the beast. "Don't worry, you're forgiven," he murmured to his pet. After all, it was only a couple of Noxu. They were disgusting creatures anyway. Supremely expendable.

Lantz waited for his answer.

So did Raige. "We have the Order on their knees, Wyvern." The warrior stared at him. "I say we stay right here and demand their surrender."

"And what do we do when their allies show up?" Fionnula demanded in a crisp tone, striding in just then with the Red Queen a few paces behind her. "Try to think beyond typical male bravado, Raige. Any minute now, some Lightrider could open up a portal and bring a regiment of wood elves or giants or who-*knows*-what through to give us more than we're prepared to handle."

"She's right," mumbled Viola, folding her arms across her chest.

The sea-witch nodded. "We made our point, accomplished what we came for."

Raige smirked. "If you ladies are too frightened to proceed, just leave the fighting to us men."

Viola bared her fangs and hissed at him.

The sea-witch propped her hands on her hips and looked expectantly at Wyvern. "Nathan?" she demanded, tapping her foot.

He didn't answer for a moment.

Both his sorceress fiancée and his strongest fighter had made good points. He *had* accomplished his main goal—simply to strike the Order in a show of strength to demonstrate to all of Dark-kind that he would be a better sorcerer-king than old, frail Zolond.

But, on the other hand, Raige had an excellent argument as well. Why not launch a second wave of attacks and finish the Order off?

Unfortunately, Wyvern found himself struggling to make the decision as the three waited. It was most unlike him, but the reason was simple.

He had a bloody concussion from that final wand blast!

He'd managed to set aside the dizziness and pain in order to deal with the dragon, but now that Taz was under control, his head was throbbing so badly that he could hardly think.

"Somebody make that blasted chalk man stop pounding on the walls!" Wyvern snapped. The reverberating booms from Aelfric's fists echoed through the castle and filled his skull with agony.

"I'll enchant him with a song, dear," Fionnula promised.

"Good," Wyvern growled, then glanced at the others, refusing to show weakness in front of his followers. "I'll give you my decision shortly. First, I must return this creature to his stall. Then I'll take a short respite in my chambers and see what Shemrazul wishes us to do."

It was never a bad idea to seek guidance from his demon father. Besides, Wyvern desperately needed a few minutes alone to refresh himself. His clothes were caked with dried blood, and, in truth, the room was still spinning.

"In the meantime," he said to the navigator, "set the coordinates for the Karakum Desert, but don't activate the jump unless I give you the order."

"Yes, sir!" Lantz saluted him, then hurried off to the control room.

At that moment, the upper half of the Noxu corpse fell out of the chandelier and crashed to the floor.

The dragon whipped his head around and eyed the corpse hungrily.

"Don't even think about it," Wyvern warned Tazaroc, then scowled at the blood spattered everywhere. "The rest of you, get busy!" he snapped at the rank and file. "I want this place shipshape by the time I come back!"

They scrambled to obey, and Wyvern headed off to take the dragon to his stall on the basement level of the ten-story fortress.

No rest for the wicked. It had been a long night, but it wasn't over yet. Still, as he led the dragon down the dark stairwell, Wyvern savored his victory.

His only regret this night was that Jake hadn't stayed around to see it. No doubt his future son and heir would've been impressed...

Wherever he was.

CHAPTER ONE
Through the Portal

A t that moment, Jake Everton, the seventh Earl of Griffon, was hurtling down a brilliant tunnel of light that tracked along one of the Earth's ley-lines.

Seconds ago, however, he had been standing in the midst of the battle raging back at Merlin Hall.

Pure chaos had engulfed the palace grounds as the Dark Druids sprang their sneak attack, and Jake was still slightly dazed by all that he had seen.

Big, tusked, ogre-like Noxu warriors with axes and spears on the rampage.

Wand duels flashing in the onyx autumn night.

Billows of smoke choking the air as the great boxwood maze went up in flames.

One minute, he was standing on the palace lawn with the world burning down around him, the warlocks' invading forces coming at him from all sides, and his rugged head of security, Derek Stone, bellowing at him to go; that, after the Dark Druids' prophecy about him, neither mortals nor magic-kind could afford for him to be captured.

Next thing he knew, he was flying through the Grid.

As much as he hated being sent away like a child, Jake knew Derek was right. He had to get out of there, or the consequences could be disastrous for everyone.

Oh, to be sure, if he stayed, Jake knew he could continue inflicting serious damage on the enemy—like what he and his Gryphon had done a short while ago—crippling the fearsome dirigible, *The Dream Wraith*, to stop the enemy's air assault.

But creepy, half-demon Lord Wyvern had already tried once before to kidnap him.

The Nephilim warlock apparently wanted to claim Jake as his heir, make him the so-called Black Prince of their sinister brotherhood.

Deep down, Jake was secretly terrified that Wyvern might somehow succeed in recruiting him over to the dark side, for, frankly, he could not say with a hundred percent confidence that he did not have a bit of an evil streak in him.

Especially right now—moments after one of the sky pirates aboard *The Dream Wraith* had fallen to his death.

Jake was trying not to think about the sickening fact that he had just accidentally killed a man.

A bad one, yes. The airship's gunner had been aiming to shoot him and Red right out of the sky. But, truly, Jake had not meant for the fool to stumble overboard and fall to his death. He'd been aiming for the swivel-gun!

Nevertheless.

When you were only thirteen and had already killed a bloke, it did not bode very well on the moral scale.

Especially when you had a prophecy hanging over your head, warning that you might grow up to be the most powerful leader the sinister Dark Druids had ever had...

The mere thought made Jake slightly queasy—and the rocketing speed of Grid travel wasn't helping much with that.

Obviously, the best thing that he could do for everyone was to get the blazes out of there, posthaste. He knew the stakes, and understood it was too dangerous to stay.

Besides, if anything happened to his friends because he was being stubborn, he would never forgive himself.

His cousin Isabelle was already in extremely bad shape.

The delicate fifteen-year-old empath was on the verge of passing out, blood trickling out of her ear and nose from all the rage and hatred churning over the palace grounds.

Prince Janos, their vampire friend (who secretly adored her), had roared at Jake to get Izzy out of there before dashing off with a snarl to go and dispatch more enemies.

The vampire was right. There was no more time for delay. So Jake went, taking the others with him, including his Gryphon, Red, and his best girl, Dani O'Dell.

Or rather, Dani was the one taking them.

For it was she, not Jake, who had recently been chosen to become a future Lightrider—elite agents of the Order, who alone had the ability to open portals and conduct traveling parties safely through the Earth's innate energy Grid.

Her trainer, the wood elf, Lightrider Finnderool, had ordered the Irish lass to take Jake and the others somewhere safe. With the Dark Druids pressing the attack, no adult Lightrider could be spared for the task.

It was now on the shoulders of the dauntless redhead to get them out of there, and she was to choose the place.

Dani was forbidden to tell anyone what destination she had in mind.

Wyvern and his minions would not hesitate to torture the information out of any captive taken in battle who might know where Jake and the other kids had gone.

Whatever happened, Janos had said, they had to keep Jake out of the warlocks' clutches, or things might get even worse than they already were.

It was hard to imagine that was even possible, but Dani had her orders, and so did he.

And now, here he was—warping along through the Grid at unimaginable speeds.

As per usual with portal jumps, his lean, solid body had dissolved into a loose cluster of shining molecules that somehow managed to keep together in a sort of cloud as he careened toward supposed safety.

Not even Jake knew where Dani was taking them.

He just hoped the carrot-head knew what she was doing, because she'd only had a few weeks of training so far.

Jake knew for a fact that she'd only opened a portal *once* by herself before—in class, under the watchful eye of the haughty wood elf.

Since Jake had no desire to be instantly incinerated inside the Grid, he had balked at going. But when the cutest girl in the world begged you to trust her...

Ah well. He was helpless against those big emerald eyes. Lord knew Dani had trusted him enough times in his mad schemes.

Even so, Jake could only pray he came out on the other side with all his molecules intact, all his body parts returned to their proper places. He was already enough of a freak with his two talents— telekinesis and the ghost-sight. The last thing he needed was to arrive on the other side of the world somewhere with his blasted arm sticking out of his forehead.

Well, it seemed he was about to find out. For as the din of battle and the smell of smoke faded behind him, the glowing circle of the terminus came into view ahead.

Jake gulped in molecule form. *Here's hoping.*

* * *

If Jake was hoping, Dani O'Dell was downright praying, her molecule-heart in her molecule-throat.

She'd done a lot of brash, brave things in her many adventures with Jake and the gang, but never before had she been responsible for all her friends' lives.

Crikey, she was barely twelve!

But so be it.

Guardian Derek Stone (who could be quite scary) had thundered at her to take them away, and Master Finnderool himself had ordered her to do this. If her stern elvish teacher believed that she could do this, then Dani had to think Finnderool was probably right. She had yet to witness any occasion when the princely wood elf had ever been wrong.

Probably why he's so arrogant.

And so, whisking across the miles at the back of the line of portal travelers, Dani waited on tenterhooks to see if everyone would congeal on the other side with all their bits in order: arms, legs, heads, hands, noses.

Internal organs!

She winced at the thought.

Jake had led the way, thank goodness. If he'd refused, she supposed there was little hope of anyone else being willing to put their lives in her hands.

But he'd gone; he'd trusted her. That meant so much.

Red had flown into the portal after his handsome young master, and the aristocratic Bradfords, Archie and Isabelle, had followed, along with Archie's sweetheart, super-witch Nixie Valentine.

At the last minute, Dani had also spotted her new friend from class Brian, a young Guardian-in-training, who was as new to his craft as she was to hers. The tousle-headed American boy had been running around on the palace lawn in the middle of the battle, looking bewildered.

Dani had beckoned to him to join them; she didn't want to leave her friend in danger. Besides, Maddox had run off to fight alongside his Guardian mother, Rayvn, and every traveling party needed at least one Guardian present; those were the rules.

Guardians were the Order's trusty soldiers and bodyguards, gifted with extra-sharp senses and fighting skills.

Thankfully, Brian had leaped into the portal without even questioning her (unlike certain blond young earls of her acquaintance).

After all of her Grid passengers had filed into the portal ahead of her, finally, it was Dani's turn to go.

With her little Norwich terrier, Teddy, whining anxiously in the satchel on her shoulder, she had stepped into the shining tunnel, closed the entry point behind her, and promptly dissolved into shimmering bits of light.

And now, here she was, insubstantial as a plume of sparks popping over a bonfire as she raced toward the terminus with her first traveling party.

Just like a real Lightrider.

Half of her was proud. The other half was terrified. She could only pray she hadn't messed up the coordinates.

Those long strings of numbers representing places were difficult to memorize or recall even under good conditions, let alone in the midst of a battle.

Mother Mary, she'd been so scared back there that she could barely remember her own name, let alone any numbers.

But, from the moment Master Finnderool had ordered her to get Jake and the others out of there, Dani realized that it was up to her. So she had racked her brain to think of a good place to bring everyone.

A safe place.

Unfortunately, she hadn't many to choose from. At this early stage of her Lightriding career, she had only memorized the coordinates of a few destinations.

No matter. Determined to carry out her orders, she had lifted her left arm, where she wore the leather training gauntlet affectionately known as the Bud of Life. It was full of clever gadgets and embedded with a communicating device so the Lightrider-in-training could check in with his or her teacher back at Merlin Hall.

With trembling fingers, Dani had dialed in the set of coordinates she was most sure of. The one place in all the world where no one would ever think to look for them.

Her favorite place, in truth. The first set of coordinates she'd ever bothered learning.

Confident in her choice, Dani had carefully entered each number into the Bud of Life. It had taken her a few tries, but she'd finally got the portal open.

Now, as the glowing circle of the terminus grew larger and larger ahead, she prayed she had not misremembered any of those tricky numbers. Otherwise, she had no idea where on the globe she and her friends might've ended up.

Then the tunnel spat her out the other side, and darkness engulfed her. She went stumbling forward onto the grass.

After the dazzling brilliance inside the tunnel, she had to blink rapidly a few times to force her vision to adjust to the night, and the first thing she did was glance down at herself to make sure she was all there.

Right. Good. Whew. Beneath her stood her feet in sturdy brown half-boots that laced up to her shins in black woolen stockings; the tidy dark blue skirts of her Lightrider uniform were hardly even wrinkled from the jump.

Her arms were fine. Her hands were there, too; she glanced at each. The Bud of Life on her wrist looked unscathed, thank goodness.

Briefly clutching her head, she found it firmly perched atop her neck and shoulders where it should be. That was a relief. Her heart was pounding, too, so it must've returned to its proper post inside her ribcage.

Then she quickly scanned her passengers by the bluish-white glow of the still-open portal.

Sure enough, there was Red, Jake's magnificent scarlet-feathered Gryphon to her left, shaking his eagle head as if to clear it.

Jake stood a few feet beyond his lion-sized pet, looking a little queasy from the ruthless speeds of Grid travel. But the boy hero was on his feet, leaning forward, hands planted on his thighs as he strove to steady himself. All his cute parts seemed to be in order. *Whew again.*

Dani looked to her right and saw Archie and Isabelle both intact, each recovering from the jump as best they could. Though both aristocratic siblings seemed a little speed-sick from their journey, Dani saw that they were safe.

Poor Izzy had to be feeling at least some relief being a hundred miles away now from all the hate and fury on the battlefield. But she would need assistance.

Straight ahead, the black-haired and ever-gothic Nixie Valentine sat on the ground with her hands planted behind her. Her delicate face looked even paler than usual as she strove to regain her equilibrium. But to Dani's relief, the young witch had also reappeared with all her necessary parts.

Brian, likewise, was all in one piece, calm, sturdy, and good-natured as ever. The dark-haired American boy was already on his feet and scanning the area, looking ready to do all the usual things that Guardians did when they were on duty, protecting people.

He sent Dani a wordless nod, confirming that all of their conductees had made it safely through the portal.

Miracle! thought Dani. But there was one more traveler to check on.

While Brian took a few paces around the grassy area where they had landed, assessing their whereabouts, Dani set her satchel on the ground and opened the flap.

At once, Teddy scampered out and started running around to all the kids, checking on them in turn and giving each a reassuring lick.

When Dani saw her wee dog complete from his twitchy black nose to his waggy stump of a tail, only then did she nearly collapse with relief.

I did it! I can't believe I did it.

Her first Grid jump as a Lightrider had been a total success. Her body didn't care to celebrate her victory, though; her knees were still all wobbly, her stomach churned, and for a second, she thought she might either puke or burst out in hysterical tears after the fact like a cakehead.

Instead, a fleeting thought of Finnderool's usual annoyed frown helped her claw back the necessary businesslike attitude.

Tamping down her emotions, Dani turned around and firmly pressed the CLOSE button on her gauntlet.

Instantly, the bright, round portal winked shut. The kids were plunged into deep autumn darkness.

The first thing Dani noticed was the silence. The only sounds were the chirp of a few surviving summer crickets and the panting of all her friends striving to catch their breath.

"I-is everyone all right?" Jake finally asked. Even he still sounded slightly shaky.

By the moon-glow, Dani saw her bold young beau straighten up. She couldn't believe what he had done back there, flying up on Red to battle the airship, armed with nothing but his telekinesis.

The boy was an utter loon. Brave, of course, but clearly quite mad.

She didn't know whether to hug him or slap him silly.

There were a few grumbles and groans in answer to Jake's question, but everybody mumbled that they'd live.

Jake nodded, took a deep breath, then flipped his blond forelock out of his eyes. That was always a good sign.

"Right. Good job, carrot." He turned expectantly to her. "Where are we, then?"

It was always oddly comforting when Jake seemed ready to take charge. Even if he was bluffing, he always seemed to know what to do.

Dani gazed at him, still a little in awe of him for how he'd performed back there. She couldn't help hoping that she'd impressed him, too, with her Lightriding prowess.

"Where have you brought us to?" he asked, and waited for her answer.

Dani couldn't help smiling a little. "Don't you recognize it, Jake?"

By the moon's silver shine, she saw him furrow his brow. He propped his hands on his waist and took a puzzled look around. His gaze followed the wide gravel path nearby. Though it was overgrown with weeds, the path stretched like a pale ribbon in both directions, winding off into the trees of a parklike setting.

"Hold on..." Jake lifted his head slightly and squinted toward the distance, where faded pastel turrets loomed above the black trees. They were shaped like scoops of ice cream. "I don't believe it." He pivoted to face her, an incredulous grin spreading across his handsome face. "You brought us here?"

"Yep." Dani grinned back.

"You know this place, coz?" Archie asked, still sounding groggy.

"Oh, aye." Jake began laughing.

Dani laughed too, glancing over at the bespectacled boy genius. "He certainly does."

Then she and Jake exchanged a tender glance.

Elysian Springs Pleasure Gardens.

The old, abandoned amusement grounds had been Jake's hideaway back in the days when he was an orphaned pickpocket, roaming the streets of London.

He had always been safe here, after all his escapades.

Not even the bobbies, like good ol' Constable Flanagan, had ever managed to track Jake to Elysian Springs, Dani knew.

And neither would wicked Lord Wyvern.

CHAPTER TWO
Safe Haven

"You clever, clever girl," Jake murmured. Standing in the moonlit clearing by the waypoint, he could not stop smiling at Dani O'Dell. She had picked the best place in the world for their refuge.

"I thought you'd be pleased, milord," she said, and dropped a teasing curtsy.

Jake looked around at his friends with a broad smile. "Relax, you lot," he said. "She's done it. We'll be safe here."

"And where exactly *is* here, coz?" Archie asked.

Jake was glad to see that, finally, the rest of the gang was starting to recover from the portal jump—and the battle before it.

"Yes," said Nixie, who had apparently arrived with her sarcasm intact. "It's all ginger peaches that you two chuckaboos know where we are, but would you mind telling the rest of us?"

As the petite, black-haired witch started climbing slowly to her feet, new kid Brian hurried over to assist her. She *did* still look a bit wobbly after the jump.

But before the obliging Guardian could reach her, Archie shooed him away with an almost jealous look and stepped in to do the honors himself. "I daresay we're in the middle of nowhere, Nix."

"Hardly, coz," Jake said, feeling unexpectedly roguish to find himself back in his old hideaway. "Miss Lightrider has brought us to the best hiding place any bloomin' mumper could want."

Dani giggled at Jake's use of the old Cockney slang that had been their native tongue before Miss Helena and Master Henry—the shapeshifting governess and tutor to the Bradford family—had gotten hold of them.

The boy genius, however, did not speak Cockney. "How now?" Archie pushed his spectacles up higher onto his nose and squinted into the darkness. "Wherever we are, it looks deserted to me."

"Aye, that's what makes it perfect." Jake glanced around with a wave of nostalgia while Dani knelt down next to Isabelle and patted the traumatized empath on the shoulder. "We're at Elysian Springs Pleasure Gardens, everyone, the abandoned carnival grounds. Ages ago, they used to have music and shows here, games and food, fireworks and circus freaks. Jugglers and whatnot... Anyway, this is where I sort of used to live."

"You *lived* here?" Nixie dusted bits of dried leaves off her black skirts after sitting in the grass.

Jake nodded, relieved to see she still had her wand in case they ran into any trouble. He was sure of *her* battle skills and his own, but the Bradfords and Dani were more limited in what they could do, and Maddox St. Trinian, their usual Guardian friend on their adventures, had deserted them to go racing off into the battle to fight alongside his Guardian mum, the fierce Ravyn Vambrace.

Of course, Jake could understand Maddox's higher loyalty to his birth mother, but he would've felt better if the tough older boy were here right now. (Even though he was an unrelenting grump.)

As for the new Guardian, Jake had only just laid eyes on this Brian kid moments ago for the first time.

Dani had mentioned her American classmate before, however, and, in truth, Jake had been less than thrilled to hear his best girl chatting on about some other boy.

But that was beside the point. Jealousy was for idiots, anyway.

Like Maddox, who could not seem to manage his feelings for Isabelle like a rational human being. He was always growling about their vampire friend, Prince Janos, having a soft spot in his undead heart for the pretty blond empath.

Be that as it may, the only thing that mattered at the moment was whether this Brian chap was any good in a fight.

Which remained to be seen.

For his part, Jake was feeling rather drained after using his telekinesis so vigorously against the airship, but at least he had Risker, his magical dagger from Odin, sheathed on his hip.

It also helped considerably that Red was there to protect them, for only a suicidal fool would dare anger the Gryphon.

With that, Jake decided they'd be perfectly fine here, at least for a while. All they had to do was stay out of trouble and kill some time until the adults sent someone from Merlin Hall to fetch them once things calmed down back there.

Naturally, his chief concern was keeping his friends safe—and calm—in the ongoing crisis of this night.

"Elysian Springs used to be fashionable back when Queen Victoria was just a young princess," Dani told the others, for she loved this place even more than Jake did. "I was shocked when I saw the map in Lightrider class and realized there was a waypoint here all along!"

Maybe that's why this place always drew me, Jake mused, resting his hands on his waist. He gazed toward the Grand Pavilion in the distance, with its whimsical turrets. "I wonder if any of the carnies are still here," he said.

"Carnies?" Archie echoed, furrowing his brow.

Dani nodded. "Some of the *unusual* folk from the carnival freakshow were allowed to keep on living here after it closed down. They were quite kind to us. Should we go and visit them, Jake?"

Jake shook his head with regret. "As much as I'd like to, it's probably not a good idea. Best if no one knows we're here. Plus, I wouldn't want to risk putting them in danger because of us. Don't worry," he told the others. "The carnies won't bother us. They're good folk. They never ratted me out to the constables, anyway."

"The bobbies were always after Jake back in his pickpocket days," Dani said fondly. "But, for some reason, not even Constable Flanagan ever thought to check this old place." She glanced around with a wistful sigh. "I used to love coming here."

Teddy barked twice with excitement, clearly seconding that.

"I'm glad you brought us here, Dani," Isabelle spoke up, finally beginning to recover, it seemed. The older girl was still sitting on the grass, Dani on her right and her solicitous younger brother on her left.

Ever the perfect English gentleman, Archie had given his sister his handkerchief from his waistcoat pocket. Thank heavens, Izzy's nose and ear had stopped bleeding, Jake saw with relief.

He, too, had once experienced a nosebleed from overusing his powers—and the ear bit, as well. It wasn't pretty, but it wasn't fatal, as long as you stopped overstraining your abilities.

As relieved as he was to see his gentle cousin feeling better, he'd known deep down that she would be all right.

Isabelle Bradford might look like a sugar-spun angel, with her lovely face and long golden curls, but she was much tougher than most people ever dreamed. After all, the Order didn't pick just *any* girl to become a Keeper of Unicorns.

Still blotting the blood away from the side of her neck where it had trickled out of her ear, Izzy glanced around at the parklike setting. "I've always wanted to see this place. You both spoke of it so fondly."

"How are you feeling, Iz?" Nixie asked. "Need a healing spell?"

"No thanks." Izzy gave her a wan smile. "I'll be right as rain in a moment."

"Well, as soon as we're ready to go," Jake said, "I'd be happy to give you all a tour of this old place. Might as well! We've got nothing else to do until we hear from Merlin Hall."

"I wonder what's happening back there," Dani said uneasily, then scooped Teddy onto her lap and hugged him. "Do you think it's over yet?"

No one answered for a moment.

"Probably not," Jake admitted. "Soon, though, I should think."

"Did you *see* Aunt Ramona back there?" Archie asked. "She was astonishing."

"She's even more formidable than I imagined," Nixie, sole pupil of the Elder witch, agreed.

The others nodded.

They had never seen Great-Great Aunt Ramona in action before. The mighty white witch rarely made a display of her powers. Over time, she had come to mistrust magic in general...

Then everyone fell silent, each clearly pondering the disaster still in progress back at the palace. Their initial relief to find themselves safe gave way to gnawing fear over the outcome of the battle—and what the Dark Druids' raid on Merlin Hall was going to mean for the entire magical world.

It seemed that the war the Order had long feared had finally begun.

Archie glanced with desperation at his sister. "Mother and Father are still back there."

Nixie took his hand, but Izzy gave her brother a dazed nod. "I know. And Miss Helena, and Henry. And Derek."

"And Maddox," Nixie murmured.

"And Janos," Jake said.

Izzy sent him a soulful glance, her eyes full of fear.

The telepathic bond she shared with the vampire prince was something not even *she* understood.

Dani patted Izzy's hand. "Yes, but don't worry, Janos is immortal, more or less. I'm sure he'll be perfectly fine. And Maddox is awfully strong. Smart, too."

Izzy gazed at her uncertainly, but Archie clenched his fist and stood. "I cannot believe Lord Badgerton betrayed us! What a devil."

Jake folded his arms across his chest and shook his head. "You know, I never liked him."

"And he *really* didn't like you," Dani mumbled. "Especially after you flung mashed potatoes on him."

Jake arched a brow. "That was an accident!"

"Aye, sure it was, Jake," she teased, and the others chortled at the memory of the mishap in the dining hall.

"So, what's the plan, Lightrider?" Brian asked, turning to Dani. "And where exactly is this place? In the world, I mean?"

"Oh—sorry. We're in London," Dani said absently. "On the south bank of the Thames, to be exact."

"London?" Brian's eyes widened. "Wow..."

Jake turned to the newcomer with a quizzical look. "What, you've never been?"

When Brian shook his head, Jake couldn't help but scoff.

Teddy yipped, as though he, too, found it absurd that anyone could never have been to the capital of the entire British Empire before.

"Brian's from America, Jake, remember?" Dani chided. "When they recruited him for the Guardian program, Tex brought him straight to Merlin Hall from a waypoint on top of an Indian mound near the small town in Indiana where he's from."

"It's not that small," Brian mumbled. "We have a train stop."

Jake couldn't help grinning. "Blimey, one whole train stop. Aren't you a man of the world."

Archie shot him a disapproving frown for his jest, then turned to Brian. "An Indian mound sounds fascinating, though."

"Oh, we've got tons," Brian said with artless enthusiasm. "I found an arrowhead there once!"

Jake drew breath to offer another cheeky quip, but Isabelle must've sensed it coming.

"Behave, coz," she warned him, then rubbed her temples, still looking rather pained. "Can we please just focus on the plan?"

Jake swallowed his humor and tossed the new kid a breezy smile. "Sorry, mate, just havin' a bit of fun. Plan's simple." He flipped his forelock out of his eyes and shrugged. "We stay put for a while here, like I said. Wait for things to calm down back at the palace. Then we'll let the adults know where we ended up. We can call Aunt Ramona in a bit through that speaker thingamajig on Dani's gauntlet." He gestured at the redhead's forearm.

Everyone agreed that all sounded acceptable.

For his part, Jake figured that giving his friends a tour of his old hideaway would help to keep everyone's minds off their many justified fears. "Good," he said with a firm nod. "Then follow me, you lot."

* * *

"And me!" Spilling her dog off her lap, Dani jumped to her feet and ran eagerly after Jake as he began marching down the moonlit path.

Teddy bounded along by her heels, as happy to be back at Elysian Springs as she was. A city dog, he had always loved coming here, where he could run free.

Catching up to her beau, Dani seized hold of his arm, smiled at him, and privately breathed a sigh of relief. Trust ol' Jakey-boy to know what to do.

Bossy and sarcastic as he usually was, she found his confidence hugely reassuring in a crisis. Never mind if it was half bravado. Somehow, it was enough.

It always got them through.

"Wait up!" Nixie called.

Jake and Dani paused and turned around. They'd almost lost their tour group already in their excitement to revisit their old stomping grounds.

Back in the grassy area where they'd landed, Archie was pulling his sister to her feet.

Dusting off her skirts, Isabelle glanced down at herself and saw where the blood had dripped from her nose and ear onto her pale gown. "Ugh, I look a fright. I hope we don't see anyone, or I'll probably terrify them. They'll think I'm a ghost."

"Nah, ghosts are sort of grayish and see-through," Jake said cheerfully. "What you *really* look like at the moment is, ahem, *someone's* vampire bride."

Dani smacked him for his teasing remark, but any allusion to Janos was the one sure way to cheer Isabelle up.

The reminder of Janos's flirtatious joke about marrying the girl someday when she grew up brought a startled smile across Izzy's face.

"Very funny, coz," she said wryly—but blushed.

"Uh, 'scuse me..." Brian was staring nervously at Red. "Does your Gryphon bite?"

Dani looked back and saw her friend standing frozen while Red sniffed him curiously.

"Only if you're evil," Jake said.

"I'm not!" Brian answered, shaking his head, his eyes wide.

When Jake furrowed his brow at the boy, Dani glimpsed both perplexity and mischief in his expression. Jake's bemused stare seemed to say, *"You're kind of a sheltered one, aren't you?"*

She fought back a laugh. She'd been thinking the same thing.

Brian might have been born with the heightened senses and vicious fighting skills of a Guardian, but she doubted he would've lasted a day in the rookery.

Not with that gullible air of innocence he had about him.

Since the American's naiveté was obvious, Jake, the street-smart Londoner, relented on him, much to Dani's relief. She knew better than anyone that Jake's teasing could be a bit *much.*

"Don't worry, mate." He took a kinder tone as he walked back toward Brian and the Gryphon. "Let me introduce you to Red. I inherited him from my family. He can be extremely dangerous in a fight, but he'd never hurt *us.* Just think of him as...I dunno...a giant, friendly guard dog."

"That flies," Archie added.

The girls laughed, and Red snuffled with indignation.

Teddy ran over to his large, feathered friend, yipping as if to say he'd suspected all along that the Gryphon might be a fellow canine.

"If you say so," Brian mumbled uncertainly.

Then Jake hooked a thumb toward the young Guardian and looked at Dani. "Who is this chap, now?"

"Oh—sorry!" Still slightly in shock after the battle, Dani only now realized she had failed to do the formal introductions. "Everyone: this is my friend Brian from class."

If he had a last name, she didn't know it.

"Finnderool and Master Ebrahim had our groups—the Lightriders and Guardians—team up for drills, since that's how we'll work in the field. We always seem to end up as partners. He's really nice," she added sincerely, embarrassing the newcomer a little.

Then she told Brian everyone else's names.

"Good to meet you all," he said with a modest smile.

As the whole gang welcomed him into their midst, Dani was glad he was there. The sturdy boy had a calm, measured way about him, and besides, having seen him in action, she knew that if they ran into trouble, Brian could be a big help.

He wasn't as tough or experienced as Maddox, but, then again, he did not bring all the tension that the moody older boy carried around with him into their group.

Poor Maddox, he really had become a bit of a malcontent, especially since things had gone wrong between him and Isabelle.

Of course, in Dani's experience, bad moods in boys of seventeen or so were to be expected. Each of her rowdy elder brothers who'd attained that grand old age had gone through the exact same grumpy phase. For her part, she just hoped Maddox was safe back there at Merlin Hall.

Brian, for his part, looked impressed to find himself in the company of the semi-famous Jake, Lord Griffon, "the boy from the prophecy," as well as the scientifically renowned Dr. Bradford.

Nixie, too, was highly regarded in magical circles for her advanced abilities. And as for Isabelle, well, most boys' eyes nearly popped out of their heads when they saw her.

Dani was relieved that Brian managed not to act like a jingle-brains around the beautiful older girl.

He was, she decided, a good egg.

"Well, c'mon, you lot," Jake said. "Come down to the edge of the water. I'm going to take you out to see my old island."

He stepped off the path and marched through a dark grove of trees, striding down to the reedy edge of one of the old canals. "Grab a swan boat and follow me."

Beaming, Dani ran after him down to the little canal, where a row of faded swan-shaped pedal boats floated, their white wings stained green with algae at the waterline. Tethered to a low beam that ran for several yards along the edge of the canal, the swans seated two people each. Dani climbed eagerly into Jake's boat at the front of the line, taking Teddy with her.

Jake freed the swan's tether from the beam and tossed the loose end of excess rope behind their seats. Then he stepped into the boat and sat down beside her with a smile, planting his feet on the pedals. "Just like old times, eh, carrot?"

Dani nodded, settled her dog on her lap, and put her feet into position as well.

Behind them, their friends followed suit. Archie and Nixie clambered aboard the second swan, while Izzy shared the third with Brian.

"You have to pedal backwards first to get away from the side, then go forward and turn the tiller to start heading that way." Jake pointed toward the man-made lake, still concealed by the trees.

Red spread his wings and lifted into the air, hovering overhead as the three boats clumsily backed up and splashed loudly as they worked to turn forward. The process of getting faced in the proper direction was both frustrating and fun.

At last, they all managed to form a line. The Gryphon followed overhead as the three boats began trundling down the old, narrow canal.

Teddy's little stump tail never stopped wagging as Jake and Dani pedaled along. The dog had always loved going on the swan boats, and so did she.

The canal wound through the overgrown park until it joined the largest of Elysian Springs' three man-made lakes. At one spot, a dead branch had fallen off one of the trees and blocked the way like a turnpike bar, but Jake moved it aside with his telekinesis.

They pedaled on.

Before long, the kids reached the sprawling lagoon and headed out across it in the moonlight, the ripples of their passing creating little waves.

Already, Jake's island came into view out in the middle of the lake. Dani was relieved to see the gazebo still standing.

Though a cold breeze swept across the open water and chilled her, she couldn't help but smile, gazing at the spot where they'd had so many fun times.

It had been ages since she had visited this place.

Back when her dear pickpocket had been homeless, the island's fanciful gazebo—weathered and worm-eaten as it was—had become Jake's castle.

Now he had a real one, and a title to go with it.

She shook her head and marveled as they floated toward it. Truly, those days seemed like a lifetime ago.

But one thing was certain. Of all the many wonders and amazing lands she had seen since their adventures had started, to Dani, Elysian Springs would always be the most magical place in the world.

In a strange way, this park was home.

Then a wave of guilt struck her. Here she was, feeling so happy to be here, safe with all her friends, while people were probably dying back at Merlin Hall.

Her smile faded and a shiver of fear ran through her.

Jake sent Dani a knowing look.

She could see in his eyes that he was worried, too. Though neither spoke the question aloud, Dani knew they were both wondering whether the battle at Merlin Hall was over yet...

CHAPTER THREE
The Balance Keepers

Ramona Bradford's gray hair had fallen from its usual tight bun in the fray. Strands of it blew in her face as the Elder witch stood panting, still clutching her wand in her bony fingers.

The battle had ended moments ago, more or less, except for a few small skirmishes between some Guardians and a handful of Noxu stragglers.

But Wyvern and his Dark Druid brethren had fled, routed by the mighty Ring of Negation spell that she had just unleashed.

Sweet Hecate, she had not needed to resort to a spell of such magnitude in centuries, but at least it had worked. She blew a strand of hair out of her face in relief.

Though the spell had drained her entirely, the blast of power had knocked the Dark Druids off their feet, then sent them fleeing like cowards, disappearing in black puffs of smoke.

They were gone.

Now the Order was left to assess the damage. The cost had been high. Ramona feared they were all but defeated. Eyes stinging in the smoke, she looked around slowly at the devastation in a state of disbelief.

In all her three hundred and thirty-three years of life, she never dreamed she'd live to see such things. The great maze was burning. The acrid smell of the smoke was awful, the screams from the tortured trees horrific.

It seemed impossible, but somewhere in the center of the vast green labyrinth, the Old Father Yew was dying.

Out by the meadows, the very ground had been vandalized, torn asunder by the tunnel that Lord Badgerton had dug to let the enemy in.

Traitor. Ramona quivered with fury at the thought of that vile, pompous shapeshifter. One of the Elders, no less!

She did not know for how long Badgerton had been secretly siding with the enemy, but she was certain that, one day, he would get what he deserved.

The Dark Druids were not foolish enough to trust anyone who'd already betrayed one side.

The fool might not realize it yet, wherever he'd slunk off to, but Ramona had no doubt that the shapeshifter lord was already doomed. It was only a matter of time.

Suddenly, she wobbled on her feet as a wave of exhaustion washed over her. *Oh, I'm too old for this.*

Coughing a little from the smoke, she turned to gaze toward the battered palace. Merlin Hall was locked down tight, but at least her wizard colleague, Sir Peter Quince, had put out the remaining rooftop fires.

As for her own role, Ramona had been kept busy stopping Fionnula Coralbroom from entering the great library of Merlin Hall. The obnoxious sea-witch had been trying to raid their priceless collection of ancient grimoires.

Precious as the spell books were, Ramona had been more concerned about the hundred youngsters and handful of adult civilians huddled in the library's secure basement.

Still shaking with terror and rage, she wearily pushed her blowing hair out of her dirt-streaked face. It was all so shocking.

The lawn was littered with dead gnomes, a few warrior centaurs and humans, and charred Greenfolk. The groans of wounded Guardians reached her on the wind.

But, amid all their losses, Ramona was profoundly grateful for at least one thing: Jake and the children had whisked away to safety.

She'd seen the brilliance of the portal opening amid the fight.

Though she knew not where they had gone, the little band of rascals had been through so many scrapes before, always coming through reasonably unscathed, that at least she could take comfort in knowing they'd look out for one another until things settled down here. Then she could send someone to fetch them.

Probably Derek Stone and Miss Helena, Isabelle's governess...

Then Ramona's eyes welled with tears as she stared across the lawn at the spot where the chief Elder, Balinor, lay dead on the ground.

She closed her eyes for a moment. But no rest for the weary. Old and exhausted as she felt, she forced herself into motion, slowly heading over to where a few Guardians were standing around the body, looking at a loss.

One of them was Ravyn Vambrace, but Ramona didn't see the warrior woman's son, Maddox, anywhere. Perhaps the seventeen-year-old had gone with Jake and the others. She hoped so. He was a promising young fighter.

Then the soldiers stepped back to a respectful distance to let Ramona have a moment alone with her fallen friend.

Balinor's owl let out a mournful screech, circling overhead.

Her tears thickened as she looked up at the old wizard's grieving familiar, and then down at the Order's slain leader.

She wasn't even sure who had killed him.

She was still standing there in a most uncharacteristic daze when Peter (who ran Merlin Hall from day to day) walked over and joined her, looking battered and worn out.

His tortoiseshell spectacles were askew and his black scholar's robe was singed, but at least he was alive.

The usually glib fellow stared down at the murdered head wizard for a long moment, then turned to Ramona, his silver tongue failing him for once. He said nothing.

At that moment, Prince Janos whooshed down from the sky, instantly taking human form again as he strode over to them.

When Wyvern had retreated, the vampire had changed into his bat form and followed the Dark Druids to see where they went. After all, a spy was exactly what the vampire prince had long been.

"Have they gone?" Peter asked dully, ashes streaking his face.

Janos glanced regretfully at Balinor's corpse, then gave the two of them a grim look. "Afraid not. They've retreated into the Black Fortress, but it's still parked on top of poor Aelfric. I saw no lightning on the towers yet," he added with a halfhearted look of hope. "It seems they're not quite ready to jump yet."

Peter frowned. "I wonder why. Are they waiting to make sure they have everyone on board?"

"Or..." Janos hesitated.

"What?" Ramona said.

The vampire rested his hands on his waist. "I hate to say it, but they could be planning a second wave of attacks."

Ramona nearly panicked. "We can't hold them off again! We barely survived the first wave!"

"I'll go collapse Badgerton's tunnel," said Peter.

"What good will it do?" she exclaimed. "The dome of charms that protected this place for centuries is all but gone! They'll get through it easily right now if they try again."

"How long to repair it?" asked Janos.

"Oh, many hours to regrow some semblance of protection, and the wands of all our best mages," she said, shaking her head. "A full repair will probably take months, especially now, without Balinor's help."

Janos lowered his gaze. "I could try to get into the Fortress and, ah, cut Wyvern's throat?" He arched a brow at Ramona.

"Egads, I'm sure that won't be necessary!" said Peter. "You'll never make it out alive."

Janos shrugged. "'Alive' is a relative term in my case. Besides, I do have cause."

"Indeed," murmured Ramona.

Wyvern had killed the poor fellow's whole family, burning his harem of vampire brides and their dastardly hatchlings alive.

Apparently, the Nephilim had used the same, strange, cuff-like Atlantean weapon to melt the very stone of Castle Gregorian that he'd employed tonight to set the roof of Merlin Hall ablaze. The silver gauntlet Ramona had seen on Wyvern's arm shot forth blue flames. The whole palace could've been lost if not for Ramona's genius nephew, Archie, who knew the secret chemical mixture required for putting out Greek fire. (Baking soda plus a few other items—but not water.)

She shuddered. It was all so horrible.

Janos awaited his orders with a dark look.

"I must say, it's tempting," Ramona admitted.

"Don't encourage him," Peter chided her, turning to Ramona again. "Come now, my lady. I highly doubt they'll try again tonight. You battered the blazes out of Fionnula, and Wyvern was in very poor condition when we drove them off. Janos is simply thinking like a Guardian. As he should. Still, let's not be hasty." Despite his optimistic words, the scholarly wizard's tone was uneasy, his face haggard. "There's no need to jump to the worst possible conclusion. Believe me, I've done that once already tonight and have yet to learn the cost."

Ramona nodded sympathetically. In truth, the poor wizard looked like he'd aged five years since the moment earlier this evening, when Wyvern's trickery had led Peter to accuse his own beloved wife, Jillian, of being the traitor in their midst.

Everyone knew he doted on his "Jilly-bean." Wyvern must have also realized that Peter's love for his non-magical wife might be his Achilles' heel. He'd managed to deceive him.

Peter had broken Jillian's heart and his own earlier tonight with his furious accusations, mistaking *her* for the traitor—before discovering that the real Judas among them was Badgerton.

Unfortunately, his leadership role as the youngest of the Elders required Peter to keep a stiff upper lip in this moment of personal crisis and see to his duty instead of his marriage.

The weary wizard gave Janos an appreciative clap on the shoulder. "Just keep an eye on those blackguards for us for now, would you? I think we all need to take a breath here. But if you see them preparing to return for a second strike, alert us at once."

"As you wish." Janos nodded, then pivoted and walked away, turning first into a man-sized column of black smoke before flapping up into the skies again in the form of a bat.

He screeched to Balinor's owl to follow him, recruiting the bird to help with sentry duty. The owl swooped away after him to assist in keeping watch on the Dark Druids from the skies.

"Handy fellow to have around," Peter said, capable of only a halfhearted quip at the moment, as he watched Janos disappear into the night.

Ramona nodded but said nothing. Her mind was already churning.

There was no time to lose.

She took leave of Peter and marched inside, bypassing the chaos teeming in the halls and the lobby.

The healers swirled about, assisting the wounded. A she-elf asked Ramona if she needed medical attention. The Elder witch waved her off and hurried on, crossing to the stately marble staircase that led up from the entrance hall.

On the way, Ramona noticed that many of the grand chambers on the ground floor had been sacked. The ballroom, some of the parlors, even the enchanted art gallery.

It only increased her rage. By the Blessed Isles, if Zolond was behind this attack, she would never forgive him.

Or herself.

Everywhere, civilians still cowered. Frantic people flocked around the Elder witch, seeking reassurance, and tried to tell her what they'd seen. But Ramona brushed them off with a few empty platitudes on her way to the stairs. She had no comfort to give them at the moment.

Not now.

First, she needed answers.

Heading for her chamber, she was relieved to see that at least the Noxu hadn't made it this far into the palace. But with every step, her anger grew. Guilt soon joined it.

How could I not have seen this coming?

Had her secret dealings with Zolond—and more importantly, their past relationship—blinded her to the threat?

In recent months, the Elder witch had been engaged in private, unofficial peace negotiations with the Dark Master, both of them (supposedly!) trying to prevent a full-out magical war that so many on both sides sensed coming.

Though Ramona had remained sensibly wary of her old flame, she had eventually come to believe he was negotiating in good faith. Zolond claimed he was too old and world-weary to bother launching some terrible new war. He was one of the few still alive who, like her, remembered just how horrific total war between wizards and warlocks actually was. He was comfortable with the way things had been for so long: good and evil more or less balanced in the world. So he'd said.

The question was, had he duped her?

Or was there more to all this than met the eye?

The possibility that her once-beloved Geoffrey de Lacey might've betrayed her all over again—just like when they were young—struck like a knife in her heart.

As she marched down the hallway, Ramona swore that if he had deceived her, if he had been manipulating her all this time, merely keeping the Elder witch distracted while he plotted tonight's treachery, she would destroy him.

So what if it meant ending her own life as well?

She'd been ready to die for at least a hundred years. Three centuries was far too long for any sensible person to live. But *he* had done this to her.

To both of them.

Centuries ago, in the Renaissance age, as two young fools in their teens, both highly gifted in magic, they had pledged to be together for all time, joining their fates forever through the fearsome Montague and Capulet spell.

As much as she regretted that rash decision, she had made good use of the blood tie between them. For the past three hundred years, she had forced the Dark Master to behave by the simple threat of ending her own life, like Juliet in Shakespeare's play, for then, because of the spell that bound them, he would die instantly as well.

It was Zolond's greatest secret, and her own. Ramona did not believe in suicide, of course, but she would've done it gladly as a last resort to contain the Dark Druids' evil and save countless lives.

After all, she knew better than anyone that there was nothing Zolond feared more than death—and who could blame him?

He had spent the past three centuries in league with the demon Shemrazul. So, when death finally came to claim the Dark Master, it was down, down, down to the Ninth Pit of Hades that Zolond would go.

The Horned One had granted him great magical power during his long lifetime, but it came with a price. He still owed the demon his soul.

And yet, as she approached the door to her private apartments, Ramona warned herself not to jump to conclusions, the way Peter had with Jillian.

There was still one good reason to hope that Zolond was not behind tonight's attack: the simple fact that she had not seen him here.

Only Wyvern and a handful of other Dark Druids.

Supposedly, Zolond was taking a much-needed sabbatical in the Balefire Mountains. He had told her he had left Wyvern, his second-in-command, in charge.

Of course, that could be part of the lie. As the leader of the Dark Druids, the old sorcerer-king might've simply remained inside the Black Fortress, commanding his troops from a distance.

There *was*, however, a slim possibility that Zolond knew nothing about tonight's raid, had had nothing to do with it.

At the moment, Ramona didn't know what to believe, but she intended to find out. It was time to put their longstanding bond to the test.

With that, she opened the door to her chambers and stepped into the sitting room. After pulling the door shut firmly behind her, she leaned against it for a moment and took a deep breath. *I will get to the bottom of this.*

Half of her braced for confirmation of what would surely feel like a very personal betrayal. The other half hoped stubbornly for the best: that her dear Geoffrey was still true to her, in his way, innocent of any involvement in this, and willing to prove it by helping the Order in their hour of direst need.

Humph. She shook her head cynically. To think that it should come to this! That Dark Master Zolond, of all people, might be the Order's best hope for survival—if only for the next few hours—until repairs on the dome could start to take effect.

Pushing away from the door, Ramona crossed the parlor to the small, round table, where she sat down grimly before her white crystal ball.

It was time to confront the Dark Master.

Closing her eyes, she rested her hands on the pure quartz sphere and strove to calm her mind. Unfortunately, she was so shaken by the night's events that, much to her frustration, she could barely concentrate.

Finally, after a few deep breaths, she managed by sheer force of will to project herself out of her body and into the astral plane.

For a second, darkness engulfed the Elder witch.

She heard the softly chiming notes of the ethereal music in this neutral zone that she and Zolond had conjured for their secret meetings in the ethers.

Then she opened her spirit eyes and saw the white, curling path that led across a purple void with big crystal stars.

At the end of the walkway was the drifting charcoal gazebo where they had been holding their parleys. Its shape and colors dissolved slowly upward, bit by bit, like a runny watercolor painting that defied gravity.

To her surprise, Zolond was already there.

Why, she had assumed she'd have to summon him. But, in the distance, she could see him pacing around slowly in the gazebo.

What on earth is he doing?

Strange musical notes joined the customary chimes from the stars that flashed here and there and twinkled in the purple clouds.

Ramona furrowed her brow, not knowing what to make of this. Had he come to gloat?

Suddenly, long, discordant notes whined in the distance, scratching and squeaking like a dragon's claws on a chalkboard.

She winced, confused. It was dreadful!

Instantly on her guard, Ramona wondered what on earth the old devil was up to. Was this some new form of torture the Dark Master had devised?

Gripping the astral version of her wand, she forced herself forward. The rumble of thunder she brought with her wasn't on purpose; this setting they'd created merely responded to their emotions.

Zolond heard the growl of thunder rolling toward the gazebo and turned.

Each time Ramona looked at him, even here, in the astral plane, she still caught glimpses of the well-bred, bookish lad she had once loved.

An elderly gentleman now, slight of build, with snow-white hair and the stately manner of a retired butler, the Geoffrey of today looked as though he were in his mid-seventies, as did she. But, in truth, he was three years older than Ramona: three hundred and thirty-six.

Fossils, the both of us. Elder witch and Dark Master alike, they had been too long in this world.

Zolond turned when he noticed her coming, and Ramona's jaw dropped as she spotted the source of that dreadful noise: the old fool was attempting to play the violin!

She scoffed, remembering the musical talent he'd shown in his youth. Well, he'd lost any skill he might've developed over the years, to be sure.

His efforts at this late date sounded like two werecats fighting.

"Well! This is a pleasant surprise." Zolond lowered the violin from his shoulder as he waited for her to arrive. "Evening, ol' girl. Didn't expect to see you here tonight."

"What on earth are you doing, you daft old loon?" Ramona demanded as she whooshed up to the gazebo with a mere thought.

He grinned with a flash of his old charm and glanced down at the instrument dangling from his grasp. "Trying to tune this old thing. Haven't played it in years. I fear it shows. The strangest thing—I suddenly found myself in the mood to give it a go again. Funny, eh? Thought I'd serenade you if you came along, and here you are. So what song would like me to..." His smile faded as he noticed her stark expression. "Ramona, what's wrong?"

"As if you don't know," she whispered bitterly. Her voice had all but fled.

Facing him like this, the possibility that he might've betrayed her yet *again* was overwhelming.

He cocked his head with apparent confusion.

"Wyvern attacked us!" she cried, too angry for eloquence.

"What?" Zolond went motionless.

"That demon-spawn just attacked Merlin Hall!" She cursed her voice for trembling, but her throat felt tight. "He had an army of Noxu warriors and half the Dark Druid Council by his side."

Zolond stared at her with a look of shock.

Ramona gathered her composure. "Tell me right now: are you behind this?"

"I have no idea what you're talking about." The violin promptly vanished, and the bow in his right hand became his wand, the scepter of the sorcerer-king. "When?"

"Moments ago! I swear, Geoffrey, if you had anything to do with this, I will *never* forgive you. If it's war you want, by all that's holy, it is war you shall have!"

Her threat reverberated mightily into the purple void.

His eyes turned to ice. "Tell me *exactly* what happened."

Thunder rumbled louder with her wrath. "They besieged the palace. Balinor is dead. They've burned the Old Yew!" she burst out, and a sob escaped her, to her shame.

"What?" he whispered.

"You dare feign innocence? You are the sorcerer-king! This is your doing—I'm no fool! But perhaps I am, for you have surely deceived me."

"No!" Zolond took a step toward her. She sensed no deception. "I am not a part of this, Ramona. I swear. You must believe me."

"Must I? Even though you serve the Father of Lies?"

He stared at her in dismay. "I can only give you my word." He searched her eyes. "Whom did you see?"

Her heart pounded. Heaven help her, she wanted to believe him. "Wyvern led the raid. But the vampire queen, Viola Sangray, she was there too, foul creature. And your insane field marshal, Archeron Raige. Fionnula Coralbroom. The wood elves said that they could sense your filthy prophet, Duradel, somewhere nearby, but no one actually saw him. Oh, and let's not forget Captain Dread of *The Dream Wraith*. He was up there battering the dome from above with the airship's guns."

Zolond's pale eyes turned black as he absorbed this information. "He broke through your shields?"

"Damaged them, yes. Fionnula assisted, I believe. But," she admitted stiffly, "they had help. One of our own turned traitor."

"Who?" he asked, marveling.

"Boris Badgerton. He...he dug a tunnel underneath the dome's shields, and let Wyvern and his army in."

"But isn't he an Elder?" Zolond exclaimed.

She nodded. "Representing the shapeshifters."

"Baal's beard," Zolond murmured. "When did this occur?"

Ramona rubbed her forehead wearily. "It started over an hour ago. We just now repelled them. I swear, Geoffrey, if this is your doing—"

"It is not!" He moved closer. "I vow to you, Ramona, I had nothing to do with this. You know I have no desire for war. We're both too old for this nonsense. But blazes... If Wyvern has indeed killed the Old Father Yew, then the balance between dark and light is all awry at the moment." He looked at her. "Both our sides face collapse."

"I'm aware of that! Why else would I be here?" she snapped. "Something must be done, and at the moment, you're the only one who can stop that Nephilim filth from coming back and—finishing us off."

Zolond's lined face turned grim. "Yes. I see..." His gaze wandered as he considered. "Now it all comes clear. Wyvern has been scheming behind my back..." He looked at her again. "He's finally made his move. Still, I had no idea he would do something so rash. Do not fear. I assure you, he will be punished this very night. I will deal with him at once."

She stared at him through the astral plane, and Dark Master Zolond stared back.

Obviously, he was a most accomplished liar, but, as deeply as they were connected by the Montague and Capulet spell, she could sense no lies from him.

"The truce that's kept both sides in check for hundreds of years has been broken, as of now," Ramona informed him. "If you indeed plan to get Wyvern under control, then you'd better hurry. The Black Fortress is still stationed just beyond the bounds of Merlin Hall. He could return at any moment."

"That's not going to happen," Zolond said in a voice of iron. "I can be there within a quarter hour. But first, Ramona, you must promise me one thing."

"You dare ask for favors?" she cried, outraged.

He ignored her glare. "Once I've dealt with Wyvern, I want to see you again. In person."

She was taken aback—and not at all sure that was a good idea.

"Will you meet with me just once...for old times' sake?"

Ramona harrumphed, then drummed her fingers on her folded arms.

"We can negotiate a new peace treaty for the future, since this one's destroyed. Well?" he asked.

"I hardly think that is appro—"

"Promise me!"

Time was of the essence, so Ramona rolled her eyes. "Oh, very well!"

"Good." Zolond tugged at his black silk waistcoat, looking pleased. "Then I shall be there shortly. Tell your forces not to attack me when I appear. This is between Wyvern and me. Keep your fighters back, or someone could get hurt."

Ramona nodded with relief and ignored the lump in her throat. He had not betrayed her.

Thank you, old friend.

"Good luck," she forced out.

His lips twisted. "Luck? My dear lady, I wear the Black Crown. Luck has nothing to do with it, I assure you. Farewell."

Amused at his arrogance, she nodded goodbye.

Then he disappeared.

A moment later, Ramona zoomed back out into the present world as well.

Upon opening her physical eyes again, she glanced toward the window of her room. An ominous tremor ran through her.

Never in her long, long life had she ever imagined that a day would arrive when the fate of the whole Order rested on her ancient bond with Geoffrey de Lacey. He had always been the most fearsome warlock she had ever known.

Still, she did not envy him going up against Wyvern and the Dark Druid Council by himself. She stared out the window at the moon.

Let's hope the old scoundrel hasn't lost his touch.

* * *

So, Zolond thought, incensed, *the devil's whelp dares launch a coup against me?*

He understood exactly what this meant.

As the Dark Master returned from the astral plane to the present reality of his large, cozy cavern in the Balefire Mountains, he would have liked to claim he was surprised.

But he had gained an inkling of Wyvern's intent about a week and a half ago, when Ramona had told him of the Nephilim's attempt to abduct her nephew, Jake, from the boy's estate of Griffon Castle.

Ah well. Zolond drew a deep inhalation through his nostrils and let it out slowly. Such scheming was to be expected when one allied oneself with the evilest companions one could find. Treachery was in their blood.

Especially Wyvern's.

No matter. Zolond did not lack for options regarding his response to this brazen challenge to his authority. But there wasn't a moment to lose.

His holiday was officially over.

It was time to take back control of the Black Fortress.

With that, he pulled on his simple black jacket, placed his bowler hat calmly on his head, and picked up his scepter, which now took the form of a walking stick.

The Master's Ring on his finger glowed an angry shade of lime-green, tiny tendrils of ominous purple magic already wafting up from the stone.

Zolond turned toward the door to call in his reptilians, but it suddenly occurred to him that if, indeed, Wyvern meant to make a play for his throne, then Zolond's own successor, his great-great grandson, Victor—the Black Prince—could also be in serious danger.

I should warn the boy. Take measures for his protection.

Zolond sighed. He did not speak to his headstrong grandson often. The Dark Master was hardly the sentimental type.

But there was more to it than that. The truth was, he didn't like the way the boy was being raised, in isolation, in a state of constant pressure and training. Alas, it had been necessary to keep the Black Prince hidden and apart from the world; indeed, *both* worlds—the magical and the human one.

There were too many people out there to whom he was a threat. Victor's parents had died years ago because of that very fact.

For his part, Zolond had done his best to give the boy every possible advantage. Shadowedge Manor was practically a palace out in the English countryside, with elaborate gardens and opulent chambers. He had supplied Victor with an army of servitors and had given him the best possible tutor/bodyguard that he could find...

Whisking aside a lingering flicker of guilt, Zolond reached for his black calling candle.

The Dark Master wasn't much for family, but he could not deny having a certain soft spot for his grandson.

In truth, Victor reminded him just a bit of himself, long, long ago, back when he used to be mere Geoffrey de Lacey.

Then Zolond lit the calling candle and waited for the secure communication channel to connect...

CHAPTER FOUR
Heir of Darkness

Victor de Lacey was annoyed.

It was past midnight, and he had just fallen asleep, when his sensei, the samurai-wizard Master Nagai, had barged into his chamber and dragged him out of bed for another, random, middle-of-the-night training challenge.

"You must be ready at all times, Your Highness. Do you imagine your enemies will give you warning?"

Such was the life of the Black Prince.

So now here he was, out on the torch-lit training ground behind Shadowedge Manor, dodging javelins being hurled at him by Nagai's helpers, a trio of tusked Noxu half-trolls.

While knocking their spears aside with his telekinesis, Victor simultaneously maintained the illusion of a charging war elephant he had conjured off to his left, *and* continued walloping his assigned target—a pile of enchanted bricks—with crackling bolts of energy from his alderwood wand.

His three-fold challenge was to avoid getting skewered by the spears, keep the elephant illusion convincing enough to fool an enemy, and smash that vexing pile of bricks down to rubble.

So far, the elephant was holding steady, thanks to the spell that Victor whispered now and then under his breath.

That part was relatively easy.

Victor had always been good at illusions. It was the first magical talent that had shown itself when he was only five.

Large as life, the big bull elephant swung its gray trunk back and forth, flapped its ears, and trumpeted angrily as it stood at the edge of the garden, looking as real as you please.

The Noxu's stray javelins flew right through the figment.

Deflecting their spears was not too difficult for him either, although doing both at once when he was still half-asleep *was* a bit of challenge.

The brick pile, though, *that* was another story.

Sitting there stubbornly some thirty feet away, this part of his teacher's latest midnight challenge was giving him the most trouble—as usual.

"Concentrate!" Nagai barked.

Victor pursed his lips, gripped his wand tighter, and redoubled his efforts to destroy the brick pile, flashing out a lightning bolt of energy that struck another chunk off the side.

"Not good enough! Again!"

Victor gritted his teeth. It was not simply that earth had always been his weakness, out of the four classical elements.

It was that, frankly, those enchanted bricks were not just stubborn. They were downright obnoxious, and their taunts were starting to get under his skin.

When not in use as a training tool, the enchanted bricks looked like ordinary building materials, neatly stacked up in a square sort of tower, four feet wide and ten feet high.

But when activated—when Nagai woke them from their slumber— the bricks opened their eyes, peered out into the night with little faces, and promptly began taunting him.

"Nice try! Missed me!"

"Ha, ha! You loser!"

"Weak!"

"Ach, you're ugly!"

"What are you, stupid?"

"You're never going to succeed, you dolt. Why don't you just give up?"

The rude little bricks mocked and jeered, blew raspberries at him, pulled faces, and stuck out their tongues.

"Missed again! Too bad, so sad!"

"Get your eyes checked, mate. You need spectacles."

Victor glowered at them. *Nobody* spoke to the Black Prince that way! Except those insufferable bricks.

He wanted to kill them.

But that was the whole point.

Master Nagai expected the future Dark Master to keep a cool head at all times. To remain unflappable, unemotional, detached.

The way the future head of all evil on Earth ought to be.

It wasn't easy when one was being insulted by inanimate objects.

Unfortunately, the more Victor let those niggling little voices get to him, the less control he had over his magic.

Thus the lesson.

Meanwhile, all Victor really wanted was to go back to bed.

Well, that wasn't actually true. He wanted, oh, many things. To meet a few girls would be nice. Not that he had any idea how to talk to them.

Mainly he just wanted to get out of this place once in a while. For, stately as it was, luxurious in every room, Shadowedge Manor was but a gilded cage.

This place was *so boring.* All there was to do was train, train, train, study, study, study, and listen to Master Nagai saying blah, blah, blah.

Warlock royalty? Ha.

Victor was a prisoner here, plain and simple. His whole existence boiled down to two basic rules: stay put and do as you're told.

All by myself.

The elephant began to flicker as Victor fumed and his attention wandered.

"Focus!" Nagai snapped his black metallic war fan shut into its wand form and lobbed a fireball at Victor.

He jumped back, then glared at his teacher, while the smoke from the singed grass by his feet filled his nostrils.

"You don't have to blow me up!"

"Tsk, tsk! The elephant is fading! I can see right through it." Nagai swept a graceful gesture toward the illusion, then flipped his samurai battle fan open again and continued fanning himself impatiently with it.

He was an imposing figure, the wizard warrior-monk, with his piercing eyes, his partly shaved head, the rest of his long, graying hair slicked back into a tight topknot.

His long black samurai robes, the kamishimo, swirled around his lean body as he paced, ready to scold, correct, or criticize at any moment.

Victor heaved a sigh, then mumbled, "Yes, sensei."

What choice did he have?

He dutifully fixed the elephant with a firmer repeat of the spell, but harrumphed. The ronin was indeed a harsh taskmaster, but that was not surprising. Nagai's life had made him what he was.

His father had headed a Buddhist temple shrine in Japan, where young Nagai had been raised and trained by deadly warrior monks. After spending his entire childhood under their discipline, he left the monastery and eventually made his way to Edo Castle, where he entered the service of the shogun as a samurai.

There, Nagai had been fascinated by the *tezuma* magic of the court magicians as they performed their theatrical illusions. A stranger in a new place, the lonely young samurai had sought these men out and persuaded them to teach him the tricks of "hand lightning," as it was called.

But the playful illusions and artful sleights-of-hand these low-level conjurers performed to entertain the shogun and his court soon led Nagai's curious mind down darker paths...toward real magic.

Somewhere along the way, he encountered a traveling sorcerer, who was impressed enough by the young samurai to begin initiating him to learn the ways of dark magic.

But when the superstitious shogun discovered Nagai's new hobby, he was outraged. Such dabbling in the dark arts would bring down a curse upon the whole palace, he claimed. Nagai was thus disgraced, and the shogun declared that ritual suicide was the only remedy.

Nagai had declined that honor.

So, the shogun ordered the other samurais to kill him, but they could not. His magic, combined with his fighting skills, made him too strong.

It was only his prior training at his father's temple that prevented him from slaughtering his former colleagues. He restrained himself for the sake of his family's honor and accepted banishment as his fate instead. He left the shogun's castle for the last time, and then sailed away from Japan.

For years, Nagai had wandered the world as a ronin, challenging wizards and warriors alike on his journeys, and ever increasing his powers.

Eventually, he heard about the Dark Druids, and then came looking for Grandfather.

That was how Dark Master Zolond had first found him. When Nagai discovered he could not defeat the ancient English warlock, losing to the Dark Master again and again, the ronin finally became a true samurai once more, choosing Zolond as his new overlord.

He had been devoted to the old Englishman ever since—almost as much as Grandfather's royal reptilians.

Given Nagai's wide knowledge of magic, martial arts, court etiquette, and the world at large, Zolond had put him in charge of molding Prince Victor in the same strict spirit that the warrior monks had once trained *him*.

All of which meant there was no use arguing with this particular teacher.

Nagai could crush Victor if he chose.

Of course, the ex-ronin wouldn't *really* hurt him; he wasn't allowed. He was probably tempted to, though, from time to time, Victor mused.

The sourpuss Japanese wizard never really saw the humor in his only student's pranks.

Ah well. A boy of nearly fourteen had to amuse himself somehow.

In truth, the only time that Victor felt real fear of Master Nagai was when he donned his full samurai armor (especially his horned helmet and blank ebony mask) and unsheathed his katana.

Then the tolerant teacher became fairly terrifying.

Little did Victor know that such an episode was about to unfold.

At that moment, he heard a familiar voice some distance behind him.

"Your Highness! Your Highness!"

He could barely hear his imp servant calling him over the constant mockery of the bricks, the trumpeting of the elephant, and the garbled snuffles of the Noxu.

But it was enough to break his concentration; Magpen sounded truly alarmed. The war elephant vanished. In the nick of time, from the corner of his eye, Victor saw a spear flying at him and caught it midair in his hand.

Nagai quickly made the Noxu pause their next volley, and held up his hand to silence the bricks.

Victor turned around to see his servant come bursting out of the mansion's back doors and race across the elegant stone terrace, waving both hands in the air to get his attention.

"Y' Highness, come quick!"

"What is it, Mags?"

Magpen skidded to a halt at the top of the stone stairs, his red frock coat askew.

The blue-skinned imp, as a species, was not normally inclined to wear more than a loincloth.

If that.

Fortunately, Victor had trained the imp to dress like a proper servant in any noble household. They'd had a set of red-and-white footman's livery made for the little fellow to match that of the two dozen human-seeming servitors that Grandfather had conjured to work at Shadowedge Manor from an extra set of silverware.

At least Magpen was real. Victor didn't have a dog or a cat or even a turtle, but he supposed his imp servant was the next best thing to a pet. The creature was useful, and, though he was often annoying, Victor found him amusing at times.

Magpen had grown to love his little clothes, each set specially tailored to fit his diminutive size.

Like most imps, he was only about three feet tall, with spindly arms and legs and, in his case, a plump belly. Most imps were thin—the lowly, kicked dogs of the evil hierarchy—but in the service of the Black Prince, this one ate well.

Victor made sure of that.

Magpen had thin tufts of bristly gold hair that sprouted from the tops of his pointy ears. They matched the fancy gold trim around the lapels of his livery coat.

He was bald across the top of his flattish head, like any imp, which was why he so delighted in wearing one of those white powdered wigs on formal occasions at the manor, like all the other footmen.

He thought he looked so grand with that thing on his head that it was hard to drag him away from a mirror.

In any case, something had clearly put the imp in an agitated state. He hopped down the stone steps from the terrace onto the lawn that served as a training ground.

"What's going on?" Victor inquired.

Magpen leaped onto the grass. "It's the Dark Master, Your Highness! H-he's come through for you on a candle-call!"

"What? Now?" Victor's eyes widened.

Magpen bobbed his head, pointing to the house. "He's waiting, sir! He wants to talk to you!"

"Go." Nagai nodded.

Victor was suddenly so excited that he nearly missed his sheath entirely with his wand. Sliding it into place, he sprinted across the grass and bounded up the stone terrace steps.

"Which candle?" he asked as Magpen followed him into the house.

"Your bedchamber, Highness." The imp's bare feet pattered across the polished marble floor behind him as he shadowed Victor down the hallway. (He refused to wear shoes. That was where even Magpen drew the line. Only when there was a blizzard would he accept snow boots.)

Victor strode down the hallway, passing marble statues in niches and large oil paintings on the walls.

"I wonder what he wants!" He swung around the newel post, then paused so abruptly that Magpen ran into his leg. "I'll bet he's called to ask me what I want for my birthday!"

It was coming up at the end of the month: October thirty-first. Samhain, or, Hallowe'en, as outsiders called it.

Magpen clapped his hands eagerly. "Yes, that must be it, sir, I'm sure!"

After all, the sorcerer-king was a very busy man. The great warlock only called two or three times a year.

"Do you know what you're going to ask for this year, sir?" Magpen said eagerly.

Victor laughed. "You'd better believe it!"

Magpen had no trouble keeping up as Victor pounded up the grand staircase. Imps were good leapers, a bit clumsy, but nimble.

Birthday presents could be pretty outrageous when they came from the most powerful wizard in the world.

Last year, Grandfather had given him a Galileo Spyglass. Forget the twenty-times refracting telescope that its inventor, the great astronomer had told the public (and the Pope) that he'd used to trace the stars and view the distant planets. The truth was, Galileo's secret, full-strength telescope, touched with magic (just as the Inquisition had suspected!) could reveal the busy worlds going on about their business in distant galaxies.

Victor had largely tired of it after a week.

The year before that, Grandfather had sent him a Bauble-nut Tree, which grew jewels instead of fruit. Protected indoors year-round in its big clay pot, the little tree had yielded its first crop this past summer. Diamonds, rubies, sapphires, and an emerald or two.

Why, Magpen himself had been a gift several years ago to keep Victor company and serve as his unwitting court jester.

But the best part of Grandfather's annual gifts—or as occasional rewards whenever Master Nagai gave him an especially good report— were the spells that Zolond magically imparted into Victor's personal grimoire.

Any conscientious mage took careful notes on everything he learned, from hexes to curses, incantations to potion recipes.

Victor kept his growing collection of knowledge in a little black spell book. Each year on his birthday, a new spell appeared on one of the blank pages straight from Grandfather's mind: a gift from the Dark Master to his heir apparent. And, Hades, that old warlock knew some good spells.

"Well, sir?" Magpen prompted as they reached the top of the stairs. "What are you going to ask for, mighty prince? Or is it a secret?"

"No, it's not a secret." Victor paused outside his chamber door, then he lowered his voice in case Grandfather could hear him inside. "I'm going to tell him I want to go to London for a while. I'm so sick of being here! No offense," he added hastily when Magpen's face fell.

The imp looked wounded, as though Victor had merely tired of his company.

"It's not you, Mags. I just want to see more of the world. People. *Girls*. I want...a life!"

"Oh." Magpen gazed up mournfully at him, then heaved a sigh, lowered his head, and stepped back. "Yes, master."

Victor frowned. *Great.* Now he felt guilty. "Stay out," he ordered Magpen, quickly remembering he was the scion of all evil. "I'm sure this won't take long."

Then he went into his room and banged the door shut in his only friend's face.

When he walked into his chamber, the head of the sorcerer-king appeared atop the flame of the thick black candle on his desk: a moving, three-dimensional portrait sculpted by smoke.

At once, the ominous look on Grandfather's stern, craggy face told Victor that the old man hadn't called to ask about his birthday.

"Ah, good," the Dark Master said, terse as ever. "You're awake."

"Yes, Your Majesty." Victor didn't dare sit down on his nearby bed, but gave the smoky image of the sorcerer-king a formal bow. "I was training with Master Nagai."

"Hm. I am most pleased to hear it. Unfortunately, lad, there is no time for pleasantries this evening—er, eager as I am to hear of your progress," he added, as an afterthought. "I'm afraid I have received a most disturbing bit of news tonight that may well affect your security.

"No need for worry, of course," he continued. "I shall soon have it sorted. Still, it is prudent that you be advised of the situation. And

Master Nagai. At ease, Victor," Zolond added, nodding his permission to be seated.

"Thank you, sir." Still sweaty from his ordeal outside, Victor merely leaned against the nearest twisty, Gothic spire of his four-poster bed.

"Difficult training?" Zolond asked.

Victor smiled and thrust his hands into his pockets. "Your samurai keeps life interesting, sir." But he sensed Zolond's churning displeasure with whatever had occurred, and Victor grew concerned. "What is it you wanted to tell me?"

Zolond pursed his smoky gray lips. "Yes. Erm, you'll have heard of Lord Wyvern."

"Yes. Mortal son of the most unholy Lord of the Ninth Pit." Victor bowed his head at the mention of the great demon, Shemrazul, as he had been taught.

The Horned One was the guiding spirit of the Dark Druid brotherhood, and the Dark Master was his representative on earth.

"Correct," Grandfather said. "Well, it seems the dear fellow has taken it into his head to try to seize my throne."

"What?" Victor's stomach dropped.

He pushed away from the bedpost, every muscle tensing.

"Don't be concerned, boy." Grandfather's attitude became businesslike. "This happens every so often. Some young upstart full of his own stink takes it into his head to challenge my power. It'll happen to you, as well, when you're the Dark Master. But it's of no consequence. Many have tried before Wyvern, and they all have failed. I shall be rid of him soon."

"O-of course, sir," Victor agreed.

But the thought of his grandfather raising a hand against the son of Shemrazul made him queasy. Wouldn't the demon be...a bit peeved if Zolond killed his son?

Zolond glanced downward, as though checking his fob watch. "I haven't much time, I'm afraid. I just...wanted to tell you myself that they may come after you tonight, since you are my heir. But never fear. You'll be quite safe. Just do as Nagai says. Oh, and don't be alarmed when you see a couple of dragons land on the lawn."

Victor's eyebrows rose. "Dragons, sir?"

"I'll be sending a pair of my reptilians to guard the house—in a somewhat altered form."

Victor grinned. "I can't wait to see them."

Zolond smiled back and shook his head. "Boys and their dragons. Run along, now. Fetch your samurai for me. I wish to advise him on your security. And do give Magpen my regards." Grandfather glanced toward the door, and Victor suddenly heard little bare feet running away from the spot where the imp attached to them had been eavesdropping.

"At least he is loyal," Zolond said with an indulgent smirk.

Victor smiled warmly. "It is good to see you, sir."

"Likewise, m'boy." Zolond nearly faltered for a moment, as though there was something more he wished to say. Then his craggy face hardened again. "Oh, and Victor?"

"Yes, sir?"

"I have not forgotten your birthday."

Emboldened by his grandfather's kinder tone, Victor took a step forward. "If possible, sire, I should so like—"

"Victor! War is upon us. We'll discuss it later."

Stung, he lowered his head. "Forgive me, sire. I understand."

"Yes, yes. Go now. I must speak to Nagai." Zolond's gray, wispy image gestured impatiently at him.

Victor swallowed his embarrassment with a nod and hurried out of his chamber to go and get his sensei.

This sounds bad. If Grandfather had to kill the Nephilim son of their demon-god, Shemrazul was sure to punish him somehow.

Then Victor remembered he was only thirteen. Who was he to question the Dark Master?

Best not to meddle in things he did not understand. It was enough to know there was yet another enemy out there who wanted him dead. Just one more to add to the list, along with every blasted member of the Order.

Victor leaned over the banister and yelled down the steps for his sensei, but Nagai was already on his way, thanks to Magpen.

Victor let his fierce Japanese trainer into his room to speak to the sorcerer-king.

He left them in privacy, pulling his chamber door shut after Nagai had stalked in. Then Victor remained in the hallway, unsure what to do.

Uneasiness filled him. Visiting London seemed so unimportant now. Even his birthday. Baal's beard, the more Victor learned about life as the Dark Master, the less he liked it.

Unfortunately, for the Black Prince, fate was fate.

CHAPTER FIVE
Jake's Hideaway

Jake laughed, pedaling the swan boat for all he was worth, for the voyage to reach his island in the middle of the lake had inevitably turned into a race.

"Land-ho!" Brian yelled, pulling ahead. Everyone else's legs were tired from the difficulty of churning the rusty pedals, but the Guardian had been powering his and Isabelle's swan boat relentlessly.

"Supernatural strength—no fair!" Dani hooted.

Jake knew they were making too much noise, but he let it go for now. Everyone desperately needed a respite from all of the danger and gloom.

Let them have their fun, he thought. They could use it.

Him included.

There was a brittle air to their merriment—great tension just beneath the surface.

"My legs have turned to pudding! Er, not literally," Archie said. It was an important distinction when one had a witch for a sweetheart.

Isabelle chuckled and gave them all a cheeky wave as she and Brian passed. "Toodle-oo!"

"Oh, I'd splash you if it weren't so cold!" Dani retorted, and Teddy yipped playfully.

Only the dog's cheer was genuine, however, Jake suspected.

The rest of them were simply trying to put the disaster at Merlin Hall out of their minds for a little while. Jake hoped his friends were having more success at it than he was. For his part, he kept having flashes of the moment when the sky pirate had fallen to his death.

Having visited Hades himself once, Jake had a fairly clear notion of where the criminal had ended up. He just hoped the poor blighter he'd accidentally killed never decided to pay him a ghostly visit. To be sure, the memory itself was enough to haunt him.

"Boo, hiss!" Dani yelled as Brian and Isabelle pulled up to the island first.

The Yank laughed and sprang out of his swan boat. Isabelle tossed him the rope, and he secured it between two boulders. Then he handed Izzy out of the boat. The soon-to-be debutante lifted the hem of her gown daintily over the water as she stepped out onto dry land. She thanked him, dusted herself off, and looked around at the island.

In the next moment, Jake's boat bumped against the shore, rocking and creaking. Archie and Nix arrived third.

"You lost!" Dani teased.

"At least we didn't sink along the way," Archie replied. "I count that as a victory; these boats are ancient."

"They're fun, though, you've got to admit," Nixie said.

Brian assisted them, taking hold of their swans' ropes and securing them on the rocks so they didn't float away.

The rest of them clambered out, and nobody mentioned Merlin Hall, as if by tacit agreement.

After all, it was important in life to understand there were things you could control and things you couldn't. Things that happened *happened*, and the best you could do was deal with the situation as it stood.

At the moment, there was nothing they could do but wait.

They should hear something soon, Jake was sure.

Until then, whatever twists and turns unfolded on this deep, dark, seemingly endless night, he was determined to take them in stride as best he could.

In the meantime, he had decided to focus on his friends. It seemed like the easiest way to keep from obsessing over myriad distressing questions that still had no answers.

"Yay, Teddy, we're here!" Dani put the little brown terrier down on the pebbled ground.

At once, Teddy darted about, sniffing everything.

"You know exactly where you are, don't you, boy?" she said, then raced after her dog toward the ramshackle gazebo several yards away.

The wooden structure was octagonal, its roof mossy, its foundations choked with overgrown, dried-out weeds.

"This is where I used to sleep a lot of nights after I ran away from the orphanage," Jake told the others. Isabelle gave him a sad look, but he wasn't looking for sympathy.

He'd survived.

Red landed on a large, flat boulder by the water's edge, then prowled over to join them.

"I'm freezing," Nixie said. "I think I'll start a fire."

"No!" Jake stopped her as she reached for her wand. "It could draw too much attention. We can't risk being seen. We've been too noisy as it is."

Brian nodded. "He's right. We should probably keep it down."

"Do you know how to conjure blankets?" Dani asked.

"Hmm, I should be able to do that..."

While she stepped away to concentrate on a mental review of any relevant spells she'd memorized, Jake led the others up the creaky wooden steps into the faded garden folly.

"Welcome to my former home," he said with a gesture at the place. "It's not much, but we should be comfortable here for a while."

* * *

Um, comfortable? Izzy thought. No doubt the ancient gazebo had been charming in its heyday. But now? With some trepidation, she scanned its moldering rafters, full of cobwebs and old swallows' nests.

At least the solid lower half of the walls offered shelter from the wind, which had been bone-chilling out on the lake. And so—after checking for spiders—she sat down on the dusty wooden floor, leaning back against one of the posts.

Jake began regaling everyone with madcap stories of his pickpocket life; they were supposed to be funny. And they were. But Izzy sensed the pain behind his picaresque tales and knew that her cousin was merely trying to entertain everyone, distract them from their fears.

It was good of him, but it wasn't really working.

Anxiety hung like a cloud over the whole group. Their emotions were plain to her, as an empath.

Oh, Brian was fairly serene, as was the Gryphon, of course. But Jake seethed with uncertainty, guilt-ridden over the fact that he had just accidentally killed one of the sky pirates back there. Archie was putting on a brave face, bless him, but he was terrified for their parents.

Isabelle wasn't, much. Mother was too sensible to do anything overly foolish, and Papa recognized his own limitations. The elegant Viscount Bradford was a diplomat, not a fighter. Izzy had a feeling they'd both be all right.

Then she moved on, assessing the others.

Nixie remained strangely unflappable, off by herself, preparing to conjure blankets. Though she was only twelve, she somehow maintained the most magnificent air of sangfroid. As the cynic—often, the pessimist—of their group, her usual mode of always waiting for the other shoe to drop must have prepared her well for a crisis.

Dear little Dani was another story, though. The redhead's trusting nature rose and fell in waves between hope and dread—and her dog's mood followed right along. Poor Teddy wagged his tail or whined nervously, depending on how his owner seemed at any given moment.

As for Izzy herself, she scarcely knew *what* to feel. This had been, without question, the most confusing night of her life.

Much, much earlier this evening, she had spent a short but poignant hour with Janos on the moonlit deck of the ship the diplomatic party had taken out onto the Mediterranean to visit the merfolk.

It seemed like a lifetime ago instead of a mere few hours.

While the others dove into the sea to go and warn King Nereus about the latest threat from the Dark Druids, Isabelle had remained behind. It was not just that she needed a break from all the formality and diplomatic protocols that were a part of traveling with her parents.

She'd wanted a chance to speak privately to Janos about the tragic death of his hatchlings, and to present him with the Floating Flowers— an old childhood toy that Aunt Ramona had once given her.

Izzy had brought them along specially in her mountain of luggage to share with her dear vampire friend.

She hoped it had helped him as the brokenhearted vampire grieved his poor, murdered children.

"I know they were nightmares," he had said wistfully, *"but they were my nightmares."*

She'd glimpsed the brief tears in his eyes when she'd offered her gift, but he'd accepted. One by one, they had sent the Floating Flowers aloft into the starry sky over the ocean to honor the memory of each innocent vampire child that Lord Wyvern had killed when he burned down Janos's castle.

It was hard to imagine such cruelty, but the Nephilim warlock had done it from sheer spite.

Janos could barely forgive himself for not being there to protect them, but he'd been out on a mission with the Order.

The strange part was that Izzy knew better than anyone how conflicted Janos felt about the fact that his hatchlings were dead.

She did not sense him mourning his vampire brides in the least, but the children were another story. As their father, he had loved the misbegotten creatures as best he could, yet the Guardian side of him knew full well that his wicked little hatchlings would be pure evil by the time they grew up.

He had been determined to teach them only to drink the blood of animals, but his wives had disagreed with that.

Thus, a part of Janos felt relieved that his dangerous brood was no more on this earth—and, for that, he could not forgive himself.

And yet commemorating them with the little magic sky lanterns seemed to ease at least some of his grief.

Just when Izzy and he had finished sending up the last of the Floating Flowers from the deck of the yacht, suddenly, they both had received a wave of sharp inner warning—she as an empath, he through his Guardian instincts.

In an instant, they both knew something was terribly wrong back at Merlin Hall.

At once, they had called the diplomatic party back to the ship, and were soon underway. Ranjit and Tex, their official Lightriders, had conducted them there with all haste.

But Isabelle could never have imagined the hellish scene that awaited them when they stepped out through the portal onto the palace lawn.

She squeezed her eyes shut, trying to route the bloody images and awful sounds from her mind. So much anger and ugliness. Such evil and hate.

And Janos was still back there.

As was Aunt Ramona.

Unfortunately, Izzy was afraid to do more than steal the briefest peeks around the edges of her inner awareness to try and determine whether the people she loved were even alive.

She *believed* that they were, but she was afraid to probe for greater clarity for fear of distracting them.

Janos could be in the midst of a death match with ten enemy fighters, for all she knew. Those were the sorts of odds he seemed to like, and he would feel her scanning him.

She did not dare break his concentration.

Same with Aunt Ramona. The Elder witch might be uttering the incantation for one of her devastating spells against the warlocks at this very moment.

Izzy took a deep breath. She could be patient. She could wait. What choice did she have?

Because, in her gut, she knew that the fight for Merlin Hall wasn't over yet.

She could feel the spiritual warfare taking place in those invisible realms barely known to the sorcerers. With a shudder against the deepening chill, she forced her attention back to the here and now.

Opening her eyes again, she gazed at her friends as they all chattered on. Cousin Jake was explaining how the bearded lady of the carnival had described that they used to have fireworks over this lake, long ago.

"Bearded lady?" Archie echoed, scrunching up his nose.

Jake shrugged. "She made the best elderberry muffins. She used to give me one when I was hungry."

Izzy got up, dusted herself off, and joined the group, only half listening to her cousin's tales.

Looking around at the lake and the run-down pleasure grounds, she knew one thing: this was a good place.

It might look sad now, but there were decades' worth of good feelings imprinted on the atmosphere here, countless happy memories.

Despite the present gloom of this coal-black night, she sensed the lingering radiance of much joy in this location. Dani had chosen well.

There had been laughter and dancing, a world of whimsical entertainment, romance and wonder. Friends by the thousands having fun. Generations of performers eager to dazzle their audiences...

As Izzy watched her rascally cousin telling some cock-and-bull tale about his past exploits, playfully bragging about outwitting the constables, Izzy smiled to herself.

No wonder Jakey-boy had made this place his haven. Somehow, it fit. She smiled and folded her arms across her chest as she listened.

Maybe someday some enterprising soul would bring the pleasure gardens back to their former glory.

I hope so. If the park was ever resurrected, she'd be first in line to buy a ticket. And she would come at night.

So she could walk the graceful promenades with Janos.

* * *

"Hey, vampire!" someone rudely called the moment Janos landed on the ground in human form.

He'd come back briefly from his spying mission, not because there was anything essential to report, but he figured Derek might find the information about Wyvern's escaped dragon useful.

Circling in bat form overhead, he had witnessed the commotion around the open drawbridge of the Fortress a short while ago, the Noxu fleeing the castle in terror. Intrigued, he'd flown closer. A few darting passes had gained him a discreet peek into the great hall, where he'd seen Wyvern bring the vicious beast back under control.

Thank God it didn't get out.

He had met the dragon before in his past dealings with Wyvern, but its presence inside the Fortress had slipped his mind. Rather an important detail, that.

Leaving Balinor's owl to keep watch, Janos had returned to warn Derek they had a bloody dragon in there, just in case the Guardians were considering storming the Fortress, since, for once, they knew where it was.

Of course, Janos personally thought such a move would be madness, but no one ever listened to him.

He was the black sheep of the Order, its prodigal son, and rude tones of voice were all he ever got around here.

Especially from Maddox St. Trinian.

"Janos!"

Striving for patience, he paused on his way to the entrance of Merlin Hall, then turned in the graveled courtyard and waited for the seventeen-year-old Maddox to close the distance between them.

The tall, black-haired lad marched toward him, all brooding intensity, as usual, though blood-flecked and looking a little beaten up after the battle.

Janos schooled his face into a nonchalant smile but fully expected another tedious confrontation.

"Maddox," he said, refraining from using his favorite nickname for the serious young Guardian. After all, the boy deserved his respect. He had fought well in the battle, made his mama proud—though Ravyn, for her part, had probably killed more than either of them tonight.

"What can I do for you?" Janos asked as he joined Maddox.

"I need to ask you something."

"Yes?"

The lad was never much for talking, but instead of spitting his question out, he floundered, staring at Janos almost in distress for a second.

"What's the matter?" Janos asked.

Maddox looked away with a huff, dragged his hand through his hair impatiently, and scowled at the ground.

"I'm in a bit of a hurry, if you don't mind. Still in the middle of a mission here—"

"It's Isabelle!" he blurted out.

The boy suddenly had Janos's full attention. "What about her?" he asked quietly.

Maddox grew even more tongue-tied, his cheeks coloring by the light of the maze's still-simmering fires. "I, um, I *know* you have some sort of bizarre...telepathic ability to communicate with her, and I just...um...I wondered..."

Janos lifted his brows, rather enjoying this. "Yes?"

"I just want to know if she's all right. Have you, er, talked to her? Mentally or whatever?"

"No, I have not," said Janos.

Maddox looked flabbergasted at this reply. "Why not? Don't you care if she's safe?"

"She's safe."

"But you just said you didn't—"

"Use your Guardian instincts, man." Janos clapped Maddox on the shoulder. "Mine would be going mad if she were in danger. What do yours tell you?"

Maddox frowned. "Well, that she's...safe, I guess. But can't you just ask her where she is?"

"I don't go prying into the girl's head unless it's an emergency."

"This *is* an emergency, Janos. I want to know where she is!"

"And why is that?"

"Don't *you?*" Maddox retorted.

Janos narrowed his eyes. "We don't need to control her, Maddox," he said slowly. *Idiot kid. You really know nothing about females, do you?*

"I'm not trying to control her!" Maddox scoffed, but his face flushed bright. "I just want to know if she's in a safe place. What's wrong with that?"

"Well, for one thing, we weren't supposed to know Jake's location for security's sake, remember? Until the danger had passed. The Dark Druids are after him."

"Yes, but—"

"Secondly, you saw the condition she was in before they went through the portal. Her powers were already taxed beyond her ability to bear. For that reason alone, I would not seek to make contact. I would not risk hurting her just to put *my* mind at ease. She needs time to recover. I can wait until the time is right for *her*."

Maddox heaved an impatient sigh.

"Relax," Janos said. "She's got Jake, Red, Nixie with her—and let us not forget the formidable Dani O'Dell. I'm sure she'll be perfectly fine, wherever she is. Anywhere is safer than here at the moment. The Black Fortress hasn't left yet. On that note, I need to speak to Derek. Have you seen him?"

With a sulky look, Maddox nodded toward the entrance of the palace. "He's coming out now. Guess he's looking for you, too."

Janos glanced over his shoulder and saw the master Guardian prowling out of the charred doorway with Ravyn Vambrace a step behind. "Er, no, mate. I think he's looking for *you*." He turned back to Maddox with a rueful half-smile. "You disobeyed orders, remember?"

Maddox cursed under his breath as he, too, realized it was time to answer for ignoring Derek's command to stay with the group.

"Just think..." Janos said in a low tone as the two Guardians spotted them and headed their way. "If you had done as you were told, you'd be with Izzy right now. But you had to go and be a hero, eh? Just like your birth father."

Maddox gave him a withering look.

"Maddox!" Derek boomed.

Having been, himself, on the receiving end of Stone's rebukes more times than he could count, Janos relented on the matter of Isabelle. "If she reaches out to me, I'll let you know as soon as I hear anything."

"Thanks," Maddox mumbled, then visibly braced himself for a scolding.

Poor kid. Janos suppressed a chuckle. Not only did Derek have his sternest glower on, but Ravyn's coal-black eyes could've drilled holes into her son. The warrior woman had been proud of the fighting skills

Maddox had displayed tonight, but apparently, she had just found out that he had disobeyed a direct order.

Now poor Stick had to deal with the both of them.

"Tsk, tsk," Janos said in amusement as they approached.

"Shut up," Maddox muttered.

"Whatever you do, don't talk back. Trust me on that."

"I don't need advice from you," Maddox said under his breath.

Janos shrugged, then turned to face his former team leader and fierce female colleague.

"St. Trinian! Inside," Derek clipped out.

"Yes, sir." Maddox dropped his gaze and marched grimly into the palace. Ravyn stared at him with icy disapproval as he passed, then she followed him in.

He really has my sympathies, Janos mused, then snapped back to attention. "Derek! I have news." Janos strode over to the brawny, brown-haired Guardian and quickly explained about the dragon. "Just thought you should know. I'd better get back there."

"Good work." Derek started to turn away, then paused. "Er, Janos? Any word from Isabelle and the kids?"

"No." Janos shook his head and prayed Derek didn't ask him to try to make contact with her. "No news is good news."

"Is it?" the rugged warrior asked.

"Yes." Janos nodded firmly. "If there was a problem, she'd tell me."

"Understood. If that situation arises, get a Lightrider and go. I'll tell Tex to stand by, just in case. Take as many men as you need. Whatever happens, Jake must not be captured."

Janos nodded, then returned to his mission.

A moment later, he was winging his way back up into the night sky and across the sprawling grounds of Merlin Hall.

He could see the Black Fortress still sitting where he'd left it, on top of Aelfric. The chalk giant had calmed down; Janos wondered if they'd put a spell on him.

Probably.

Halfway across the dark landscape, he briefly pondered his sense of relief that Derek had not ordered him to contact Isabelle. There was more to Janos's reluctance to do so than the excuses he had given Maddox—though all of them were true.

His unspoken reason was actually cowardice.

His darling Isabelle, his light, the one pure thing in this foul, ugly world, had glimpsed him in his true vampire form for the first time tonight before he'd sprinted off to join the battle, and Janos wasn't quite sure how to face her after that.

He'd had no choice. He was strongest in that form, and his former vampire acquaintances had been closing in on old Dame Oriel for the kill.

Well, he had saved the clairvoyant Elder. But he still wished Isabelle had looked away.

For all he knew, she might never speak to him again, telepathically or otherwise. She might be too repulsed.

After all, he was quite the nightmare under that appearance: fangs, claws, the whole, hideous bit.

Not *quite* the stuff of young ladies' infatuations, to put it mildly.

In short, if his one true friend in this godforsaken world was horrified by him now, he was in no hurry to find out.

CHAPTER SIX
Joining Forces

Zolond finished his brief candle-call with Master Nagai concerning his grandson's security, then it was time to hurry to Merlin Hall before Wyvern caused any more mayhem.

That Nephilim upstart was not going to get away with this.

The Dark Master promptly called in his trusty troop of elite reptilians to explain the situation to them.

At least *their* loyalty was sure, he thought, appreciatively watching his half-dozen bodyguards come trotting in in single file. Each about seven feet tall, with crocodile heads and powerful humanoid bodies, dressed in ancient Egyptian style garb, Druk and the rest of the royal reptilians lined up before him and stood at attention.

"We must leave at once," Zolond informed them. "It seems Lord Wyvern thinks he can make a play for my throne."

Low gasps escaped the lizard men. They glanced around at each other in shock, and some started hissing and growling.

"Tut-tut, boys, never fear," Zolond said with a wave of his hand. "He will be freed from this delusion shortly. I trust I can rely on your full cooperation?"

The reptilians bowed.

Druk, their captain, stepped forward. "We serve the sorcerer-king only. Do with us as you will, Your Majesty."

Zolond gave his elite bodyguards a wan smile. "Thank you, boys. Knew I could count on you. Very well. Gird yourselves for battle and follow me outside. We must away."

The reptilians grabbed their weapons from the corner of the cave, then marched after Zolond, who walked outside, idly swinging his walking stick.

As all six reptilians joined him outside in the chilly night, he gestured to them to line up on the flat, grassy area in front of the cave, where his sedan chair sat.

"Swift travel is needed," he explained, and as he walked down the line of them, murmuring incantations under his breath, each tall lizard warrior bowed down, accepting a light tap on the forehead from Zolond's walking stick/wand.

One by one, they began transforming into the shape their master required—still reptilian in nature, but larger.

Much larger.

Unlike Wyvern, Zolond was not a true dragon lord, but it was well within his power to turn his bodyguards into towering, winged beasts.

Druk roared, welcoming his new form. Now a great, olive-green dragon with amber eyes, Zolond's head bodyguard let out a blast of fire from his mouth and stretched out his wings, then flapped up out of the clearing to make room for his brethren, who were all undergoing the same change.

Zolond smiled, looking up at his terrifying troop. "Magnificent."

Then Zolond transformed his sedan chair into a proper chariot while his bodyguards took a moment to adjust to their imposing new shapes.

It was hardly the first time he had changed them into dragons, but it had been a while.

When they were ready, he sent Bhisk and Etah off to guard Shadowedge Manor, but the other four, he kept for himself.

Then he waved his walking stick once more, magically hitching them to all four sides of the chariot.

They made quite a sight with their leathery wings, ivory teeth, and baleful golden eyes.

He wryly hoped Ramona was impressed when she saw the sorcerer-king of the Dark Druids arrive in his royal state coach.

Probably not. His lips quirked. She was a tough old bird.

Climbing up into the vehicle, Zolond sat down and collected the reins. "I want all of the traitors arrested and destroyed," he announced. "The Red Queen. General Raige. Fionnula Coralbroom, the sea-witch. The shapeshifter lord, Boris Badgerton. And"—Zolond sighed—"I regret to say, Duradel."

"Even the prophet, sire? Is he not the favored of Shemrazul?" Druk rumbled, his voice mighty in his huge dragon form.

"It does not signify," Zolond said in a hard tone. "We must make examples of them all. But leave Wyvern to me. No one questions my power," he uttered into the night. "None dare challenge my throne. Wyvern must be made to pay. I don't care if he is Shemrazul's son. I will not tolerate such defiance. Now, fly!"

The dragons roared in unison, sending bone-chilling echoes across the mountains. Then they began to gallop, stretching out their wings.

Reaching the side of the mountain, they leaped into the air, and the gilded chariot took flight.

Zolond felt his stomach lurch until the vehicle straightened out. In truth, this was not his favorite way to travel, but sometimes a chap had to make the proper sort of entrance.

Gaining altitude, the dragon coach flew at top speed. The racing wind threatened to whisk away his bowler hat, so Zolond tugged it forward with a low incantation and caused it to reveal one of its other forms: not the dramatic but impractical Black Crown that he wore for ceremonial occasions, but the simple iron circlet that he liked to refer to as his war crown.

This, at least, wouldn't blow away.

That small wardrobe change also helped to put him more in the mood for the task before him. It had been a long time since he'd had a proper fight. He quite believed he was looking forward to it.

The Balefire Mountains sped by far beneath them in all their bleak beauty. But there was too much ground to cover without some magical assistance. For a lesser warlock, this might've been a problem, but he was the Dark Master.

Lifting his hand in a fist, Zolond aimed the Master's Ring at the sky over the front dragon's head. The team continued flying in formation.

"Steady!" Zolond clenched his jaw, concentrating.

With a heave of mental effort and a mighty blast of power flashing forth from his ring, he caused a square opening to appear in the night sky ahead.

It ripped open with a violent tearing sound. The edges of the rift were the blue-black of night, but the realm beyond was filled with a swirling gray fog.

The forced opening through the reaches of time and space offered Zolond a quick but temporary shortcut through the ethers.

This would take him to Merlin Hall in moments—before Wyvern could fire up the infernal mechanism and jump the Black Fortress to some unknown location far away.

Zolond urged his dragons onward, and, bravely, the reptilians flew straight into the rift.

As the carriage entered the thick, cloudy mists of this formless place, Zolond knew they were not alone in the ethers. He could feel the presence of many faceless spirits of gigantic size.

The creatures who dwelled on this plane of existence were every bit as ancient and evil as Shemrazul; whether they were as powerful as the Horned One remained to be seen.

Mankind had long known them as the principalities and powers of the air.

Wyvern might have the favor of his father, Shemrazul, but Zolond also had allies of his own among their kind. Even now, the towering spirits granted him passage.

He raised a hand in salute as he drove by.

Unlike Shemrazul, chained down in his fiery chasm, the demons of the air could move with the winds, tainting the layers of atmosphere surrounding the earth.

Though their force of will was great, their bodies were as formless as wisps, transparent, with no more substance than swirling puffs of cloud.

One of the crystalline air demons nodded to Zolond, then obliged him on his way by grasping the vast miles of space and drawing them together to shorten the distance of his travel.

Zolond wasn't really sure how it worked. The how and why of it were mortal questions, anyway. These creatures inhabited another dimension, another plane of reality.

For them, it was a small matter to manipulate space and time in this formless realm.

The crystalline devil—a cloud giant who obviously recognized him—reached toward the south and grasped the horizon as though it were a vast gray tablecloth, then pulled the fabric closer.

Though Zolond and his dragons seemed to move for a moment in slow motion, floating weightlessly, the beasts pumping their leathery wings, while time hung suspended, it was mere seconds before the far end of the rift opened up before them.

In the blink of an eye, they flew out the other side of the square hole in the sky directly over Merlin Hall.

It was jarring, the return to normal speed and the inky darkness of the night sky.

Below them, however, Zolond saw the fires still burning in the maze beneath Merlin Hall's greatly weakened dome. Even he was shocked to see the Old Father Yew in flames. The wise old tree had lived for thousands of years.

At that moment, Zolond knew he was witnessing the end of an age. The realization shook him. It was so unsettling that it took him a moment to get his bearings.

Peering down from his carriage, he saw the damage to the roof of the big Baroque palace. Corpses of Noxu and Order folk alike littered the grounds.

Why, Ramona could've been killed tonight, Zolond thought suddenly. And that meant that he, too, would've perished, because of the secret spell that bound their lives. His expression turned steely.

Then Zolond began his descent.

* * *

Meanwhile, through the mullioned windows of his bedchamber in Shadowedge Manor, Victor watched, amazed, as Grandfather's two promised dragons flapped down slowly onto the lawn.

The wind from their powerful wing beats swayed the treetops, eddied the fallen leaves everywhere, and blew out the training ground torches.

Heart pounding, Victor left the window and dashed across his room.

Magpen ran after him. "Master, where are you going?"

Victor did not bother to answer, already out in the hallway and bounding halfway down the stairs. His little servant raced after him.

Finally, something interesting had happened around here!

Bursting out the front door, he ran over to the dragons. The mighty beasts stood perhaps twenty feet high and took up much of the flat, sprawling front lawn.

"That was fast!" Victor greeted them.

When both dragons bowed down to him—for Grandfather's reptilians were most courteous creatures, exacting in protocol—they lowered their snouts almost to the ground and angled their wings back in abeyance.

It was a magnificent sight, though Victor barely came up to their scaly olive-green chests.

"Your Royal Highness," the dragons greeted him with deep, rumbling voices.

It was rather thrilling. "Which ones are you?"

"I am Bhisk, if it please you, sire."

"And I am Etah, oh great Son of Darkness."

Victor grinned. "Well, it's awfully good to meet both of you! Thanks for coming. Say, you don't really think there'll be a problem here, do you?"

"If so, we stand ready to defend you, Your Highness." Bhisk's voice rattled the windowpanes across the front of the rambling Tudor mansion. "We serve the Dark Master and his heir, the Black Prince."

"I'm glad of that," Victor said heartily. "I'd hate to have either of you as enemies."

"We are honored, oh most terrible Scion of Doom."

Victor was a little embarrassed by their compliments.

Just then, Nagai strode out from around the corner of the manor, still barking orders at his troop of Noxu.

Victor paused at the formidable sight of his sensei arrayed in his samurai armor. Nagai had not yet donned the expressionless black mask, but the horns that rose like a half-moon from the top of his helmet gave Victor chills. His katana gleamed at his hip.

Victor noticed the warrior had called up for service all two dozen of his Noxu guards. Some of the ugly blackguards looked groggy, but they were armored up as well, and hefted their double axe-headed spears, serrated blades, and spiked clubs.

As Victor's head of security, not just his tutor and trainer, the Japanese man was dispatching the half-trolls off to various posts all around the manor, the roof, and the woods surrounding the compound.

With all these measures in place, Victor had no doubt that any sort of foe Wyvern might send to try to kill him stood no chance at all.

What a fool Wyvern is. Suppose hypothetically, he mused, that the earl succeeded in his coup against Grandfather and managed to assassinate them both. *Then what? What's he going to do for an heir, for starters—snatch someone off the street?*

Amusement quirked Victor's lips. He'd heard the rumors that the Nephilim could not father children because of his half-demon bloodlines.

It was one of the ways that the dreaded Almighty limited what their side could do.

Well, if that was the earl's plan, A) it was absurd; B) It wasn't going to work; and C) It didn't even make sense.

One had to be *born* the Black Prince, loaded up from birth with generations of innate magical skills. *Doesn't everybody know that?*

Unless...Wyvern knows something we don't.

Victor's smirk faded. Perhaps he ought to take this threat a bit more seriously. He tilted his head, studying the night-clad woods.

Nagai had taught him that the worst thing you could do was underestimate your opponent.

Grandfather was the sorcerer-king, but Wyvern was a formidable foe. Younger, stronger. *And* he had the favor of his father, the Horned One. It seemed almost unthinkable, but...

What if he wins? What if Zolond can't beat him? What then?

Victor knew the answer at once. *Well, then they're going to come here and kill me, obviously.*

As the possibility of his own death started sinking in, the prospect of it ever actually happening struck him as ridiculous.

He had a birthday coming up! He was only thirteen. Locked up here, he hadn't even experienced a proper life yet.

But Grandfather? Victor's frown deepened at the thought of his ancient, somewhat frail grandsire going up against a demon-born warlock.

Victor had seen Nathan, Lord Wyvern, a few times for himself. A well-dressed, powerfully built man in his prime, the earl stood some six and a half feet tall and might be considered handsome by some.

At first glance, Wyvern was certainly a striking figure, with short brown hair and cold gray eyes. But on closer inspection, his strangeness emerged.

The careful observer might note first the odd heaviness of his square jaw; that was because the Nephilim sported double rows of teeth in his mouth like a shark. At least, that was what Victor had heard. He had stared at the man when he'd seen him, trying to decide if the rumor was true.

He couldn't tell. Either it was just a lie the earl put out to intimidate others or he'd learned how to hide it.

What the earl could *not* hide was his six-fingered hands. He was unique, all right.

Victor wondered uneasily how Grandfather had found out about Wyvern's rebellion, then he saw Nagai approaching.

The warrior was just finishing up with the Noxu. "You four, watch the gates. Kill anything that approaches. You have your orders. Now, go."

His mind made up that he would participate in his own protection, Victor strode toward the samurai. "What can I do, sensei? I want to help."

"No. You will do nothing, Your Highness."

"What?" Victor stopped in his tracks. "You can't be serio—"

The armored samurai lifted his chin; his face was like stone. "Go back inside."

Victor's temper snapped. "What's all my training for, then? Nagai, you know I am capable—"

Even the dragons' eyes widened when Nagai suddenly roared at him, *"Do as I say!"*

Victor folded his arms across his chest and glared at his sensei, katana or not.

"I said go, Highness. Now."

"But I can help."

"Not this time."

"Why don't I ever get to do anything interesting?"

"You have a duty."

"Yes. To crush all those who come against me," he replied. "You know I can fight. You trained me yourself, both in magic and the martial arts of your homeland."

"To fight now is not your task, Victor-kun," Nagai said in a softer tone, using the Japanese honorific. "Your only task at this time is to survive into adulthood and become the Dark Master in turn—Your Highness," he added, remembering courtesy.

After all, Victor outranked his mentor.

By a lot.

Still. The samurai's refusal to budge here was plain.

Victor scowled, but realized they both had their orders.

Glancing around at the distant Noxu and the towering dragons nearby, he heaved a sigh. So be it. If these people (and creatures) were prepared to give their lives for him, the least he could do, he supposed, was cooperate.

His shoulders drooped, but he swallowed his protests and trudged back inside.

Like a good boy.

He slammed the front door behind him, though, then slouched across the entrance hall while Magpen stared at him, wide-eyed.

"Master?" The imp followed, wringing his long-fingered hands. "What's happening?"

Victor glanced darkly at his homely little servant. "Nagai wants me to stay *inside*, where I'll be *safe*. He thinks I can't do anything."

"Oh, but you can, sir," Magpen said.

Victor turned to him all of a sudden. "You're right."

There was a *lot* he could do—from the comfort of his own bedchamber.

"Come on!" In the next heartbeat, Victor was in motion once more, bounding up the stairs two at a time, the imp at his heels.

When he reached his chamber, he let Magpen in, then locked the door behind them. "Get me my crystals."

At once, the imp hurried over to the towering, ornate wardrobe by the wall, pulled its double doors open, and took out a sleek wooden box engraved with the lunar phases.

Magpen brought the box over to Victor, who set it on his bed.

He did not bother with his wand. It was too dangerous. Not knowing what sort of ghastly spells the Dark Master might unleash against Wyvern tonight, he did not dare interfere with some juvenile effort of his own and risk accidentally mucking things up for the old man. He might cast a curse or send some spell that could warp or even cancel out what his grandsire was doing.

Victor could, however, lend the old man the considerable force of his concentrated will, and channel his strong, youthful energy into Zolond's protection.

The Dark Master probably didn't need it, in truth. But Victor had to do *something*.

This was his *grandfather*—the only blood kin that Victor had left. Zolond was about a million years old, and he was about to face off against the supernatural son of a demon.

With that, Victor opened the box containing his crystal collection and gazed down appreciatively at the twenty-four jewel-like stones.

Merely lifting the lid, he could feel their power at once.

They gleamed and sparkled in the mystical glow of the candles that Magpen was lighting around the chamber, setting up for Victor's working.

With great fondness, Victor trailed his fingertip over the crystals and gemstones, feeling the energy that each exuded. They felt like old friends.

Well, he'd had the set since he turned seven—another birthday gift from Zolond. The sorcerer-king had spared no expense.

Each stone came from the best mines around the world for its type, and was larger than most mages could afford, about golf-ball-sized, but not round.

No, they were each raw and beautiful, left in their natural shapes and forms for the most part.

Victor considered his choices, then made his selections: black tourmaline, onyx, obsidian, hematite, quartz. The strongest stones for protection he possessed.

As Magpen hopped over and pulled the curtains to aid concentration, Victor arranged the crystals in a circle, marked out on the points of a star.

Magpen handed him a glass of water; Victor took a sip, then stepped into the middle of the circle and sat down, folding his legs as he did during the half-hour of meditation that Nagai made him do every day to focus his mind.

At once, he could feel the crystals' power encircling him.

"Which candle, Your Highness?" Magpen was already standing on the footstool beneath the wall shelf lined with various magical candles.

Victor considered. "Dragonsblood."

The imp lifted the crimson pillar candle off the shelf, carried it over to Victor, and set it atop the low iron candle stand in front of him.

Victor lit it with his wand, then dismissed the imp with a nod. Magpen bowed and withdrew.

When his servant was gone, Victor took a deep breath, closed his eyes, then cleared his mind.

Almost instantly, he could feel the protective energies gathering around him. He spoke a few informal words to himself to enhance his intention with greater clarity. The energies grew stronger with that and slowly began swirling within the bounds of his magic circle.

Victor let them churn faster, let them grow and intensify, until the room fairly vibrated with them.

Only then did he focus his thoughts on his grandsire, and cast all his passionate youthful energy forth through the ethers to shore up the old man's defenses.

It did not occur to Victor to worry about his own.

He was evil like that.

CHAPTER SEVEN
A Warlock's Wrath

Wand-scepter in hand, the iron crown cold on his brow, the wind whipping through what was left of his hair, Zolond fixed his icy stare on the swiftly approaching Black Fortress below.

He braced for landing atop the ramparts of the spiky-towered castle as the dragons made their descent.

It was time to bring that upstart Nephilim to heel.

Assessing the situation as he approached, he saw the drawbridge still open. Aelfric the Long Man groaned on the green hillside beneath the weight of the castle on his chest.

In the next moment, the reptilians made a soft landing, quite expert at these maneuvers by now.

Indeed, their transformation back to their usual humanoid, crocodile-headed forms was almost instantaneous the moment their scaly green feet touched down on the wide ramparts.

Likewise, the sorcerer-king's gilded state coach turned back into a modest sedan chair at once.

Grik hurried to open its door for him, and Zolond calmly stepped out.

"Fine work, my friends. You may go."

"Go, sire?" Druk asked in alarm. "Leave you—at such a time?"

"This is between me and Wyvern." Zolond smiled, touched by his loyal guard's anxious stare. "Tut-tut, dear lizard, that miserable cur is no match for me, I assure you. Now go inside...and let me work."

Zolond adjusted his war crown and twirled his wand in his fingers with a wry smile.

Druk did not look happy at the command. "As you wish, sire."

The four reptilians obediently retreated, taking the sedan chair with them as they trudged into the nearest tower.

From below, on the front face of the castle just then, Zolond heard the giant drawbridge slam closed. The last Noxu must've returned.

In the next moment, the pumping, fiery core of the infernal engine that powered the Fortress's jumps awoke with a grinding noise that quickly grew to a roar.

Why, he'd arrived just in time.

Down in the bailey between the castle's outer walls, the metal cylinder swiveled up from its brick housing.

Clearly, the traitors had decided to flee before the Order had a chance to bring in some of their allies.

Somewhere inside, Zolond knew, the bridge crew were putting on dark glasses.

The boys were ready to go.

Good. That meant he had taken Wyvern completely by surprise. *Let's put this devil's whelp in his place.*

Zolond refused to worry about what Shemrazul would have to say about this. He would cross that bridge when he came to it. For now, he had cloaked himself as best he could from the demon's penetrating awareness. But he realized full well that, after this fight, the Horned One he'd served for so long would deem him a traitor.

So be it. It would make his eternity in Hell even more horrible than he expected, but he was already doomed, so what did a little more pain really matter?

After all, Ramona was worth it.

Raising his scepter, Zolond started with an irresistible summoning spell, drawing Wyvern to him, molecule by molecule, against his will.

In moments, his overly tall second-in-command began materializing on the ramparts in front of him, his form translucent, ghostlike at first. The bewilderment on Wyvern's face amused Zolond greatly.

The warlock earl glanced down at himself, as though he could not believe what was happening.

But Wyvern's confused look turned to one of dread as the would-be usurper realized the Black Fortress was about to jump—while he was stuck outside.

For his part, Zolond didn't care. An alchemist or magical scientist at heart, he'd invented the mechanisms that ran this blasted castle, after all. He knew it could be survived...probably.

But Wyvern looked terrified.

And that was the whole point.

The Nephilim wasn't afraid of much.

For a few seconds, he could feel the younger warlock resisting with all of his will, but the Dark Master's power was too great even for him. Also, the rebel was no doubt tired from his unauthorized raid on Merlin Hall.

"Are you mad, old man?" Wyvern shouted as soon as he was fully formed across from him.

"That is no way to address your king."

Wyvern cast about, unable to escape Zolond's hold on his person. "We're about to jump!" he cried.

"Indeed," Zolond said with a slight smile.

By now, the wind from the dynamo was blowing. The metal column spun around and around in its housing, ever faster, while the brilliant ball of glowing energy danced atop its pedestal.

The vibrational hum throbbed, deafening, around them.

Lightning began to crackle overhead. Its blinding brightness illuminated both warlocks in savage blue flashes.

Then the glaring arcs—white, cobalt, amethyst—shot forth from the energy ball, leaping out to each of the four pointy turrets. The lightning sped on, running now in between the four spires on the corners to form a magnificent circuit.

"We cannot be out here right now!" Wyvern yelled in a panic above the din.

"Are you frightened, Nathan?" Zolond asked with a mocking smile. "I hear you've been a naughty boy."

As the dynamo pounded on, whirling and whirling, driving the lightning, the Fortress began to shimmer in and out of reality at its current location.

Wyvern glanced anxiously at the device.

They both knew it could not be shut off once the coordinates had been entered on the panel inside and the whole system had been activated.

"You'll kill us both!" the earl shouted.

"We'll see." Obviously, it was safer inside. It wasn't as though Zolond had ever tested this before on himself. He hadn't the slightest idea what might actually happen.

But it'd be fun to find out. He enjoyed the exhilaration of risking catastrophe. One had to be reckless to become a truly great warlock—

and perhaps a bit mad.

As much as he was enjoying terrifying Wyvern, Zolond's own pulse pounded at what he meant to do. Outwardly, he remained nonchalant about the chaos whirling around them.

If he hadn't turned his bowler into the iron circlet, the Black Crown itself might've blown away—the very object Wyvern apparently wanted, along with the scepter-wand in Zolond's hand, and the Master's Ring, glowing a furious green on his finger.

"You young sneak! Wish to challenge me, do you?" he chided Wyvern over the howling wind. "Well? What are you waiting for? I'm standing right here!"

"We'll be torn to shreds if we don't get inside, you fossil!" Wyvern yelled. "We can sort this out once we've reached our coordinates!"

"No. Now."

"You're insane!"

Zolond grinned. Wyvern hauled back and lobbed a bolt of magic at him in frustration. Zolond deflected it easily.

"Oh, Nathan. Really?"

The earl cursed. But rather than stay and fight him, the braggart Nephilim turned around and ran toward the nearest tower door.

Zolond flicked his wand and tripped him. Wyvern sprawled on his belly.

"Tsk, tsk, my lord. Whatever would your father say to see you running like a coward?"

Zolond walked after him, then began buffeting the traitor back and forth, slamming him against the battlements again and again without even touching him.

Finally regrouping, his haughty face bloodied, Wyvern wrenched free of his magical chokehold and leaped to his feet with a snarl.

"Your time is done, you traitor!" Wyvern said, pointing at Zolond with one of his freakish six fingers.

Zolond broke the finger with a snap.

Wyvern bellowed and clutched his hand.

Zolond fought a smile. It really was too bad Ramona couldn't see this. *Still some life in the old dog yet, eh, my girl?*

Of course, if this were merely a physical battle, Wyvern would've crushed him. After all, the half-breed was herculean of stature, while Zolond was ancient and frail.

But the Dark Master had honed his sorcery for more than three hundred years.

And he was angry.

Which explained the dread in Wyvern's eyes when he looked at him.

That's right. Zolond stared at him matter-of-factly and watched Wyvern put the danger together in his mind. If the Dark Master could do that to his finger with a mere thought...

Rallying, Wyvern let out a furious cry and struck back with a sudden release of force.

The bolt of power he shot forth from his palm knocked Zolond off his feet and flung him over the side of the wall into the courtyard below.

Plunging downward, he quickly broke his fall with a cushion of air to slow his descent. But, as he landed on his stomach, he heard a clank. His war crown had slipped off his head in the fall.

Now it rolled across the brick-edged courtyard.

And that left the sorcerer-king seriously annoyed.

Up on the ramparts, Wyvern climbed to his feet and hurried on toward the same tower door he had been trying to get to before Zolond had so rudely stopped him.

"Oh, Nathan!" he called, projecting his voice so it rang like a thunderclap. "Just where do you think you're going?"

Zolond murmured a spell that turned his own arms into huge tentacles like those of a Kraken. The left tentacle he slithered across the ground, retrieving his crown. But the right he stretched forth longer and longer, across the courtyard and up the castle wall to wrap around the fleeing earl's waist. He dragged Wyvern over the edge of the wall, slamming him down in the courtyard.

"Stay and fight like a man."

Just as Zolond retracted his arms back to normal and placed the iron circlet back on his head, the Black Fortress shifted out of reality there on the hill beside Merlin Hall and went hurtling out through the void.

At once, excruciating pain ripped through Zolond's body. He let out a roar, knocked to the ground. He heard Wyvern's bellow of agony as well.

It was nothing like gliding through the gray clouds of the rift, as he'd done earlier, and nowhere as painless as he'd heard that the experience of traveling through the Grid with an authorized Lightrider was.

This resembled falling through a tornado fraught with broken glass at unimaginable speeds, with lightning bolts flying past on all sides.

The thunderous wind stole the air from his lungs; the whole castle rattled as they whizzed through the nothingness. The frigid cold was intolerable, the pressure immense. His eardrums felt like they would burst.

Zolond crawled over to the brick housing of the machine and hugged the base of it to keep from being flung off into the void. All the while, the throbbing of the infernal device beat like goblins' drums in his chest.

By the lurid glow of the pulsating energy ball, he looked over to see how his foe was faring.

The younger warlock glanced around too, trying to get his bearings. Then he noticed Zolond eyeing him and sent him an evil sneer.

Zolond surmised they were both thinking the same thing: to weaken the other during the jump in order to strike the winning blow first the moment they landed.

The Nephilim was not without skill as a sorcerer, Zolond knew. But it was his brute physical strength that gave him the advantage in this bizarre situation, allowing him to at least move his powerful body under the crushing gravitational forces bearing down on them both.

Zolond could do nothing but lie there, helpless. Even Wyvern struggled to lift his left hand a few inches off the ground. His lips began moving and his biceps bulged beneath his finely tailored shirt as he strove to keep the hand raised to cast a spell.

Zolond couldn't hear the earl's words over the howling of the gale and the frantic pounding of the machine, but it dawned on him that the young upstart actually had the nerve to speak an Assassin's Arrow at him.

With a gasp, Zolond recoiled from the deadly curse, but the fiery dart of glowing magic dissolved in the whirlwind before it even reached him.

Halfway through its arc, the orange arrow of the curse was ripped to pieces, which were then sucked up into the void like wisps of smoke.

Wyvern cursed at his failure, then seemed determined to kill Zolond with his bare hands, if need be.

The oversized earl rallied his strength, then began dragging himself inch by inch across the few feet of ground between them.

Zolond watched him in alarm, still unable to move from the gravitational forces. He narrowed his eyes in growing fury when Wyvern managed to grasp his ankle.

The hatred in the Nephilim's eyes as he inched nearer made Zolond realize that the brute meant to strangle him.

Suddenly, they arrived at the coordinates with a bone-jarring jolt, slamming into place at their destination, wherever this was.

Zolond felt mighty forces surging around them, huge gravity, a tearing sensation as the hole they had punched through reality flew to mend itself back together.

The void was slow to release them from its black grip.

As the machine continued its pulsating drumbeat and the gales began to slow, Zolond realized this would be his best opportunity to immobilize the Nephilim for once and for all.

But did he have the strength left to do it?

His whole body felt battered and so very old, his bones as weak as matchsticks, his skin like paper. In short, the sorcerer-king was drained of nearly all power, while Wyvern could still summon the strength of his demon father...

A strange thing happened at that moment, however. As his weary molecules began settling into this new physical realm, Zolond suddenly perceived a faint thread of energy from afar begin flowing into him. *What on earth?* He had no idea where it came from.

Not from *him*, to be sure.

No, it seemed to emanate to him from a great distance. *Ramona?* But she wouldn't dare presume to assist the Dark Master.

Besides, this unexpected infusion of energy felt hot-blooded and vigorous.

Young.

Victor! Zolond suddenly realized—and nearly laughed. Of course. *Why, you little scoundrel.* But at his age, he was not too proud to appreciate the long-distance boost. He just might survive this after all.

The Fortress was still finishing the jump, blinking in and out of reality at its new location.

He could smell the noxious fumes from the energy ball, feel the ions hanging in the air as the lightning began to dwindle. It was all rather dizzying.

But Zolond fought the disorientation of that nightmarish trip. He'd been alive too long to let anything faze him. Ignoring the ghastly, sizzling sensation racing across his skin, he strove to clear his head and come up with a solution.

Honestly, the Order didn't know how easy they had it, with Gaia always so accommodating toward their side. The Dark Druids had to use the most cunning magic, the most forbidden science to achieve what the Order trained mere junior Lightriders—children—to accomplish with ease.

Fortunately, Wyvern was as dazed from the jump as he. The earl's grip loosened on his ankle just a little; Zolond took that as his cue.

Half to preserve the shattered truce with the Order and stop a useless war, half to save his own life, Zolond (with a little help from his grandson) forced himself back into a state of battle readiness before the jump had fully completed.

Mentally sifting through his wide repertoire of spells at top speed, he lifted a yet-translucent hand, summoning up all the sinister magic that had been forced into the Master's Ring by the Dark Druids' founders.

The second he felt the solidity of the machine's brick housing at his back, he let out a raspy war cry and hurled a blast of pent-up power through his ring and the wand-scepter at once. The double blow hit Wyvern in the head at point-blank range.

And knocked him out cold.

"Ha," Zolond whispered with a grim smile, his chest heaving. "That'll teach ya."

Then the machine shut off and the cylinder swiveled back down into its housing.

The doors that let out into the bailey flew open instantly. Reptilians and bridge crew members alike came running out to find the "frail" Dark Master standing over the unconscious Nephilim.

Zolond gave the crewmen a frosty look to let them know he was back, and most displeased with every one of them.

"Take him away," Zolond ordered them. "No—wait." First, the traitor must be bound.

Zolond glared at the crewmen who had foolishly obeyed Wyvern's treasonous orders. They would all be dealt with, in turn, and he saw how they quaked in their boots, for they knew it too.

But first, Zolond conjured a set of adamantine chains just like the ones that trapped Shemrazul in the Ninth Pit of Hades.

The thick, unbreakable silver chains wrapped themselves magically around Wyvern's ankles and wrists; they snaked around his waist, hog-tying the proud Nephilim.

The crew members cowered. While the reptilians glared and hissed, flicking their forked tongues in disapproval at them, Zolond levitated the unconscious earl off the ground with his walking stick—all two hundred plus pounds of him.

Then he floated the Nephilim into the castle as easily as though he were walking a dog on a leash.

When he went into the Black Fortress, guiding his levitated burden before him, Zolond did not speak a word to anyone. He didn't have to.

Every staff member he passed stared at him with shocked dread, then cleared out of his path and hung their heads. No doubt they sensed his fury and disgust with them all.

There was an old saying: *If you're going to kill the king, you had better kill the king.*

Well, Zolond wasn't dead yet. But those who had dared to move against him soon would be.

The other insurgent Dark Druids did not show their faces. They probably hadn't even realized yet that he was here.

"Where are the others?" he asked Escher, his trembling lieutenant. "Raige, Viola, the sea-witch?"

"I-in their chambers, sire."

"Hmm." Zolond deemed it likely they were still recovering from the battle at Merlin Hall and had retreated to their rooms to brace for the jump.

Only a couple of minutes had passed, after all, since the Black Fortress had vanished from the hillside atop Aelfric the Long Man and reappeared here, wherever they were.

The interim felt much longer to Zolond, of course, thanks to that horrific ride through the void. But most of the crew, the half-troll mercenaries, and the other Dark Druids probably hadn't even noticed that he was in the building.

How could they know Ramona had warned him about what was going on behind his back?

Still pondering the best way to deal with the other members of the failed coup now that he had neutralized the ringleader, Zolond personally took Wyvern down to the most impregnable cell the Black Fortress contained.

This would only be a temporary haven, of course. The traitor had much worse in store for him. *All in good time.*

For now, Zolond dumped the earl on the stone floor of the cell in a clatter of chains, then slammed the iron door shut and triple-locked it.

More was needed.

"*Belua lapis viventum...*" Murmuring one of his favorite incantations into his fist, Zolond conjured a handful of dust, then blew it off his palm and watched it grow and quickly congeal into a living stone gargoyle.

Seven feet tall, the fiery-eyed thing had horns, fangs, and long, lanky arms that ended in deadly claws. It hissed and stretched restlessly.

"Guard the door," Zolond ordered it. He conjured a second one for added security.

Next he saw to it that both of Wyvern's dangerous pets were secured, lest either beast try to help its master. He had the surly manticore caged and the temperamental dragon, Tazaroc, chained in his large stall near the loading bay.

Zolond was eager to punish the earl's rebel followers, but first, there were the Noxu to deal with. The barbarian mercenaries seemed to have become confused in their loyalties, and thus were of no further use to the Dark Master.

In their barracks, the half-trolls were celebrating their plunder.

Cocking his head toward one of the ventilation grates, Zolond could hear the echoes of their coarse laughter and bestial snorts of glee.

What to do, what to do...

Zolond walked up the black stone stairs from the basement, leaving the two gargoyles to guard the Nephilim.

"Hmm, how shall I punish them?" he mused aloud.

The various uniformed crewmen who were following him around whimpered uncertainly.

Zolond smiled. "I know..."

Lifting his hand, he invoked a contagion that infected only troll species. That seemed efficient.

Zinjo Fever was one of the few things the dull-witted Noxu feared. The dread disease was harmless to others but killed their kind almost instantly.

Admittedly, sending a pestilence was tricky work, even for the Dark Master. It required immense concentration, and Zolond was worn out from the night's events. First, he closed his eyes, secure in doing so despite having traitors lurking in the castle.

With his four trusty reptilians surrounding him once more, Zolond knew he didn't have to worry. He whispered the spell for Zinjo Fever into his right hand.

Though he kept his eyes closed, concentrating, he knew the Master's Ring took on a sinister glow.

He could feel the gathering pestilence tingle and burn the flesh of his palm slightly, like hot spices. He cradled the growing handful of red smoke for a moment longer, letting it intensify.

Then he opened his eyes, craving vengeance on all who'd disobeyed him. When the scarlet smoke in his hand glowed hot, Zolond released the fever with a snarl.

At once, tendrils of red smoke began traveling down the black granite hallways of the castle, curling up and down the stairwells, reaching their way into every chamber, until all of the Noxu were falling to their knees, gasping for breath.

Pleased, Zolond turned next to the bridge crew. The gray-uniformed officers of the castle-ship backed away from him.

"I want a full report of all the jumps Wyvern ordered since I left," he told Escher.

"Y-yes, sire, right away. Back to your posts!" Escher snapped at his subordinates.

Half the bridge crew had been following Zolond around in a terrified daze.

"W-we had no choice but to obey the commander, Your Darkness," said the navigator, Officer Lantz. "We were only following orders."

Without warning, Zolond turned around and hurled a bolt of magic at him, sealing Lantz's lips so there was nothing beneath his nose but smooth skin, down to his chin.

The mouthless navigator's eyes widened and he made a muffled sound of terror.

"Do you think I care for your excuses?" Zolond did not bother telling him that the silencing spell usually wore off in about nine hours. Let him suffer. "You heard the lieutenant. Get back to your posts and await my orders!"

The bridge crew fled back to their places, two of the others leading Lantz, who was doing his best to scream without a mouth.

"Now then," Zolond murmured to the reptilians. "I must deal with my unfortunate colleagues." He paused, saddened. "I wonder if any of the Council refused to join Wyvern's adventure. Surely a few must've stayed loyal to me."

"We are with you, sire, come what may," Druk said. The other three reptilians nodded and closed ranks around him.

Zolond was gratified by their loyalty. At least someone around here appreciated the sacrifices he had made for this organization.

Everyone else seemed to need reminding that it was he, not Wyvern, who wore the Black Crown.

Unfortunately, Zolond was wearied to the core of his dark soul by all that had just transpired. If that hurling journey through the void and his duel with the Nephilim weren't grueling enough, the subsequent series of spells he'd performed since his arrival had taxed his powers to the utmost.

If it weren't for the boost from his cocky young heir, Zolond feared he might've collapsed from exhaustion by now. A slight smirk crooked his lips. *Good lad.*

Still, was it wise to go up against the rest of the insurgents in this depleted state? When he thought of the Drow prophet, Duradel and his mystical mind tricks, Raige's deadly skill at arms, the Red Queen's bloodthirsty cunning, and, of course, the newcomer, Fionnula Coralbroom, the treacherous sea-witch who had nearly overthrown King Oceanus of the North Sea's mer-clans, Zolond decided there was no need to rush these confrontations.

They could wait until he had regained his full strength. His mind made up, he stalked to the bridge.

The crew backed away from him. Lantz was weeping. He tried to beg for mercy through gestures, dropping to his knees.

Zolond scowled. "Oh, dry your eyes, or I'll close those too." Seeing Lantz's terror, he took a whit of pity on the man. "Relax. It'll wear off in a few hours." Then he brushed off the anxious navigator and went over to the instrument panel that controlled all the guestrooms.

His solution was easy and efficient. With the flick of a switch, Zolond simply locked all the guestrooms, diverting power from the dynamo in order to contain his powerful prisoners.

Shushing the bridge crew, he then closed his eyes and added a sealing spell around each guestroom door to prevent his captives from using transport spells to escape.

Without this final layer of security, the vampire queen could've easily turned herself into a puff of black smoke and slipped out through the crack beneath the door. Raige might've managed to blast his way out of his chamber with one of his many artful weapons. And Hades only knew what tricks Coralbroom had up her sleeve.

But a sealing spell from the Dark Master himself would make sure that all the turncoats stayed put until he was good and ready to deal with them.

If they gave him any trouble, why, he'd use the ventilation system to fill their chambers with fumes to knock them out.

He could've simply killed them that way, but he wanted to know how far this had gone. For that, he'd have to question them. *Then* they could die. For now, he would spare them.

With these measures in place, Zolond was satisfied that it was safe now to go and catch his breath in his private quarters.

Leaving Itro to stand guard in the bridge room, lest any of the crew members succumb to one of Duradel's mind tricks or an Oebedire Spell from the sea-witch, Zolond ordered the reptilian to kill anyone who tried to get past him.

None of the bridge crew looked remotely inclined to try. Not after what had happened to the navigator.

"Now, then." When Zolond turned to the lieutenant, sweat poured down the man's pasty face.

"Y-yes, Your Darkness?"

"Set a course for Antarctica," Zolond said.

The reptilians glanced at him in surprise.

Escher blanched. "The, er, the spot you've directed us to before, sire?"

"Yes. Near the Feldspar Chasm." Zolond smiled. "I know just the perfect ice cave to contain that sneaky son of perdition."

The underworld would learn what happened to those who tried to cross Dark Master Zolond.

Escher swallowed hard. "Aye-aye, sir."

As the lieutenant began giving his men orders, Zolond left the bridge, his head held high.

Only one thought filled his mind now, and it was not the coming wrath of Shemrazul, but how soon he could claim his reward from the Elder witch.

Ramona had promised to meet him in the real world if he got rid of Wyvern, and he'd done just that. Well, now she owed him. A deal was a deal.

And he intended to collect.

CHAPTER EIGHT
Shifting Loyalties

In badger form, shapeshifter Boris, Lord Badgerton, limped through the shadows of the Black Fortress on his wounded front paws, his weaselly little heart pounding in utter panic at this unexpected turn of events.

Zolond was back? Egads, he had been horrified when that dragon got out, but this was a far worse calamity!

What the return of the Dark Master might mean for *him*, an ex-Elder who had joined forces with Wyvern, Badgerton dreaded to contemplate. Indeed, the past several hours had been so overwhelming that it was all a bit of a blur.

With Peter and Ramona catching on to the fact that the traitor in their midst was none other than himself, Badgerton had spent half the night finishing the massive tunnel that Wyvern had ordered him to dig so that his Noxu forces could invade by an underground route, bypassing the magical dome protecting Merlin Hall.

Badgerton had done it, his betrayal of the Order complete.

He refused to feel sorry as he hurried on, scurrying as fast as he could go down one of the black, polished corridors of the guest wing. Those self-righteous prigs back at the palace had never shown him the proper respect.

Besides, Wyvern had promised him a vial of the Proteus Power, which would allow Badgerton to change into any shape he pleased, not just a specific species of mammal.

It was all very well being a badger, of course. They were brave, and vicious when provoked. Loyal to their own clan. Excellent diggers, as well—the engineers of the animal kingdom.

But it *was* rather limiting, as magical gifts went, and all his life, others with wider-ranging powers tended to look down on him, even poke fun.

Boris Badgerton could not abide people making fun of him.

Which was why he despised that rotten brat, Jake, who poked fun at everyone—even the skunkies, Badgerton's adorable niece and nephews. (Oh, how he hoped the triplets were safe! The battle had grown rather more dangerous than Badgerton had anticipated back there.)

In any case, it was seeing how Ramona Bradford so often used her position to protect her unruly young nephew from the punishment he richly deserved that had helped drive Badgerton over to the dark side.

So, no. He wasn't a whit sorry for betraying the Order.

In his mind, it was over anyway, and the best thing to do now was move on.

If only he could get the images of the invasion out of his mind, along with the sick feeling in the pit of his stomach.

In his ordinary human form, he had watched the battle from the ramparts of the Black Fortress for as long as he could bear, then retreated to the guest chamber he'd been assigned inside the spiky black castle.

They were very clever, those magical guestrooms the Dark Druids had devised. You could turn the mirrored walls into any sort of setting you wished.

Anxious as he was over the night's events, it had comforted Badgerton greatly to be able to transform his chamber into the familiar likeness of a cozy underground den.

There, he had waited, trying not to listen to Aelfric's groans or the explosions from above as *The Dream Wraith*'s guns battered Merlin Hall.

Instead, he focused on cleaning himself up after all his labors. Though he'd washed away all the dirt from digging the final stretch of his treacherous tunnel and had changed into clean clothes, his hands were bloody, his fingers killing him.

He winced even to move them. The skin was raw and blistered, the nails ragged and torn. Even his palms were scratched and inflamed.

So, when Wyvern and the others returned—and the dragon was back under control—Badgerton had ventured out of his chamber to go and ask Lady Fionnula to fix his injured hands with a healing spell. It would be easy for her, if she was anything like the witches of the Order.

Unfortunately, the voluptuous, black-haired sea-witch had marched right past him, stomping off to her room after a short but loud argument with General Raige.

Badgerton had heard a bit of their exchange echoing up the corridor from the great hall moments after Wyvern had led his orange beast away.

It seemed Raige wanted to stay and press a second wave of attacks, while Fionnula insisted it was too dangerous, it was not in the plan, and they should leave at once.

Having missed his chance for a magical healing, Badgerton had no choice but to wait for the temperamental sorceress to get over her snit and come out of her room. Then he would simply try again to ask for the favor.

But what had unfolded while he waited in the hallway outside her chamber had shocked and horrified him.

The other Dark Druids remained in their rooms, apparently unaware of what was happening. Raige, Badgerton surmised, was busy binding his many wounds.

The Red Queen could be heard inside her chambers, singing dirges for her courtiers, who'd apparently had their heads lopped off by Janos during the fight. Fionnula, meanwhile, was in a mood as dangerous as the sea after getting trounced by old Ramona Bradford, and blind Duradel was meditating, searching the ethers for insight into their next move.

As for Wyvern, after returning his escaped dragon to its quarters, the Nephilim earl must've gone down to the basement to brag to his demon father about his victory, for he did not return.

In order to visit Shemrazul in person (though Badgerton did not know why anyone would want to), the Dark Druids had to go down to the bottom level of the Black Fortress and enter a mysterious ceremonial chamber called the Throne Room.

Supposedly, it had a bottomless pit in the floor from which Shemrazul would rise to give the Dark Druid Council their instructions for what mayhem to cause next.

Apparently, that was as far into the mortal world as the demon could venture in physical form. Great adamantine shackles around his ankles held him chained to the bottom of the Ninth Pit.

Badgerton supposed that was probably for the best.

At any rate, that was Badgerton's best guess for where Wyvern had gone, but he had not been able to confirm the earl's whereabouts until the jump a short while ago, when things had started to go so very wrong.

Still pacing in the hallway outside Fionnula's door, Badgerton had been waiting for the sea-witch to get over her pouting and heal his torn-up hands when he realized the Black Fortress was getting ready to jump.

There wasn't time to rush back to his room, so Badgerton had braced against the wall during the castle's unnerving leap through time and space.

It made one confuzzled in the head, warping in and out of reality like that, only to blast into being again someplace far away. It reminded him of Lightrider travel, which Badgerton had tried once and refused to subject himself to ever again. What a nauseating experience! He didn't care how long it took to get to his destination; he was a carriage man.

But once the jump was completed and he'd shaken off his dizziness, Badgerton noticed some sort of commotion coming from the direction of the control bridge.

He'd headed warily in that direction, his animal instincts sensing trouble.

The next thing he knew, he'd watched an impossible sight pass by the intersection of the hallways ahead, and he'd frozen in his tracks.

A little old man with snow-white hair around the edges of his mostly bald head had calmly strolled past, surrounded by a troop of tall, green lizard men who looked like they had just stepped off the wall of some pharaoh's tomb.

But worse—far worse—the elderly gent was floating the unconscious and chained Lord Wyvern down the hallway with his wand.

Badgerton had flung himself backward into the shadows and nearly had an apoplectic fit. He had never seen Dark Master Zolond in person before, but who else could it be?

He had pressed himself against the wall, heart pounding in terror. *Sweet Proteus, we're doomed,* he had thought.

Once Badgerton was sure the sorcerer-king was out of earshot, he tried knocking quietly on the doors of his allies' chambers to warn them, but the four Dark Druids had either barked at him to go away or ignored him altogether—just like the top Magick-folk at the Order always had!

It infuriated him. Did no one *anywhere* respect a shapeshifter?

But, considering that each of his new allies had at least twenty ways that they could kill him, Badgerton had huffed off, offended, and decided to leave the thankless blackguards to their fates.

None of his efforts would be worth anything to him if he ended up dead. Whatever the Dark Master did to them at this point was on their own heads.

Abandoning his efforts, he had changed into his much smaller animal form and, from that moment on, done his best to stay the bloody blazes out of sight.

For a few minutes, he had crept around the onyx hallways, trying to figure out what to do. Then he spied the weird tendrils of red smoke weaving through the corridors like loosed snakes.

And the half-trolls started dropping dead.

Next, massive outer doors had slammed down over the ordinary doors of all the guest chambers. This was followed by the spontaneous creation of gleaming magical barriers around each room, sealing the occupants inside.

It was astonishing.

Badgerton could hardly wrap his mind around what he had just seen—or believe how quickly the triumph of this night had turned to abject defeat.

They were supposed to be celebrating right now, but instead, Wyvern was under arrest, and all of his most powerful co-conspirators were caged like dogs in their rooms.

And they didn't even know it yet, the fools!

Somehow, he, the *lowly* shapeshifter, was the only one who had managed to stay free! Ha. *Well, now what?*

Unfortunately, hiding in his room was not an option, for while the others had been locked *in* their chambers, Badgerton found himself locked *out.*

The same sort of hulking iron door that had slammed down over the others' guest rooms had also covered his, he saw; the same magical glow that shimmered around their doors had likewise cut him off from his safe haven.

He shuddered in dread, feeling quite alone all of a sudden.

Up until the moment he had seen the Dark Master ambling down the hallway with his floating captive, Badgerton had been feeling merely anxious over his betrayal of the Order.

The sight of the mightiest warlock on earth swiftly reordered his priorities, however. Pure terror took over. His survival was at stake, but badgers fought best when they were cornered.

There was no telling what the Dark Master might do to him if or when he found him in the castle. Why, the old maniac had killed his own Noxu troops with some sort of poison—to say nothing of that unfortunate fellow who had gone rushing by without a mouth.

Ugh, dark magic had always made him queasy, but Badgerton scraped his wits together as best he could.

Think.

Obviously, his best chance of survival lay with finding a way to free his powerful caged allies. Let *those* four take on Zolond together, if Badgerton could just get them out.

He had no idea how to accomplish this yet, but one thing was clear: he had better figure it out quick if he ever wanted to see dear little Prue, Charlie, and Welton again.

* * *

Prue Badgerton crouched down with her brothers, Charlie and Welton, and countless other civilians in the cavernous basement of Merlin Hall's ancient library, where they'd been ordered to shelter from the moment they'd heard the opening salvos of the Dark Druids' attack.

Most of the people huddled in the sprawling, dimly lit stone space were school-aged children, but there were a few non-magical adults, like prissy Miz Jillian, Sir Peter Quince's wife. She was the one in charge down here, more or less.

Everyone else with any sort of useful powers was out on the palace lawn, fighting the Dark Druids. Even the knee-high gnome servants of Merlin Hall were out there doing their part.

But Prue and her brothers were stuck down here with all the useless ones, because that was exactly what they were, she thought bitterly.

Never had she despised her own disappointing magical ability more than now. What on earth good was it being able to turn into a skunk? All you could do was stink on people, and that wasn't very impressive in the grand scheme of things. Though it was sometimes amusing.

Like the time she and her brothers had gotten that horrid Dani O'Dell and Archie Bradford point-blank in the woods at Merlin Hall. Ha!

Unfortunately, the memory did not cheer Prue up the way it used to, because, since then, Jake had still picked that irritating little Irish nobody over *her* for his girlfriend.

Prue really wanted a beau—and it had to be a good one. Someone important. With powers. And cute. And with a title, obviously.

If Jake or someone else who met her criteria had picked her, then maybe she wouldn't be huddled down in this cold, dark basement right now, trying to figure out how to save her own life, and that of her brothers, because those two were basically useless. Well, at least they both did what she said at all times. They trusted that, as firstborn, she'd figure something out.

And she jolly well better, thought Prue. Because there was no dashing young rescuer coming for *her*, a mere skunk-girl.

As usual, her survival and her brothers' was on *her* shoulders.

At the moment, she wasn't sure if anyone in this vast, dank space was going to live out the night.

Stupid Elders. Prue fumed. *If they're so smart, why did they put us down here, where there's no way out?*

If the Guardians and wizards did not repel this attack soon, and the invaders broke into the library, everyone down here was going to be trapped; they were probably dead.

Everyone in the basement had heard the warlocks buffeting the library with relentless bolts of magic. Weapons, too. The cathedral-like building had shuddered at each blow, but its stone walls held.

The stained-glass windows must have broken, though, for although the thunder of the magical blows had stopped, the faint smell of smoke had begun seeping into the basement from under the cracks of the three sealed stone doors. They'd be lucky if they didn't suffocate. *I hope they let us out of here soon.*

For now, the chancellor's prim wife was doing her best to comfort the half-hysterical brownie librarian, Mr. Penwick Calavast, who was pacing back and forth in agitation by the foot of the stone stairs.

Prue could just make him out by the light of the few lanterns people had brought along as they fled.

An eccentric little fellow, about four feet tall, with round spectacles and a paisley waistcoat, the fuzzy-toed brownie was beside himself with fear that some of the books in the vast collection upstairs might be damaged in the fray—or worse, stolen by the Dark Druids.

No doubt the evil warlocks would like to get their hands on some of the rare grimoires tucked away in the restricted section.

So would Prue.

The rebellious notion had occurred to her (they often did) when she'd first heard the whispers in the darkness around her.

"Lord Badgerton betrayed us to the enemy..."

"...He dug a tunnel and let them in!"

Her brothers must've heard the murmured rumors rippling through the crowd as well, because all three shapeshifter triplets began glancing around uneasily to find people everywhere giving them shocked glances and dirty looks.

"What are they looking at us for? We had nothing to do this!" skinny Welton whispered, pushing his spectacles up higher onto his big nose.

"It can't be true," huffed Charlie, the second-born, as he gripped the shoulder straps of his knapsack.

Prue had ordered him to carry it for them when the evacuation order had come.

Charlie, of course, had tried to load it up entirely with sweets and snacks, while Welton had tossed in the adventure book he was reading, but Prue gathered more practical supplies and put them in there as well. Honestly! What would the pair of dunces do without her?

Poor Charlie wasn't very bright, but at least he could be intimidating to people she didn't like.

Largest and huskiest of the litter, though by no means the leader, he glared back at the onlookers to warn them what they'd get if they kept gawking.

No denying, this was bad.

Prue knew, moreover, that her sharp tongue and Charlie's fists could only protect the three of them for so long.

Welton began gnawing his lower lip with his bucked teeth the way he always did when he was scared. Which was often. He was, obviously, the runt. "What are we gonna do, sis?"

Prue's quicker mind was already churning on the problem. To be sure, her animal instincts smelled serious danger to the three of them, though (for once) they'd done nothing wrong.

Charlie might deny that Uncle Boris had done this, but it didn't sound like much of a stretch to Prue.

She was furious. What an idiot! How could their uncle—who supposedly loved them!—go off like this and ruin their stinking lives? Didn't it occur to him that his actions would turn their whole family into total outcasts?

Even if Uncle Boris was innocent—which, deep down, Prue rather doubted—if the Elders *believed* he was a traitor, they'd probably send some Guardians at once to take the skunkies into custody to find out whatever they might know.

Which was zero.

But who was going to believe them now, if their own kinsman, the patriarch of their clan, turned out to be a traitor and a liar?

Besides, people *always* discriminated against skunks and weasels, ferrets and polecats, wolverines and badgers of all kinds as it already was!

Sometimes the ignorant even mistook them for rodents—*ew*—which could not be more insulting, thank you very much.

So, with one unfair strike already against them on account of their very natures, plus their own somewhat deserved reputations as...Prue preferred *rambunctious*...who knew what all they might be subjected to?

Hours of interrogation, probably.

Maybe even torture. Well, no, the Order was too squeamish to torture people.

Not like the Dark Druids.

It made you wonder who would win sometimes, because one side wasn't afraid to do *anything*, and the other side was.

"Do you think this might actually be true?" Charlie asked in a low tone.

"He *was* acting really weird at supper tonight," Welton said. "Remember how he lost his voice all of a sudden at the table? What on earth was that about?"

"No idea," Prue replied. "But forget about him. We have to worry about ourselves now. We're clearly on our own." She sent a hard-eyed glance around the dark stone basement. "We need to get out of here."

Charlie furrowed his brow. "But Prue, there's a battle going on outside."

"Yes, I know that, genius. Not this *instant*. I mean as soon as they let us out."

Her brothers stared at her uncomprehendingly.

Prue fought for patience. "Don't you get it? Uncle Boris has betrayed the Order! Everybody's going to hate us now!"

"Uh, don't they already?" Welton mumbled.

"Maybe you, but not me!" she shot back, refusing to believe it. "At least, not until *now*. And it's all our stupid uncle's fault, so he can go hang for all I care. As for us, we need to get away from Merlin Hall before they send the Guardians to arrest us."

"What?" Welton gasped so hard that he choked on his own spit.

Charlie's eyes widened. "Arrest us? But we didn't do anything!"

"They're not gonna care!" Prue said angrily. "They need a scapegoat to cover up their own failure to be properly prepared for something like this. Someone's always got to take the blame, and I don't see Uncle Boris down here, so that only leaves us!"

Charlie gulped. "M-maybe he's up there fighting?"

Prue scoffed. "Are you serious? There's no way. He might be a badger, but he's fat and out of shape. He's not going to risk his own life unless he's got absolutely no choice. He'd be down here pretending to protect us, but he's not.

"The logical conclusion is that either the Guardians already caught him or he ran away. And that's exactly what *we're* going to do," she said. "But we're not leaving empty-handed."

"What do you mean? Where are we gonna go?" Charlie asked.

"And what about Mother?" Welton whimpered. "Do you think she's going to get arrested, too?"

"Probably," Prue said.

"We need to help her!" Charlie cried.

"We can't." Prue looked at him matter-of-factly. "Oh, come on, she's annoying, anyway. All she ever does is nag."

"But she's our mother. We can't just leave her behind."

"Think! *As* our mother, the main thing she'd want is for us to be safe. And that means getting far away from here. Especially you, Charlie," Prue added sweetly. "Everyone always blames you for everything, poor thing. If they're going to accuse anyone of assisting Uncle Boris, it'll probably be you."

His eyes widened. "You think so?"

Prue nodded sincerely. She needed him on her side. But getting her main henchman in line was usually quite easy.

Not even Welton could argue with her logic.

Prue laid a firm hand on each brother's shoulder, the caring big sis. "Don't worry, boys, Mother will be fine. Either she'll tell the Order what she knows and they'll release her, or if they bully her, she'll faint and play dead. She's a hedgehog, remember? She's an expert at playing the helpless female. They'll believe her. But on the off chance that she *does* know something about Uncle Boris's plan, she's clever enough to lie her way out of it."

Welton frowned. "Then...couldn't we do that, too?"

"Welton, I am not going to stay here and be *unpopular!* Do you want to be an outcast?" Prue fairly hissed. "Look at how everyone's staring at us already!"

The boys did.

"You two can do what you want," Prue informed them, "but I'm getting out of here. I never liked it here, anyway! Everyone's so full of themselves because of their stupid magical powers. They all think they're better than us."

The boys exchanged an uneasy glance, then gave her a chastened look.

"What do you think we should do, then, sis?" Charlie mumbled.

Relieved they'd given in, Prue beckoned them closer, and when all three put their heads together, she whispered her plan...

* * *

A plan was starting to form in Badgerton's mind, but he still wasn't sure it would work.

Scared as he was, he had pursed his snout with determination and pressed on down the black corridor, desperate to find a way to save himself.

Clearly, that meant saving the other Dark Druids, so they, in turn, could save Wyvern.

Then, perhaps, if they all worked together, they might stand a chance of surviving the Dark Master's wrath.

Though still rather terrified, Badgerton had forced himself to calm down, deciding that the first order of business was to take a stealthy look around to try to get a better picture of what exactly was happening here. A bit of spying was in order.

So he'd begun doing just that.

But he felt very sorry for himself, indeed. Honestly, he was beginning to wonder if he would ever receive the Proteus Power. False promises!

But he brushed off his impatience. The all-shapes potion hardly mattered at the moment. He'd be lucky to get out of this alive, in any form.

Limping on down the jet-black corridor, he winced over his bloodied paws and kept to the side of the hallway. Thank goodness for the darkness!

Feeble wall sconces lit the winding obsidian hallways at regular intervals, but it was easy for an animal the size of a small beagle to hide in the shadows.

Then Badgerton spotted a large, heaving lump in the middle of the floor ahead, heard groaning and gasping, and hesitated.

Another half-troll barbarian had collapsed to the floor in his death throes.

There was no getting around it. Badgerton forced himself forward and scampered past the dying brute.

As he hurried by, it was strange being at eye level for once with one of the hulking Noxu. The creature writhed on the floor, choking for air, all its armor, blades, and clubs of no use against this sort of enemy.

Foaming drool dripped off its tusks.

Ugh, the thing stank! Badgerton grimaced and hobbled on, but as he neared the end of the guest hallway, the situation grew even direr.

A pair of Zolond's horrifying lizard men approached from the hallway ahead. Badgerton huddled down close to the floor, his pulse hammering.

He held perfectly still, fearing that if they saw him, the reptilians might try to gobble him down for a snack. Even fierce badgers had their limits against upright-walking alligators.

Badgerton didn't even breathe as the strange creatures prowled by without noticing him, thank the gods.

After they had passed, he realized they were on their way to check the other Dark Druids' doors, making sure they were securely imprisoned in their rooms.

Badgerton gulped and crept on. It was very easy to get lost in this endless labyrinth of midnight hallways, but he had his tunneling instincts to guide his way. Eventually, he found his way back to the corridor, where he was able to peer into the bridge some distance away.

The busy control room was brighter. He could see the crew bustling around. Judging by the orders he overheard the lieutenant give, he realized they were preparing the Black Fortress for another dizzying jump.

Where to this time? he wondered. Then he heard one of the officers mention Antarctica and could not believe his ears. *What on earth? They must be joking.*

But there was no sign of humor in the bridge room. No chuckles, not so much as a smile. Only a grim, businesslike quiet.

From his stealthy spot nearby, Badgerton could feel the tension in there, though the crew did their best to work in spite of their obvious terror.

He could not see the whole bridge room, however, so he lifted his head and sniffed the air with his keen animal senses. *Aha.* His nose told him that Zolond wasn't in there anymore, but he could smell at least one of the reptilians.

Badgerton crept closer until he spotted the tall, scaly fellow posted by one of the control panels. He eyed the crew sternly, making sure they did their jobs—or else.

The humans smelled frightened of making one wrong move.

Badgerton's devious mind weighed matters and quickly concluded that the set of buttons and levers the reptilian was guarding must have something to do with the locks on those big metal doors keeping the rebel Dark Druids inside their chambers.

Hmm. A possible option was becoming clear.

When the right moment came, perhaps he could use his small, unassuming size to his advantage. He could sneak onto the bridge, slip past the lizard somehow, and then quickly jump up onto the control panel and start pressing buttons until he set his allies free.

The thought of having to perform such ghastly heroics made him shudder with dread, but Badgerton knew he had no choice.

He wasn't sure *when* he should attempt it—he was in no hurry, to be sure. But that was probably his best hope of survival.

He stifled a whimper, but only managed not to cry by thinking of his precious little skunkies. *Yes.* He wiped away a tear, feeling noble. *I must be brave...*

For the children!

CHAPTER NINE
Forebodings

Jake's uneasiness grew the longer they waited. The air of fun they had stubbornly manufactured could only last so long. By now, it was whittled down to a nub.

What do we do? he kept wondering. He had brought his friends to the relative safety of his island, where they'd at least have some shelter in the decaying gazebo.

But although he kept his thoughts to himself, he was really starting to worry.

Dani's attempts to contact Merlin Hall through the little speaker gizmo on her Lightrider training gauntlet continued to fail.

After the first hour passed, Isabelle finally made a brief attempt to reach out telepathically to Janos.

This failed, too.

"Usually, he's the one who creates the connection, not me," she said. "But I can try again."

They discouraged her from doing so. No one wanted her to push herself after she'd already overtaxed her powers so greatly. She gave in without much of an argument, admitting that she was terrified of distracting the vampire anyway. For all they knew, Janos might still be fending off dozens of enemies.

So, they waited.

And waited some more.

Jake had never been terribly good at waiting.

He felt half ready to explode with suspense.

Tick-tock, tick-tock. He counted the moments, burning to know what was going on back at the palace.

Red, meanwhile, continued circling overhead, gliding like a hawk on the currents of air as he kept watch for any sign of danger that might be approaching.

As the first hour crept into the second, Jake grew increasingly restless. As the unspoken leader of the group, he knew they could not stay out here all night.

It was the middle of October, almost cold enough for frost, and his aristocratic cousins were not cut out for a night of homelessness. Nixie had managed to conjure some blankets, but in the morning, they'd need food, and then what? Elysian Springs wasn't up to the job.

He had to bring them someplace warm, where they'd all be safe.

Unsure where to go at this hour, he continued scanning the gloom of the quaintly faded pleasure grounds and pacing slowly over the weathered wooden floorboards of the ancient gazebo.

The warped planks creaked beneath his feet as he brooded on the question and his own sense of responsibility for his friends' welfare. His gaze traveled past the three swan boats bobbing gently on the shore and out across the glittering black surface of the man-made lagoon. For a moment, he stared at the distant mass of straggly trees surrounding the water.

I can't believe the Dark Druids attacked us. Now that it was behind them, he realized he was still a bit in shock. It was strange how emotions from momentous events only seemed to hit you after the fact.

Well, if his friends were experiencing the same sort of odd, delayed reaction, so far, everyone was managing to keep a stiff upper lip about their situation.

Archie and Brian sat on the boulders by the waterside, skipping stones across the lake. Those two seemed all right. But after all of Henry's training in chivalry, Jake was growing ever more concerned about the three girls.

They huddled around the steps of the ramshackle gazebo, trying to stay warm. Maybe he should've allowed them to build a fire. Jake knew he was right to forbid it, but he still felt bad.

Skinny Nixie looked particularly miserable. Without an ounce of fat on her bones, the petite witch shivered in the cold, wrapped in a blanket and holding Teddy on her lap for warmth.

Isabelle sat leaning her head back against one of the gazebo's posts, eyes closed. Even dauntless Dani was beginning to look peaked, frightened, and pale.

She kept checking her gauntlet, shaking it like she feared it was broken, and then listening to the little gadget from which they should've long since heard Aunt Ramona's voice crackling out their next instructions.

Or Derek's voice. Or Aunt Claire's or Uncle Richard's or Finnderool's or even Sir Peter's...

Unless they were all dead.

Everyone was thinking it, though no one dared say it aloud.

Jake was starting to feel it was imperative that they find out what in the blazes was going on—aye, as quickly as possible.

Because this was bad.

And for Jake, deep down, this silence from the adults had him privately fighting his worst fears. He had already lost his parents to the Dark Druids' schemes as a baby.

True, the recent news that Jacob and Elizabeth Everton, Lord and Lady Griffon, might still be alive after all this time had restored his faith that maybe, someday, he might find out what it was like to be part of a real family.

But he was a firm cynic...and seeing was believing.

Tonight, the possibility that the evil warlock brotherhood had also destroyed every *other* adult he had finally let himself care about or trust had him balanced on the very knife edge of rage.

Unthinkable as it was, though, he knew it was possible. Knew what Wyvern was capable of. He had fought the Nephilim lord himself, after all—or, at least, had tried.

The half-demon earl had quickly neutralized any threat he'd tried to pose.

As much as it chagrined him, Jake knew he wouldn't even be here right now if the towering warlock had really wanted to hurt him.

On the contrary, Wyvern had been pleased by Jake's fighting spirit, laughing at his efforts like a proud father. The truth was the Nephilim earl could've killed him with a wave of his freakish, six-fingered hand if he had wanted to.

But no. To Jake's astonishment, Wyvern had tried to recruit him, instead.

Because of some daft prophecy, the madman wanted to claim Jake as his son and heir apparent, officially making him the so-called Black Prince of the Dark Druids.

Jake had told Wyvern exactly what he could do with his offer. Then he had fought the Nephilim with everything he had.

And had quickly learned it wasn't near enough.

It still made him slightly ill to think of how easily the half-demon earl had held him down, face flat in the dirt.

Ugh. Jake could not remember his true father, but if that was what it was like having a dad, then he was better off being an orphan.

The only thing worse than having Wyvern for a dad would be having Fionnula Coralbroom for a mother. Those two were a couple now, ever since Wyvern had sprung the sea-witch from her jail cell beneath the ocean.

What a perfect match. Jake despised them both.

Unfortunately, the last he'd seen them, the deadly pair had been dealing out damage to everyone in their path back at Merlin Hall.

Which was why the silence from the palace was driving him mad. He was especially worried about Derek, his beloved bodyguard and mentor. His personal hero, really.

Wyvern had nearly killed the master Guardian once before. What if he succeeded tonight in finishing the job? Miss Helena would be heartbroken, since Derek and she had just become engaged to be married...

As Jake's thoughts continued to torment him, his empath cousin must've sensed his distress, for she dragged her eyes open and gave him a melancholy look.

He knew she was suffering too, torn as she was between Janos and Maddox. Both of her admirers were in danger tonight—to say nothing of her diplomat parents, who'd insisted on remaining behind to help in any way they could.

Jake dropped his gaze, striving to keep himself together. He had to stay strong for the others. Rather than giving way to fear, he focused his mind on their next move.

Right. Might as well face it. If the Order had indeed been vanquished by the Dark Druids tonight, the kids needed to know it, and soon.

Because that meant no one was coming for them, and they were on their own.

At least Jake, of all people, knew how to survive as a kid with no adults to turn to.

He paced again across the gazebo. The longer this silence dragged on, the more he concluded that it was up to them to figure out what to do.

As usual, they'd have to save themselves. But why was he

surprised? A faint, bitter smile skimmed his lips.

Figures. Adults were never there when you needed them.

It had been true when he was a half-starved pickpocket living by his wits on the streets, and it was just as true now that he was wealthy and titled. They all *said* they cared, of course. Told you to trust them.

But when push came to shove, they were nowhere to be found. No, a kid was on his own in this world. He was lucky enough if he had a pet and a few good friends.

Suddenly, Jake could not bear another minute of standing around doing nothing.

If their survival was up to them, then he was taking charge, done waiting for those blasted, incompetent grownups. Dying, he thought sardonically, was no excuse for their abandoning him again.

"What time is it, Arch?" he asked his cousin in a hard tone.

Over by the waterside, Archie took out his fob watch and squinted at it in the moonlight. "Quarter past one, coz."

"One o'clock in the morning?" Dani cried.

"*Two hours* we've been out here now?" Brian shook his head with a dire expression.

"It's even past my bedtime," Nixie mumbled.

Archie clicked his fob watch shut.

Jake jumped off the stairs of the garden folly and landed nimbly in the dirt, then glanced around at his friends. "Listen up, you lot. This is getting us nowhere. We need to find out what's going on. I propose we head for Beacon House. That's the Order's London headquarters," he told Brian and Nixie, in case they didn't know.

The rest of them had been there before.

"The mansion's got plenty of bedchambers, and Mrs. Appleton's cooking is a dream. We can't just stay out here all night," Jake continued. "We're all exhausted, hungry, and cold."

"You'll get no argument from me," said Nixie. "How far?"

"Just across the river and up the Strand," Jake answered. "We could walk there in an hour."

At that moment, Red flew down from the dark sky.

"Becaw," the Gryphon said placidly to Jake, meaning, of course, that the coast was still clear.

Well, that was good news, at least.

Dani shook her head and rose to her feet. "I don't think we should leave the waypoint."

Jake huffed. "I'm going to go mad if we have to keep standing around here—"

"Just hold on and let me try again!" Impatiently flipping the communication switch on her gauntlet, Dani lifted her hand, speaking into the wrist piece as she paced around the gazebo. "Hello? Is anybody there? Lady Bradford? Sir Peter? Miz Jillian? Dame Oriel? Master Finnderool? This is Dani O'Dell reporting! Can anyone hear me?"

They listened with bated breath, but after a while...

Still nothing.

After another long moment of silence, Dani dropped her arm to her side. "Have they forgotten about us?"

"Impossible." Archie frowned, folding his arms across his chest. "They're probably just dealing with the aftermath of battle. Tending the wounded, putting out fires. It's only logical. Give them time to deal with those emergencies. We'll be fine in the meanwhile."

Izzy nodded wearily. "We wouldn't wish to be a burden at a time like this."

Brian shrugged. "Maybe they just figure we'll be safer where we are."

"Or maybe," Nixie said, "they're all dead."

Archie turned to his best girl with sudden outrage. "How could you say such a thing? What's wrong with you? Apologize at once!"

Nixie held her ground. "You know we're all thinking it."

"No, we're not!" Archie shouted. "That's my parents back there, Nixie! Just because you don't like yours—"

"Archie!" Izzy said sharply.

"Keep your voice down," Jake ordered them all, taken aback by this outburst from the normally mild-mannered Archie. "The whole point of us not building a fire was to avoid drawing attention to ourselves. Cheese it, man!"

Archie harrumphed and turned his back on them, glaring toward the lake. "They're not dead," he said. "I won't allow it."

Behind him, everyone exchanged awkward glances.

Blimey, Jake thought. The boy genius had the longest of fuses, but on those rare occasions when Archie went off, it was usually with a bang.

To be sure, Jake had been on the receiving end of his temper more than once.

Izzy climbed to her feet. "Come, brother, Nixie didn't mean anything by it. She was only speaking her mind." She sent Nixie a sympathetic glance. "The worst thing we can do is start fighting amongst ourselves.

The truth is, none of us know what's going on at Merlin Hall right now."

"That's why we should go to Beacon House," Jake said.

"Yes, but what if we leave the waypoint and they send someone to fetch us and we're not here?" Dani protested.

"How can they? They have no idea where we've gone, remember? Look." He strove for patience. "I don't want to scare anyone, but, um, there's another reason we should go to Beacon House."

Dani frowned at him. "What do you mean?"

He hesitated, not wanting to panic them. "It's, um, possible that the attack the Dark Druids launched tonight was broader in scope than just the raid on Merlin Hall."

They all stared at him with looks of dawning horror.

As Jake glanced around at them, only Brian looked back at him with grim understanding.

Thanks to his Guardian instincts in matters of war, it seemed the new kid was the first to catch on.

"What exactly are you saying, Jake?" Izzy murmured.

Jake gave up trying to be diplomatic for the sake of clarity. "What we saw tonight was the start of a war, my friends. You do understand that, don't you? These are the Dark Druids. They're not playing games."

"He's saying the warlocks might've launched simultaneous attacks on various Order strongholds all at once," Brian explained in a low tone.

Jake gestured at the American with gratitude. "Exactly. Including Beacon House. If that's the case, we need to know."

The others were all still staring at him, looking aghast.

Dani covered her mouth with both hands, her eyes wide and staring. Isabelle bit her lip and looked away, her eyes misting.

Nixie whispered some arcane swear word, then shook her head. "He's right. It *is* possible."

Red growled, and even Teddy whined nervously.

"Let's not jump to any rash conclusions, please," Archie clipped out, his face somber as he pivoted to face them once more.

"I'm not sure it's all that rash, coz," Jake said. "There are thirteen warlocks on the Dark Druid Council, but I only counted five at Merlin Hall. The others could've been attacking elsewhere, and we just haven't heard about it yet."

"So, what do we do?" Izzy wrapped her arms around herself.

"Do you think that's why no one's answering my attempts to hail them?" Dani said with a gulp.

"There's only one way to find out." Jake strove to keep his voice calm and authoritative. "Like I said, let's go have a look at Beacon House. If it's all clear, then we don't need to worry. We'll be safe there while we wait. The mansion is protected by multiple layers of ancient spells and enchantments, after all. And I'm sure Mrs. Appleton would be happy to look after us. She's the housekeeper and cook at the residence," he told Brian and Nixie.

Brian gave Jake a firm nod. "I'm with you."

Jake nodded back. What a relief to have a Guardian around who wasn't always making fun of him, like Maddox.

"What if we get there and it's true?" Nixie asked in a dark tone. "If the Dark Druids have taken Beacon House, what then?"

"I know! We could go to Everton House," Dani said anxiously. "Jake inherited a mansion on the far end of London—"

"No, carrot, we can't go there." Jake shook his head. "Too obvious. That's the first place Wyvern will look for us. I've got to assume he's still after me—and Uncle Waldrick's with him now. He and Fionnula both know exactly where Everton House is, remember? They'll lead Wyvern straight to us."

Dani let out a small sound of distress and went over to Jake's side. He put his arm around her shoulders, trying to comfort her. "Don't worry. If Beacon House has fallen, we'll take rooms at an inn somewhere nearby and lie low till we figure out our next move. Steady on, everyone. If we just stick together, we'll get through this. We always do."

"Hear, hear," Archie murmured.

"Becaw," said Red, his golden eyes gleaming in the night.

Jake was so glad Red was there. He smiled at the Gryphon, then glanced around at his friends. "Right, then. If everyone's ready, let's get back into the swan boats. We can row the rest of the way to the park exit; it'll be faster."

Several sighs could be heard as they all wearily left their posts around the island and headed back to the boats.

Red flew off ahead to scout out any dangers that might await them.

Jake glanced up at his pet with gratitude, then set his feet on the pedals and got to work. All three swans headed out the other end of the lake, then glided along through the quaint, winding waterways that crisscrossed the bleak autumn landscape.

Before long, the park's main gates appeared ahead beneath a faded white archway. The kids ended their voyage and climbed out of the swan boats, leaving them at the reed-choked end of the canal.

Then they walked up to the wrought-iron gates. Overhead, the old, faded sign on the archway read, *Elysian Springs Pleasure Gardens*.

Jake and Dani exchanged a grim glance, wondering if they'd ever see this place again.

"It's locked," Brian reported.

Jake went over to investigate.

"I can get it," Nixie said, wand in hand.

"No need," Jake said, for the chain securing the park gates was still as loose as he remembered.

Though the rusty padlock was still fastened, the gap between the two gates was not difficult for a wiry kid to squeeze through. Dani led the way. While she showed the others how to shimmy through the narrow opening between the gates, Jake waved at the Gryphon flying by overhead.

"Don't let anyone see you," he called to his pet as loudly as he dared. "You're a gryphon, remember? You're not supposed to exist! You need to stay out of sight."

Red dismissed his advice with an indignant snuffle, as if to say, *"I've been to the city before! I know what I'm doing, thank you very much."*

Very well, the Gryphon did know how to be stealthy, Jake supposed. The beast could leap from roof to roof if necessary. Besides, it was very dark out, considering the hour.

Red pumped his wings and headed up into the clouds, then it was Jake's turn to squeeze through the gates, the last to follow.

As he stepped through them, he was surprised at how much smaller the gap seemed now that he was a well-fed thirteen-year-old.

This unexpected evidence of how much bigger he'd grown pleased him. Why, if he ever *did* get to meet his parents, they probably wouldn't even believe he was the same bald little baby that his mother had handed off to the water nymphs all those years ago. Putting the past firmly out of his mind, Jake caught up to the others.

Then they all set out together on their chilly autumn hike through the dark streets of London.

CHAPTER TEN
Under New Management

Zolond dispatched the reptilians to various posts: He stationed Itro on the bridge, and sent Grik and Zoss to patrol the guest corridors to make sure the Dark Druids stayed locked up.

Since Bhisk and Etah were guarding Victor, this left only Druk as Zolond's personal bodyguard, but that was plenty.

He could always conjure more gargoyles if he felt he needed extra protection. Confident he had the situation in hand, Zolond walked back to his chambers, his heart surprisingly light for a man who had just earned the particular hatred of a demon. He swung his walking stick/scepter like he hadn't a care in the world.

Anticipation filled him to see Ramona Bradford in person again after all these years—the feisty slip of a girl he had once loved, centuries ago, when the word *love* had still had a meaning to him.

He had not seen her in ages. Zounds, he was actually rather nervous at the prospect, which amused him immensely.

But would he see hatred in her eyes when they met? Or something else?

Should be interesting, at least, he thought, ambling down the polished black corridor to his private apartments, and trying with all his will to block out his psychic awareness of Shemrazul raging.

Alas, the demon's fury was too strong to ignore entirely.

"You will pay for this, old man. How dare you betray me? I gave you everything. We had a deal. Have you forgotten? I own you!"

Zolond gulped and focused harder on the corridor before him.

"You're nothing without me. You swore an oath of fealty. You imagine that you can simply break it? We're in this together, Geoffrey. It's too late for you to turn back now. I made you the sorcerer-king! You're mine. I

chose you, and you chose me."

"*I chose wrong,*" Zolond mentally replied.

Shemrazul let out a roar from the depths of the Ninth Pit that echoed up audibly throughout the Black Fortress.

Druk looked around in alarm, searching for the source.

"Horned One's a little peeved," Zolond murmured.

"Y-yes, sire," his tall, scaly guard replied.

They kept going.

Again, Zolond distracted himself from Shemrazul's tantrum by giving some thought to his other colleagues who were still unaccounted for.

There were thirteen members of the Dark Druid Council in all, including himself, but Ramona had mentioned only seeing a few.

Perhaps some remained loyal to me. Zolond wearily hoped so.

He could not imagine the Cajun swamp witch, Mother Octavia Fouldon, turning against him, nor the necromancer, Deathhand the Abomination.

He had known old Tavey for an age. Indeed, he'd opted to ignore her slight infatuation with him since she was young.

And Deathhand was a loner who chose very few friends, one of whom was Zolond. The plague mage simply wasn't the type to stab one of the rare humans he liked in the back. If he had a problem with you, he'd tell you to your face. Then cause you to decay in some horrific fashion.

Professor Labyrinth, the great Austrian mind doctor—and Victor's own therapist—was hardly the violent type. An academic and researcher, Labyrinth would not have been involved in this, Zolond was sure, and the fog enchantress, Lady Nebula Vail, would've sided with the psychiatrist.

The two were great friends and enjoyed working together. They usually saw eye to eye.

Then Shemrazul managed to break back into Zolond's thoughts.

"*Oho, you spoke rightly indeed when you said you chose wrong, my dear Geoffrey,*" the harsh voice taunted. "*Especially tonight. You dare lay a finger on Nathan? Imprison my son?*"

"*He betrayed me,*" Zolond answered stoically, refusing to be moved.

"*Well, that's rich!*" The demon laughed angrily in Zolond's mind. "*You fool! I helped Nathan rebel against you because you betrayed me. You know I have long wanted the Order put down, but you refused to act.*"

You think I don't know why?"

Zolond deigned not to respond.

"I am well aware of your plan, you know. I see now your treason is complete. So, go, Geoffrey. Go running back into the arms of your foul Elder witch. But she cannot save you now. No one can. You are mine forever...the second you die."

Zolond could almost smell the sulfurous fumes that awaited him.

"Oh, I can be patient," Shemrazul promised from deep in his pit. "Your spells can only preserve you for so long. One day, time will catch up to you, warlock. You will be dust. And when that day comes, what a welcome party I'm going to throw for you! I'll invite all of Hell."

Zolond shuddered, but kept his chin high, resolute.

He could feel Shemrazul shaking his horned head at him. "So be it, then. I can wait. I've got nothing but time. But I promise you this. An eternity of pain awaits you, the likes of which your puny mortal brain cannot even fathom. It's going to be so...much...fun."

As the chilling threat reverberated in his head, Zolond caught a glimpse of his own reflection in the shiny black doors to his chambers; he noticed he was looking rather pale.

Druk went in ahead of him, making a sweep of the apartments before beckoning him in. Zolond then posted his faithful retainer outside the front doors to keep watch; all he really wanted now was some privacy.

As soon as the door clicked closed, he let out a weary exhalation, feeling every one of his three hundred and thirty-six years.

In truth, he was a bit shaken up by Shemrazul's wrath.

Then he took off his war crown, changed it back into a bowler hat, and hung it neatly on the coat hook in the corner of his cozy little parlor.

I really am getting much too old for this.

Not that dying sounded like a better option—especially now. But it couldn't be too far off. He'd best start taking a more active role in Victor's training...

Still amused by his grandson's interference in the fight tonight, Zolond rested his walking stick in the umbrella stand and loosened his cravat. Then he dragged himself over to the dressing table in his bedroom, where his black crystal ball waited, and plunked down into the chair.

He was feeling weaker than ever as he set his hands on the obsidian orb.

It took him a moment to summon the strength simply to reach her.

"*Ramonaaaa...* Ramona?" With a final heave of strength, he shoved himself into the astral plane.

Weightless, he whooshed across the sparkling purple dreamscape to the drifting charcoal pavilion.

"Ramona, can you hear me? Where are you, woman? I have news."

It took her a while. She must've stepped away from her crystal ball.

"Yes?" she finally demanded, sounding prim.

She did not join him in the gazebo, but peered down on him through her crystal ball.

Her face loomed huge in the dreamscape sky, its bony contours slightly distorted by the orb's curve.

Zolond sighed. Her refusal to come down to him made it clear that she still wasn't sure whether she could trust him.

"It's all sorted," he informed her. "I've contained the situation. Look out your window and see for yourself. The Black Fortress is gone."

She pursed her lips. "Yes. I saw. Good."

"So? I've done what you asked." He turned up his palms and shrugged. "Wyvern is in chains, and, very soon, I shall put him in a place where he can cause no further harm. I've upheld my end of the bargain. Now it's your turn."

"Oh, Geoffrey," she mumbled.

"There's no backing out now! A deal's a deal, my girl. So, tell me. When and where in the real world can I finally see you again?"

* * *

After she'd finished speaking with Geoffrey, Ramona slid her hands off her crystal ball, her awareness returning to her chamber.

Which reeked of smoke.

But so did every room in Merlin Hall now, after the fires.

Her friend and fellow Elder, Dame Oriel, the chief clairvoyant, sat perched on the armchair in the corner of Ramona's parlor, waiting for news.

"Well? What did he say?" Oriel asked in a hushed tone, her short purple hair dusted with ashes.

"It's done," Ramona reported. "Wyvern's contained. The Black Fortress has jumped away. Zolond didn't say where."

"And?" her friend prompted with a worried look.

Ramona shrugged. "I agreed to meet him somewhere on neutral

ground."

Oriel winced. "When?"

"As soon as possible. Once the chaos dies down a bit."

Oriel gazed at her anxiously for a moment. "I wish you would not do this. It's too dangerous."

"I haven't got much choice; these are the terms he set. At least he did as he promised." Ramona hesitated. "I see no harm in giving him a chance to explain himself, anyway."

"No harm? Ramona! He can't be trusted! This could be a trap."

"Oh, I'm aware of that, ol' girl," she said with a weary smile. "Don't worry, I shall stay on my guard the whole time. However, Zolond and I do need to discuss rebuilding the truce between the Order and the Druids."

"I suppose," Oriel said with a frown. "At least let me go with you."

"Certainly not. I adore you for volunteering, but no." The Elder witch rose from her chair. "For one thing, we both agreed to come alone, and for another, I cannot vouch for the safety of anyone else. Don't worry. Zolond can't harm me or he risks his own life, remember? I'll be perfectly safe. Now, enough about me. How are you?" Ramona folded her arms across her chest as she gazed at her clairvoyant friend. "Are you all right? Fionnula prevented me from coming to your aid, but I saw those dreadful vampires menacing you."

Oriel brightened and waved off her concern. "Twas the young vampire who saved me!"

Ramona arched a brow. "Janos?"

"Oh, you should've seen him! I thought I was dead, but then he appeared out of nowhere, grabbed me 'round the waist, and leaped clear up onto the palace roof. Snatched me right away from them! He's very strong," she said with a dimpled smile.

Ramona gave her a stern look. "Don't go all giddy, or I'll throttle you, I swear. At your age!"

Oriel laughed, ever the free spirit. "He is a beautiful young man, though. At least, in human form."

"Humph," Ramona said.

Any female within a quarter mile of the black-haired and too-charming vampire prince seemed to get that same silly twinkle in her eyes—Isabelle, Ramona's darling niece, most alarmingly of all.

The bond that had formed between the two distressed Ramona in the extreme. It was almost as dangerous as her own connection to

Zolond.

"All I know is that Janos saved my life," Oriel said. "And I recall he once saved Jake's—then Red's and Derek's and Ravyn's and, one might even argue, that of the angel, Celestus—"

"Oh, you've made your point," the Elder witch grumbled. "I suppose he did well enough tonight. At least you're safe."

Oriel chuckled. "Oh, come, Ramona, he's not so bad." She heaved her slim body up from the comfortable chair, her gauzy, jewel-toned robes flowing around her.

"Are you sure about that, hmm?" Ramona turned to her friend with a searching gaze, one fist propped on her waist. "Come, you're a clairvoyant; how do you read him?" For Izzy's sake, she had to know. "Myself, I don't trust him."

"Well, of course not," said Oriel. "He's a vampire and a spy. Trusting such a person overmuch would not be wise. However..." A thoughtful look skimming her fine features, the clairvoyant furrowed her brow, glanced away, and pondered her impressions of the Order's prodigal son. Then she spoke slowly. "I would say...Janos lives and breathes remorse. And is in constant pain."

"Oh?" Ramona was taken aback by this revelation. "He certainly hides it well."

Oriel shrugged. "Not to me. And probably not to Isabelle. She is so tender-hearted, your niece. No wonder she can't help but—"

"No! Please, don't say it." Ramona held up her hand. "It's more than I can take right now, with the night we're having. One disaster at a time, if you don't mind."

Oriel grinned. "As you wish, my lady," she teased. "I suppose we all have to do what you say, now that you're the chief Elder."

"Ugh, don't remind me," Ramona muttered. But with Balinor's death, someone had to do it.

"Better you than me," Oriel said, giving her an affectionate pat on the shoulder.

Ramona sent her a grateful smile. "Now, then. You must promise me you will tell no one of my plans to meet with Zolond."

Her friend rolled her eyes with a great sigh.

"Oriel!"

"I will keep silent," she agreed. "But I still think it's a terrible idea."

Ramona arched a brow. "Sometimes a terrible idea is the only kind one has."

If she was honest with herself, though, Ramona was excited at the prospect of seeing Geoffrey again after all this time.

She told herself they were only meeting on magical business. High-level negotiations, face to face. It was her duty!

Now that she was the head witch of the Order, and Zolond remained ruler of the Dark Druids, the possibility of a lasting peace between their sides seemed closer than ever.

Maybe that was why fate had brought them together in the first place.

But her clairvoyant friend knew better. With a smile and a comforting pat on the back, Oriel followed Ramona out of her chambers. Then both women headed back outside to see what else they could do to help.

Another little troop of gnomes trudged past them in the white marble hallway. The grumpy, knee-high servants were carrying rags and cleaning supplies; one rested a wee broom over his shoulder.

"Poor things," Oriel whispered after they'd passed. "We lost a lot of them tonight. They fought bravely, as best they could."

Ramona gave a sad nod. Her thoughts returned to Balinor. "We have more vacancies to fill on the panel of Elders."

"Hmm, you're right. We need a shapeshifter, for starters."

They turned a corner and continued down the next hallway, where another elvish healer finished binding the knee of a wounded centaur.

"They're going to put me out to pasture," the centaur groaned.

"Nonsense." The healer rose. "Just keep your weight off that hoof for a few weeks."

"Ahem! Your Ladyships," the centaur said, seeing Ramona and Oriel approaching.

Alerted to their presence, the silken-haired wood elf rose gracefully and turned. Then both creatures bowed with respect to the two old ladies. Ramona managed a smile, though it was not nearly as warm as her friend's.

Oriel had always been the sociable type; Ramona was usually all business.

Unfortunately, though, as head Elder, Ramona supposed it was her duty to comfort everyone, so she mumbled vague reassurances to the anxious pair as she went by. It seemed to help. The centaur quit whining and the she-elf hurried on to seek her next patient.

"You know," Oriel remarked as they reached the top of the grand staircase, "Sir Peter could take your old post, representing the mages."

Ramona nodded. "He certainly deserves it."

"He's very capable," Oriel agreed.

Below them, the lobby was still in chaos, but at least there were no more Noxu. They exchanged a bracing glance, then started down the stairs.

"I must say, I'm worried about him, though." Ramona glanced at her friend. "He might be smiling on the outside, but Jillian's the center of his world. Do you think she'll ever forgive him for accusing her of treason?"

"In time. But...I wouldn't hold my breath." Oriel grimaced.

"I'll have to apologize to the poor woman myself. I fell for Wyvern's deception as much as Peter did. When I saw Jillian couldn't speak, I, too, thought she was the traitor."

"It was a dirty trick Wyvern played on us all," Oriel said with a scowl. Then they came to the bottom of the stairs. "Where to, chief?"

Ramona looked around, ignoring the groans of the wounded and the weeping of the bereaved. "I need to find Derek Stone."

"Why? Are you going to send him to bring back the children now?"

"Not yet. They'll be fine. They've quite proven they can take care of themselves."

"Do you know where they went?"

"No idea," she said. "Don't worry, I'll get in contact with little Miss O'Dell in an hour or so. There's too much else to do at the moment." She nodded toward a pair of muscular Guardians carrying a dead Noxu mercenary out of the palace, leaving a trail of blackish-red blood droplets behind them as they went. The half-troll's blood was still dripping from its tusked snout.

Oriel grimaced. "Quite right. They're much better off elsewhere until all this is sorted."

"Indeed, having another of their *adventures*," Ramona said with a sardonic smile.

"All right, then." Oriel propped her hands on her waist. "What shall I do?"

"Go and let Finnderool know it's safe now to let the children and other civilians out of the library basement."

Oriel nodded and started to turn away, then paused. "Why do you want Derek Stone, anyway, if not to bring the children back?"

"Because"—Ramona gave her a conspiratorial smile—"I'm going to make him an Elder."

"Head Guardian?" Oriel gasped, then laughed as Ramona chuckled. "Oh, in that case, I am coming with you. I'll go pass your orders on to Finnderool in a moment. First, I have *got* to see Derek's face when you tell him he's been promoted."

Ramona grinned. "Do you think he'll be surprised?"

Oriel giggled. "I think the great warrior might faint!"

At that moment, they spotted young Maddox St. Trinian helping carry out another dead troll. Ramona summoned the lad and asked him if he had seen his mentor.

"Yes, ma'am, he's questioning Waldrick Everton in the jail." Maddox pointed to the small, squat building across the dark grounds. "Shall I escort you ladies?"

"No need. We can see ourselves there," Ramona said. "Carry on."

"Yes, ma'am." Maddox sketched a bow, then strode back to his grim task, and the two Elders continued on their way.

CHAPTER ELEVEN
The Defector

Though not exactly *thrilled* to find himself a prisoner once more, Waldrick Everton was grateful at the moment for the rusty iron bars of his cell, as they kept certain angry Guardians of his acquaintance *out*.

The hard, scruffy face of Derek Stone glared at him through this meager barrier: the square jaw clenched, one cheek bruised, his broad forehead smudged with black smoke from the battle.

It was downright unnerving, especially by the flickering illumination of the lanterns hung from the little jail's low ceiling.

Derek's steel-gray eyes gleamed with a vengeance that could've pierced armor.

Waldrick could not deny the warrior had cause.

Egads. Jake's wicked uncle knew full well that the brawny fighter hated him.

Unfortunately, Derek Stone was the least of his worries, for Waldrick had made a great many powerful enemies tonight, when he had switched sides.

Again.

He was trying not to think about what each of the terrifying Dark Druids might do to him for this if they ever got the chance.

The knowledge that he'd earned the monstrous Lord Wyvern's wrath made Waldrick yearn to dive under the covers of the cot in his cell and hide until his lanky knees stopped knocking.

Why, oh, why were these sorts of dreadful things always happening to him?

He felt quite sorry for himself about it all. Surely no man in history had ever been caught between such a terrible rock and a hard place before—or in his case, a Stone.

His situation was stark. But after what he had done tonight, defecting from the Dark Druids, Waldrick knew the protection of the Order was his only hope of long-term survival.

He had information to barter about the Dark Druids' plans.

Of course, Waldrick was well aware that everyone here despised him. Especially longtime family friend Derek—Mr. No Fun—ever noble and true, he thought cynically.

The two of them had a long, unpleasant history together; in their boyhood, Derek had been best friends with Waldrick's elder brother, Jacob, the firstborn, Jake's charismatic father.

Why, the warrior had even been the best man at Jacob and Elizabeth's wedding. Of *course* Jacob hadn't picked Waldrick for the honor—his own brother!

Instead, he'd chosen this commoner.

When Derek grasped the iron bars at that moment to lean on them after his exertions in the battle, Waldrick jolted backward with a small shriek. "Stay back! You're not allowed to come in here!"

Derek's lips crooked in a half-smile that made his rugged face even more terrifying—a dark, angry lion of a man.

Waldrick gulped and kept his distance from the rough-mannered nobody. It was true, Jacob used to put up with a lot from Waldrick when they were boys. He *had* to; Waldrick was his little brother.

But even in childhood, Waldrick always got the feeling that his brother's rough-and-tumble friend could see right through him. Perhaps, even all those years ago, Derek's latent Guardian instincts had sensed that Waldrick's seething resentment of his glorious, golden-haired, older brother sometimes grew ugly and spiteful.

Waldrick did not deny he had let his jealousy of Jacob get the best of him once, years ago.

But there was still time to fix his mistake.

And that was why he had done this suicidal thing tonight, betraying Lord Wyvern and all his hideous allies.

To undo his crime.

"What are you playing at—Wally?" Derek taunted, still pinning him in an icy stare. "Is this some sort of trick? I know you think you're very clever."

"It's no game." Waldrick managed to ignore the boyhood nickname he had always hated. "Look, I know you don't like me—"

"*Like* you? You killed my best friend. And murdered his wife."

"But I didn't—that's just it!" Waldrick cried. "I mean, I thought I did—yes, very well, I tried, I admit it—but I failed! That's what I'm telling you! You know my case; you heard every word of my trial before the Elders. Fionnula coated the bullets in my pistol with some mad potion that turned them into, I dunno, mere magic pellets that didn't *kill* Jacob and Elizabeth, but only put them in a state that mimicked death! They're alive, Stone. I've seen them with my own two eyes."

Derek stared skeptically, but perhaps he'd heard rumors about this, for he did not look shocked in the least.

He didn't even scoff.

Waldrick's heart sank. This was not the reaction he'd been hoping for. *Oh no.* Maybe his huge, earth-shattering news was no news at all.

Perhaps the Order's spies had already caught wind of the Dark Druids' horrid Lightrider project in the basement of the Black Fortress.

Waldrick desperately hoped not. He was banking on using this and other inside information to buy himself merciful treatment from the Order.

"Look. I know what I did to them was wrong, Stone. I-I fully admit that. Believe me, I had plenty of time to ponder the error of my ways during the past year and a half I spent in prison."

"Till you escaped," Derek growled.

"What choice did I have?" Waldrick cried. "When Wyvern showed up and broke me out, I didn't *want* to go with him. They made me! He and Fionnula. He broke her out of prison, too, before they came and got me. I tried to decline their invitation, believe me, but that six-fingered freak would've killed me if I had refused to cooperate." Waldrick shuddered. "You should've seen how he commanded all those vicious, wild dragons outside the dungeon. Then he marched in and killed the guards. He's insane! He's literally demonic."

"What did he want with you?"

Waldrick hesitated, trying to determine which information to hold close to his vest until he got a promise of lenient treatment.

"Waldrick?" Derek warned.

"He wanted to know all about Jake," Waldrick blurted out. "'You're the boy's uncle,' he said. 'You should know better than most how to get to him.' He's determined to recruit my nephew for the dark side. There's some sort of prophecy about him, I don't know." Waldrick shook his head. "For my part, I would've much preferred to stay in my cell and serve out my sentence. But I don't fancy dying, so I did as he said."

"What did you tell him about Jake?"

Waldrick shrugged. "Not much. I barely know the boy. He hates me."

"Well, you did kill his parents."

Waldrick started to protest, and Derek corrected the record with a long-suffering look.

"*Fine.* They're still alive, so you claim. Suffice to say, your jealousy is the reason Jake grew up in an orphanage. You're lucky I found him," Derek added with a warning glower. "So, what else? What happened once Wyvern broke you out?"

Waldrick took a deep breath and went to sit on his cot, still shaky after his mad dash through the battle. "When we left that Order dungeon, I went with Wyvern and Fionnula to the Black Fortress. There, I was given fine rooms. Made comfortable." He wrung his hands anxiously as he spoke.

"We know that you were with Wyvern when he went to Griffon Castle and tried to kidnap Jake," Derek informed him. "We know you went there to try to retrieve the vial containing your extracted pyrokinesis out of the family vault."

"You really think I want that horrid gift back? Again, I just went along with whatever they said," Waldrick insisted, then shrugged. "I had always assumed my brother destroyed the vial years ago, just like he told me. It was Wyvern who claimed otherwise. I didn't understand how the warlock could possibly know the vial was still there, intact, until I discovered the truth for myself. The Dark Druids have been holding my brother captive all this time."

"You actually saw him—alive?"

"Yes! Both Jacob *and* Elizabeth. They're unconscious, and Lord only knows how long they've been that way. But as for my pyrokinesis, good Lord, I honestly don't want it back anymore! I did for a time, badly—I admit it. But I see now that Jacob was right; it's too dangerous. I don't even trust myself with it anymore.

"Retrieving it from the vault was all Wyvern's idea." Waldrick shrugged. "He expected me to be useful. They're all dark magic users of one sort or another, and they wanted me to do my part. But, as far as I'm concerned, it is a dreadful gift."

He still had nightmares sometimes about accidentally setting things on fire with the hellish talent he had inherited.

Like peasants, villages...

"Look," Waldrick said, wearily rubbing his forehead. "I know I'm a terrible person—"

"Yes," said Derek.

"But it turns out I'm not quite as bad as I thought! At least I'm not a murderer, because Jacob and Elizabeth are *alive*. So are many other Lightriders, being held captive this way. The Dark Druids have them all in glass coffins deep in the bowels of the Black Fortress. They're in a comatose state, being kept alive by some huge machine. It seems to be one of Zolond's infamous experiments."

"And you know this how?"

"I went snooping around inside the Black Fortress one day. When I discovered the chamber where they're being kept, I knew I had to come and tell the Order. That's why I defected! Don't you see? My brother and his wife can still be saved."

Derek stared at him.

Waldrick waited on tenterhooks, trying to read Derek's reaction. His heart pounded, but not like it had a short while ago, in the middle of the battle, when he had fled the Black Fortress and run like a rabbit straight into the fray.

Barreling out onto the battlefield, Waldrick had skidded to a halt and flung himself to his knees, hands in the air, voluntarily surrendering to a group of Guardians.

It was the bravest thing he'd ever done in his life.

Maybe the only brave thing.

There was no going back now, that was certain.

Wyvern had roared at Fionnula to stop him, kill him, apparently grasping his intent when he'd seen Waldrick go sprinting by.

But Derek and the other Guardians had kept him alive and brought him to safety in this squat little stone building across the grounds, away from the palace itself, and untouched by the blaze.

The building turned out to be a small jail with a few holding cells, but Waldrick didn't mind one bit. Aye, being in Order custody was the safest place for him right now.

Provided Derek stayed on the *outside* of those bars.

"Why should anyone trust you after all you've done?" the warrior demanded.

"Bring an empath in if you don't believe me! Find Isabelle and have the chit question me. I'm perfectly willing to have her read me so you'll know I'm telling the truth."

Stone's wary eyes narrowed.

Waldrick stared desperately at him. "Wyvern's got plans, Stone. Strange doings are afoot inside the Black Fortress. There's a lot more I can tell you, but that's all the information I'm sharing for now, until the Elders grant me a deal. I want it in writing that I'll receive leniency."

"Why, you brazen— You are in no position to be making demands!"

Waldrick cowered from him, when suddenly, an unseen female called primly to the warrior from outside the jail.

"Oh, Guardian Stone?"

Waldrick gasped and recoiled, recognizing the voice of his ancient kinswoman, Great-Great Aunt Ramona.

Oh, no. He backed against the wall of his cell.

The thought of what the Elder witch might do to him after all his misdeeds was even worse than the notion of Derek tearing him limb from limb.

A witch of her power with a grudge to bear was dreadful to contemplate.

Even Fionnula was a little afraid of her.

Waldrick had not had to face Aunt Ramona since his trial in the Yew Court. And even then, the rest of the Elders were present, so the stern old dowager baroness had to restrain herself.

Fortunately, Aunt Ramona did not come into the jail. Perhaps she did not want to see him, either.

"Oh, Guardian Stone, a word with you, please?" the Elder witch called from outside.

"Yes, ma'am! On my way!" Derek barked in a soldierly tone, then turned to Waldrick. "Behave yourself—or else."

Giving him one last dirty look, the Guardian pivoted and marched out, sending two of his grim-faced underlings back in to stand guard outside Waldrick's cell.

Once the warrior had disappeared, Waldrick drifted forward again, feeling safer now. Eager for news of the battle, especially whether the Black Fortress had left yet, he pressed his face between the bars as best he could, trying to peer around the stone corner into the little hallway.

He listened intently, but the voices outside were too muffled for him to hear. Still, he was curious. *Wonder what that crazy old bat wants with him.*

CHAPTER TWELVE
Another Prisoner

The Ninth Pit of Hell reverberated with the roars of the Horned One. Shemrazul was in the throes of a temper tantrum the likes of which his strange assortment of minions had not seen since that whole embarrassing debacle on Calvary.

He thrashed his dragon tail and wrenched uselessly at the adamantine chains around his ankles. He stomped his cloven hooves and punched the canyon walls so hard that it started an earthquake on the far side of the world.

He howled and he yowled, screamed with rage and frustration, until, finally, Baphomet over in the Tenth Pit, where he, too, was chained, poked his giant goat head up over the edge of his canyon with a scowl. "Quiet down over there!" he shouted. "I'm trying to sleep here!"

"Don't tell me what to do *ever again!*" Shemrazul roared back. He stood panting for a second. "You think I don't remember what happened the last time I listened to you people? So just *shut up*, goat face!"

"Well, you don't have to be rude. It's on *your* ugly head if you wake up the boss," the other demon added, before sinking back down into his own canyon.

Shemrazul flicked a sulky glance down at the river of lava bubbling by beside his massive cloven hoofs. Glowing bright orange and radiating unbearable heat, the river flowed into a fiery sea where Satan himself was bound in chains at the bottom.

Realizing he should probably be grateful for his colleague's reminder, Shemrazul gnashed his sharp teeth but kept his mouth shut in the interest of letting the Beast get his beauty rest.

Instead, he began pacing back and forth along the flat stone landing beside the river, where he had spent countless millennia, and where he would remain.

With a pout on his long, narrow face, the demon slouched over to his skull-covered throne, flicked his once-angelic but now batlike wings out of the way, and plopped down angrily to brood.

His minions—an assortment of blue-skinned, pointy-eared imps and lesser red devils, plus a few far stranger creatures—cowered around him, anxiously watching his every move.

They could never be sure when he might lash out and throw one of them into the river, stomp them into jelly, or express his disapproval by temporarily destroying them again in one way or another.

Shemrazul was nothing if not inventive when it came to finding new ways of snuffing his minions out of existence for at least a few minutes before they popped back into being to annoy him once more.

Growling to himself, he shook his horned head at the sudden ruination of his plans—just when everything seemed to be going his way!

Typical.

The Almighty really had the most obnoxious sense of humor when it came to torturing His turncoat fallen angels.

Well, Shem wasn't laughing. All of his best mortal instruments had flown the coop. Failed him in one way or another. He shook his head in disgust.

That was what came of having to rely on humans. Sneaky little meat sacks. Double dealers!

He could not believe Zolond had chosen his old attachment to that insufferable Elder witch over the debt he owed to all of Hades and to Shemrazul personally for three centuries of unwavering support. Some thanks!

And now his own supernatural, half-breed son, Nathan, had allowed himself to be vanquished by the old man! How humiliating.

Shem had had such high hopes that Wyvern would make him proud someday, fulfill all his plans to invade the earth with the locust army he had guided Zolond in creating years ago. Now the larvae were almost ready to hatch beneath the desert sands, and there was no one to run the show!

Useless, the both of them. When he snorted in disgust, sulfurous fumes puffed from his nostrils.

When he thought of Wyvern's other Dark Druid henchmen trapped in their stupid chambers, unable to get out, he raked his clawed fingers on the arm of his throne, leaving deep gouges.

Oh, this was only a temporary setback, of course, and he would get it sorted somehow. But all of his followers would be punished in due time for their incompetence.

Ah well. He still had hope for his chosen grandson.

Beautiful, wicked Jake.

The raw power the boy had displayed in disabling *The Dream Wraith* at such a tender age had delighted Shem as he observed the former pickpocket's heroic feats through Wyvern's eyes during the battle.

Oh, yes, the Griffon heir was definitely the one.

Shem was not about to honor Zolond's grandson by making Victor de Lacey his vessel on earth anymore, not after the grandfather's betrayal.

No. Their whole family line must be punished. Wyvern would have to see to that, in due time.

Shem brought his thoughts back to his new target: young, bold Jake Everton.

Why, he would make a magnificent Black Prince and the most dreadful ruler the world had ever seen, one day.

Like all demons, Shemrazul was always thinking of the future, planning, scheming, setting things up. The only way any devil could get a respite from Hades and enjoy earthly life was through the willing service of some human or another.

But human lives were so short, while *his* lasted forever. It seemed like he had to replace his Dark Masters every few years.

He preferred to possess men with powers, rank, wealth, intelligence, courage, and a sketchy conscience, or better still, no conscience at all.

The young ex-thief was the perfect type of lad to become Shemrazul's representative on earth, once he was grown.

It would take years of training, with Wyvern and Fionnula looking after the boy, molding him, and raising him as their own. And then, one day, good ol' Jakey-boy would become the Dark Master, in turn. He'd have the world at his feet.

Oh yes—Shem smiled—Jake belonged with them. Especially now that he'd made his first kill.

That it was an accident did not matter to Hell in the slightest. It was a start.

Unfortunately, the young scoundrel had slipped away, escaping through a portal with his horrid little do-gooder friends.

Shem had sent six of his most loyal underlings to find his chosen child and bring him to the Black Fortress, but so far, there was no news.

"Report!" he bellowed into the air, losing patience. That trait had never been his strong suit.

Within seconds, a blue, pointy-eared imp ironically named Jolly appeared alongside the strangest little creature in Shem's entourage, known simply as Eyeball.

Eyeball had skinny arms and legs attached to a round body with a single eye in the middle of his stomach. This made him an excellent observer and an obvious choice for a spy.

"Well?" Shem demanded.

The blue imp cowered. "N-nothing yet, sire."

Shemrazul narrowed his eyes and drummed his fingers. He was tempted to blow them up—it would probably make him feel better—but he restrained himself in the interest of speed.

"Keep searching. I want him found. Did you see anything, Eyeball?"

"No, Your Awfulness," the thing answered. "But I'll keep looking everywhere."

"Blast it, what's taking so long?" Shem whined.

They both bowed and scraped in terror.

"Forgive us, master!"

"It's a big Earth, sire!"

Muttering about excuses, Shemrazul decided to give his little monsters more help.

With a snap of his clawed fingers, he summoned a squad of Nightstalkers. A full baker's dozen: thirteen.

True, the three phantom assassins that Wyvern had foolishly sent to kill Jake in Sicily had failed.

What a blunder it would've been if they'd succeeded, Shemrazul thought, shaking his head. To be fair, though, he had not yet revealed to Nathan his eventual plan to make young Jake a part of the family.

Shem had wanted it to be a surprise; he liked to keep his followers guessing.

Still, he was well aware that the only reason the Nightstalkers had failed in Sicily was because of the sudden arrival of that ridiculous vampire, Prince Janos, and his darkling blade.

His ex-Guardian instincts had led him to the boy in the nick of time, whereupon the vampire prince had helped Jake fend off the three spectral assassins.

But this time, Janos would not be there to meddle. Shem knew for a fact that the smarmy bloodsucker was still at Merlin Hall, helping the Elders sort out the aftermath of Wyvern's splendid attack. At least *that* had gone well.

Anyway, all of this simply meant that, wherever he was, Jake was unprotected.

Now all they had to do was find him.

In short order, the Nightstalkers appeared, floating up to the edge of the canyon above. They peered down over the cliff for a moment, their faces hidden, as always, by strange metal gas masks.

The charcoal tatters of their hooded robes fluttered in the hot breeze as they came streaming down over the side of the canyon in two orderly columns, gliding and weightless, silent and fast.

The man-sized spectral assassins landed in two rows of six before Shemrazul. Large as he was, they only came up to his knee.

Their leader descended slowly, taking his place in front of his troops.

They all bowed in unison to the Horned One, then awaited their orders, their slow, eerie breaths rasping behind their masks.

Even Shemrazul wondered what Nightstalkers looked like under those masks.

On second thought, perhaps he didn't want to know.

"I have a job for you," he said.

They stood stoic, awaiting their instructions.

"Find me the boy, Jacob Everton, the Griffon heir. You are not to harm him, but bring him to the Black Fortress unscathed. I want to hear from you the moment you pinpoint his location. I have no idea where he has gone. A Lightrider took him through a portal, so he could be anywhere on the cursed globe.

"But search quickly," he commanded them. "You must find him before the Order can send Guardians to secure him. And, just to reiterate, you are not to harm this young man. He is...important. Have I made that extraordinarily clear?"

The Nightstalkers seemed disappointed. But, levitating in their ragged black robes, they bobbed their hooded heads slowly in unison.

"Ah, don't worry, assassins," Shem said, "I won't spoil all your fun. As long as you bring me this boy, you can do as you like with all his friends. Kill the little vermin, for all I care. And the Gryphon, too, if you can manage it. That creature has caused me enough aggravation." He waved a hand. "Dismissed."

A ripple of excitement blew through the Nightstalkers' gauzy black robes at their mission and the promise of an evening's hunt. The leader garbled out a few indecipherable orders to his crew.

Then the group of Nightstalkers gave Shemrazul a bow in perfect unison.

Shem waved a claw to dismiss them, and the phantoms shot straight up out of the canyon to zoom off in all directions, exiting Hades.

As they scattered to the four winds to scour the Earth for his grandson, the Horned One sank back sullenly in his chair to wait.

"What should *we* do, oh, Your Dreadfulness?" Jolly asked with trepidation.

But before Shem could answer, Blobby suddenly appeared, all a-tizzy. The cheerful monstrous blob was one of the half-dozen underlings Shem had sent out in the first round.

All of his gelatinous slime quivered with excitement. "We spotted him, sire—Jake!"

Shemrazul sat up straight. "Where?"

Blobby writhed eagerly. "In London, oh Terrible One!"

"London?" A puzzled smile broke slowly across Shemrazul's face.

What foolish children! They had the whole Earth to choose from, and they only went there? That wasn't far at all.

Then he remembered his annoyance with his subpar helpers and exploded Blobby just for spite. "You couldn't tell me this two seconds ago—before I sent the Nightstalkers out to the ends of the earth?" he boomed at the mess scattered on the nearby rocks. "I told you to *report*."

"But I just did, sir," said the unhappy pool of slime. Blobby's gooey bits began sliding back toward each other.

"Well, you're *late*," Shemrazul growled.

Blobby lumped back together, popped up again, and dusted himself off with amorphous arms. "Honestly, we...hoped you'd be pleased at the news, sire."

"I am never pleased. That is my policy. Don't you know that by now?"

It was a lie, though.

Admittedly, Shem was a *little* pleased at the news that his incompetent minions had finally pinned down his grandson's location. Why, he'd have the boy here in his new home with his new family in no time.

"Where exactly in London did you see him? It's a big city."

Blobby still looked upset. "On the south bank of the Thames, sire, approaching Vauxhall Bridge. They mean to cross the river."

"Hmm," Shem murmured, tapping his claws on his throne. Then he relented. "Excellent work, Blob. Tell the others I said so."

He liked to keep them guessing. Occasional praise was as important as fear, if you really wanted to control someone.

Worked like a charm.

"Oh, thank you, Your Darkness!" His goopy minion bounced in place. "It's an honor to serve—"

"Get back to London now, all three of you. It's a big city; don't let the boy out of your sight. Stall him until the Nightstalkers get there if you have to. But be careful. I know he can be...difficult. It's part of his charm." Shemrazul sat back in his throne and smirked with pride at the thought of the lad's talent for causing mayhem. Jake would fit right in with the rest of the family.

"The phantoms will capture him and bring him to me," Shemrazul said. "There is no need for you lot to try to tangle with him directly."

"Oh, that is good news, sire," the blue imp said. "We were a bit nervous about that."

Eyeball gave a worried nod. "We saw what he did to that dirigible!"

Blobby's only response was a wriggly shudder. No doubt he was frightened that Jake would splat him with his telekinesis if he made him angry. There were only so many insults any poor blob could take in one night.

"Well, there are Nightstalkers on the way, so quit whining. Now, stop wasting time and get out of here! Don't lose him—or I will make you sorry!"

The three little monsters shrieked and disappeared, scrambling back to their spying mission.

Then Shemrazul shut his eyes and focused on the Nightstalkers, searching the ethers for his usually more competent henchmen.

Once he'd made telepathic contact, he informed them to get to London, posthaste, and narrow their search around Vauxhall Bridge.

Yet worry gnawed him as he waited for the next report from the field. Why could he not sense the boy for himself?

It was disconcerting.

He knew that Jake would have been shielded inside the portal for those few brief seconds during the jump. But Grid travel was blink-of-an-eye fast.

The moment Jake and the other children had emerged on the other side of the tunnel to wherever they had gone, Shem should've been able to detect their whereabouts rather quickly.

Thanks to lingering aspects of his original angelic nature, he possessed mighty telepathic powers that allowed him to see into the hearts and minds of men, just like any garden-variety guardian angel.

He could search any mortal's worst fears and deepest desires, discovering how best to manipulate him or her.

Unfortunately, these idle musings on his own angelic origins suddenly gave Shem a startling idea of why he had not been able to sense Jake himself.

He sat up straight, alarmed at the possibility.

Oh dear. That had to be it. Something was definitely blocking his telepathic search for the kids...

Or rather *someone.*

Shem's stomach clenched with deep, instant knowing. He swallowed hard as his suspicion deepened.

Yes. An old enemy was near.

He might not be able to sense Jake at the moment, but when he closed his eyes and reached out with his mind, *oooh,* he could feel someone else out there.

A vision suddenly swept through his mind. A figure standing on the roof of some Gothic-style building.

A man in a neat black suit. A formidable silhouette.

No...not a man. The glint of moonlight on the Brightwield blade in his hand gave him away.

Shem drew in his breath, aghast, as the figure suddenly unfurled white wings. "You!"

"Hello, Worm. Thought you got rid of me, didn't you?"

Shem jolted on his throne as the quiet taunt from his former colleague penetrated his mind. Rage flooded him instantly. "So...it's true. You're alive."

"Always," his enemy whispered through the spirit realm.

"You stay away from my grandson! You hear me?"

"You'll never take him," came the soft-toned reply.

Unnerved, Shem rose from his throne. "I'm warning you, Celestus! I cut your wings off once; I'll do it again!"

"Hmm, yes. I still owe you for that," his age-old counterpart said serenely. *"Lucky for me, I know an excellent healer."*

Shemrazul recoiled with a snarl at the mere mention of the terrifying one who had put him here.

Then he cast about desperately for some way to scare his foe. "Enjoy my Nightstalkers!" he taunted.

The Light Being snickered. *"Child's play."*

"Come down here and fight me on my own turf, you sniveling coward! You think we hurt you before?" Shem shook his fist at the sky. "You haven't seen anything yet!"

"Ah. Well, there's just one problem with your threat—Worm. How do you propose to do anything to me when you are locked up down there," he said slowly, relishing every word, *"and I am up here, free?"*

Shemrazul threw his head back and roared so loudly at his insolence that all of Hades went quiet for a moment.

"Celestusssss!" he thundered at the bloodred sky.

But this time, there was no answer.

PART II

CHAPTER THIRTEEN
Something's Out There

As Jake led his weary band of followers out onto Vauxhall Bridge, his heart sank at the thick fog gathering on the river.

Oh, perfect. Just what this night needed.

It was not that Jake was *afraid* of the fog. Obviously. Who could be afraid of a little mist? Certainly not a lad who had just crippled an airship with his bare hands, he told himself.

And yet...

From the time he had been but a wee pip surviving on the streets, he had always found something so sinister about the dense fogs that occasionally rolled over the city. Cold and soupy, they were known as *London peculiars,* part fog, part pollution. Utterly eerie, like a live thing, some huge, formless creature.

It used to unnerve him when he was little, how stealthily the London fogs arrived, gray, ghostly tendrils stretching down the streets, blotting out the rooftops, wrapping around everything in sight, even the lampposts, like cold, clammy fingers trying to choke out the light to leave everyone in darkness.

With a scoff, Jake turned up his collar against the chill and marched out onto the bridge, determined to ignore his outgrown childhood fears.

The fog had no intention of letting him do so.

Its phantom swirls glided menacingly around him and his friends as they walked across the empty bridge. It coated their faces with a fine layer of slimy damp and sent the night's chill straight into their bones when they were already exhausted.

Some eight hundred feet ahead of them, the far end of the elegant city bridge floated in and out of reality, as though it might be a bridge to nowhere.

On the other side of the river, they caught glimpses of distant buildings shrouded in the fog's woolly billows, like the clouds themselves had come down to swallow the city whole.

A spooky mood promptly settled over the whole group.

Knowing his friends would take their cue from him, Jake forced an outward air of nonchalance, refusing to ponder his growing sense of danger—or the more practical fear that the fog might cause him to get lost.

Don't be barmy, he scoffed at himself. He had walked through London hundreds of times before, even in the dead of night. He knew this city like the back of his hand, and his goal was simple: to get his friends to Beacon House, where they could all take refuge until they heard from the adults.

Provided, of course, that the Order's city headquarters had not *also* been raided by the Dark Druids tonight.

Jake shivered. Since that possibility was almost too terrifying even for him, he tried not to think at all, and just kept walking.

As they made their way across the empty bridge, he glanced down at the river flowing by beneath them. The water looked oily and black in the darkness.

A fleeting memory of his mudlarking days skimmed through his mind. It seemed like a lifetime ago, but it had only been about a year and a half. He shook his head, marveling at the drastic change in his existence.

And yet not everything had changed. For what the sight of the swirling black water reminded him most of all was how badly he had wanted back then just to be a regular boy with an ordinary life, a normal family.

A real home. Parents.

Deep down, he ached for that still. But at least he wasn't starving anymore, he told himself. He had his relatives, a brilliant best girl, a magnificent pet, plenty of gold, a roof over his head (owned a few different houses, actually).

But normal life? No.

It continued to elude him, and he'd probably never know what it was like. There was nothing normal about having telekinesis, the ghost-sight, and a terrible prophecy hanging over one's head.

He let out a sigh and walked on until, at last, they reached the far side of the bridge.

Jake was glad to leave the river behind. The mist was always thickest over the water. Now all he had to do was navigate his way through London Towne.

He knew the way, of course. It was easy. Yet his sprawling hometown felt strange and unfamiliar in the fog.

The mist cloaked long-memorized routes in vaporous gloom, making him doubt his own two eyes; it played tricks on the hearing, as well. The dampness in the air distorted sounds, concealing their sources. Carriages could appear quite suddenly out of the mist and you'd never see them coming...

Determined to make no missteps, Jake shepherded his friends in a right-hand turn onto Millbank Street, which hugged the north shore of the Thames.

Before long, the ominous hulk of Millbank Penitentiary loomed, fortress-like, on their left. Red circled the jail, no doubt startling any prisoners who might've been looking out their cell windows just then, the rascal.

"Stop fooling around!" Jake chided his pet in a hushed tone. "Somebody's gonna see you!"

Red tossed his head as if to say he was only having fun, then swooped off into the mist to land atop the next building.

Jake could just make out the Gryphon's noble silhouette standing proudly at the edge of the rooftop as he waited for them to catch up.

On foot, it took them considerably longer. Nixie nodded at the big, forbidding jail as they walked past it.

"Did they ever toss you into that one, Jake?" she teased, her hands tucked down in her coat pockets.

"Who, me?" He flashed a smile, determined to lighten the mood. "Nah, only Newgate and the Clink."

Dani just shook her head, but Brian glanced at him in surprise.

Jake shrugged. "I was pretty bad."

"You're not that good now, really," Archie drawled, and Jake guffawed. On second thought, he wasn't sure if his straight-arrow cousin was serious or joking.

All he knew was that it was weird, indeed, seeing Millbank Street so deserted. It was usually clogged with carriages and all manner of traffic.

"Could we please walk faster?" Izzy grimaced as she nodded toward the prison. "This place feels horrid."

Jake sobered instantly. He knew the empath disliked coming to

London. There were six and a half million people jammed into this city, far too many minds for her to try to block out all at once. And to be sure, the men locked up in the Millbank Penitentiary had to be among the worst of the lot: nasty, angry, and violent.

With that, the kids picked up their pace to protect the empath's delicate inner senses.

"I didn't know you can still read people when they're sleeping," Nixie remarked.

"Sometimes they have dreams." Izzy sent another fearful glance over her shoulder at the jail.

"I'm so sorry, Izzy. This is my fault." Dani took the older girl's arm with a fretful look while her dog clicked along at her heels. "I should've brought us somewhere easier for you. I didn't think of it—and now you're suffering."

"You did brilliantly, Dani," Isabelle assured her. "Don't worry, I'll be fine once we get away from this spot. I'm much stronger than I used to be, just a bit weakened by the battle at the moment."

She did start looking better once they got past the jail, Jake was glad to see. They kept going straight on Millbank, where the row of wrought-iron street lamps stretched out endlessly ahead.

The left side of the avenue was lined with fine shops and hotels, various government buildings, and occasional side streets. But on the right, the river flowed by, so there was nothing to see but empty docks and dark wharves, abandoned at this hour.

Moored boats of all kinds swayed at anchor, creaking eerily in the fog.

They saw almost no one out and about, not even the bobbies on patrol. The murky streets were empty, the genteel shops shuttered; even the pubs had closed down for the night.

A total of one delivery wagon rolled by slowly: a milkman making his rounds. He eyed them with suspicion from under the brim of his cap as he drove by, but did not stop to ask why a bunch of kids were out walking down the road in the middle of the night. He didn't even wave.

"Well, he was friendly," Archie mumbled.

"Welcome to the city, coz." Jake cast him a wry smile.

But he was glad that at least they all had each other. For, at the moment, in this dark and spooky night, it felt like he and his friends were the last people alive in all the world.

Pools of darkness collected under shop awnings, and painted

wooden signs creaked now and then overhead, dripping dew. The kids' reflections in shop windows appeared unexpectedly as they passed, reminding him of ghosts. But not even the spirits were out tonight, as far as Jake could tell.

The fog thickened and the eerie feeling intensified.

Jake peered anxiously down each side street that opened up on their left as they kept going straight. He glanced over his shoulder now and then as well, his old thief's senses on constant high alert.

Maybe it was just the events of the past few hours catching up to him in the form of nervous exhaustion. It had been a rough night. But as the tingling sensation on his nape turned into a full-blown shiver down his spine, he finally admitted to himself that he felt like they were being followed.

Watched.

Stalked.

He could swear he heard little, pattering footfalls scampering after them, but every time he glanced furtively over his shoulder—trying not to be too obvious so as not to terrify his friends—no one was there.

Heart thumping, Jake glanced up at Red, who continued bounding along from rooftop to rooftop, keeping watch over them. He was glad the beast was up there. If anything hostile approached, the Gryphon would alert them and charge before the threat arrived.

Besides, if they were attacked, it wasn't as thought they were powerless. Jake had Risker and his telekinesis. Nixie had her wand, and as for Brian, well, they'd just have to see whether the new kid was any good as a Guardian or not.

"It's creepy out here," Dani finally said, while Teddy hurried nervously behind her. "I have an idea! Why don't we sing to cheer ourselves up?" At once, she began an old familiar round: *"Hey-ho, nobody home! No food, no drink, no money have I none—"*

"I don't think that's a good idea," Jake interrupted.

Brian nodded grimly. "We should probably keep quiet."

"I don't see why," Dani said with a pout. "There's nobody out here but us."

Don't be too sure.

Jake and Brian exchanged a wary glance. Jake was glad the Guardian was keeping on his toes. Maybe the new kid would prove useful in a fight after all.

Suddenly, a flicker of movement in the shadows of a side street caught Jake's eye. He stopped so abruptly to stare that all of his friends, following, bumped into him, one after another.

"Sheesh, watch where you're going!" Nixie said.

Ignoring the pileup behind him, Jake stood riveted, peering intensely down the intersection on their left. He cursed the fog, conspiring with the darkness to mask the world around them.

"Something wrong, coz?"

Jake didn't answer. Instead, he concentrated with all his senses and the ghost-sight, as well, holding his breath and scouring the darkness.

"Brian?" he asked in a low tone. "You got anything?"

The Guardian kid came up beside him and narrowed his keen eyes, peering into the night for a long moment. "Nope."

"You sure?" Jake stood stock-still, ready to use his telekinesis if anything charged out of the fog at them.

"Nothing at the moment," Brian murmured, speaking only to Jake. "But something's definitely out there."

"Aye. I feel it too." When Jake noticed Dani gazing at him in alarm, he remembered all of Henry's lessons in chivalry again. No need to scare the girls. "Right. Well, never mind, you lot," he said, moving on. "I thought I saw something, is all. It was probably just a stray cat. Or a ghost."

"Ghost?" Brian aimed a worried look at Jake.

Who grinned. "London is a haunted city, mate."

"Now you tell me," Brian muttered.

"Surely Red would alert us right away if there was any trouble." Archie nodded up at the Gryphon, who was poised on the edge of a bookshop roof.

Red's golden eyes caught the glow of the street lamp below him as he watched from above.

"Agreed." Jake nodded, but felt uneasy all the same. "Let's just keep moving. The sooner we get to Beacon House, the better."

They forged on. But they hadn't gone far when Brian drifted to a halt, staring down an alley in between two shops.

"What is it, Bri?" Dani asked.

The Guardian wrinkled his nose, paused, and looked around. "I thought I heard footsteps a little ways back. But now there's just this awful odor. Does anyone else smell...rotten eggs?"

"Wait, you smell *sulfur*?" Archie asked. "As in brimstone?"

"Well, that can't be good," Nixie murmured.

"I don't smell anything," said Dani.

"Be glad." Brian wrinkled his nose. "It's like Beelzebub farted."

Jake chortled, and even Archie grinned, but the girls gave the boys withering looks.

Nixie grimaced. "It's probably just trash in one of these back alleys. People are pigs. Can anyone else smell it?"

"Teddy can." Isabelle hesitated, gazing at the dog, who was panting nervously. "For my part, I-I must admit, I've got a most...unsettled feeling."

"What are you sensing?" Dani turned anxiously to the empath, but Jake was watching Red scout out the way ahead. Something had got the beast's attention.

The Gryphon zigzagged back and forth across the street, his lion paws pushing off the friezes near the tops of the buildings as he flew.

"I'm not sure," Izzy said in a halting tone. "There are so many minds here, it's hard to separate one from another. But it feels like—I hate to say it—something evil coming closer."

"Let's pick up the pace," Jake said. "Don't worry, when we reach Beacon House, we'll be safe." *Hopefully.* "C'mon."

Teddy whined, but the kids pressed on, huddling closer together as they hurried through the mist.

Brian tried to lighten the mood a little farther on when they came to a life-sized, painted wooden cutout of the great Admiral Horatio Lord Nelson posted outside the entrance of a pub.

Above the recessed doorway, gilded letters proclaimed it *The Victory.* Its hanging wooden sign depicted the famed sea captain's mighty warship, with which he had destroyed most of the French fleet in the early 1800s, during the Napoleonic Wars.

As for the great historical hero himself, there he stood—resplendent in his Royal Navy uniform, with his gold epaulets and his bicorne hat, his black eyepatch and his missing arm—for all his glory, reduced now to welcoming pub visitors in for a pint.

Brian grinned and slung his arm around the flat, man-sized figure. "Argh, look, maties! A pirate."

"For shame, sir!" said Archie. "That is Admiral Lord Nelson, y' heathen. One of the greatest war heroes in all of British history."

"Is he really?" Brian lifted his eyebrows and lowered his arm from the cutout's shoulder. "Huh. Must've been the eye patch that threw me. No offense."

Archie harrumphed. "Nelson joined the Navy when he was barely our age. He got the eye patch because he sacrificed an eye for King and country—and his right arm, as well."

Every British schoolchild knew about Horatio Nelson, but the name was clearly new to the Yank. Brian looked impressed, but Dani heaved a sigh.

"Can we quit dawdling, please? Teddy's getting tired. He wants to go to bed, and so do I." The carrot-head picked up the little terrier and carried him for a while.

As they all walked on, Jake found himself mulling the life of the great English hero. Having just stepped away from a bloody battle himself, Jake pondered Nelson's famous courage. He couldn't even imagine giving up *either* an eye or an arm, let alone both. That would be like...well, losing his powers.

He shuddered at the thought. That would leave him defenseless.

In any case, the kids soon saw the dashing Lambeth Bridge on their right, with its showy red arches. Just beyond it, they came to the spot where the new riverside park was being built in honor of the Queen.

Victoria Tower Garden, it was to be named—an open, grassy space right next to the Palace of Westminster, the famous buildings where Parliament met.

For now, though, the future royal park was still under construction, especially the river wall they were building to keep the Thames in check. The stretch of land there needed to be built up from a low, muddy shore into a nice, smooth wall, and the land for the park itself had to be leveled out before they could plant the grass, flowers, and trees for people to enjoy.

With all that construction underway, the site of the future city oasis was a big, ugly mess. Towering, steam-powered Hercules cranes had been brought in to lift and lower the heavy granite blocks into place for the river wall.

They should've just asked me, Jake thought wryly. He could've used his telekinesis.

There were piles of gravel, pallets of bricks, mounds of mud the workers had dug out and needed to cart away, coal bins and smokestacks for the steam engines, frumpy little padlocked sheds where, Jake guessed, shovels and picks and other equipment were probably stored overnight.

What an eyesore. He preferred the view ahead, where stately

Westminster waited, about a third of a mile up the road. Reaching it would put them at about the halfway mark to Beacon House. Gazing up the road, Jake found it comforting to see Big Ben glowing, strong and steady as ever, driving back at least some of the fog.

"C'mon, you lot. We've still got a ways to go."

Izzy yawned and Dani set her dog down again, then the kids continued up Millbank, wondering aloud why it turned into Abingdon Street right there for no particular reason.

All except Archie.

The boy genius had slowed to a halt beside the future park site, studying the builders' progress with interest.

Absorbed as he was in the construction project, it was he—not Jake, not Brian, not even Red—who first noticed the strange little creature scampering up the crane.

Behind him, Jake heard his cousin gasp.

"What the devil is *that?*" Archie cried.

CHAPTER FOURTEEN
Lesser Devils

Jake spun to face his cousin. "What? Where?"

"*That!*" Archie pointed wildly at the crane they had just passed. "There! See it?"

Between the darkness and the fog, Jake couldn't see much of anything, but he heard metal bits clanking in the vicinity of the crane.

Everyone else stopped and came back, staring curiously into the dark construction site, trying to spot whatever was making the noise.

"What did you see?" Jake asked his cousin.

Archie looked baffled, his gaze locked on one of the Hercules cranes. "I-I'm not entirely sure. Some sort of animal, I think, only..." He faltered. "It had arms and legs like a human. About my height, maybe a little shorter. Slender."

"Probably just some kids fooling around," Dani mumbled. "Troublemakers, I'll bet. My brothers would definitely try climbing that thing if they thought no one was looking."

"I don't hear anyone," Brian said, his head cocked to listen.

But Teddy must've heard—or smelled—someone, for he growled, the scruffy fur on the back of his neck bristling.

In the next heartbeat, the little terrier exploded into furious barking, tore free of Dani's hold on his leash, and went charging into the construction site.

"Teddy!" Without a second's hesitation, she raced into the darkness after her dog.

Jake and Brian both launched into action, chasing her.

Red must've heard the dog barking. He cawed with alarm from somewhere up the road—perhaps as far away as Big Ben. Jake wasn't sure, but he trusted that the Gryphon was coming.

As for Teddy, Jake couldn't see the terrier, but his yapping reverberated through the construction site and across the river.

Jake's stomach tightened, for he'd lost sight of Dani as well amid the sinister swirls of fog. "Dani!" he yelled, his heart pounding.

Brian raced up a slag heap and crouched down atop it, scanning the darkness. "Dani, get back here now!"

"Do you see her?" Jake asked.

Brian squinted. "She's headed toward the river."

Jake strode deeper into the park while Teddy's barking became even more savage. "Blast it, carrot, you can't simply run off like th—"

"Jake!" Brian said in a shocked tone. "Look."

Still crouched atop the slag heap, Brian pointed upward. Jake paused, turning to him. He had been searching at his own eye level for Dani, and at ground level for her dog. But, uncertainly, he followed the upward angle of Brian's extended finger.

And then he saw it—a hideous humanoid animal of some sort, shimmying up the crane's smokestack.

"Nixie, light!" Jake shouted.

"On it!" the witch yelled back from the street.

I knew we were being watched. Jake didn't take his eyes off the strange, wiry creature. But dread for his best girl seized him. "Dani, get over here, now!"

"I'm not leavin' Teddy!" she hollered back, hidden by the fog. "I think he's cornered a rat or something!"

"It isn't a rat," Jake replied. "Forget the dog—" he started, but knew he was wasting his breath. "Go," he told Brian, who had also seemed spellbound by the strangeness of the blue-skinned creature. "Bring her back if you have to drag her. I'll watch this thing. If it moves, I'll blast it with my telekinesis."

The young Guardian nodded, leaped off the slag pile without hesitation, and ran in the direction of Dani's brogue-tinged voice, instantly vanishing into the mist.

It was now just Jake and the creature, staring at each other.

The skinny, pointy-eared thing had frozen once it realized it had been spotted, as though unsure whether to flee or hold its ground.

"What are you?" Jake demanded. "Why are you following us?"

It snickered but didn't answer, and continued wriggling higher up the smokestack—like some tropical islander climbing a palm tree to pick some coconuts.

At that moment, the illumination spheres that Nixie had conjured left the tip of her wand like big, pale, shining bubbles, and slowly ascended over the construction site.

A dozen pale orbs of soft, glowing light floated up into the fog and began spreading out across the future park, lighting up the small sections of it beneath them.

When one of the orbs passed the creature on the smokestack, Jake got a better look. He rather wished he hadn't.

The creature had blue skin, a hooked nose, and a rail-thin body dressed in nothing but a loincloth.

Instead of running away, as Jake had rather expected, it peered down at him with a sly gargoyle's sneer. "We know who you are, Jakey-boy," it taunted in a crackly, high-pitched voice.

Jake blinked at its use of his name, but held his ground.

"You're *ours*," it continued. "The Horned One has decreed it—Your Highness!"

"Your Highness?" Jake retorted as a chill ran down his spine.

"You will be the Black Prince. You can't undo the prophecy—especially now that you've got blood on your hands!" A crazed cackle suddenly burst from the creature's lips, and Jake recoiled.

How could that thing possibly know about the sky pirate he had killed tonight by accident? Unless...

"Wyvern sent you!"

"No-ho, but his daddy did! Tonight, you will join us, Lord Griffon."

"No, I won't."

"You, we want," it said eagerly. "But the others? Your little friends? They're *doomed*!"

"Dani!" Jake thundered, turning toward the river as he suddenly realized he did not hear Teddy anymore. "Brian!"

He was suddenly alone in the fog, and when he spun around to face the creature, it was gone.

Fear gripped him.

He sensed a powerful evil approaching.

Then Jake saw it. The towering shadow on the wall of Westminster Palace, at the edge of the park. He stared in horror. Surely his eyes were playing tricks on him.

Blacker than black, the huge, horned silhouette spanned the whole stone wall of Parliament, and it was moving. It swished its dragon tail as it turned and shifted tattered batwings. Its clawed fingers curled into fists by its sides.

Red eyes gleamed from the wall, searching the night.

Were they staring right at him?

Jake took a step backward.

The shadow let out a frustrated snarl.

His mouth went dry. What was it that imp had just said? Wyvern hadn't sent them. His daddy had. *Shemrazul...*

We need to get out of here.

"Dani!" he yelled, suddenly turning toward the river, his heart pounding. *"Dani O'Dell, answer me right now!"*

"Where'd she go?" Archie asked, hurrying out of the darkness just then.

Jake whirled around and had never been happier to see his eccentric cousin. Nixie and Isabelle were right behind him, running into the park site from the street.

"Egads, coz, you're as white as a ghost."

"Look—!" Jake pivoted and started to point at the wall, but the demon's silhouette was gone.

"What is it, Jake?" Nixie asked.

He swallowed hard, his heart thumping. "D-did you all hear that horrible sound? Like a-a snarl?"

"No." They shook their heads.

"What did you see?" Izzy asked with a penetrating stare.

Jake fell silent, still rattled by the realization that something worse than he'd ever imagined was hunting them.

And yet he wasn't sure whether Shemrazul had actually seen him. The terrible gaze of those gleaming red eyes had swept right past him, as though he were invisible.

"Never mind." Jake decided to tell his friends about it later. Right now, he just wanted everyone to get to Beacon House. Besides, the demon was gone. "I-I thought I saw something, is all. Probably—just a shadow." He cleared his throat, a little embarrassed that they could tell he was scared, and turned away. "C'mon, Dani went this way."

He strode ahead once more, his senses on high alert. Glad as he was to have the trio's reassuring company nearby, a part of him wished they hadn't followed, after that nasty little creature's threat against his friends.

It made him jittery—and all the clutter of this blasted construction site made him feel claustrophobic, boxed in.

"Nix, come on!" Archie said when the witch hung back.

Jake turned and saw Nixie standing motionless, her astonished gaze trained upward.

"Imps!" she said, and pointed.

"Oh, is that what you call 'em?" Jake muttered, but then he saw his cousins glancing around in shock.

"Good Lord," Izzy whispered.

Jake followed her stare and was startled to find there were imps all over the park site.

As soon as Nixie's illumination orbs revealed their presence, the lesser devils burst into gleeful laughter and scattered. They began running amuck around the kids, twirling like acrobats around the crane's arm, racing on tiptoes across the stacked bricks, and somersaulting along the half-built embankment.

Others juggled chunks of coal, then hurled them at the kids with the most unpleasant snickers. Jake and his friends ducked.

"Hey!" Jake yelled. "Stop that!"

"All hail the Black Prince!" one yelled in a squeaky voice, and the others joined in.

"All hail the future Dark Master!"

"We are your humble servants, Your Highness!"

They began cheering for Jake, but only to mock him, he knew.

His friends looked appalled. They'd heard about the prophecy, of course.

"Hail Prince Jake! He'll destroy the Order one day! The evilest Dark Master ever born!"

"Shut *up*!" Jake barked, but they merely laughed like he'd just proved their point. "Go away!"

They persisted.

"I don't think I like imps," Nixie remarked.

But, of course, the blue-skinned imps weren't the only ones pestering them. There were red devils, too—just like in the old theater pantomimes, with horns and tails and nasty little pitchforks.

And there were...other things.

"What is *that*?" Isabelle asked, pointing at a blob-like creature that was staring at them from the roof of the nearest shed. It looked like a giant scoop of tapioca pudding with a face.

The blob shrieked and leaped away when Jake spotted it, boinging off the shed to land in a quivering heap yards away, atop a stone block waiting to be added to the embankment.

"What ridiculous creatures," Nixie said. "If they're from Hades, you'd think they'd be scarier than this."

"Scary enough for me, thank you very much," Jake muttered, though he was thinking of the shadow demon on the wall.

Archie adjusted his spectacles, as though he'd doubted his own eyes. "I daresay, at least we've found the source of Brian's sulfurous fumes."

This brought Jake back to the task at hand. "Let's go. We've got to find Dani and him and that stupid dog and get the blazes out of here." He walked on.

Nixie snickered as she followed. "Oh, come on, Jake, you're not actually scared of these little critters, are you?"

He didn't answer.

He didn't care to tell them about the shadow, nor could he bring himself to repeat the blue imp's sickening warning that all his friends were doomed.

Of course, devils *lied*. It was simply what they did.

But Jake wasn't taking any chances. "Stick together," he ordered. "And grab anything you can find to protect yourself."

"Really?" Archie looked at him.

"Really." Jake paused, not wanting to scare them. "Just in case."

Hearing the seriousness in his voice, they quit dawdling.

Nixie slapped her wand against her palm. "Well, I'm ready."

"Sis? Here." Archie jogged over to an abandoned shovel leaning against the nearby shed the blob creature had fallen off of, and handed it to Isabelle, taking a pickaxe for himself. "Crude, but serviceable."

"Thanks, brother." Izzy gripped the shovel and hefted it like the Keeper's Staff, with which she regularly trained.

"Let's go. Dani!" Jake yelled again, striding ahead into the fog. "Dani! Brian! Where are you? Curse this fog!"

"Where are they going?" little mocking voices asked all around them.

"I don't know. We'd better follow."

"We shall attend you, Your Highness! *Hee, hee, hee!*"

The imps and devils followed Jake en masse, watching and tittering, as he and the other three marched through the construction site.

Strangely, the creatures kept their distance. Instead of closing in, they peered down from their perches on cranes, sheds, and brick piles, harassing the kids as they passed with mocking comments, rude whistles, and taunting laughter.

A couple of the red devils jabbed pitchforks in their direction, but none actually attacked.

"I think they're afraid of us," Nixie said.

"I doubt it," Jake said under his breath.

"Maybe they're just afraid of Red." Izzy nodded upward as the Gryphon arrived on the scene.

His wingspan cast a shadow over the little miscreants everywhere as he swooped down beneath Nixie's glowing spheres. Red let out a war cry, and the lesser devils screeched, then scattered like ants.

The imp swinging around the crane arm like a gymnast wasn't fast enough. Red snatched him off the structure by his wrist and flew away, tossing him into the river; Jake heard the splash.

Then the Gryphon circled back.

"Red, find Dani!" Jake yelled.

"Becaw!"

Red went. He flew above the orbs where the fog was thinner and made a pass around the whole site, scanning the ground with his sharp eagle eyes.

"Caw!" The Gryphon suddenly zoomed toward the far corner of the future park, by the river.

Watching where he flew, Jake, Archie, Isabelle, and Nixie raced after him. The Gryphon helpfully hovered over a certain spot till they arrived.

To Jake's huge relief, they soon found Dani and Brian there, unharmed. Teddy as well.

Joining them, Jake now saw the reason the dog had gone quiet. Teddy wasn't barking anymore; he was growling.

Against a huge stone block, the terrier had cornered an oddity the likes of which Jake had never seen before—and that was saying something.

"Egads," Archie said. "What is he?"

"No idea," Nixie murmured.

The bizarre little creature was only as tall as a child of four or five. It had a body as round as a ball, skinny stick legs that ended in a pair of red shoes, and skinny arms with white gloves on its hands.

A large, single eye stared out of the middle of its belly. The eye blinked once, but for the most part, stayed fearfully fixed on Teddy.

With its back pressed against the big stone block, the funny little thing appeared to be panting, cowering away from the snarling terrier.

"Teddy, you're frightening him," Izzy chided. "Leave him be! Dani, make him stop."

At that, the carrot snapped out of her speechless daze and snatched her dog up in her arms. She wrapped her fingers around Teddy's snout to quiet him.

"Go on," Izzy told the frightened little monster with a gentle wave. "Shoo."

At once, the peculiar wee eyeball fellow ran off into the shadows, pattering off in his little shoes.

Archie started laughing, but Jake turned angrily to Dani.

"Why didn't you answer me?" he demanded, though he was weak-kneed with relief to see that she and Brian and Teddy were safe.

"Huh?" Dani mumbled, looking dazed.

"You nearly stopped my heart! Oh, never mind. Let's get out of here." Jake took her by the elbow and began firmly leading her back toward the street.

"But—did you see that?" Dani said, going along without argument. "Did the rest of you see that, or am I losing my marbles?"

"We saw it," Nixie said.

"What the devil was it, I wonder?" Archie said.

"Who cares!" Jake answered. "It doesn't matter, anyway. Something's wrong, everyone. If you haven't noticed, these creatures don't belong here."

"There are more?" Dani asked.

"Look around!" Jake retorted, still cross at her for disregarding her own safety. Then he gestured to Red to go ahead of them, since the imps and devils were clearly afraid of the Gryphon.

Red dropped to the ground and prowled along ahead of them rather than flying. The creatures melted out of his path, some hiding in the shadows.

"Criminy," she whispered.

"Why aren't they attacking?" Brian murmured, bringing up the rear. "They could take us if they wanted to. They've got us outnumbered."

"Maybe that's not their job." Jake gave the Guardian an uneasy glance.

Suddenly, one of the devils bounded over to stand before him after the Gryphon prowled past. "Oh, most terrifying Highness, please don't go!"

Red whipped around and snarled.

The devil cringed from the beast, but held his ground. "I mean you no harm!"

"Good. Then get out of my way," Jake said. "We're leaving."

"But we have a song for you, sire." The devil waggled his eyebrows.

Jake frowned. "I don't care."

"Aww," said a bunch of the imps.

"We practiced for days! Please?" This fellow was smarmy, with his oily smile and thinly penciled mustache.

"Yes, please, please, please, Your Highness?" they all started whining. "Let us sing our pretty song for you and your friends!"

"It could be enchanted," Nixie warned.

"It's not enchanted, cross my heart, hope to die. Come, you'll enjoy it, and it won't take much of your time."

The creatures were not taking no for an answer.

The red devil gestured with his pitchfork to his mates like he held a conductor's baton. "Hit it, boys! A-one and a-two..."

The creatures all started humming a jaunty yet menacing tune in some minor key, stepping into a large circle around them.

"Goodness!" said Isabelle.

Red hissed, glancing about.

"I don't like this," Brian murmured. "We're surrounded."

"I know. Just go along with it," Jake said under his breath. "Watch the ones behind us."

"Can't you zap them or something? Then we run."

"I don't want to set them off. Too many, like you said. And these things are bloody fast."

Still humming their song's introduction, the creatures joined hands like they were playing ring around the rosie and began swaying back and forth in time with the firm, implacable beat. Then they started to sing:

> "Ha, ha, ha, you're in trouble now,
> Trouble now,
> Hail to the new Black Prince!"

"Wait, why? Why are we in trouble?" Jake demanded.

> "Tra, la, la, He'll terrify the world now,
> He's the boy we must convince!"

"You're not going to convince me of anything."
The determined singers sang louder and faster.

> *"Fa-la-la-la-la!*
> *The rest of you are all quite dead."*

"Hey! Don't threaten my friends!"

> *"Ha, ha, ha, it's so funny now,*
> *Funny now,*
> *All the bad children should've stayed at home in BED!"*

The Gryphon roared.

All the creatures screeched and ran away.

In seconds, they had vanished.

The night was quiet and dark.

"Huh! Would you look at that," Archie said, glancing around at the empty park site. "They're gone."

Dani beamed. "Good boy, Red!"

But Jake's blood curdled when he lifted his gaze and saw that it was not the Gryphon who had scared the lesser devils away. "Everybody, be quiet. *Now.*"

CHAPTER FIFTEEN
Surrounded

Three Nightstalkers were gliding up Millbank Street.

The spectral assassins were almost invisible in the fog, but Jake's ghost-sight gave him a talent for spotting such creatures.

They were still some distance down the road but surely would've heard Red's roar, if not that awful song.

They floated about eight feet off the ground, the tattered edges of their hooded cloaks blowing behind them as they approached.

Their faces were concealed by the sort of ventilator masks that Archie used when he was playing in his lab with dangerous chemicals.

"What's wrong?" Dani whispered, giving Jake a wide-eyed look, but he kept his stare fixed on the wraithlike creatures zooming up the road.

They had reached the edge of the park at the same spot where the kids had first entered the construction site.

Jake gulped. "We're in trouble, you lot. Don't make a sound. Stay calm. Crouch down. Nixie, douse the orbs. Quick."

Nixie did. "Why, Jake?"

Thank the Lord the creatures had not spotted them yet in the darkness. For once, the fog might actually work in their favor.

His friends followed his gaze and saw the three sinister phantoms for themselves; even Brian turned ashen.

The Nightstalkers were carrying scythes, which seemed an especially bad sign. The last time Jake had encountered them, they had wielded long knives.

Nixie lifted her wand uncertainly—not that it would do her any good. "What are they?"

"Nightstalkers. This is what attacked me in Sicily." Jake's heart pounded faster. "I'd have been dead if it weren't for Janos and his darkling blade."

Izzy looked at him sharply.

"There's three more coming up the river," Brian reported, glancing back toward the park.

Aye, Jake saw them. "Blast it, those little miscreants were stalling us," he whispered. Scanning for an escape route, he could've kicked himself.

Janos had specifically lent him a darkling blade for their diplomatic journey to various kingdoms with Uncle Richard and Aunt Claire. Such swords were prized by vampires, who could appear either as solid flesh or a puff of black smoke; the darkling blade worked as a weapon in either form. Thus, it could kill phantoms like these. Janos had insisted that Jake borrow the weapon, just in case. But the whole group had been in such a scramble to reach Merlin Hall that Jake had left it in his blasted, blinkin' luggage.

"There!" Archie said, keeping his voice down as he pointed toward the ornate roof of Parliament. "Two more atop Victoria Tower!"

Izzy looked around slowly. "They're everywhere."

Teddy whimpered while the imps gathered, eager to watch their doom.

Red moved in front of the kids, opening his wings as though he could shield them from the spectral assassins. Unfortunately, Jake doubted there was much that even the Gryphon could do against evil spirits.

"How do we kill these things, Jake?" Brian asked in a taut voice.

"We can't. They're phantoms, wraiths. Normal weapons pass right through them. My telekinesis was of no use against them either. I know of only two things that can hurt them: holy water and a darkling blade, like Janos carries."

"Well, there's holy water right across the street." Dani nodded toward Westminster Abbey.

"She's right," Jake said. "We need to get inside the cathedral. They'll have plenty of holy water in there."

"Except the church is huge, and the entrance is not exactly close," Archie whispered. "We'll need to go up the street and around the corner to reach the door. The Nightstalkers will see us."

"Not necessarily," Nixie replied.

They all looked over at her.

"I have a new trick." The witch sounded confident, but Jake saw fear in her dark eyes. "I've been studying invisibility spells lately. Ulwyn's

Umbrella is the strongest one I have, but we'll need to move together in a clump—as if we're all sharing one, big, dome-shaped umbrella."

"Fantastic, Nix," Jake said. "What should we do?"

She waved them closer. "Everyone, huddle together as tight as you can. Wait—let me stand in the middle." Nixie pushed into the center, then the rest of them did as she said and held on to each other in order to stay tightly packed.

"C'mon, Red. You too." Jake beckoned, and they had to reshuffle their arrangement, putting the Gryphon in the center, since he was the biggest.

The kids lined up on either side of the beast: Jake, Nixie, and Archie huddled close to Red's left side, with Dani, Izzy, and Brian on his right. The carrot-head clutched Teddy in her arms, her hand poised to hold his snout closed to keep him from barking. Red folded his wings down and curled his tail across his back to make himself as compact as possible.

Still, Nixie looked worried. "I'm only able to do a ten-foot diameter at best, and I'm not sure how long I'll be able to sustain it. But it should be enough to at least get us out of here. It was invented by an elvish spy. The Fae know what they're doing when it comes to magic, trust me."

"It'll work. It has to. Don't worry, we can do this," Jake said, then glanced at Red. "Keep your tail in tight, boy."

"Right." Nixie nodded. "Arms and legs and tails have to stay concealed beneath the dome. Whatever part of you that sticks out beyond it will be visible. Now, everyone, be quiet. I need to concentrate." She lifted her wand over her head and began murmuring an incantation.

Something about the determination on her pert face reminded Jake of Aunt Ramona. Within seconds, a silver shimmer fountained up from the tip of Nixie's wand and formed a small dome over their heads, like an ordinary umbrella.

But it grew quickly.

Jake was fascinated. The magical barrier that her incantation was creating resembled a thin layer of clear, flowing water; it cascaded down around them in a domed circle, hiding them bit by bit from prying eyes. It descended past their shoulders, then at waist level, until it went all the way down to their feet.

When it hit the muddy ground, its silver shimmer disappeared, and they all looked at Nixie.

"Did it work?" Archie whispered.

She nodded. "No talking. They can't see us now, but they could still hear us. Try to keep your footsteps light, and Dani, make sure Teddy doesn't bark."

Without a word, Jake tugged on Dani's arm. Since they had all grabbed hold of Red and each other, that moved the whole group forward at a cautious pace, one foot after the other.

It took a tremendous amount of self-discipline not to run off in a panic or scream as the Nightstalkers glided closer from all directions and began methodically searching the park.

The kids gripped each other harder as the phantoms floated past.

When one flew by just a few feet overhead, scythe in hand, its hooded face turning this way and that as it searched for them, they could hear its rasping breath beneath the gas mask.

It moved on, passing so close that the torn edges of its cloak trailed over their heads as it glided by.

Everyone winced but resisted the urge to brush off the black streamers of cobwebby fabric. Somehow, they all stayed silent.

Of course, the lesser devils had seen where the kids had been standing when Nixie cast her spell, so they gave the phantom assassins a general sense of where to look, pointing and gesturing.

Somehow, Jake and his friends managed to elude them. Under their dome of invisibility, they progressed farther and farther from their original spot, and even managed to make it out of the construction zone, back out onto the road.

But the Nightstalkers were on the move.

The three that Brian had seen gliding up the river now skimmed high across the park site to join their colleagues on Millbank, about twenty yards behind the kids.

Meanwhile, the pair atop the roof of Parliament were gliding down the front wall of the government building, blocking the way ahead in their search.

Jake could feel his friends' fear. It was palpable as they tiptoed up Abingdon Street, clinging to one another beneath their cloaking umbrella. Even Red seemed a little intimidated, silent on his lion paws.

A few yards farther on, Abingdon widened greatly into the Old Palace Yard, where the magnificent statue of King Richard the Lionheart sat astride his horse. While the Nightstalkers zoomed this way and that around this broader section of road, the kids hurried on as fast as they dared, until the Old Palace Yard narrowed briefly into Margaret Street.

Very soon, Jake knew, they'd be able to make the left-hand turn that would take them to the north entrance of the cathedral.

They were almost at the corner where the wide, grassy plaza of Parliament Square opened up, with its bronze statues of dead politicians posing atop thick granite pedestals here and there.

The Nightstalkers were growing frustrated—as though they sensed the kids nearby, but couldn't see them and didn't understand why.

The largest one let out a piercing screech, which turned out to be a signal of some sort. Apparently, this was the leader, judging by the bandolier across its chest and its somewhat less raggedy garb.

Jake held his friends back as the whole troop of Nightstalkers swarmed into the narrow passage of Margaret Street to receive their orders. More must've arrived, for there were at least a dozen of them at this point.

The kids stood motionless, holding their breath.

"They are here," the leader rasped. "Kill!"

The kids shuddered as a group and slowly began crouching down under the dome to make themselves as small as possible.

The Nightstalkers swirled all around them, back and forth, sniffing for them through their gas masks.

It was unnerving, and Jake wasn't sure what to do. Janos wasn't coming this time, but even he would've been too badly outnumbered in this situation.

What are we going to do? They couldn't crouch here all night, hiding in plain sight outside of Parliament.

The kids ducked as one of the Nightstalkers zoomed just over their heads.

Exchanging worried glances, they rose without a sound after it had passed and forged on, inching forward step by step.

Finally, claustrophobic Margaret Street spilled out onto Parliament Square Garden, a broad, green space across from the Parliament buildings.

Lampposts brightened the square's dark, foggy lawns; the tall trees edging its borders stood leafless with autumn. The big, dark statues glistened in the wet.

To their right stood Parliament, where Big Ben glowed in the Clock Tower. To their left lay glorious Westminster Abbey—where the kings and queens of England had their coronations, and many great poets had their tombs.

And where the holy water waited.

Based on his prior experience with this kind of enemy, Jake was fairly confident that the Nightstalkers wouldn't be able to follow them into the church.

But when he looked ahead, he didn't like all that open space in Parliament Square, either.

Old medieval Margaret Street had felt too cramped, but Parliament Square seemed too open and exposed. If Nixie's spell failed, there was nothing to hide behind except the row of trees around the border and the granite bases of the statues.

Ignoring his dread, Jake kept tiptoeing forward with his clump of friends at his back. It wasn't much farther.

They had left most of the Nightstalkers behind, but a few were coming out onto the square and flying around, on the hunt, trying to sniff them out.

It was bizarre seeing spectral assassins pouring into a major tourist destination. Jake felt cold as he watched them flying back and forth along the graveled walkways and sniffing at the statues.

Devoid of its usual tourists and picnickers, protesters and handcarts selling trinkets and snacks, and, of course, the self-important MPs hurrying back and forth from Parliamentary sessions, the sprawling square looked eerie.

Tearing his gaze off the Nightstalkers, Jake scanned the route to the cathedral's magnificent front doors.

Almost there.

Glancing to the right as he guided his friends into the left turn, Jake's heart lurched when he saw the phantoms' silhouettes flying past the face of Big Ben, like witches on brooms.

The rest of the Nightstalkers arrived in Parliament Square and continued circling like sharks, growing angrier by the minute.

Jake was telling himself that if the church doors were locked, he could just use his telekinesis to blast them open. It seemed sacrilegious, but in this case, God would probably understand.

Just then, the leader rasped out an unintelligible command.

The other Nightstalkers nodded. Then the whole group turned their scythes upside down to use the wooden ends as clubs. They started swinging and poking at the empty air beneath them with their long sticks. Apparently, they had concluded the kids were here somewhere, only invisible. One good whack should expose them.

Panic took hold among his friends as the wraith assassins flew closer, as though sensing their general whereabouts. The tiniest of whimpers escaped Dani, and one of the Nightstalkers must've heard.

It zoomed over to them, weapon raised. When it thrust its wooden stick straight into their midst, the blow struck Red's back.

The Nightstalker screeched; everyone screamed, including Nixie. The shielding umbrella failed. As the Nightstalker flipped its scythe right side up, the kids fled in all directions.

Pure horror gripped Jake as he watched the phantom assassins chasing his friends with the blade ends of their scythes. For a heartbeat, he did not know which way to run, which one to try to help first—not that there was anything he could do against these foes.

Then two of the creatures zoomed toward Jake.

He tried to run, but they were too fast. The first to reach him gripped him by his right arm.

This shocked him.

How could it grab *him*, but when *he* tried to strike back, his fist whooshed right through the creature? It was as useless as trying to punch a ghost.

As Jake struggled against the Nightstalker's hold, he saw his friends doing their best to make their way to the cathedral. Red was swooping back and forth, trying to get a few of the phantoms to chase him, but they weren't interested.

The Gryphon wheeled and darted and rounded back again, while the kids ran around, ducking every which way from the Nightstalkers' blows and trying to reach the church entrance.

Meanwhile, Jake had a different sort of problem. The Nightstalker that had seized his right arm began lifting him off the ground.

"Hey! Put me down!" He kicked his legs, trying to get his feet back onto the ground, but a second phantom arrived and grabbed his left arm.

Together, the creatures carried him higher.

"Don't fight, Your Highness," one gurgled. "We wouldn't want to drop the Black Prince."

"*I am not the Black Prince!*" Jake roared.

"Yessss. The Horned One has decreed it."

"No! I refuse—" Then he saw one of the Nightstalkers nearly split Dani in two with his sickle, and he was ready to make a bargain. "Let my friends go, and I'll come with you willingly."

"You'll come with us, willing or not. And your friends will die," hissed the one on his right.

Then the pair of them lifted him three, four, five feet off the ground. Jake was powerless as they floated higher than the wrought-iron fence, then as high as the naked trees ringing the square.

He wasn't sure if he ought to struggle anymore. Being dropped—or thrown down—from this height would have very unpleasant results.

Not that he had much choice. Their grip on his arms was viselike.

"Jake!" Dani screamed, seeing them carrying him away. Teddy began barking like mad.

There was nothing Jake could do, dangling at the mercy of creatures that he knew had none. Panic overtook him; it was rare that he found himself completely helpless.

In a few more seconds, he'd be on a par with the roof of the cathedral.

That was when he saw the flock of doves that lived atop Westminster Abbey suddenly flutter up from their cozy night perches and swirl about in a cloud of white wings.

Something had disturbed them, and when Jake glanced over in a panic, expecting to see one of the Nightstalkers posted there, he spotted a black-clad figure—much like Janos had appeared on the roof of the church in Sicily the night he'd come to save Jake, led there by his Guardian instincts.

But this was no vampire.

The figure standing at the edge of the ornate Gothic roofline held a brilliant silver sword in his hand—and suddenly unfurled powerful white wings.

Jake's mind went blank.

It can't be...

Then a brilliant column of white light shot down from the dark sky and landed in the street near Archie.

Another slammed into place by Dani and Isabelle.

A third appeared between Nixie and Brian.

Then the white-winged figure took a running leap off the roof of the cathedral, descending with masterful control.

It all happened in the blink of an eye.

Sword in hand, wings outstretched and angled just so, their old friend Celestus swept down a few yards until he flew even with Jake and his captors. His otherworldly blue eyes gleamed, his bright blade flashed, and he skewered the Nightstalker on Jake's right.

The creature burst into a rain of ashes.

The one on the left fled with a terrified squeal, dropping Jake—but Celestus quickly clasped his forearm.

"I've got you," the angel said, holding him firmly.

"You're alive!" Jake blurted out. "A-and you've got your wings back!"

"Nice of you to notice," the angel said coolly, his fierce gaze on the square as he lowered Jake safely to the ground.

Jake found his footing on the cobbled road, but couldn't stop staring. "You saved my life! Thank you. Listen—I saw something back there—"

"I already know. That's why I'm here. Run," the angel ordered him in a low voice. "This is not your fight—yet."

With a flick of his wings, Celestus turned about-face in midair, lifted his sword, and charged after the fleeing Nightstalker.

Jake watched in wonder for a second, then turned around. What he saw amazed him.

The three other warrior angels protecting his friends were badly outnumbered, but did not seem concerned.

Jake wondered if they were the same team of Light Beings who had come to Wales with Celestus a year ago, when the demon Shemrazul had tried to escape Hades. The four warrior angels had fought the hideous demon back down into the Ninth Pit, where he belonged.

And now, here they were, battling the Nightstalkers.

Jake remembered Janos telling him once that the only weapons comparable to darkling blades were Brightwields—the swords the Light Beings carried.

No wonder Celestus' thrust had turned the Nightstalker into ashes.

But although the warrior angels' arrival had helped even the odds, Jake knew that he and his friends were not out of danger yet.

Dani ran over to him and grabbed his shoulder, turning him to face her. "Are you all right?"

He snapped out of his daze with a nod. "Let's go!" he called to the group.

The others also looked entranced by the wondrous sight of the Light Beings thrashing the sinister Nightstalkers, but to Jake's relief, everyone was still alive and on their feet.

Red roared, flying low zigzags around them to shepherd the kids back into a group.

"Follow me, everyone!" Jake said. "Never mind the holy water; Celestus said we need to run."

"Sounds good to me," Archie muttered, while Brian looked dazed by the arrival of real, live angels.

"C'mon!" Jake urged, then raced toward Big Ben, dodging around the corner of Westminster Palace.

With Red bringing up the rear at a gallop, Jake led his friends a stone's throw down Bridge Street, then they crossed the empty street to enter the parklike setting of the brand-new Victoria Embankment.

The wide, sandy walking path here was well lit by gas lamps, and would take them all the way up to Beacon House as it followed the curving north shore of the River Thames.

Jake did have to use his telekinesis to blast the park gates open, however. The river walk and gardens were officially open only during the daytime.

No matter. This would be the safest way for them to go, and the easiest. Jake hurried his friends through the busted-open gates, then pulled them shut behind his Gryphon.

At once, they all started walking up the dark, tree-lined pathway, anxiously glancing over their shoulders now and then to make sure they weren't being followed.

The din of the fray soon faded behind them.

When they were finally sure they'd escaped the Nightstalkers, they paused for a moment to catch their breath.

"Did you see Dr. Celestus' new wings?" Dani burst out, as though she could no longer contain herself. "I'm so glad he's all right! Oh, I had a feeling we would see him again soon! I found a white feather one day not long ago in our suite at Merlin Hall when I was tidying up. I couldn't figure out where it came from. I just *knew* it was a sign—and now he's back!"

"With some awfully good timing, I daresay," Archie said, and the others nodded.

"I'll have to tell my mother about this." Brian folded his arms across his chest with a solemn stare. "She's always believed in angels—she's got angel figurines and knickknacks all over our house—and now I can say I've seen four real ones with my own two eyes." He shook his head. "I can't believe actual guardian angels saved our lives tonight."

"They do that," Jake said ruefully, but he couldn't help wondering if the demon's presence on the wall of Parliament was part of the reason the angels had been authorized to come to their aid. Either way, he let out a long sigh of relief.

"We'd better keep walking," Isabelle said.

Everyone groaned, but knew she was right. Wearily, the kids continued on, heading up the wide, graveled path in the direction of Beacon House.

For his part, Jake was starting to wonder if this night would ever end.

CHAPTER SIXTEEN
Shifty

"**W**ake up," Welton said, nudging Prue after she'd dozed off with her head on Charlie's shoulder. "Something's happening."

Blinking sleep out of her eyes, Prue lifted her head and followed the runt's nod toward the front stairs of the library basement.

Hmm. Welton was right.

The wood elf, Master Finnderool, had just come gliding down the stone stairs with speedy grace. When he reached Miz Jillian's side, he leaned toward her ear to pass along some discreet message.

"They must've unsealed one of the doors," Charlie said, rubbing his eyes with a yawn. "I can smell fresh air."

Welton beamed. "Maybe they're finally going to let us out of here."

"Then you two had better be ready," Prue murmured, keeping her gaze fixed on the front of the basement.

A moment later, the Lightrider wood elf sprang back up the stairs, and Miz Jillian turned to the crowd.

The brownie librarian, Mr. Calavast, finally quit pacing and looked up at Sir Peter's wife expectantly.

Lifting the hem of her skirts with a dainty motion, the woman went to stand on the fourth or fifth step up, so that everyone could see her.

"Ladies and gentlemen, may I please have your attention!"

The crowd's curious murmurs quieted down.

"I have a wonderful announcement! The Black Fortress has gone. The battle's over. We've been given the all-clear. So, please rise to your feet—"

Exclamations of relief and hoots of joy interrupted her speech. Here and there, applause burst out across the dim, cavernous space.

She allowed a brief celebration, smiling as she waited for the applause to simmer down.

"Master Finnderool and his helpers will be unsealing the other two exits momentarily. I'd like to thank each and every one of you for your patience this evening during this distressing ordeal. At least now it's over. I would ask that we all *please* leave the basement in an orderly fashion, two by two. I know that everyone is eager to see their loved ones again outside, but stampeding for the exits will only clog the doors. This way, we can all get back to the palace safely." She clapped her hands twice. "Now then! You may begin queuing up."

Across the basement, the schoolchildren and adults of lesser magic or no magic at all began climbing to their feet, dusting themselves, and stretching a bit after sitting for so long on the cold stone floor.

"One more thing!" Miz Jillian held up a hand. "Will the Badgerton triplets please see me at the front as you exit the building?"

She did not explain why, but Prue, Charlie, and Welton looked at each other, aghast.

A few knowing glances were cast their way, but most people around them were too excited about getting out of this creepy cellar to bother with them.

Prue's pulse raced. *We have to get out of here.*

It was just as she had feared. The three of them—who had nothing to do with any of this—were doomed to get tangled up in Uncle Boris's bad deeds. Thankfully, Prue had already made a plan.

First up: escape.

Since now nearly everyone was standing, it would be easy for the skunkies to slip out of here in their much smaller animal forms. If they kept to the edges of the basement, no one would even notice them.

But which way should they go?

Still in person form, Prue stood on her toes and looked around, considering her options.

Well, she had no intention of leading her brothers out by the front door. She wasn't a fool. If they went that way, they would immediately be taken into custody.

But which of the other two exits offered a better chance of escape? Urgency thrummed in her veins, and she told herself to hurry.

The hundred schoolchildren packed into the library basement were herded into three large clusters, which, in turn, formed into vague lines, filing slowly toward the exits.

Theoretically, while the civilians walked out two by two, as instructed, it should be easy for the triplets in skunk form to scurry up the stairs, bypassing the line, as long as they hugged the wall and managed not to be spotted by any bossy adults.

Prue did not really like her options. She was trying to make up her mind which exit would be the safer, when, suddenly, she noticed a curious thing.

Mr. Calavast, the brownie librarian, was unlocking a small, narrow door on the back wall with a sign on it that said: *Staff Only.*

The desperate brownie must've been in a hurry to check on the library upstairs, because, after unlocking it with his key, he flung the staff door open, sped through it, and failed to close it all the way behind him.

Prue elbowed both brothers. "Transform!" she ordered them.

At once, the triplets jerked their heads to the side and shrugged their shoulders briskly in a move they had long since perfected; in an instant, three young skunks appeared in their places, the skinny one still wearing his glasses, the husky one still carrying his knapsack.

"Follow me," Prue said to her brothers in skunk language (which would've sounded like naught but a series of squeaks and squirrelly chitters to any human listener). Then she took the lead, scurrying off to the shadowed edges of the basement wall.

With her brothers right behind her, she galloped toward the *Staff Only* door. When she reached it, she nudged it open a tad wider with her cute little black nose, then slipped through it into the inky darkness of a cramped, cobwebby stairwell.

Welton whisked in behind her, then came Charlie. Mr. Calavast was already out of view; brownies moved with incredible speed, which was why they were so efficient as workers of all kinds.

Prue began hopping up the dark narrow steps, pausing to look back briefly. "Charlie!" she squeaked. "Get the door!"

She didn't want anyone following them. There must be no witnesses to what she intended to do.

The chubby skunk obeyed, scampering back to pull the door shut behind them. Satisfied, Prue continued jumping up the steps, using her long, luxurious, striped tail for balance.

The staff stairway turned one corner and then another, twisting its way up to the main floor.

At the top, she had to nudge a second door open. Then she peeked out into the library, looking this way and that.

What she saw shocked her.

Prue was not the scholarly type, nor was she at all sentimental, especially when it came to the Order. But even she was taken aback by the haunting sight of the towering library shelves swathed in smoke.

The only sound was Mr. Calavast's fuzzy bare feet pattering up and down the aisles as he ran about, checking everything and muttering anxiously to himself.

When she heard the brownie speed off toward the circulation desk, she eased out of the doorway to get a better look around, signaling to her brothers with a flick of her tail that they should stay back. She just wanted to get a better sense of what she was dealing with here.

Creeping a few steps out into the library and sniffing for information, though the heavy smoke in the air burned her nose, she stood on her hind legs and peered through the bookshelves.

It was difficult to see much. Skunks did not have the best eyesight to start with, and it was dark as midnight and smoky. Nevertheless, she soon ascertained that the smoke was not coming from inside the library.

Nothing in here was on fire. Lifting her gaze, Prue saw she had been right: some of the stained-glass windows had been shattered during whatever magical fight had taken place here.

The smoke was drifting in from outside, wafting through the giant holes in the building where the windows used to be.

Those empty sockets were perhaps what shook her most. Much of that gleaming, colorful glass had been centuries old. She hoped Sir Peter could repair them with a spell or incantation...

But a grim feeling sank in as Prue realized that not everything could be fixed with the wave of a wand.

Like her family's reputation.

Not after this. The Badgertons were done for. Disgraced.

Beyond the gaping hole of what had been the rose window at the front of the cathedral-like library, she beheld the orange glow of a huge bonfire illuminating the black night sky.

Her nerve faltered as she realized it was coming from the direction of the great maze, where the Old Father Yew lived.

Now even that was on fire?!

She swallowed hard, terrified to think of how close the Dark Druids must've come to destroying the entire Order tonight—and it was all Uncle Boris's fault?

For a second, she thought she might throw up. But in the blink of an eye, her courage hardened again. All the more reason to forge ahead with what she planned to do.

If she and her brothers had no choice but to fend for themselves in the world henceforward, she did not intend to leave this place empty-handed. The three of them would need all the help they could get to survive on their own.

Across the echoing space of the library just then, Prue heard the front door open.

Someone came in.

"Yoo-hoo! Mr. Calavast? Are you here?" The pleasant female voice resounded across the echoing space. "I've come to check on you."

"Oh! Dame Oriel. Y-yes, here I am! How kind." The brownie librarian hurried to greet his visitor.

They began chatting, but Prue mostly tuned out their conversation, scanning the way up to the restricted section.

"There, there, are you all right?" the Elder asked.

"Well enough, I suppose. It's all such a mess! Fortunately, it doesn't seem as though anything was taken. There were some small fires around the edges, but thankfully, none of them reached the books."

"Thank heavens," Oriel said. "I know Fionnula Coralbroom was trying to blast her way in here, but I understand Lady Bradford held her off."

"My goodness!" said Calavast. "Well, it's over now. The library should be all right, I daresay—as long as it doesn't rain before these holes are fixed. Oh, it will take an army of helpers to get this place cleaned up. There's a layer of soot all over everything..."

Soot.

The mention of it gave Prue an idea. While the two adults commiserated, she crept back into the stairwell, where her brothers waited.

"All right. Calavast is distracted at the moment," she told them in skunk language. "I'm going to go get us a spell book. Here's what I want you to do—"

"What, you're going to steal it?" Welton said, looking scandalized.

"Consider it a permanent loan," she replied, giving him a snide stare.

Charlie frowned. "Uh, I don't think you're supposed to steal from the library, Prue."

"Leave the thinking to me, Charles. I wouldn't want you to hurt yourself."

"But sis." Welton twitched his nose to push his spectacles back up higher onto his snout. "Don't you need a wand to do magic?"

"I bought one at the last Fairy Market, remember, genius? It's in Charlie's knapsack. Now, quit asking questions. We don't have time for this! We have to get out of here. You heard what Miz Jillian said. The Elders are already looking for us. If *you* want to get arrested by the Guardians, be my guest, but I'm getting out of here. Are you with me or not?"

Both boys hung their heads and mumbled that of course they were.

"Good. Now, here's the plan. I'm going to go and find us a *serious* grimoire. We're on our own now, and that babyish beginner book Mother gave me isn't going to be much use.

"Now, after I've gone, I want you to count to three hundred to give me some time, then sneak over to the edges of the library and find one of those fires that burned out. I want you both to roll around in the soot to camouflage your stripes. That'll help us blend in when we get outside and make a run for it.

"And watch out for all that broken glass. I don't want you cutting up your paws for when we need to run, which will be soon."

She peeked out the door again. "It looks like the back wall of windows are intact, so that way should be safe. Meet me by the exit in the back corner. It's farthest from the palace; it leads out onto the grounds. From there, we'll head for the woods as fast as we can run. Got all that?"

The two boy skunks nodded.

"Good luck, Prue," Charlie grunted.

"Thanks. Both of you, be careful." With that, Prue scurried out of the stairwell, heading to the right. Her heart pounded as she ran over to one of the small piles of ashes where a wand blast had landed. There, she rolled over like a dog doing a trick.

Wriggling on her back for a few seconds, she did her best to get soot all over her bold white stripe; this should help her hide under the cover of darkness. Then she flipped up onto all fours again and scampered on.

Next stop, the restricted shelves.

Alone now, she moved silently along the back wall. She had never minded sneaking around. In fact, she was rather good at it. And she knew exactly where she was headed.

The restricted section was where all the best grimoires were kept— the ones that only advanced magical students could borrow—like Jake's weird friend, Nixie Valentine.

Some of the spell books were so powerful that they weren't even allowed to leave the library at all.

I'll bet one of those would be most helpful. Why not? She had a wand, and she wasn't afraid to use it. *I might not know very much about magic yet, but I'll figure it out as I go. How hard can it be?*

Determined as ever, Prue made her way over to the spiraling metal staircase that led up to the restricted collection. There, she turned herself back into a girl, albeit a girl whose face and clothes were smudged with ashes like war paint. She ducked beneath the chain cordoning off the staircase—as if that was going to keep anyone out. Then she began tiptoeing up the spiral stairs without a sound.

Calavast was fussing to and fro behind the circulation desk, and Dame Oriel was still fluttering around him, trying to be helpful.

Prue lifted her gaze as she continued sneaking up the metal staircase. The moon shone in through one of the empty window sockets. From outside, she could hear someone crying; others were giving orders as they sought to organize the chaos left behind by the night's invasion.

When she reached the top, she stepped off onto the gallery overlooking the main library. At once, she stole into the nearest shadowed aisle and quickly started scanning the shelves by moonlight.

Her heart pounded with excitement at the mad risk she was taking. Problem was, she wasn't quite sure what she was looking at here. She was no scholar; clever by nature, yes, but she'd never had much reason to apply herself before.

Usually, if any bad grades arose or teachers weren't nice to her, all she had to do was sniffle and cry a little, and Uncle Boris would say, "There, there," pat her on the head, and make sure her problems went away. He was an Elder, after all.

Or had been.

All Prue could figure was that the Dark Druids must've promised him major benefits for going over to their side. He wasn't stupid.

That must be it, she thought. *I'll bet he's probably going to be a really important person on their side now.*

She had no problem with that. Power was power. Still, it would probably be a while before they all found each other again, so she'd better find a grimoire with a wide range of useful spells to see them through...

Prue kept looking, doing her best to hurry.

Many of the spell books were tomes too thick to lug around in skunk form, even for Charlie. (She congratulated herself for making Charlie bring his knapsack of supplies. Now at least they'd have a way to carry the grimoire when she found the best one.)

She rejected whole rows of them. A lot were in Latin, so she couldn't even read them, and many were so old and fragile that their yellowed parchment pages looked like they'd fall apart at first use.

Here's something. She pulled a slim leather-bound volume with gilt letters off the shelf. *This one's in good shape.* The gold letters seem to twinkle in the moonlight as she read the cover:

ARVATH'S ARCANIUM
A Classic for the Ages
Newly Updated for Our Day
with a Preface by Dr. Belinda Glooms,
Headmistress of Brambles Academy of Magick

There was even a quote on the cover from Balinor himself: *"This essential resource belongs on the bookshelf of any working mage."*

It sounded promising. Prue quickly flipped through the pages and found a wide range of spells waiting inside. In the dark, she could just make out some of the chapter headers: *Conjuration, Summoning, Illusions, Hexes...*

Perfect. Hugging the mysterious volume against her chest, Prue left the restricted section, crept back down the spiral staircase, and hurried toward the corner exit farthest from the circulation desk, where she'd told her brothers to meet her.

They'd better be there, she thought, keeping her footsteps as light as possible. She didn't see them as she strode over, then suddenly—

"Watch it!" Welton whispered.

"Oh. Sorry," Prue muttered.

The boys had done such a good job of hiding their stripes that she had nearly stepped on Welton's tail.

"Did you find a good spell book?" he whispered.

She nodded, bending down to open the flap of Charlie's knapsack. She slid *Arvath's Arcanium* in with her wand beside the ridiculously babyish *Little Owl's Beginning Book of Magic*, as well as the money she'd had the sense to bring along—and what little remained of their snacks.

Prue rolled her eyes to find that Charlie had already eaten nearly everything. His gluttony erased any twinge of guilt she might've felt about making him carry the book. There was a reason that their husky middle brother usually took the most blame for their escapades.

No one believed weakling Welton could hurt a fly, and Prue was too good at playing innocent. Therefore, if they *did* get caught with the stolen grimoire, it might as well be Charlie who got the blame, as usual. He was the one who'd be carrying it in his pack.

She secured the buckle and looked at him. "Are you going to be able to run carrying that much weight?"

"No problem," he said with a proud squeak.

"Good. I'll get the door." Still in human form, Prue pulled the heavy door open as silently as possible, and her brothers slipped out one by one.

She stepped outside after them with a shiver, then pulled it shut behind her with a soft click. To her relief, no one was nearby on this side of the building. The students and civilians were all flowing out of the three larger exits of the library into the quadrangle.

Still standing at the top of the few stone stairs that led down onto the grass, Prue changed back into her animal form.

Then the skunkies set off into the night. They ran as fast as they could before anyone saw them, making a beeline for the woodlands surrounding Merlin Hall.

Her heart pounded; Prue found their escape both terrifying and thrilling. All they had to do was make it into the forest, and then, even if they were seen, they would most likely be mistaken for ordinary skunks.

Well, except for the knapsack.

It didn't matter in the end.

They slipped away without a trace.

Maybe this all was for the best, she reflected. Everyone hated them here. Glancing back resentfully at Merlin Hall one last time, she didn't care if she never saw this place again.

Then she led her brothers—still in skunk form—into the dark, familiar safety of the autumn woods.

Welton giggled nervously, twitching his tail. "We did it!"

"Where are we going?" Charlie whispered as they rustled along through the fallen leaves.

"Who cares!" Prue shot back. "Anywhere but here. Now, both of you, shut up and follow me..."

CHAPTER SEVENTEEN
The Black Prince

"Grandfather! I'm so glad you're safe." Victor gazed in relief at Zolond's smoke-sculpted face atop the calling candle.

"It was a dashed close thing," the Dark Master admitted. "And, by the way"—he arched a brow—"don't think I am unaware of your interference tonight."

"Who, me, sir?" Victor flashed an innocent smile.

Zolond snorted, but gave way to a disapproving chuckle.

"I hope it was helpful, sir."

"It was. And most unexpected." The old man studied Victor for a moment, as though seeing him in a whole new light. "You lent me your strength right when I needed it most. 'Twas good of you."

"Glad to be of service, sir. I had to do *something*." Victor faltered, perilously close to admitting that he cared.

Such sentimentality would not be welcome, he knew. Two dark souls like himself and his grandfather ought not to form attachments with other people at all—or, at least, should never admit to it.

Victor cleared his throat. "So, er, will you be calling your dragons back, now that you've contained the situation?"

Zolond shook his head. "Not yet. To be quite honest, I would not say the danger is entirely passed. I have everything under control now, of course, but...keep your guard up over the next few days. I will be leaving Bhisk and Etah with you until we can be sure how all of this will settle out."

Concerned, Victor nodded. "I see."

Grandfather saw his uneasiness and smiled. "Don't worry, lad. As I told you, things have calmed down. You should go to bed. It's, what, two or three in the morning? I could use a bit of rest myself. I'm old, if you haven't noticed. And I have...an important meeting in the morning with"—he lifted his chin—"a representative from the Order."

"Really?" Victor said.

"Hm, yes. I have the dubious honor of explaining why Wyvern attacked Merlin Hall, unprovoked, and broke the truce."

Victor whistled at this startling information. "What if they don't believe you?"

"Then there will be war. But don't worry, they will."

"You seem very sure."

Grandfather paused. "They're sending someone I...trust."

Victor stared at him, perplexed. These were astonishing words. He was not aware that the Dark Master trusted anyone.

Hold on, Victor thought. Surely Grandfather didn't mean he was meeting with *her.*

Oh, he'd heard the rumors about Zolond's youthful romance centuries ago with a powerful young witch.

Ramona something.

She had chosen the Order, while he had joined the Dark Druids. Over time, she'd become an Elder, while he'd clawed his way to the top of the black brotherhood. Though they had been sworn enemies ever since their break, as far as anyone knew, somehow, between them, the pair had managed to keep the truce between the two sides intact for many long years.

After all, even Victor had been taught that a full-out magical war was a prospect too terrible to put either side through, let alone the mundane world of ordinaries who had no idea magic even existed.

"Who are you meeting with, sir?" Victor asked cautiously.

Zolond pursed his thin lips. "It does not signify. What matters is making sure the Order understands this was an unsanctioned attack, and that Wyvern has been dealt with. On that note, I must go—"

"Oh, sir?" Victor interrupted, unwilling to miss this rare chance to tell his grandsire what he craved this year for his annual gift. After all, Victor's Hallowe'en birthday was only a week and a half away.

"Yes, boy, what is it?" Zolond cocked his smoky head impatiently.

"Erm, before you go...w-would it be all right if I told you what I *really* want for my birthday this year?"

Zolond's snowy eyebrows shot up. "Such audacity!" he said mildly. Then he gave Victor a dry look of amusement. "So, that's your real motive for helping me tonight?"

Victor laughed, fairly sure the old man was teasing. "No, sir! I did it because I thought perhaps you wouldn't mind an ally, considering your own top henchmen have proved so treacherous."

Zolond smiled. "Indeed. Blood is thicker than water, I warrant. Very well, then, Your Highness. What do you want for your fourteenth birthday?"

Bracing his hands on his thighs, Victor leaned a little closer to the calling candle, his heart pounding with eagerness. "I want to go to London."

Grandfather's eyebrows shot up.

"I don't mean alone, of course." Victor straightened up again. "I know that wouldn't be safe because of who I am. But Master Nagai could come. Or even...you, perhaps, Your Majesty. If you are not too busy with ceremonies and such."

Samhain was *the* high holiday for their side, after all.

"Hmm." Zolond narrowed his eyes, considering.

"Please? I mean, it's no extraordinary request, surely, just to be able to see the capital of one's own country, is it? Anyone can go there, so why not me? I daresay I'm old enough to start going out into the world, finally. You know I can't just stay locked up here forever with Magpen and Master Nagai—"

"Easy! Let's not get ahead of ourselves. Let me think for a moment."

Victor obeyed, holding his breath.

"Tell you what. You will serve as my assistant in this year's Samhain ritual atop Mount Woe, and then I will take you to London myself for a few days."

Victor's eyes widened. Had he heard right?

The Dark Master had not just agreed—and offered to take him there personally, no less—but he was giving Victor the unprecedented honor of assisting in the All Hallows' Hail to the Dark.

Grandfather looked amused to see he had rendered Victor speechless. All Victor could think was that the old man must've been impressed, indeed, by his assistance earlier tonight.

"Master Nagai will have to come along, as well, but tell him I said he'll have to dress like an Englishman. He'll draw too much attention to us if he goes to London in his Japanese garb."

Victor nodded, still slightly in shock. "Y-yes, sir. Thank you, sir!"

"Well, it *is* your birthday. And I hear you've been diligent in your studies all year, so...why not?"

Victor smiled from ear to ear. "I can't wait. Thank you, Grandfather!"

Zolond bowed his head in acknowledgment; he seemed amused at Victor's joy. "Now, then. It's far past your bedtime, and mine. So, I bid you a fond goodnight—grandson."

Victor bowed to the sorcerer-king. "Goodnight, sir."

"Rest well."

When Zolond disappeared from atop the calling candle, Victor blew out the flame.

Still in awe, he rose from the edge of his bed where he had been perched and walked dazedly across his bedchamber to let Magpen in.

The imp had been eavesdropping, of course. He bounded in at once. "Oh, master! At last!"

Magpen danced about, knowing how much Victor had been yearning for this.

"I guess he appreciated my help." Victor began to pace, anticipation for the trip already zinging down his nerve endings. "Oh, Magpen, this is going to be tremendous!" He spun around and grinned at his servant. "I'm finally going to get to see the River Thames, and Big Ben, the Tower of London, Buckingham Palace—! And girls," Victor added heartily. "Girls *everywhere*, I reckon."

In truth, that was the tourist attraction that interested him most.

"Oooh, girls," Magpen echoed. "What are those, then?"

Victor snorted. "Exactly."

Because, in truth, for all his fearsome magic, he had never successfully talked to one. Not a real one, although he had conjured a few to gather 'round and tell him how wonderful he was.

He suspected it wasn't the same.

Illusion girls could only do and say the sorts of things a mage conjured them to carry out. And that grew boring fast for any self-respecting lad.

Real girls, now, there was a challenge. And, frankly, for all his well-honed powers of death and destruction, the delicate creatures terrified him. On those few occasions when he'd had the chance to try to meet one, his simple effort to offer a normal greeting, such as *"Hello, how are you?"* came out sounding more like *"Heh-hubble gleck-loo?"*

Smooth.

In short, he usually tripped over his own tongue, humiliated himself with his ineptitude, and then just wanted to run away as fast as possible.

One young lady with strawberry-blond ringlets and a turned-up nose had giggled at his awkwardness once. Victor had been seriously tempted to turn the haughty miss and her whole family into amphibians—or worse.

But, of course, if he ever gave way to that kind of temperamental, knee-jerk response, they'd lock him up here at Shadowedge until he was thirty.

That was why Nagai was always harping at him about self-control. He could hurt people. With ease.

But, of course, if he ever did, they'd make him sit down for another *talk* with the loathsome Professor Labyrinth.

The one man Victor truly feared.

With a shudder, he thrust the pasty-faced image of the bearded, bespectacled psychiatrist out of his mind and quickly returned his thoughts to the much more pleasant subject of the female race.

Talking to them had to get easier, surely. There had to be some sort of trick to approaching these strange, fascinating beings, with their bonnets and parasols and dainty fans... But he was never going to figure it out stuck here, as always, in his gilded cage.

Just then, the mantel clock bonged two soft notes, tolling the hour. It *was* late, he thought.

Victor knew he ought to get some sleep. Nagai would no doubt have more schoolwork and training challenges for him in the morning. The emergency of tonight would not matter in the slightest to his sensei.

But although Victor lay back slowly on his bed, lacing his fingers beneath his head, he stared up at the ceiling and could not possibly go to sleep.

London!

Finally, he would get to see a little bit of the world he'd one day rule when he followed in Grandfather's footsteps and became the great and terrible sorcerer-king.

He could hardly wait for Hallowe'en.

CHAPTER EIGHTEEN
A Light in the Dark

At last, Beacon House came into view through the scraggly trees that adorned the Victoria Embankment. Still a safe distance from the rambling Tudor mansion, Jake halted the group on the graveled path.

For a moment, they all gazed in silence at the giant rooftop lantern that the huge house was named for shining out amid the drifts of fog.

"So, that's the place?" Brian glanced at him.

Jake gave a grim nod. Now came the hard part: making sure the Dark Druids hadn't seized control of the Order's London headquarters.

Red and Jake would do this by themselves. Once he could confirm that the building was secure, only then would he beckon his friends in to take shelter.

In the meantime, they could wait out here. It shouldn't take long. Jake just hoped he could keep his eyes open long enough to carry out his mission.

Almost too tired to think, he drew a deep breath of chilly night air. It helped revive him a bit. Then he turned to his friends and called Red over.

The Gryphon had prowled a few steps ahead of the kids, but he needed to hear the plan too. Jake couldn't do it without him.

"All right, everyone. This is it. We're almost in the clear. You might as well take a seat for a while." He nodded at the lonely park benches along the path. "Here's the plan. Red, you and I are going to fly ahead and scout out the situation."

"Becaw!" Red pawed the ground in approval.

Jake looked around at the others. "If I see any sign of the Dark Druids, believe me, I'll be *right* back, and we'll have to move on. But if it looks promising, then Red and I will land on the roof and sneak in through the cupola door to check inside the mansion. As soon as I know whether it's safe, I'll come out onto the back terrace and call you in."

"I could go with you," Brian said.

"Nah." Jake gave the earnest young Guardian a grateful glance. "You'd better stay here and look after this lot. But thanks." Jake turned to Dani. "You know the city as well as I do, carrot. If anything goes wrong, get everyone out of here."

"And leave you behind?" By the light of the gas lamps lining the path, she frowned at him.

"I'll be fine. I've got Red," he assured her, glancing at the Gryphon. "If we get into a scrape, we'll just fly away."

"Very well," Dani said uneasily. "Where should we go? We're far from the waypoint now."

Jake thought about it for a moment. They used to hide from the bobbies in the rookery, but the old neighborhood wasn't close, nor was it safe at this hour.

They had just passed Waterloo Bridge, however, on their walk along the Victoria Embankment, and the three rowboats he'd noticed moored beneath it caught his eye.

"There." He pointed at them. "Borrow those boats below the bridge and row downriver as fast as you can. The current's strong here. Without the trains running, that'll be your quickest way out of the city."

"What, steal them?" Archie said.

Jake shrugged. "If you must. Better than dying, coz. Desperate times."

Archie frowned. "That phrase is becoming uncomfortably familiar of late."

Dani heaved a sigh and looked at Jake. "Just promise you'll be careful."

"Promise." He smiled at her. If the others hadn't been there, perhaps he'd have even pressed a farewell kiss to her cheek. But he remained all business as he turned to his Gryphon. "Right! Well, come on, Red. Before I fall asleep on m' feet."

"Good luck, Jake," Isabelle said, leaning against a tree trunk that glistened with dew. "For what it's worth, I'm not sensing any particularly evil people nearby."

"Good to know."

"Stay on your guard anyway," Nixie warned him.

"Will do. See you all soon." With that, Jake swung up onto Red's back and gripped his leather collar. The Gryphon's warm, fuzzy back was so soft and comfy he could've laid his head down on the big beast's neck and gone to sleep.

Shaking off fatigue once more, Jake focused on the task at hand. "All right, boy. Let's circle a few times first and see what we can see."

Jake steeled his courage as Red took a few running strides then leaped into the air. He held on tight as the Gryphon pumped his wings, moving higher through the swirls of mist.

He could feel his friends staring after them, but he left them behind, telling himself they would be safe there. Whether it was true, he could only hope.

Red rose past the bare tree branches, but continued following the course of the path below until the blanket of fog still churning over the river hid it from view.

To his right, Jake caught glimpses of the Thames, black and silky as it slithered through the city. Fortunately, there was no sign of any more Nightstalkers or those bizarre little imps.

Ahead, the light from the huge yew-tree lantern glowing in the cupola atop Beacon House grew stronger. As they approached, Jake scanned its gardens that backed onto the Thames; he also spotted the Order's private barge moored at the river's edge behind the mansion. His gaze skimmed the carriage house, then the turreted roof of the creaky old mansion, but there were no warlock minions that he could see posted there, keeping watch.

A good sign.

Red banked to the left, rounding the manor as they made their first pass toward the front. Below them stretched the Strand; it was so strange to see the busy thoroughfare empty at this hour. Only one lonely carriage trundled past below; Red and Jake whooshed by unnoticed overhead in the darkness.

Jake kept scanning the ground below. The front face of Beacon House looked exactly as it should in the middle of the night, silent, the lanterns by the front door dimly shining. Its immediate surroundings looked quiet, too.

Up the road to his right hulked the familiar outline of old St. Mary-of-something church. Across the Strand from Beacon House, the various buildings of King's College took up several blocks.

But there were no Dark Druids.

So far, so good. Maybe Izzy was right. Maybe they simply weren't here. That would be a welcome change of luck after the night they were having.

Jake urged Red a little lower, making a second pass around the house at closer range. He tried to see in the windows, but the blinds were drawn for the night.

If enemies had taken the place, he reasoned that they'd probably have Noxu or servitors peering out the windows to watch for any attempt by the Order to take it back.

Increasingly hopeful, Jake rounded the headquarters one more time, then murmured to Red to land on the rooftop. It was time to get inside.

The Gryphon landed on silent paws near the center cupola, running a few paces, then slowing to a halt. Jake was always amazed at how quiet Red could be for an animal weighing several hundred pounds. He supposed it was Red's lion side that made the beast so stealthy.

Jake swung off Red's back and whispered to him to follow. The flat main section of the manor's roof stretched all around them, black and broad. Turrets poked up from the corners, broody in the fog, but straight ahead, the tall center cupola shone like a miniature lighthouse.

He had to squint as he approached, for his eyes had long since adjusted to the night. The giant lantern in the cupola had given Beacon House its name; the metal yew-tree design superimposed over the glowing light served as a signal to any magical creatures in distress that they could find refuge in this place.

Walking silently toward the little door that opened off the side of the cupola, Jake glanced at the yew-tree symbol with a heavy heart. The nightmarish sights, sounds, and smells of the battle were still fresh in his memory—including the horrible image of the Old Father Yew burning in the great maze.

Anger hardened Jake's heart against the enemy as he reached for the door knob. The Dark Druids had taken enough from them tonight. They better not have taken Beacon House, too.

The metal doorknob was slippery with mist, but it turned with ease, much to Jake's relief. Unlike the street-level doors, the rooftop entrance was normally left unlocked for the sake of any of magic-kind who might arrive seeking safety in the house.

He glanced over his shoulder at the Gryphon. "Ready?" he whispered.

Red nodded, his golden eyes gleaming with courage. Jake inched the door open slowly, taking care not to let it creak.

Unfortunately, even by human standards, the doorway was small and narrow; the Gryphon had to squeeze his wings in tight to be able to fit through.

From there, they crept down the spiraling metal staircase, and, with every step, Jake listened intently.

Beacon House was very quiet. Only two people lived here on a permanent basis: Mrs. Appleton, the housekeeper, and Mr. Mayweather, the butler. *If the Dark Druids have done anything to them...*

His jaw tightened. But, again, he warded off his worry. So far, he had seen no signs to indicate that the enemy had been here. Meanwhile, behind him, Red accidentally bumped Jake in the shoulder with his beak and nearly knocked him down the last couple of steps.

"Ack!" With no choice but to leap off the stairs, Jake landed nimbly on his feet in the hallway below. He caught his balance at once, but knew he'd made a rather loud thump. "Red!" he whispered. Jake rolled his eyes. "Blimey."

"Becaw," Red mumbled, contrite.

"I hope nobody heard that. C'mon. We'd better hurry, in case they did." He headed down the dim third-floor hallway, drawing on all his stealthy skills as a former thief, and listening for all he was worth.

At times like these, he envied the Guardians with their extra-keen senses. But the thought of Guardians only made him worry about Derek and Maddox and Ravyn and Janos and Ibrahim and everyone he'd left behind.

Focus! he scolded himself. The sooner he made sure Beacon House was secure, the sooner he could bring Dani and the others inside, where they'd all be safe. *I hope.*

For a few more quiet paces, Red and he continued down the third-floor hallway, but suddenly, Jake froze, hearing muffled voices coming from somewhere nearby. He held up his hand; at once, Red crouched down into battle mode.

Lifting a finger over his lips, Jake motioned to the Gryphon to keep silent and follow, then began moving toward the sound with the utmost care, practically tiptoeing.

The whispers were coming from behind the closed door of a nearby guest bedchamber. As Jake approached, the indistinct murmurs crystallized into a range of different voices, oddly high-pitched and, well, silly-sounding. He furrowed his brow.

His senses on high alert, he clasped the doorknob and slowly turned the handle, heart pounding.

Ready to use his telekinesis on any foe he might find within, Jake yanked the door open without warning, and suddenly, the room went quiet.

Red peered over Jake's shoulder and sniffed the air, which held a sweet, delicious whiff of...

Gingerbread?

A grin broke across Jake's face. Of course! How could he forget? Of all the guest chambers that lined the third floor of the mansion, this must be the very room where he had put the gingerbread village and its two cookie clans last Christmas—here at Beacon House, where he knew all the little gingerbread people would be safe.

Well, he had to stow them *somewhere*, considering a wayward Christmas elf called Humbug had dusted them with enchanted sugar stolen from Santa's workshop—or rather, Mrs. Claus's kitchen—that made them come alive at night.

That explained why the tiny folk were up and about at this hour. Despite their sweet natures, the gingerbread people were as nocturnal as vampires. By day, though, they lay around, quite as inanimate as the average lemon macaroon.

Now, nearly a year later, Jake stared into the bedroom, amazed at how their pastry village had grown. Blimey, they'd been busy! A bustling gingerbread city now filled the cozy bedchamber, no doubt with help from Mrs. Appleton.

Jake clutched his chest in relief, but couldn't help laughing at himself, prowling in here ready to battle the Dark Druids. This completely nonthreatening cookie-land was the last thing he'd expected to see.

It was then that the gingerbread folk noticed him. A collective gasp arose from their tiny voices all around the room.

"Well, bless my candy buttons!" a wee voice said. "Is that Lord Jake and his noble Gryphon?"

"Everybody, look who it is!"

Jake crouched down in the doorway, afraid of stepping on anyone as the gingerbread folk rushed to see him. The next thing he knew, a crowd of gingerbread men and women mere inches tall stampeded toward the door, each one individually frosted with icing faces, colorful hair, and candy-jeweled clothes.

It was amazing how loud such small folk could be, considering they barely came up to his shoelaces.

"It's so good to see you again, young man!"

"What are you doing here at this hour?"

"Shh!" Jake said. "Thank you for the welcome, but you need to be quiet. There may be trouble afoot."

Instantly, they all stopped shouting and murmured anxiously amongst themselves.

"What sort of trouble, dear giant boy?" a candy-helmeted soldier asked.

Jake caught himself before saying too much. He did not wish to terrify them. Life was scary enough when you were only a few inches tall and quite brittle.

"Well"—he chose his words carefully—"there was...a spot of bother at Merlin Hall earlier tonight, and I just wanted to make sure everything was all right here. Have you heard any odd noises in the house tonight? Any strangers arriving over the past few hours?"

"No, sir," the tiny soldier replied. "I've been on sentry duty all night and haven't heard a thing. Of course, we only patrol the third floor. I can't confirm the status of the rest of the house."

"I understand. Thank you." Jake nodded. "I'll look around."

"Anything we can do to help, monsieur?" one of the fancy French courtier cookies asked.

Jake shook his head and rose. "That's all right. Red and I can handle it. The city looks smashing, by the way. Love what you've done with the place."

"Tasteful, isn't it?" the iced courtier jested.

They all laughed, and Jake grinned, feeling more hopeful. "Goodbye for now. I'm going to head downstairs and check the lower floors. Better move back."

He waved the gingerbread people away from the door and waited until they all had cleared off to a safe distance, then he stepped out of the room and gently pulled the door shut behind him.

"Becaw," Red remarked, standing in the hallway looking puzzled.

Jake wasn't *quite* sure what the Gryphon meant, but he shared the sentiment behind his pet's wonder-struck tone.

Proceeding stealthily down the hallway, Jake ignored the row of creepy paintings on the wall. Most were portraits of past Order luminaries; their eyes seemed to follow him as he passed by on his way to the stairs.

Soon, Red and he had sneaked down onto the second floor.

Here, once more, they encountered nothing out of the ordinary. Just more of the guest chambers like the ones upstairs.

But, revisiting the second floor, one thing was certain. Jake would never forget the night he had first met Celestus—the night Dani had been hurt so badly that she nearly died. She *did* die for a moment, in truth. Jake had seen her ghost trying to leave her body, and he had ordered her in no uncertain terms to get back in there.

She had. Then Derek and he had sped the lass here, to Beacon House, where Mayweather had sent at once for "the doctor."

The mysterious blond physician had arrived with uncanny speed, and after healing Dani, had revealed himself in his true form, wings and all, before disappearing again.

And now, tonight, Celestus had saved them once more.

A true miracle.

Shivers ran down Jake's spine when he thought of the angels showing up tonight to fend off the Nightstalkers. It seemed connected somehow to that horrible shadow demon he had seen on the wall of Westminster Palace.

"This isn't your fight—yet," Celestus had said. That certainly seemed to suggest that, in the future, it would be.

For now, Jake shook off the unnerving question of just what the angel had meant, and told himself to pay attention.

So far, Beacon House seemed secure, but they weren't done yet.

Red and he checked a few rooms on the second floor at random, then crept down the center hallway till it ended at the landing atop the grand staircase.

The landing overlooked the stately, wood-paneled foyer, which was empty.

A grandfather clock tick-tocked loudly in the silence beside the front door. A pendulous crystal chandelier hung over the foyer directly across from the landing where Jake stood, its candles unlit.

The only illumination in the high-ceilinged space came from a small, punched-tin night lantern that glowed atop a slim table by the wall.

With a nod to Red, Jake proceeded down the creaky Tudor staircase, wincing every time the ancient wood groaned beneath his feet. The staircase was made of dark, ornately carved walnut and, unfortunately, the red carpet runner did little to muffle the noise.

Red jumped silently the rest of the way to the floor below, but Jake had no choice but to tiptoe. He clenched his jaw, certain that any Dark Druid forces who might've invaded the house would have heard him coming by now.

Though nothing unusual appeared, Jake stayed on his guard, ready to use his telekinesis to ward off any enemies that might pop out of the shadows at him and Red.

Upon reaching the first floor, he sped across the entrance hall, keeping his footsteps quiet. He peered first into the parlor, then crossed to check the enchanted library.

Jake was wise enough to take only a brief peek into *that* room. The last thing he needed was to wake up the tiger-skin rug and have the thing start roaring at him, or disturb that crazy magical harp that tended to start strumming all by itself. He poked his head in just for a moment, then quickly withdrew, pulling the door shut again.

"Nobody in there, either," he whispered to his Gryphon. "I think we might just be in the clear."

He shouldn't have said it.

He realized that in the next heartbeat—when someone suddenly screamed right behind him.

CHAPTER NINETEEN
A Startling Arrival

Jake whirled around as Mrs. Appleton and he nearly gave each other apoplectic fits.

The stout old housekeeper was wrapped in her robe, a frilly nightcap covering her gray curls.

Eyes wide, she dropped her cup of chamomile tea at the sight of him. Although Jake managed to catch the falling teacup with his telekinesis, he couldn't catch its contents. The tea spilled onto the floor while the butler came running out to the landing in answer to the housekeeper's shriek.

"Hold, right there, you burglar!" Mayweather roared, and when Jake looked up, he found the frail old man in his pajamas pointing a shotgun at him.

"Don't shoot!" Jake instantly raised his hands. "It's me—Jake! J-Jake Everton, Lord Griffon! See? There! It's my Gryphon!" He pointed one finger at Red.

"Caw, becaw!" Red said anxiously, hurrying to Jake's side.

Thank goodness, when the two panicked old folks saw the mighty beast, they started calming down.

"Well, bless my eyes, Lord Crafanc! Why didn't ye tell us you was comin'?" Mayweather muttered, lowering the shotgun. (It was nearly as tall as he was.) He pressed a hand to his bony chest and strove to catch his breath.

Jake's own heart was thumping. *Egads.* That could've gone badly.

"Sweet crumb cake, you gave me a fright!" Mrs. Appleton clutched her heart. "I was just in the kitchen gettin' some tea! And now I've spilt it."

"I-I'm so sorry, Mrs. Appleton. I didn't mean to scare you. My apologies, Mr. Mayweather."

"What on earth are you doing here at this hour, young master?" the butler demanded, glaring at Jake.

It was strange to see the usually tidy, black-uniformed fellow dressed for bedtime in his nightshirt and slippers, a long, pointy nightcap dangling from his head. How to answer his question, though?

"Erm," Jake said. He hesitated to mention the catastrophe back at Merlin Hall, considering he had already scared the daylights out of the two sweet old folks. Especially when one was holding a gun. "Has there, ah, been any trouble here tonight?"

"Not till you showed up," the housekeeper said indignantly. "I knew I heard a thump."

"Er, yes, sorry—that was me." Chagrined, Jake handed her back her teacup. "I don't suppose you've heard from anyone at Merlin Hall in the past couple of hours?"

"No." Mrs. Appleton eyed him suspiciously, still looking peeved. "Should we?"

"Well... I'm afraid there has been...an incident." Jake then explained the shocking disaster in the mildest terms he could manage.

The two listened with their jaws hanging open. No doubt they had a hundred questions—so did he—but he hurried ahead to their present situation.

"My friends and I were ordered to leave immediately for our safety, and that was nearly three hours ago. We're cold, we're hungry, we're tired, and we've got nowhere else to go. So, if it's all right with you and Beacon House is still secure, I'd like to bring them in. Everybody's waiting outside: Archie and Isabelle Bradford. Dani, the girl that came here with me before—"

"Oh, yes! The little redhead that Dr. Celestus healed?" Mrs. Appleton exclaimed, her eyes as round as her tea saucer.

"Yes, ma'am." Jake nodded.

"Oh, we liked her. Remember, Ol' May?" she asked the butler.

He nodded. "A sweet child."

"Two other friends are also with us—a Guardian apprentice and a witch-in-training. She's Aunt Ramona's own protégée."

"Well, by all means, bring them in! Go on." Mrs. Appleton shooed Jake toward the door.

"Thank you so much," he said. "They're waiting out beyond the garden. I'll fetch them."

"Good, good. I'll see about some snacks for you all."

"I'll ready the children's chambers," the butler chimed in.

"Thank you both." Jake was so relieved. "I'll clean up that spilled tea for you in a moment, since I'm the one who made you drop it."

Mrs. Appleton looked astonished at his offer. "You just get those children in here. I'll see to this."

"Yes, ma'am." Jake could not deny that it took a huge weight off him to hear a few comforting words from adults. Independent as he was, this night had pushed him to the limit. Every now and then, he did manage to remember that he was still a kid.

While Jake crossed the foyer, then hurried down the main hallway of the mansion to the back door, Red fetched Mrs. Appleton a rag from the kitchen to blot up her spilled tea. Mr. Mayweather set his shotgun aside and began lighting more candles.

Jake unlocked the back door, stepped out onto the chilly terrace, and signaled his friends with a loud whistle. When a few pale faces peeked out of the shadows, he waved eagerly.

"Come on in!"

A cheer arose from the direction of the Victoria Embankment. Jake grinned as his friends burst into view, racing toward him, then stampeding in through the garden gate. They came barreling up the path past the carriage house, Teddy yipping with excitement.

When they'd dashed up the few stone steps onto the terrace, Jake held the back door for them. One by one, they filed in, everyone talking at once, asking questions, and saying how happy they were to have reached Beacon House.

Already tying her apron strings, Mrs. Appleton looked amazed as she watched them streaming in. "Poor dears, you're shivering! Mayweather, blankets for all of them! Oh, hullo, Miss Dani! So nice to see you again."

"You, as well, Mrs. Appleton." Dani came in, red-cheeked, with Teddy on his leash. "Is it all right if I bring in my dog? He's housebroken."

"Of course, dear." Mrs. Appleton shooed her in and continued greeting the others. "Master Archie! Oh, and Miss Bradford. Why, look at you—almost entirely grown up! Where does the time go? And who's this? Why, you must be the new ones. Well, come in, come in, my dears! You're all welcome here. Can I get you children a snack?"

"I think we'd all be grateful for a cup of hot chocolate or some of that chamomile tea," Jake said. "Or even a bowl of soup and some bread, if you have any."

He closed the door behind Brian, who was the last to enter.

"Why, consider it done! You know I always cook for an army, just in case." Mrs. Appleton bustled off to the kitchen.

"Everything go all right out there while I was gone?" Jake asked Brian discreetly while the others shuffled ahead into the foyer.

Brian nodded. "Nothing to report. Any trouble in here?"

"No—but I gave Mrs. Appleton a fright."

Brian chuckled, then the boys followed the others out to the entrance hall, where Dani was introducing Nixie to the two adults.

"Well, don't worry now, children. Everything's been quiet here," Mrs. Appleton said. "You just make yourselves at home."

"Could we send a message to Aunt Ramona and our parents through your Inkbug, Mrs. Appleton?" Izzy asked. "We need to let them know we're safe."

"By all means, dear! You'll find him in the library, same as always. Why don't you go and make yourselves comfy in there while I fix you up a nice, hot meal?"

"You're very kind, ma'am," Dani said heartily, and Archie nearly hugged the woman.

Mrs. Appleton laughed. "Aw, that's what we're here for, dear. Isn't that right, Mr. Mayweather?"

"Indeed," the old man said grimly.

Jake could tell by his dark expression that the butler's mind was not on making hot cocoa, but on activating whatever *other* defenses Beacon House might have. Mayweather picked up his long gun and marched off to see to his duties concerning the house's protection. Red loped after him to assist.

"This way, everyone," Archie said, visibly cheered up, despite his worries. Well, the aristocratic boy *did* like his creature comforts, Jake mused. "Nixie, my dear, and Brian, you've got to come and see. The enchanted library of Beacon House is one of my favorite rooms in all of London."

The boy genius led the way, marching across the entrance hall to the library door. But Jake dragged his feet as he followed the others, feeling wearier every moment. Then they went in.

Through a narrow, book-lined passage where the bronze busts of great writers and artists peered down from above, they walked into a large, square, high-ceilinged room wrapped in floor-to-ceiling bookshelves done in dark wood.

A rolling ladder gave access to a galleried walkway that wrapped around the room halfway up the walls' height.

Ahead, the portrait of the Order's royal co-founder, Queen Elizabeth I, all suited up for war in her silver armor, stared down at them from above the fireplace, while the stormy sea set about wrecking the Spanish Armada in the background—with just a little help from a famous English playwright with a secret wallop of magic in his pen.

A hint of a salt smell hung in the air, but for now, the Spanish galleons in the background rolled only slightly on the waves. That magical painting could unleash its hurricane on any intruder who tried to breach Beacon House.

But there were other defenses, as well. Thankfully, the tiger-skin rug in front of the fireplace did not roar and attack them, since they had permission to be there.

The magical harp on its pedestal awoke with a jangle, however. It could play screeching harmonies to drive intruders mad, but after sensing the kids' arrival and noticing their agitated state, it began softly playing a lullaby.

"Don't do that. You'll put us all to sleep," Dani said, then dropped into one of the plump brown leather club chairs.

Jake was so tired that he tripped on the fringed edge of the Persian carpet. Then he used his telekinesis to close the red velvet curtains over the tall windows and the French doors, shutting out the night.

Brian looked around at everything in wonder. Tilting his head back, he studied the gilt-lettered motto of the Order painted, frieze-like, around the base of the second-floor walkway.

Perstamus Amicitiis Defendere.

Never had the slogan seemed more fitting than tonight.

"We stand in friendship to defend," Brian murmured.

"Why, I'm impressed," Archie said as he went around lighting candles.

Brian gave a weary smile. "Don't be. It's the only Latin I know."

In the far corner, a stately floor globe tracked the locations of all Lightriders out on their missions with tiny pinpricks of light. Alas, the globe had gone distressingly dark these days, after so many Lightriders had been kidnapped by the Dark Druids.

Jake's stomach twisted at the thought of Dani ever becoming one of them, but he was too tired to contemplate it at the moment.

"So, where is this Inkbug?" Nixie asked with a yawn.

"Over here." Jake passed the wooden card catalog with its countless little drawers and stalked over to the big oak desk in the middle of the room.

Seeing it brought back a memory that would be forever etched upon his mind: the night Derek had sat there telling Jake who his parents were, explaining the existence of a whole magical world that he had never dreamed could be real.

It seemed like centuries ago.

When he reached the desk, he glanced around at his friends and was pained to see Isabelle gazing sadly at the little bonsai tree on display atop the long, narrow table that backed one of the couches. It was a miniature yew—the tree chosen as the symbol of the Order because it represented eternal life, the spirit in a person that could not be killed.

Because of their unique way of growing, ever renewing themselves, yew trees could last for thousands of years. Yet tonight, Jake had personally witnessed one's death. No—not just his death, naturally passing on his mantle to one of his tree offspring. The Old Father Yew had been murdered most cruelly, burned alive by their enemies. Jake wasn't sure if a tree felt pain; he never got the chance to ask.

Steadying himself against a pulse of rage, he reached past the handsome brass writing set on the desk and gently tapped on the Inkbug's box.

A moment later, the little caterpillar-like creature came stumbling out. Jake lifted his eyebrows. Blimey, he had never seen an insect look so tired before.

Rudely awakened in the middle of the night, the Inkbug yawned and used its front feet to rub its tiny eyes. But, ready to get to work in any case, the dutiful creature glanced up to see who had disturbed it; it looked prepared to be annoyed.

The moment it saw Jake, its antennae shot straight up; it looked astonished to see him.

"Yes, hello again," Jake said dryly. "It's been a while, hasn't it? Sorry to wake you, little fellow, but we need to send a message right away."

"It's very important," Archie chimed in while Brian stared at the insect in disbelief.

The sleepy Inkbug looked past Jake to the boy genius, its little face scrunched up with determination. Apparently, it decided that while Jake might be a bit dodgy, whatever the famously honest Archie Bradford said must be true—and quite serious, indeed.

With that, the Inkbug shook itself fully awake, then reared up onto his hind legs and nodded the upper half of its body, as if to say, *"Ready!"*

"Don't worry," Jake said. "I'll keep this short. This needs to go to any of your comrades that you can reach at Merlin Hall."

The Inkbug nodded.

Then Jake dictated a simple message: *"Dear Aunt Ramona, we are safe. The gingerbread folk send their regards."* This was a clue to their location, not a pleasantry. *"Shall we wait here? Please advise. Jake."*

As Jake spoke, the Inkbug squeezed its eyes shut, and with a look of great concentration, began twitching its antennae, sending out the transmission to one of its counterparts at the palace.

Sending the message took less than a minute.

Waiting for the answer, well, that could take all night. It just depended on whether the message got through, whether the palace was functioning at all, and, if so, how long it might take for one of the gnome servants to carry the Inkbug's message to Aunt Ramona.

If she was still alive.

If *anyone* was left alive back there.

The room fell silent as the kids each pondered their own dire questions about just how bad things might be at Merlin Hall right now, and what the Order might find once the smoke had cleared.

In mere moments, the wait grew excruciating, so Dani took the others upstairs to visit the gingerbread folk. Nixie had never seen them, and neither had Brian. Indeed, the gullible Guardian looked a bit suspicious about the whole thing, as if he suspected a prank.

"You'll see," Dani assured him. Then she led the others trooping upstairs, while Jake and Archie remained in the library, ready to pounce on any message that might arrive from Aunt Ramona.

As it turned out, they didn't have long to wait. Maybe twenty minutes.

Jake spent the interim brooding as he stared at the Lightrider tracking globe. Archie lounged on the brown leather couch with Teddy snuggled beside him and restlessly perused yesterday's copy of the *Clairvoyant*, the magical world's own newspaper. It had been left out on the library table, along with the *London Times*.

Jake could not even imagine what the *Clairvoyant*'s reporters would have to say about the events of *this* night.

After a short while, the boys heard Mrs. Appleton wheeling her tea service cart up the hallway from the kitchens. The creaking paused as the housekeeper called upstairs to let the others know their refreshments were ready.

Jake strode over to open the library door for her, and she pushed the cart in. It was draped in fine white linen and piled high with all the food they'd requested, plus a stack of bowls for the soup, a stack of mugs for the hot chocolate and tea, a cup full of spoons and utensils, and a basket of buttery biscuits that the good woman had warmed up in the oven.

"You are an angel of mercy, Mrs. Appleton." Jake followed the cart eagerly as she wheeled it into the library with a laugh.

He snatched a biscuit (rudely—he was too tired for manners) and ate it in one bite while Archie came over and peeked under the lid of the big pot of soup. Teddy begged on his hind legs nearby, and was ignored.

"Oh, that smells wonderful," Archie declared, inhaling over the soup pot. "What kind is it?"

"Potato soup, Master Archie. I also have mulligatawny heating up in the kitchen, but I brought this first because I know your sister doesn't eat meat."

Archie put the lid back on the soup pot. "You are a treasure, madam."

"She is," Jake agreed as he helped himself to a mug of cocoa.

The housekeeper beamed. "Pshaw!"

"Hullo!" Archie said abruptly. His gaze zoomed past Jake, homing in on the desk a few yards behind him. "I think the Inkbug's receiving a transmission."

Having just burned his tongue on the very hot cocoa, Jake quickly set the mug down, pivoted, and saw that his cousin was right. The Inkbug's antennae had begun to twitch.

Suddenly, the caterpillar rushed over to the ink pad that went with the writing set, nudged the lid open, and scurried across its flat surface, dipping its countless tiny feet in black ink. The creature then darted onto the nearest sheet of blank paper and began running back and forth, spelling out the message it was receiving.

The boys strode over to the desk and watched with bated breath as the Inkbug revealed the message line by line. It was definitely from Aunt Ramona. Jake recognized her terse verbiage at once:

So relieved you all are safe. Well done. Stay where you are. I've asked your godmother to fetch you. Do not wander off. She will be there shortly to collect you.

Jake and Archie exchanged a wide-eyed look.

His cousin was the first to find his voice. "You don't think she actually means—"

"Chop, chop, the Queen!" barked a deep male voice from outside.

Teddy cocked his ears.

"Blimey," Jake whispered, only now noticing the clatter of hooves and carriage wheels arriving on the street outside Beacon House.

The dog barked. Jake ordered him to stay behind and be quiet as the boys launched into motion, rushing past a startled Mrs. Appleton and barreling out into the entrance hall just as the front doors burst open.

In marched a grand retinue of soldiers in scarlet tunics and black trousers, with shiny swords and tall black bearskin hats.

With crisp, automaton-like movements, six big grenadiers from the Royal Household Division lined up in the foyer, three on either side of the front door.

Jake and Archie stared in amazement as who should come through the doorway, but Queen Victoria herself.

Short, stout, and always clad in widow's black, the ruler of the realm was the unofficial godmother of every magical child born on England's shores.

That included Jake.

Instantly, the boys bowed low to Her Majesty. Jake's pulse was thumping.

If only he could've called a warning to the others about decorum.

He cringed when he heard their pounding footsteps and riotous laughter pouring down from the upper hallway.

"I'm so hungry I could eat a whale," Brian was saying.

Izzy giggled. "Those gingerbread people *were* kind of tempting."

"Jake, you have to hear what Nixie just said about Rollio and Juniette!" Dani came skipping out onto the landing at the top of the stairs, but the words died on her tongue when she saw the royal entourage below. She froze at the railing, the other three a step behind her.

"Holy mackerel!" Brian burst out as they emerged on the landing.

"Uh, the Queen's here," Jake said, gesturing awkwardly.

Even Izzy looked shaken. Nixie just stared with her mouth hanging open.

Queen Victoria pursed her lips and lifted her fleshy chin. "Do come down, children. I have been apprised of the situation at Merlin Hall. You are to come with me."

The entrance hall was absolutely silent. Nobody moved. They were all in shock.

Jake's heart broke to think of leaving those buttery biscuits behind.

Fortunately, the future Viscount Bradford remembered his etiquette, as always. "We would be honored, Your Majesty," Archie said.

Relief passed through the group of kids. At least one of them knew how to act.

The Queen nodded, mollified by his gentlemanly words. Then the others began walking down the stairs with an air of perfect obedience, everyone suddenly on their best behavior.

The Queen turned to Mayweather and Mrs. Appleton, who had come into the foyer to offer their bows as well. "Beacon House is to be locked down," Victoria said. "The children shall come with me to Buckingham Palace."

"Yes, Your Majesty," the servants murmured.

Dani, Izzy, Nixie, and Brian reached the bottom of the stairs and approached the royal entourage. The girls curtsied, but Brian was staring in awe at the famous Foot Guards of the Household Division—until Izzy elbowed him. Then he nodded with respect to the Queen, but did not bow.

Americans, Jake thought wryly. Archie frowned with disapproval. One of the soldiers arched a brow. Jake wondered if any of them were actually Guardians. Probably so.

Queen Victoria did not seem to care about the lack of protocol from the Yank. "Now then, children. Someone from the Order will be along to pick you up from my custody by and by. Until then, you are all under my protection. Come," she said, then pivoted on her heel and marched right back out to her waiting coach.

The nearest grenadier swept a gesture to the kids that meant for them to follow. They murmured their thanks to Mrs. Appleton and Mr. Mayweather, then obeyed.

Through the open doorway, Jake saw more soldiers from the Royal Household Division assisting the chubby little monarch into her carriage. He glanced uncertainly at Red. "Let's go, boy."

"Sorry, sir, the Gryphon stays here," the grenadier said.

Jake glanced regretfully at Red, but he supposed it was better for all concerned if his pet remained at Beacon House. They did not need to cause an international incident showing up at Buckingham Palace with a real, live, mythological beast.

The Order already had enough problems.

While his cousins hurried after the Queen, Jake turned to his pet. "You stay out of sight here, Red. I'll send word once we know where we're going to be, and you can meet us there. Maybe home to Griffon Castle, maybe Merlin Hall; I'm not sure yet. Keep an eye on Beacon House till then. Maybe Mrs. Appleton will let you eat that potato soup."

"Becaw," Red said with a sad nod. Jake could not resist hugging him after all they had been through together tonight—especially taking on the dirigible. He hated leaving Red behind.

When Jake turned to go, Nixie and Brian were walking out, but Dani had just placed Teddy in her satchel, then hoisted it onto her shoulder.

"Excuse me, sir," she said to the nearest guard. "Would it be all right if I bring my dog? He's housebroken, I promise."

The manly soldier smiled at her and Teddy. "Of course, little girl. Her Majesty is particularly fond of dogs, especially the small breeds."

Dani smiled back, then traipsed out.

Jake followed.

Though their overly eventful night seemed to have come to an end at last, the jaunt over to Buckingham Palace proved rather amusing, for Queen Victoria had brought only one coach. This meant that the tiny old woman who ruled an empire upon which the sun never set was forced to squeeze into a crowded carriage with half a dozen children and one panting Norwich terrier.

The kids almost didn't dare look at each other for fear of laughing as they all squashed together, crammed into the royal coach.

"Oh, for heaven's sakes," Queen Victoria finally muttered.

If Her Majesty noted the absurdity of their situation, all jammed together like lemmings, she hid her amusement behind a façade of royal dignity. But after the short ride over to Buckingham Palace, she shooed them out ahead of her and alighted last.

One of the grenadiers handed the sovereign down.

Her dignity restored, the little queen smoothed her black skirts, lifted her chin, then nodded to them to follow, and marched into her opulent home.

Jake and Dani exchanged a marveling glance.

"We've come a long way from the rookery, haven't we, Jake?" she whispered.

"Aye, carrot, we have." Jake flashed a grin. "Actually, I'm just glad we're alive at the moment."

Dani snorted and gave him a nod.

Then they hurried after their friends, and walked into Buckingham Palace as Her Majesty's special guests.

CHAPTER TWENTY
Ice Grendels

The ice grendels were not what Wyvern had expected. Indeed, he could not have imagined them. He'd heard rumors of their existence over the years—rumors he had considered absurd. Until he had arrived in this place.

Now he wished he'd never seen them.

The wind moaned across the snowfields on the surface, but deep in the ice cave at the bottom of a glacial canyon in Antarctica where he had been imprisoned, all Wyvern could hear were his own screams.

When his shrieks of doom faded away, there was only the sound of his own panting and the ominous creaking of the ice that surrounded his captors' frigid laboratory.

They were not of this world.

Where they came from, Wyvern did not know, but they had brought with them the cruelty of scientists.

His body was contorted by the solid metal collar around his neck and bright silver steel cuffs around his wrists and ankles.

He could taste the poison they had injected into him to keep him still. It filled his mouth with bitterness, made him unable to fight.

He could hardly even see in the blue twilight of the ice cave. Only a little light shone through the bubbled teal ice that hung overhead and surrounded the cave like smooth, striated crystal.

Wyvern wasn't sure if the darkness made things better or worse, for the sight of the creature filled him with an instinctual dread beyond anything he had ever experienced.

Whatever they were, these otherworldly creatures, their sleek triangular ship nearby, and all their strange equipment did not belong here.

Zolond had left him in their care several hours ago, and already, Wyvern could feel a creeping despair.

He had dared cross the sorcerer-king, and this was his punishment.

It was the powerlessness of his situation that he could not abide. And the knowledge that he was utterly alone.

Even his father had abandoned him now. Shemrazul sent no rescue, no doubt disgusted by Wyvern's failure.

The shame of Wyvern's own dishonor swallowed him like this crevasse in the glacier had. How could he have let that frail old man defeat him?

If I ever get out of here, he vowed, fiery-eyed, *I'm gonna kill him. Take his crown. And I will rule in wrath!*

And yet, for all his fearsome mental raging, the approach of his keepers' quiet shuffling footfalls made Wyvern tremble with fear. It outraged him that, for all his physical strength and magical power, such small, delicate-looking creatures could terrify him, but they did.

He did not understand them, could not communicate with them, and so could neither reason nor plead.

Yet they seemed to be able to read his mind. It was as though they saw his thoughts quite clearly; they simply didn't care. His pleas were no more to them than the squeaking protests of a lab rat.

Wyvern knew they were telepaths, though, because they occasionally sent him expressionless commands, like: *Be still. Do not fight. There is no point. You will only damage yourself.*

How hideous they were, all of them identical, about four feet tall, with small gray bodies, oversized, hairless heads, and long, spindly limbs. Oh, but their eyes. Their huge, almond-shaped eyes were soulless and black.

Given their obvious technological advancement, Wyvern suspected they'd been Zolond's little helpers when the Dark Master had gone about creating his various monsters. Like the locust army still gestating even now in the sands of Karakum.

Wyvern could not imagine how the Dark Master had managed to befriend them. Perhaps Zolond's own scientific pursuits had established some sort of commonality.

All Wyvern knew was that his own Nephilim blood made him a highly interesting specimen to the ice grendels. They were eager to study him. He supposed he should be grateful, for at least their curiosity gave them a reason to keep him alive.

They moderated the temperature of his cell; otherwise, he would've long since frozen to death. They gave him water and offered food, but he had spit it out.

They seemed surprised by his willfulness to not eat. It had taken ten of the ugly little creatures to hold him down, then they had sedated him with some unholy potion that had put him in a state of waking paralysis.

He was only able to breathe and watch in terror as they had restrained him in a contraption like a dentist's chair and began their experiments. They drew his blood—many samples—poked and prodded at his powerful physique, examined his six-fingered hands and six-toed feet. (Wyvern noticed they had four fingers on each hand.)

Then they explored his internal organs with long, slim tools he could never have imagined.

It was this loathsome denigration that made him hate Zolond with a tenfold resolve.

As their long, chilly fingers examined and measured him and sought to calculate how he was made, Wyvern could only let out another mental howl of enmity and rage.

But when two of the little monsters approached on either side of him, he cowered, in no way able to guess their next intent.

"No, no, no," he babbled, to no avail.

One made sure that Wyvern remained secured by the straps as the other began cranking a metal wheel attached to the dentist's chair.

Plead as he might, Wyvern could not stop them. He began turning upside down on the contraption.

Though he bellowed with fury at this deliberate insult to his pride, there was nothing he could do. He had tortured others in his day, like Derek Stone, Celestus...

Now it was his turn.

PART III

CHAPTER TWENTY-ONE

A New Day

All night—or, at least, what was left of it—Jake dreamed of battle. Over and over again. Smoke. Screams. The sky pirate plummeting to his fiery death.

Nightstalkers floating by with their scythes overhead. Strange little monsters scampering through the shadows. And all the while, a huge, horned demon with red eyes stalking him through the darkness.

When he saw Wyvern reaching out with a freakish six-fingered hand to grab him, Jake awoke with a start, jolted upright, and lifted his hands to fend off the warlock with his telekinesis.

Instead, he only managed to knock a fancy vase off its pedestal across from his bed. "Ack!"

He caught it in the nick of time before it hit the floor. Still groggy and a bit confused, he floated it back up onto its pedestal against the wall on the other side of the unfamiliar bedchamber.

With the crisis averted, and no new threats popping out, he slowly recalled where he was. "Ugh."

Lord, I'm a menace. The pale fingers of morning plucked at the sheers, but he did not even remember dozing off.

Then Jake sat up and swung his legs over the side of the bed, waiting for his thunderous pulse to return to normal. Slowly, as the nightmare faded, he remembered where he was.

Right. Buckingham Palace. The guestroom he had been assigned.

Blimey, he thought, scanning it. The royal decor was fit for a visiting head of state, not some former street urchin.

Burgundy silk damask wrapped around the walls. Gilt-framed paintings glowed here and there. The fancy marble fireplace had a huge mirror over the mantel, where gold statuettes held up cut crystal lampshades.

Poufy draperies framed the window in dark green velvet; they matched the canopy over the very comfortable bed. A crystal chandelier dangled from the twenty-foot ceiling, while a lavish carpet in creams, purples, and greens stretched across the floor.

Jake spotted his jacket slung across an elegant wooden chair near the bedroom door. He vaguely remembered casting it there when he'd finally stumbled in from the sitting room last night, unable to keep his eyes open any longer.

Then he looked down at himself and saw he was still in his clothes from yesterday. He had kicked off his shoes, loosened his neckcloth, and unbuckled Risker from around his waist, but hadn't bothered undressing—or even turning back the covers.

Instead, he had been so exhausted he'd collapsed on the duvet, fully dressed. He must've slept like the dead (except for his nightmares), for he'd hardly made a wrinkle on the mattress.

With a yawn and a scratch of his chest, he wondered what time it was, whether the others had risen yet, and if there had been any news from Merlin Hall.

Last night, he and his friends had struggled to stay awake as long as they could, waiting for any sort of word, but one by one, they had nodded off.

Well, today, he intended to get answers. He reached for his knife lying beside him on the mattress, then rose and stepped into his shoes.

After splashing his face and putting himself into basic order to tackle the day, he left the bedchamber, well aware he was still pretty rumpled, all things considered.

His clothes smelled like smoke, he hadn't even noticed the hole in the knee of his trousers until this morning, and his hair (of which he'd admittedly become rather vain of late) refused to behave.

So be it.

Buckingham Palace was an embarrassing place to look so disheveled, but he was too tired to care. He needed to sleep for a week.

Grabbing his coat off the chair, he left his chamber and stepped out into the short hallway where the three boys had been given rooms.

The girls' rooms were down the opposite hallway that branched off the huge parlor at the center of the private suite where Queen Victoria had deposited them last night. Her Majesty had told her staff to wait on them, then posted soldiers outside the door for their protection.

Jake had no doubt they'd be safe as houses here. Still, deep down, he would've rather remained at Beacon House and eaten eight bowls of Mrs. Appleton's soup.

Speaking of food...

His belly grumbled as he smelled bacon. Then the sound of laughter reached him; he stepped out into the gilded white parlor and was shocked to see that everyone else was already up.

"Am I the last one?" he blurted out.

They all stopped talking and looked over.

"Jake!" Dani jumped out of her seat at the long cherry dining table where the lot of them were having a kingly breakfast feast.

Puzzled, he drifted toward them as they all hailed him with great cheer. His best girl ran to him across the dusky rose carpet full of swirling flowers, and Teddy followed, yipping at her heels. The next thing Jake knew, the carrot-head threw her arms around his neck in a huge hug.

Jake hugged her back uncertainly. "Good morning to you, too."

"It *is* a good morning. Oh, Jake!" She pulled back, her emerald eyes shining. "We've had the most wonderful news!"

"What? Tell me. I could use some."

She beamed at him. "Everyone's all right!"

"Well, not *everyone*," Nixie grumbled, nibbling a triangular piece of toast. She was not a morning person. "Balinor's dead."

"Yes, but we already knew that," Archie said from the head of the table. "We've heard from Merlin Hall, coz. Everyone we care about is safe. The Dark Druids fled; the Order drove them off."

Jake's eyes widened. "Really?" He headed at once toward the table, capturing Dani's hand and bringing her with him. "When did you find out?"

"About half an hour ago," Archie said.

"Why didn't you wake me?" Jake cried.

Dani poked him in the arm. "You needed the sleep."

"Humph." Busybody carrot-head, always looking after him.

"Our parents are safe." Archie nodded at his sister, who sat at the foot of the table. "Aunt Ramona's fine. Derek and the twins made it through all right, as well."

Relief washed through Jake. "Janos?"

"Unscathed," Isabelle said with a grateful glow in her cobalt eyes.

"What about Maddox? And Ravyn?"

"A little beaten up—you know Guardians—but they'll be fine," Dani said.

Brian chuckled as the redhead sat back down across from him.

Jake, however, furrowed his brow, skeptical. "There had to be casualties. Sir Peter? Tex? Finnderool?"

"They all made it through, coz," Isabelle said gently.

"Even Aelfric? It looked like he got crushed."

"He's alive." Izzy shrugged. "He told the Elders he thinks he'll be all right."

"What about the Green Man? He got awfully close to the fire," Jake said, "and he *is* part tree."

"His leaves got singed, but don't worry, Dr. Plantagenet is doing fine." Izzy smiled with a hint of mischief. "I'm sure he's annoyed, though. Apparently, the Dreaming Sheep escaped their pen in the chaos. The flying sheepdog is still trying to gather them all back."

"No word on Malwort, though," Nixie said, staring into space. "I hope he's all right."

They all looked at her then started laughing at the thought of the talking spider. Malwort had left Uncle Waldrick to become the witch's self-appointed familiar. Dani explained this to Brian.

"Don't worry, Nix, I'm sure he's fine," Archie said, patting her arm. "I daresay the little fellow's been through worse."

Jake chortled. "I know. He's constantly complaining about his *tragic past*."

"Complain? My little Malwort? Never," Nixie teased, throwing her last bite of toast at him, but her dark eyes danced.

Jake gave the scrap to Teddy, who scarfed it down. "So, how did you hear all this? Another Inkbug message?"

"No, Henry wrote us a letter as soon as he was able," said Archie, "and Gladwin delivered it."

"Gladwin was here?" Jake asked, sorry he'd missed her.

From the corner of his eye, he noticed Dani smiling at the mention of their favorite fairy courier.

"Briefly," Archie said, then sipped his little Italian coffee. (He'd abandoned good English breakfast tea months ago for the stronger stuff.) "She could only stay for a moment before Queen Victoria sent her off again to deliver another message. The whole kingdom's abuzz this morning, I'm sure."

"I can only imagine the *Clairvoyant*'s headlines," Nixie said.

"By the way, Jake," Dani said, "Gladwin asked us to tell you that she hopes you're all right, and that everyone was so amazed at how you crippled the airship last night."

One side of his mouth lifted in a roguish grin. "Oh, really?"

"Here." Archie reached into his vest pocket and pulled out a folded piece of paper. "It's Henry's note, if you want to read it for yourself."

"Thanks." Brushing off a brief whiff of pride over his own heroics the night before, Jake accepted the letter from Henry du Val, the boys' shapeshifting tutor. A mild-mannered scholar in his human form, in times of danger, Henry could change into a vicious wolf bent on protecting his charges.

Likewise, his twin sister, the girls' governess, Miss Helena du Val, could teach piano and etiquette lessons one moment, and then change into a lethal black leopard if anyone threatened the Bradford children.

The genteel, French-born shapeshifter twins had been hired years ago by Uncle Richard and Aunt Claire, the glamorous Viscount and Viscountess Bradford, to look after their children. As diplomats for the Order, they were often gone from home, visiting faraway kingdoms to smooth over conflicts, help solve problems between different magical peoples, and charm possible enemies into becoming allies.

Until Jake had seen his aunt and uncle's work up close in recent weeks, he had always thought that being a Lightrider was the best, most adventurous life a person could ever want. But now he wasn't sure.

From what he'd seen, the diplomats were the ones who were really at the center of things.

In any case, he skimmed Henry's letter, comforted by their tutor's steady tone—honest, but reassuring. That was Henry. He had made sure to list everyone they'd want to know about.

Relief slowly seeped into Jake's bones as he realized things really were as much under control now as could be expected, under the circumstances. The Dark Druids had been driven back, and finally, it seemed like the adults had matters in hand. *Took 'em long enough.*

"Well, then." He handed the letter back to Archie. "No wonder I found you all celebrating."

"Indeed. Here, coz." Izzy handed him a cup of breakfast tea—sugar but no cream, just the way he liked it. She really was an angel. "Cheers," she added, lifting her own cup.

Jake gave her a hearty smile. "I'll drink to that."

"Careful!" Dani warned him, and he remembered just in time not to chip the fine royal china, and tapped his teacup ever so gently against Izzy's, both of them chuckling.

Then everyone shared a whole round of cheers with their various morning beverages—tea, coffee, juice, hot chocolate—for truly, they had much to celebrate.

Jake felt the tea already starting to revive him.

"Well!" he said brightly. "It seems we're all alive, then. This really is the most excellent news."

"This is the most excellent food," Brian replied, shoveling Belgian waffles into his mouth.

Dani smiled and pulled out the chair that she had saved for Jake between her and Isabelle. "Dig in, Jakey-boy. Before the Yank eats it all."

"Who, me?" Brian teased through his mouthful.

Isabelle arched a brow. Jake sat down, still in shock that there hadn't been any additional disasters for him to absorb this morning. Lately, it seemed like it had just been one horrible blow after the next.

But this was a new day. And things must be getting back to normal, for, right on cue, his belly growled insistently.

"Crikey, I'm starving. What time is it, anyway?" He glanced around the opulent parlor for the grandfather clock, but couldn't see its face from where he sat.

Archie pulled out his fob watch. "Half past ten."

Jake lifted his eyebrows. "I *did* sleep in." Derek usually had him up at six for his rigid daily regimen of physical training before his lessons with Master Henry.

"You fought battles last night, coz," Izzy said, reaching for the butter. "You earned it."

"I suppose." Jake's mood darkened briefly at the grim reminder, but he brushed it off. "Anything else I should know?"

Dani shrugged. "Just that your Aunt Claire sent an Inkbug message a little while ago telling us we're to wait here until Derek and Miss Helena come to fetch us." Then she passed him the bacon. To be sure, the lass knew him well.

"Mother and Father can't come themselves," Archie explained. "She said they're already being sent off on a mission to tell some of our allies what happened last night."

"Huh." Jake began helping himself to bacon, eggs, toast, waffles, fruit. "I wonder who they'll choose to be the next head of the Order. Sir Peter?"

"Oh, we already heard!" Dani said eagerly, passing him the syrup next. Sometimes he'd swear she really could read his mind. He thanked her with a wink. "Wanna guess?"

"Nope."

"You're not going to believe this, coz." Archie peered over his spectacles at him. "They've chosen Aunt Ramona."

"What?" Jake laughed and set the syrup boat down. "They've made the ol' girl the chief Elder?"

Izzy couldn't quite stifle her giggle. "Poor woman. She must be miserable."

"She's gonna hate it." Nixie nodded.

The young super-witch had come to know Aunt Ramona well, ever since the Elder witch had become Nixie's official mentor in her magical studies.

It was rare for Aunt Ramona to choose a new protégée, but Nixie's powers would've made the girl very dangerous if she did not learn from the best.

Well, Aunt Ramona's outstanding abilities had now landed her the headship of the Order, and the kids couldn't help chuckling to realize how disgusted the old curmudgeon probably felt about that.

Having come to mistrust magic long ago for her own mysterious reasons, the Elder witch usually preferred not to get involved.

But, of course, everyone knew the Dowager Baroness Bradford would not refuse such a momentous duty. Someone had to lead, after all, and she had the most experience—that was putting it mildly, considering she was over three hundred years old.

Doubtful half the time that he, for his part, would live to see the ripe old age of twenty, Jake shook his head at all these unexpected developments. "Strange times, my friends. Strange times," he remarked, and picked up his fork. But then he paused and set it down again.

Having loaded up his plate, he paused, lowered his head, and sent up a mental prayer of thanks. He had so much to be grateful for this morning.

Like the fact that he was even alive. The long, awful night was over like his bad dreams. The warlocks had been driven back. His friends and relatives had been spared—thanks, in part, to Celestus and his fellow angels.

The battle at Merlin Hall aside, if the Light Beings hadn't shown up with their Brightwields to deal with the Nightstalkers, Jake doubted he and his friends would even be here.

And so, before his prayer was done, he put in a good word for the trusty guardian angel. *He's a right proper chap, Lord. You should probably promote him.*

Jake could've sworn he heard an amused voice say, *"Thanks for the suggestion."*

With a smile, Jake opened his eyes and dove in to his meal.

CHAPTER TWENTY-TWO
Courage & Consequence

Zolond was elated, his heart light. He gazed into the mirror on his parlor wall one last time and adjusted his bowtie.

He chuckled to recall the early days of their courtship, how he'd groomed himself with fastidious care before calling on her, and dressed to impress her in doublet and hose.

To this day, he still recalled the feel of his favorite black velvet jerkin; annoying as the fashion had been in those times, he had thought himself dashing indeed in his well-starched ruff.

He wondered if they would even recognize each other now, two wrinkly old things. But he didn't care. He could've changed his appearance to some handsome young stud with a wave of his scepter. But that spitfire would no doubt laugh in his face.

He smiled, too. Humming under his breath, he then set his black bowler hat on his head, reached for his walking stick, and left his apartments, trailed by two reptilians.

As he marched through the Black Fortress, he quickly schooled his face into an ominous expression. If anyone noticed the Dark Master was feeling, dare he say, happy, they would know he was up to no good.

The furious howls of his powerful prisoners raging in their rooms resounded through the jet-black halls of the warlocks' castle as he made his way to the bridge, but Zolond ignored them.

He'd disposed of Wyvern, at least. He was still thinking about what to do with the others, but their fates wouldn't be much better. For now, the thought of the Nephilim cowering before those bizarre little entities crooked Zolond's lips in a half-smile.

Approaching the bridge, he had to scold himself with a reminder to concentrate. He feared his anticipation of this meeting had him a little distracted. That was dangerous, he knew, but he couldn't seem to help it. All he could think of was her.

The hour of their meeting was set for three. He was going in early to London, though, not merely because he was excited. He also wanted to make arrangements for his trip to the city with his grandson.

Zolond did not know whether to laugh or shake his head at the thought of that lad's audacity. Well, he *was* the Black Prince, wasn't he?

An inordinate level of daring was to be expected. Cocky? Perhaps. But the boy had backbone in spades. For a moment, Zolond almost regretted that such a fine young man had been born into such a cursed bloodline. He deserved better.

But he swept aside that distressing awareness. Nothing must be permitted to ruin his strange sensation of joy today.

Instead, he mentally listed the landmarks he'd take his grandson to see.

He especially wanted to show him all the old things that had been there when he was Victor's age. Like the Tower of London, which had already been centuries old before Zolond was born. And the Temple Bar, where the executioners used to display the severed heads. Victor would enjoy that.

Ah, and the Globe Theatre, where Zolond had watched the debut performances of Shakespeare's plays. Why, yes, he decided, he'd take the lad to a show. Then they could have lunch at The White Hart, the oldest pub in London, where he and his young companions used to make merry, guzzling pints and flirting with the tavern wenches. Once upon a time, after all, the Dark Master had been a normal young man, with a normal young life.

The times had been anything but ordinary, though. If his mates in those days had had any idea he was a budding warlock, they'd have burned him at the stake. He pushed the unpleasant thought away.

Victor would probably enjoy a boat ride on the Thames. With the view from the river, he could tell the boy how London used to look before the Great Fire of 1666—and how the Dark Druids had been involved with that.

Zolond himself had only been a regular member of the warlock brotherhood at the time. It would be decades before he seized the throne from his predecessor in the usual way...

It still made him wince just a bit when he thought of wrenching the Master's Ring off the dead finger of the sorcerer-king. In due time, *he* would hand the ring over to Victor without coercion.

Sometimes he thought he'd be glad to be rid of it, rid of all this. Unfortunately, the moment it was off his finger, he would probably turn to dust, and death now held very little appeal, after Shemrazul's promises. He shuddered and, again, thrust the unpleasantness out of his head as he stepped onto the bridge.

The navigator caught sight of him and all but shrieked with his newly returned mouth.

"Sire!" said the lieutenant, snapping the rest of the crew to attention. "Commander on the bridge!"

The gray-clad men's hands shook as they all saluted and stood at attention.

Zolond almost pitied them; that was how good his mood was. "At ease," he said begrudgingly. "Set a course for some discreet landing point outside London. I have business in Town."

"Aye-aye, sir. Right away! You heard him!" the lieutenant yelled at his men.

They scrambled to obey, rushing back to their places and quickly donning their dark glasses.

Druk brought Zolond a pair. "Shall I attend you, sire?"

Pondering the carriage he'd conjure to take him from the outskirts of London into the city, Zolond glanced absently at his toothy head bodyguard, still thinking. Perhaps he would just hail a hansom cab, travel for once like the plebes. The idea struck him as charmingly quaint.

No magic. Ramona would like that.

But she most certainly would not like the sight of his crocodile-headed guards. They had both agreed to come alone. Secrecy was paramount.

"You stay here," he told the reptilian. "We have dangerous prisoners in tow. At least you won't have the Noxu to annoy you—or Wyvern. I left you those two gargoyles for extra security, just in case. Feel free to take dragon form if anyone misbehaves. I will only be gone for a few hours, anyway."

Druk gazed intently at him for a moment, worry in his yellow eyes, but then bowed. "Yes, Your Majesty."

"Never fear, ol' boy. I've always got this." Zolond tapped the Master's Ring on his finger. The very thing Wyvern had wanted—before he had become the plaything of the ice grendels.

Stakes were high in their game. Always had been. That was why his dear Ramona had wanted no part of it.

I shall destroy the locust army after our meeting, he decided on the spot. If Ramona ever found out about that particular experiment—and what he had intended to do with the resulting creatures once they were ready—she would never speak to him again. It was best to put them out of their misery before any more hatched and had to face the horror of what Zolond had done to them.

They had once been men, after all—mercenaries, who'd agreed to a job without *quite* knowing what they were getting into. Death would be merciful compared to finding oneself a monstrosity.

Ramona must never know the full depths of the evil he had dabbled in over the years.

Then the sorcerer-king put on his dark glasses and sat down on the captain's chair for the jump. With each loud pulsation of the infernal machine, he counted the seconds drawing his meeting with his lost love ever closer.

He had waited hundreds of years for this day.

Now it was finally here.

* * *

Oh, what now? Something was happening.

Badgerton scurried through a ventilation shaft in animal form, determined to find out what was going on, though he was still reeling from the latest jump.

Seconds ago, the Black Fortress had slammed into being he had no idea where, but he needed to find out.

The dizziness didn't help. The jump had thrown his furry body around in the cramped metal walkway of the ventilation shaft where he'd been hiding. He'd bumped his head pretty well and bruised his shoulder, but that wasn't the worst of his pains.

Though he'd been nowhere near the big, blinding flashes of light, the pounding vibration of the infernal machine had bellowed along the sheet metal, nigh deafening him, with his acute animal hearing.

Somehow Badgerton had bitten back his scream of pain and covered his ears with his still-wounded paws as best he could.

One more injury to add to his growing collection, he thought bitterly as he limped on, listening for voices.

He could only wonder where they'd landed this time. The last leap through time and space had brought them to the snowy wastes of Antarctica, of all places. He'd heard one of the crewmen say so.

Then Zolond had gone out briefly, floating a chained Lord Wyvern before him once more. The best Badgerton could figure, the Dark Master had marooned the earl there, like a pirate captain would a mutiny leader.

Cruel.

Well, unless Wyvern had some serious spells for warmth, he'd be dead in minutes out there. He was probably frozen solid even now, Badgerton supposed. The remaining Dark Druids would have to choose a new leader—but they were dead, too, unless he got them out.

Maybe this would be his chance.

Of course, he was still terrified of his own plan to sneak into the bridge room, jump up onto the control panel, and open the Dark Druids' guest chambers, so *they* could fight Zolond.

He, himself, had no chance.

As his hearing finally grew less muffled, he followed the sound of voices, tiptoeing down the badger-sized metal hallway until he came to a grate.

He peered through it, unnoticed.

He's leaving again, he thought, homing in on the old man in the bowler hat. But this time, Zolond wasn't taking any more of his powerful prisoners with him.

Badgerton narrowed his eyes. *What is he doing? And for that matter, where are we?*

When the drawbridge lowered to let Zolond out, Badgerton caught the whiff of a sunny autumn day.

Ah, how he missed the woods this time of year! Badgers did not belong in ductwork. More than that—sniffing harder a few times, he caught the scent of the Thames.

London?

Well, that's odd.

For a moment, he considered trying to escape here. Perhaps, if he moved quickly, he could somehow scamper out of this madhouse. London was an excellent place to slip away and blend into a crowd.

Ah, but a heartbeat later, Badgerton realized that the Order would quickly hunt him down here. Then he was doomed.

No, alas, his only hope was to go through with his heroic plan to save the day.

It was too late, anyway. His slim chance of escaping closed with the already-lifting drawbridge. The moment it slammed shut, the crew breathed a sigh of relief, then hurried back to their posts.

As did the reptilians.

When the tall, scaly lizard men passed beneath the air vent, Badgerton stared down at them in dread.

The task before him would indeed be a test of his nerve. He must take care to stay clear of those teeth. And those spears.

Queasy with fright, he gave himself a trembling pep talk as he headed back through the ductwork maze to watch the bridge room from the air grate in the ceiling, which he had already managed to find.

Right, he told himself. *Best not to think about it too much. Just act. What choice do you have?*

He reminded himself that he was brave.

Why, of all species in the animal kingdom, there were few things more dangerous than a cornered badger, and cornered he was. He took inspiration from his cousins, the honey badgers of Africa, who could rip open the bellies of lions when attacked—as long as they worked together.

Well aware he was totally alone in this, Badgerton could only gulp. But as he crept into position over the bridge room, he decided he'd use his fear to make himself even more vicious. Just like he'd taught chubby little Charlie.

His plan was simple, at least. Nor did it require much skill.

All he had to do was wait for the exact right moment, when the reptilian wasn't paying attention, then remove the metal grate, jump down onto the control panel, and get the job done.

For the children, he reminded himself. The thought of his dear little skunkies steeled his courage. With that, the shapeshifter lord crouched in the shadows...and bided his time.

* * *

Prue sat (in girl form) on a sun-dappled boulder in the rustling autumn woods a couple of miles away from Merlin Hall.

For most animal shifters, it was a relief on a normal day to escape into the forest, but especially so to her, after all the danger and destruction last night.

Since then, a golden Sunday afternoon had arrived, and Prue found herself feeling surprisingly content, even with the world turned upside down.

The skunk side of her found the woods so cozy this time of year, with the moss shining green on the fallen logs and the deer flitting up and down the trails known only to the animals. The latticework of tree branches formed colorful arches overhead, and the forest smelled of her favorite food—the delicate wild mushrooms that came into season in the autumn.

On her lap, meanwhile, rested *Arvath's Arcanium*, her coveted prize. She perused the grimoire's collection of spells at her leisure.

Her willow wand rested on the flat rock by her side, but in truth, she was still a bit wary of handling the thing.

"A wand isn't a toy," Uncle Boris had warned her when he'd handed over the money for the Fairy Market last spring. *"You may buy one, I suppose, but be careful! And don't let your brothers try it, dearheart. I don't think that would be...safe."*

A tactful way of saying they were too stupid to use it.

Prue agreed. Pleased that her uncle knew she was the smart one, she had smiled sweetly. *"Don't worry, Uncle Boris. I don't like sharing, anyway."*

He'd patted her on the head, and off she went.

And now, here she sat—with a stolen grimoire, a wand she wasn't sure how to use, and a family name that had just become synonymous with *outlaw*.

Strangely enough, Prue was warming to the role.

She turned another page, savoring her newfound freedom from any and all adult supervision. Her brothers seemed to be enjoying themselves, too. A few feet behind her, the boys (in skunk form) feasted on insects they'd found in an old log.

Prue usually pretended she thought eating bugs was gross, but deep down, she didn't, really. Other people would think so, however, therefore, she claimed that she only ate berries, mushrooms, and eggs when in skunk form.

Ah, but the real truth was she was particularly fond of wriggly grubs and crunchy crickets. She couldn't help it! It wasn't her fault. It was just instinct!

At least she wasn't as bad as Charlie, who preferred fat, juicy frogs.

Welton, on the other hand, was partial to field mice. He relished the chase, and he liked how they screeched with fright as they tried to run away.

Well, she mused, at least the three of them wouldn't have to worry about snobby Order people judging them anymore.

They were officially outcasts now. And that meant there was only one thing to do: follow in Uncle Boris's pawprints and join the Dark Druids.

Now she just had to figure out how to find him.

Arvath's Arcanium offered a range of intriguing options to choose from.

Scrying was, she believed, the usual method witches used to locate missing items or people. Unfortunately, that required two things Prue didn't have on hand: a map and a crystal pendant to dangle over it.

But it probably wouldn't work, anyway. The rumors the skunkies had heard last night claimed that Uncle Boris had escaped into the Black Fortress, which had now flown away.

So long as he stayed inside the warlocks' magical moving castle, Prue had little hope of tracking him. Everyone knew the Dark Druid stronghold was concealed from detection by a host of formidable spells.

To be sure, if it managed to elude the likes of Sir Peter and Balinor, then a neophyte magician like her would never be able to locate it.

For now, though, Prue wasn't too concerned. She and her brothers would be fine on their own for a while. Food was plentiful, foraging was fun, and they could shelter in any hollow log or abandoned foxhole they came across.

If all else failed, they could simply make a den under an outbuilding at the nearest farm.

Without adults telling them what to do, it would be, she decided, an adventure. Uncle Boris would come looking for them soon enough. Lord Wyvern no doubt had spells that could help their uncle find them.

The half-demon warlock owed the shapeshifter lord, after all. Wyvern never could've carried out his raid last night if Uncle Boris hadn't let his forces in.

Prue was rather proud of him, when she thought about it. "He'll come and get us when it's safe," she murmured to herself.

In the meanwhile, the grimoire offered numerous methods to conjure anything she and her brothers might need, like money, fresh clothes, even a carriage with servitor horses...

A smile spread slowly across Prue's face as she realized that in her hands was the means to have whatever she pleased.

At last, the full impact of the power she had seized for herself finally began sinking in. Oh, real magic was much better than being a simple shapeshifter...

She suddenly had a feeling that she was going to like her new life among the Dark Druids, once her uncle came to fetch them. Till then, she intended to relish her independence.

And figure out how to use that wand.

CHAPTER TWENTY-THREE
A Secret Meeting

"So, what are we going to do with ourselves until Derek comes?" Jake asked, lounging on a striped silk divan.

He and his friends had left the dining table, stuffed to the gills, and moved to the sitting area by the fireplace at the other end of the long, gilded parlor.

"Rest and be lazy," Dani declared. She had curled up in a velvet armchair, petting the scruffy dog perched on her lap. "I feel like a princess!"

Brian paced over to the window and braced his hands on the sill as he peered out, looking bored. "Maybe they'd let us go for a walk around London while we wait. See the sights?"

"Didn't you get enough walking last night?" Nixie drawled, twirling her wand idly between her fingers as she lay on the couch, ankles crossed.

The Guardian shrugged.

"Well, I'm not walking anywhere." Jake shut his eyes. "I'm too full of waffles and bacon. It's wonderful."

"I don't think they'd let us go out, anyway," Isabelle said with a yawn. "I'm sure the soldiers outside our door would say it isn't safe."

Jake didn't open his eyes. "Aye."

The palace people hadn't even let Dani walk Teddy herself. A self-important footman had taken the scruffy terrier by his leash and led him outside to do his business, looking slightly offended by such a low task.

When the footman had returned, Isabelle had asked if perhaps their group might join the regular public tour of Buckingham Palace. But when this request was passed along to Her Majesty, the answer that came back promptly was an emphatic no. It was best for them not to be seen.

A maid did, however, bring them some games and cards to pass the time. Unfortunately, nobody felt like playing childish games when they all knew war had come to their very doorstep.

In any case, noon came and went, and another two hours limped on with still more restless waiting.

At least they were being fed well; a line of footmen had marched in at one with a spread of sandwiches, soups, and casseroles, followed by a sweets course of fluffy chocolate mousse in crystal goblets.

Jake was in heaven.

Even Teddy ate like a king after the people were done. The servants brought him a bowl of the same rich mutton and potato stew served to the royal dogs.

A smile tugged at Jake's lips as he watched the scruffy terrier clear his plate in thirty seconds flat, then lick his chops and make one of his odd little warbling yowls to Izzy.

Dani looked at the older girl. "What is he saying?"

Isabelle laughed as she quoted: "'I could get used to this.'"

"Oh, the royal mutt, are we?" Jake scooped the little dog up before Dani could grab him. Dani smiled, watching him holding her pup.

"I hope Red's staying out of sight."

Jake nodded. "Me too."

As the servants worked on clearing the table, Nixie began shuffling the cards.

"Come on; you people are boring," said the witch. "Let's at least play a round of Old Maid."

Brian, Isabelle, Dani, and Jake mumbled that they were willing, but Archie raised a brow and dryly declined.

"Oh, too primitive for you, brother?" Izzy teased.

"Rather," Archie said as a footman brushed the last crumbs off the table into a miniature dustpan. Then his colleague whisked the tablecloth away, and both efficient fellows hurried out. "That's beside the point, however. It so happens that I have a better idea."

"Big surprise," Jake murmured with a smile.

Then Archie turned to the junior Lightrider. "I say, Dani, ol' girl. Since we've nothing better to do—"

"Hey!" Nixie said with a mock scowl.

"—would you mind my taking a look at that gauntlet of yours? I'd love to see if I can't figure out a bit about how it works."

At once, Dani hugged her arm to her chest. "You'll break it!"

"Miss O'Dell, you insult me," the boy genius said lightly. "This is *me* you're talking to."

"Yes, exactly, and we all know how much you love taking things apart and putting them back together. If you damage it, Arch, they'll throw me out of the program."

"Upon my honor, I shall do nothing of the kind! Please? Pretty please? It's killing me, you know. I need to study that thing. Just for a minute?"

She chewed her lip, debating. "I'm not allowed to take it off."

"I can work around that. Here." He pulled out a chair at the table. "Oh, come. Aren't you curious yourself how it works?"

"Well, actually, now that you mention it... I *have* been wondering what some of the buttons are for."

He bowed. "World-class brain, at your service."

Nixie snickered. "Modest, Arch."

"Oh, very well," Dani said. "Just *don't* break it. Or I'll break yer head."

"She can, you know," Jake remarked, watching in amusement.

"Oh, yes, we're all highly aware of our fighting Irishwoman's pugilistic skills," Archie said.

"You should meet me brothers," Dani said, using the brogue she usually tried to hide as she sat down beside him.

"Oh, no, he shouldn't," Jake said playfully as he sat back down across from them. "I prefer my cousin in one piece."

Brian grinned, glancing curiously at Dani as he took the chair beside her. "Mean, are they?"

"Wild dogs," Dani replied.

"She said it." Jake shrugged. "I barely survived my first meeting with the Brothers O'Dell years ago. They would've pummeled me into the pavement if it weren't for this one." He cast Dani a roguish wink.

Then Nixie dealt the cards, and the rest of them split their attention between playing Old Maid and watching Archie poke around at the mysterious device on Dani's outstretched arm.

That was how bored they were.

"Hmm," the boy genius said often to himself. And "Huh. Would you look at that. Extraordinary..."

Jake and Nixie exchanged looks of amusement at the lovable eccentric's puttering. But when he started explaining his conclusions, nobody understood a word.

Isabelle actually yawned. "I beg your pardon, Arch. If everyone will excuse me, I fear I need a nap."

"I was thinking about that myself," Jake admitted.

"Night-night," Izzy said with a smile, pushing up from her seat.

Jake and Brian quickly offered the gesture of rising from their chairs at a young lady's exit, but Archie, for his part, was too absorbed to bother. Besides, it was only his sister.

"G'night," Jake said. "Do you want us to wake you if there's any news?"

Shuffling off toward the girls' hallway, Isabelle didn't answer. Instead, she suddenly stopped, turned, and stared at the door of their suite.

Jake and Dani exchanged a curious glance.

"Isabelle," Dani said, "is something wrong?"

With a dazed look, the empath pointed toward the door. "Derek and Miss Helena are here."

"What?" Jake looked up, and Archie quit fiddling with the gauntlet.

Even Brian sat upright. "Really?"

Izzy nodded. "I can sense them somewhere in the building. They seem...nervous. I think they're going in to see the Queen."

"It's easiest for her to sense the people that she's close to," Dani told Brian as she took back her arm from the mad scientist and gave the gauntlet a quick once-over.

"Took them long enough." Nixie cast down another card. "Maybe we can finally get out of here now."

Brian cocked his head and rose from the table, listening. "I hear people coming this way."

"Maybe it's them." Jake jumped up and strode over to the drawing room door. Opening it a crack, he peered out with one eye, then turned around and nodded at the others.

Izzy was right, as usual.

Down the corridor and across the opulent state room at the end of it, Jake spotted the betrothed couple following the chamberlain into another elegant hallway that, if he recalled correctly, led to Queen Victoria's private office.

Jake had been summoned there personally once, when the Order had first found him.

I guess Her Majesty wants to talk to them first. Find out what's going on.

Jake would've liked to know that himself.

Unfortunately, one of the scarlet-uniformed soldiers flanking the door noticed him peeking out. The tall, strapping fellow pivoted, arching a brow. "Is there something you require, Lord Griffon?"

"No, no—thank you. Er, carry on."

The guard bowed his head. "Sir. It would be best if Your Lordship remained out of sight."

"Right." Feeling sheepish, Jake had started to close the door when something strange happened.

Derek and Helena had no sooner vanished down one hallway off the grand state room, than who should emerge out of another but Aunt Ramona?

Jake furrowed his brow, pausing. *What's she doing here?*

He was glad to see her, of course, but it seemed odd that she'd send the lovebirds to collect them when she was already here herself.

But, of course, they'd just made the Elder witch the head of the Order, he reminded himself, so perhaps she had more important business to see to concerning her new responsibilities than worrying about them.

Odd, though. Jake could not help thinking there was something almost furtive in the way the stern old woman gusted across the luxurious state room and hurried down the marble staircase.

Wherever she was going, she had certainly dressed to the nines in a burgundy bustle gown with a black fascinator perched on her head at a jaunty angle.

As she vanished down the stairs, Jake quietly shut the door, then told the others what he'd seen. The kids exchanged puzzled looks.

"Hmm," said Nixie, "I wonder what she's up to." As Aunt Ramona's only student, the young witch had developed a fairly close bond with her mentor. Indeed, Her Ladyship was probably the only adult on Earth the little cynic revered.

Rising from her chair, the witch went over to the window to see if she could catch a glimpse of her leaving the palace.

Isabelle followed, drifting after her, then both girls stood framed between the festooned gold curtains.

"There she is!" Nixie suddenly pointed. "There, in the black hat."

Isabelle stared through the glass with a troubled demeanor.

"What is it, sis?" Archie went over to her side and peeked out between the girls.

"I'm not sure," Izzy murmured. "But I've got a bad feeling."

Archie looked at her in alarm. "What sort of bad feeling?"

"Aye, and any idea where she might be headed?" Jake asked. Concerned, he joined the trio at the window, which offered a view off a section of the south front corner of the palace.

"Maybe she just wants to check on Beacon House," Dani suggested. She and Brian hung back.

"No." Izzy shook her head. "There's more to it than that. Something very strange is going on."

Nixie glanced at her uneasily. "What are you sensing?"

"That's just it." Eyes narrowed with concentration, the empath stared out at the street. "I could swear she knows I'm here, and she's deliberately trying to block me from reading her emotions."

"Why would she do that? She adores you more than anyone else in the world," Archie said.

Jake noticed the fear in his cousin's dark eyes as Archie moved aside to give him a better view out the window, pointing to where he should look.

Sure enough, Jake spotted the dowager baroness marching toward Spur Street with her head high and her little handbag in her grasp.

"Why isn't she taking a carriage?" Jake asked.

"Good question," Nixie said. "Or even using magic."

"This is weird." Jake looked askance at the empath. "Are you getting anything at all about where she's going?"

"Let me try again before she's out of range." Izzy closed her eyes, took a deep breath, and was silent for a moment.

The others waited, exchanging worried glances.

Izzy did not open her eyes as she reached deep into her talent. "Her emotions are all in a whirl," she reported. "This is most unlike her. Partly happy, partly scared to death."

"The Elder witch, scared?" Jake said under his breath.

Izzy's eyes suddenly flicked open, and she turned to him abruptly. "Something's wrong. I'm sure of it. Jake—you need to go after her. Now."

His eyes widened. "What?"

"Why do you say that?" Archie cried.

"Now, hold on! He's not going anywhere," Dani protested from behind them.

Izzy glanced at her impatiently.

The redhead marched forward with a stubborn look on her freckled face. "He's the boy of the prophecy, remember? The Dark Druids are after him! Last night it was Nightstalkers and imps. Lord knows what might be out there right now, still searching for him. More to the point"—she planted her fists on her hips—"when the Queen of England orders you to stay in a certain room, you'd better stay put. For all we know, disobeying Her Majesty could be, like, I dunno, breaking the law or something!"

"I'm sure it's not a *law*, carrot," Jake said. "I appreciate your concern, but if Aunt Ramona is in trouble, I'm going." She glared at him, but he turned back to Izzy. "What exactly did you get when you read her just now?"

Izzy shrugged, looking desperate and rather at a loss. "She's in danger and she knows it. Whatever it is, we can't let her face it alone."

"I'll go," Nixie said in a hard tone. "Dani's right. It's Jake the enemy wants. After all Her Ladyship has done for me, if I can be of use—"

"Nixie, no. You can't risk getting in trouble with Aunt Ramona. Besides," Jake said, "the Elders have high hopes for you. Look what they did to me for disobeying."

They'd barred him from the Lightrider program, at least for the time being.

"Jake's right, Nix." Archie nodded resolutely. "I'll go."

"You don't have magic!" Nixie said.

"It doesn't matter! I'm her nephew. We're her kin. Jake and I will go together."

Dani huffed and turned away in exasperation, shaking her head.

"There is one other thing," Izzy added. She lowered her head and studied the floor with a searching gaze, concentrating. "I get the feeling that she's on her way to see someone important. Someone...from the past."

"Oh no," Nixie murmured, lifting her fingers to her lips.

They all turned and looked at her.

"What do you mean, *oh no*?" Jake demanded.

She didn't answer for a minute, but her normally pale face had drained of any color.

"Nixie!" Archie insisted.

"Izzy's right," the witch blurted out. "You have to stop her. I-I think I know what this is. It's just, if I'm right—she swore me to secrecy!"

"Nixie, tell us what you know!" Archie said, ashen.

Jake heard the panic in his voice and cast his cousin a dark, assessing glance.

"*Oh no,*" indeed, he thought, seeing Archie's face. The last time he had seen the genius looking so unnerved, it was after he'd had another of his disastrous prophetic dreams.

Cheerful by nature, Archie didn't usually like discussing his unpleasant visions. On the contrary, he was still trying to convince himself that he hadn't *really* inherited his father's clairvoyance at all. Being a math and science prodigy was enough of a burden. But looking at him now, Jake felt rather sure that his cousin must've had another ominous vision recently. One he had not yet disclosed.

Suddenly, Izzy's "bad feeling" spread like a contagion to Jake. His stomach twisted on his lunch.

He turned to Nixie. "Are you saying you know who Aunt Ramona's going to meet?"

"I think so."

They all stared at her, waiting, but still, she balked at betraying her mentor's secret.

"Nixie, who is she meeting?" Jake demanded.

The little witch gulped and whispered, "Zolond."

CHAPTER TWENTY-FOUR
Tick-Tock

It was only a fifteen-minute stroll from Buckingham Palace to Big Ben. Ramona felt the years falling away with every stride.

Her heart pounded with excitement; her steps grew light.

She told herself that she was merely eager to see the crisis resolved in a safe and timely manner, but, of course, there was more to it than that.

If she was honest with herself, she could taste the remembered flavor from centuries ago—the thrill a young girl felt slipping off to meet her beau.

Foolishness.

In truth, Ramona was shocked at how much she still cared about that evil bounder. She mustn't let him use it against her.

Continuing up Spur Road, every now and then, Ramona glanced over her shoulder with the uncanny feeling that she was being followed.

Her decision to walk to the meeting wasn't the most secure choice, admittedly. But after the shock of last night and the many hours she'd spent after the battle trying to put the Order back together again, she desperately needed these few minutes alone to clear her head. Collect her thoughts. And prepare herself to face her treacherous former love.

The Dark Master and she had promised each other safe passage to and from their meeting. But as the new head of the Order, she had to expect that she was being watched.

No matter. She had her wand and always kept her wits about her.

With a discreet glance around, she did not see whoever was surveilling her, but they did not intimidate her—and they certainly wouldn't scare her away from the meeting.

She had waited a long time for this.

Striding for another ten minutes up the tidy, tree-lined street whimsically entitled Birdcage Walk, she found ancient memories of their youth together whispering through her mind. For a time, they had been ridiculously happy, finishing each other's sentences, causing all manner of mischief together, combining their talents to help each other's spells. Hiding together from the persecutors of those days. Smuggling away witches and fey folk the fanatics had wanted to burn.

He'd had a good heart once. Maybe, just maybe, there was a grain of goodness left in him. There had to be. Otherwise, why else would he have helped the Order last night?

Don't be a fool. He did it for his own sake. If Wyvern's coup had succeeded, he'd be dead.

And then we both would.

Ramona thrust away the troubling thought of the worst mistake she'd ever made—joining Geoffrey in the Montague and Capulet spell. She never would have agreed to it if she had known he would turn evil.

With a fretful frown, she strove to settle her nerves by taking in the fine autumn day as she walked on. A cloudless azure sky shimmered overhead, while eddies of dried brown leaves swirled across the pavement at her feet.

Golden sunshine glinted off the brass fittings of the well-polished carriages clip-clopping past her up and down the street. Despite the sun's warmth, there was just enough of a chill in the air to bring some color to her cheeks—she hoped. Because, other than that, there was so little left of the girl she used to be that Geoffrey might not even recognize her.

Soon, the Houses of Parliament and Westminster Bridge with the sparkling river beneath it came into view ahead.

On her right, she passed the broad green open space of Parliament Square Garden, with Westminster Abbey beyond it. She noticed the cathedral doors propped wide open, though Sunday services were long over. Perhaps someone was getting married.

Or buried, she thought wryly. Lucky them.

All seemed peaceful in the flat green park. Picnickers sat here and there dressed in Sunday finery. Families together enjoyed a pleasant stroll.

A passing bobby tipped his hat; Ramona bowed her head in answer.

Hm, he looked familiar, she thought, but only after the constable had passed. She dismissed the brief question; she had a meeting to get to, and she had better focus.

The Dark Master was no one to be trifled with.

Still, she always found it peculiar to think of all these ordinary mortals going about their lives with no inkling of the whole world of magic playing out right beneath their noses. Oh, a few still believed in fairies. And dragons, perhaps—especially after all the recent excavations of what the archaeologists fancied "dinosaur" bones.

There were occasional sightings of various creatures in diverse places. Plenty of ghosts raised questions in castles and haunted pubs across the land.

Indeed, most children, like the ones she spotted running amuck just now in Parliament Square, still suspected that monsters were real. But, alas, in this Age of Progress and science, most adults had lost the second sight altogether, which Ramona thought a shame.

Ah well, perhaps they were better off not knowing the truth. Because look at what magic had done to Geoffrey...

Sadness filled her. But she shoved it away, laying hold of her usual, businesslike manner—and just in the nick of time. For ahead, Big Ben towered against the blue sky, warning her it was already ten minutes till three.

No time to waste.

Upon reaching the corner, she paused and stole a furtive glance around. The sense of being followed persisted, but she saw no sign of danger.

Nor did she see Zolond anywhere. He, too, should be walking into their meeting any minute now. Perhaps he had beaten her here. He had always been prompt as a suitor. Maybe he'd made himself invisible for security's sake, she thought.

Or maybe he isn't coming at all. The thought made her desolate, which, in turn, vexed her immensely. *You cakehead! You are the leader of the Order now. Stifle your heart, you hen-witted female.*

Of *course* he was coming. This whole thing had been his idea! He was hardly going to lose his nerve and fail to appear. The Dark Master might be many things, but a coward wasn't one of them. *He'll be here,* she told herself grimly. *Now, focus.*

With that, she hurried across the street and strode right up to the wrought-iron gates outside Parliament, where two bored-looking policemen stood guard.

When she showed one of them the short note from her old friend,

Victoria—and when he, in turn, saw Her Majesty's royal seal in a circle of red wax at the bottom—he gave her a startled bow.

"At your service, my lady. You require access to the Clock Tower?"

Ramona lifted her chin. "Correct."

"Right away, ma'am. If you'll come with me." He gestured toward the nearest palace entrance, and Ramona followed him across the courtyard and through a richly carved stone archway, ignoring all the stone gargoyles leering down at her amid the Neo-Gothic splendor of the place.

In moments, the guard had led her through a smaller arch at the base of the Clock Tower, bringing her to a most ordinary-looking wooden door reinforced with a few iron bars. Across the middle of it in plain gold letters was written CLOCK TOWER.

He took out a key, unlocked the door, opened it for her, and stepped aside politely. "Is there anything else you require, Lady Bradford?"

"No. Thank you. You've been most helpful. You may go," she added as she stepped into the cramped, square space.

"As you wish, ma'am."

She nodded; he bowed to her, but sent a skeptical glance toward the staircase that started behind her and ascended some two hundred feet up into the tower.

The good fellow apparently doubted that an old lady of her advanced years could make it up to the top of Big Ben. It was quite a hike.

Oh, but she'd manage somehow. The Elder witch hid her amusement as the earnest young policeman pushed the door shut behind him. She heard the lock click, then he walked off to return to his post.

Ramona tilted her head back and looked up at the endless spiral staircase that wrapped around and around the square tower leading up to Big Ben.

Their meeting place today.

Certain spots in all manner of unlikely places around the world had been designated over the years as neutral ground between the Order and the Dark Druids.

Since Time ruled as master over all men, good and bad alike in equal measure, it seemed fitting that one such location should be home to the most accurate clock in the world. To be sure, it was convenient enough, located right here in London.

But, of course, Ramona had no intention of surmounting the tower's three hundred and thirty-four stairs on foot. She was spry, but not *that* spry, by Jove.

Instead, she slipped her wand out of its special compartment in her black silk handbag. After glancing out the door's window to make sure no one was coming, she uttered a spell, waved her wand at her feet, and then began levitating herself up the open center of the spiral staircase. She traveled straight upward with ease, ascending at a sedate vertical glide, wand in hand.

She was about a third of the way up, however, when she had to pause to let Big Ben have his say.

With a wince at the first deafening note of its familiar hourly song, she floated over the black wrought-iron banister, alighted on the stairs, and covered her ears with both hands.

The chimes were so loud here that she could feel them vibrating in her belly; after the Westminster chimes ended, then Big Ben tolled the hour of three.

Each mighty bong filled the whole tower with sound.

As soon as the third deafening note had faded away, Ramona resumed her journey, rising at a swifter pace now to avoid being late. Her heart beat faster as she reached the top of the stairs and set her feet back down on solid ground.

Wand at the ready, still unsure if this might turn out to be an ambush, the Elder witch opened the door to the plain square chamber that housed the clock's mechanical inner workings.

Zolond wasn't there.

Tick.

Tick.

Tick.

There was nothing to see in the austere room but the giant clockworks: a fifteen-foot tangle of spiky metal flywheels and rotating gears. Archie would be in raptures. Ramona smiled fondly at the thought of the young inventor, then withdrew from the chamber. Next, she went to check the narrow passages behind each of the four huge faces of the most famous clock in the world.

From this side, the faces of Big Ben looked like stained-glass windows, but only in creamy white. Ramona walked slowly from passage to passage surrounding the clockworks chamber in the middle.

She looped the strap of her handbag nervously over her forearm, but held on to her wand in case the Dark Master misbehaved.

He should be here any—

Suddenly, Zolond arrived in a puff of black smoke, transporting himself into the passage a few feet ahead of her before she could even finish the thought.

Ramona clutched at her chest. "Sweet Hecate, man! You startled me."

He chuckled as he materialized fully at the end of the narrow corridor just a few feet away.

"Greetings, Lady Bradford." The old man swept off his bowler hat and bowed politely, a faint smile—or was it a smirk?—playing about his lips.

Much to her dismay, Ramona's heart skipped a beat at the sight of her former love.

Tick-tock, tick-tock...

The way his gray eyes shone, why, he was just as she remembered him from their last parley between their two sides, about a hundred and fifty years ago.

She didn't even remember what their business that day had been, but she remembered *him*. She ignored the fluttering of her pulse and told herself it was merely amusing to see how he looked in the changing fashions of the centuries.

On that last occasion, she and her Renaissance-born counterpart had been dressed in the style of the Ancien Régime: white wigs, white-powdered faces.

He had worn a pastel silk frock coat and breeches, white silk stockings, and those big, ridiculous buckle shoes the gentlemen of fashion used to flaunt.

Her own getup had been almost as bad, with Marie Antoinette-sized hoop skirts that made it difficult to fit through doorways. The pair of them had looked like aged courtiers of Versailles, rotting together in luxury.

Now Zolond was arrayed in a tidy black suit with a gray silk waistcoat, walking stick in hand, like some eminently respectable butler enjoying his day off. She could not help smiling ever so slightly at the walking stick, well aware it must be the latest incarnation of his wand, the magical scepter of the sorcerer-king.

A hundred and fifty years ago, he had preferred to let a shiny silver dress sword serve in that capacity. He had always been so good about adapting to the times, whereas she so often felt like a relic of a bygone era, out of place and time.

"Well. Here we are again. Ramona," he greeted her, his tone raspy with age, but infused with warmth.

"Geoffrey," she replied, hoping he did not notice the slight catch in her voice.

He gazed at her in silence for a long moment. "You haven't changed a bit. Still the same stunner I always knew."

"Poppycock!" she muttered with a modest flush of pleasure.

"'Tis true. You are more yourself than ever before. And that, to my eye, is a good thing."

She gazed at him with far less severity than he deserved. "We are not here to socialize, Zolond, may I remind you."

"Yes, yes." He sighed, and his shoulders slumped. Then he drifted a few steps closer and stared up at the clock face. "I say. Impressive, isn't it? What will they think of next? The inventions these mortals come up with these days."

"They're calling it the Age of Progress. Quaint, no?"

They both laughed quietly, sharing the joke.

"So many brilliant men cluttering the world today," he said in a philosophical tone. He watched the shadow of the giant minute hand inching forward on its rounds, then nudged her. "But we all know how badly brilliant men can err, don't we?"

Ramona nodded at his regret-filled words. "I trust you've dealt with Wyvern?"

"He is at the bottom of an ice cave at the moment. Upside down, I wager," he added with a wily little smile.

She arched a brow.

"You were right. Wyvern was trying to overthrow me, with several members of my own Council assisting him. All those who participated in the raid on Merlin Hall are now in custody except for Captain Dread, but I'll track him down shortly. They all will be dealt with; I promise you that. On behalf of the Dark Druids, please allow me to assure the Order that last night's attack does not reflect the current disposition of the Brotherhood toward your side."

Searching his face, Ramona detected no lies.

"This was Wyvern's doing, not mine," Zolond added. "I hereby formally request that we return to the terms of our former truce."

She frowned but sensed opportunity. "The truce has been broken by your side, Zolond. If you wish to sue for peace, you will have to make additional concessions, as I'm sure you are aware."

He regarded her in amusement. "Tough old bird. I figured you'd say as much." He let out a large sigh. "Very well, milady. What sort of concessions did you have in mind?"

Ramona gave him a hard look, having none of his attempt to charm her. "I want our Lightriders back. All of them."

"Oh, dear," he said with mild surprise, his snowy eyebrows arched high. Then he pivoted and began drifting down the passageway. "I'm sure I have no idea what you mean."

Ramona scowled at his back and followed. "Don't play games with me, Geoffrey. I am the head of the Order now, and I will not be trifled wi—"

"What happened to us, Ramona?" he asked, turning suddenly to face her.

She bristled, offended at the question. "You chose evil over love, Geoffrey. Over me. *That* is what happened."

"And now I cannot un-choose it," he said in a low tone. "The Horned One himself has turned against me." He grimaced. "The afterlife I face now is— Oh, never mind. No use whining." With that, he pivoted and strolled on.

Ramona stared at him, a chill of fear creeping down her spine.

"Wyvern would not have attempted this coup without his father's help," Zolond continued. "Now that I've punished his son, the Beast is sure to take revenge on me."

She narrowed her eyes. "I don't understand. Why would Shemrazul help Wyvern overthrow you? You are the Dark Master."

He shrugged. "I've fallen out of his favor."

"Yes, but how? Why?"

"Because of you, my dear."

Ramona was difficult to surprise, but she could not deny that she was shocked by his answer. "Me...?"

"I was to have no further contact with you. Part of the terms of our agreement, you see. I disobeyed that order, especially of late. To meet you in battle was one thing. That could be excused. But to chat with you like we've been doing on the astral plane, *that* was something else again."

She stared at him in dread, her voice falling to a whisper. "He *knows*?"

"Mmm." Zolond nodded with admirable nonchalance.

Frightened for him, Ramona could not contain her temper. "Blast it, Geoffrey! I told you from the start that this would happen. The wicked always eat their own in the end. But your pride made you so sure that you would be the exception—" She swallowed her tirade when she saw the weary look of pain on his face.

She lowered her head and looked away, striving for patience. She felt so powerless! Truly, it was easier to suffer oneself than to watch an old friend face so terrible a fate.

Ramona looked at him again with welling distress. "Is there nothing that can be done, Geoffrey? Surely there must be some way to outwit the Beast."

"I don't see how," he said calmly. "And, in truth, my dear, I'm not sure I deserve to escape it. I've collected my rewards, done whatever I pleased my entire life. We all must pay the piper in time."

"You can't just give up! If we work together—" She huffed with frustration. "Geoffrey, I am the head of the Order now! If I rally all of the resources under my command—"

"You'll be the next one with a coup on your hands, if you try telling your agents that you want to risk helping *me*."

"But you saved the Order last night by getting rid of Wyvern! Besides, things would be different with you in the future. I feel sure that if you changed your ways, renounced evil, and did a complete about-face from this moment forward—"

He laughed, to her indignation. "No one would believe it, dear. They'd say I merely duped you somehow."

"No, because you'd provide proof!"

He arched a brow.

"If you gave us back our Lightriders and destroyed whatever monsters you've created; if you made amends to the families of all those you've hurt, then perhaps..." But Ramona's words trailed off.

Deflated, not even she knew whether what she was saying was possible.

Geoffrey shook his head. "No, ol' girl. What's done is done. There is too much blood on my hands. I am trapped. No one can help me now. Not even you."

Without warning, the quarter chime erupted from the bells overhead. Zolond quickly cast some spell that formed a bubble around them both, instantly muffling the deafening clamor.

Inside, the sphere was the soft, dark blue of a summer night twinkling with stars. It was as though he'd turned back the clock and brought them back into their own little world, before everything had gone wrong.

Then Geoffrey did something remarkable. He reached over and took Ramona's bony old hand in his own.

She gripped his fingers. Tears sprang into her eyes at the remembered feel of his hand in hers.

He was real. Flesh and blood.

Like a stab in the heart, she could not help thinking of all they had lost.

All that evil had taken from them both.

A normal life. Children. Grandchildren.

Death.

"Ah, where does the time go, Ramona?" he murmured as the Westminster chimes shook the passage around them, and the hands of the giant clock ticked on, incessant as a metronome.

She let out a sudden girlish cry of surprise as Geoffrey whisked her into his arms and danced her around the sphere a few steps.

She laughed in sheer joy, but as the chimes faded, so did their brief bubble of carefully contained happiness.

He released her and gazed into her eyes with a grateful smile. "I love you all the more for wishing you could save me, Ramona. It means a great deal."

"You love me? Still?" Though her heart quaked at his declaration, his words inspired her with a possible way out.

He shrugged. "Guilty as charged."

"Geoffrey, listen to me." She grasped his shoulders. "If there is love in your heart for me—for anyone—then I *know* you can be saved."

"Poppycock," came his sardonic echo of her own favorite word.

"Geoffrey!"

"Alas, no, my dear witch. 'Twould be a comfort to think so. But after all I've done, we both know there is no hope for me."

"My dear Geoffrey." Ramona stared the old warlock fiercely in the eyes. "There is *always* hope."

CHAPTER TWENTY-FIVE
Invisible Bonds

"*I sabelle.*"

When his familiar whisper crept into her mind, Izzy flicked her eyes open and sat up abruptly in the bed where she'd been trying in vain to relax.

"Janos!" Her heart lifted.

"*What's happened?*" he asked. "*I know you're upset. I felt it so strongly that it woke me from my coffin. Do you need my help? I heard you're in London—I can be there as soon as the sun goes down.*"

"No, no, that's all right. I'm fine." Touched by the ex-Guardian's protectiveness, she smiled and lowered her head.

Just hearing his voice at last—albeit silently, through their telepathic bond—made much of her fear for Aunt Ramona's safety recede.

She could feel him searching her, worried.

"*What is it, my dear?*"

"Oh, Janos—" She nearly broke down and told him everything, but then remembered Nixie had sworn them all to secrecy.

Not that a promise to her friend could keep her darling vampire out of her head, especially now. The closer they grew, the better they could read each other.

And so, it took only seconds for Janos to discover what she was halfheartedly trying to hide: namely, the fact that Aunt Ramona had gone off to a private meeting with the Dark Master.

"*Oh, no,*" he whispered darkly. He was silent for a second, but thankfully, Janos was always calm and cool about calamity. "*Well, goodness me. This is a bit of a pickle, to say the least.*"

"I know." Izzy nodded anxiously and folded her legs beneath her as she sat on the mattress. "All we can do is wait until she returns."

"*How could she do this? Meeting with Zolond alone? It's madness.*"

"You can't tell anyone!" Izzy warned him.

Janos was quiet for a moment. "*I don't like secrets anymore, sweeting. You know that. Secrets are part of my old life.*"

"Well, she's not *entirely* alone," Izzy said. "Jake and my brother went after her."

At this news, Janos unleashed a mental string of soldierly words a young lady ought not to hear.

"*Sorry,*" he muttered a moment later. "*Of course they did.*"

"Don't worry, they're not going to do anything," she told him with more confidence than she actually felt on the matter. "They're just going to...keep an eye on her."

"*Dearheart, this is Jake we're talking about. I need to tell Sir Peter. Don't you think? It's the right thing to do. Er, isn't it?*"

He was so cute when he was trying to be moral, Izzy thought, and her heart clenched. It was endearing how he was never quite sure of himself when it came to right and wrong. Well, *she* was sure enough for the both of them.

"No, Janos. Not in this case. Trust me. This is one secret we both have to keep."

She could almost see him shaking his head, hands planted on his waist.

"*I don't like it.*"

"Listen to me!" she insisted. "Aunt Ramona is the head of the Order now. I'm sure she knows what she's doing, or the Elders wouldn't have picked her. This is no time for people to start questioning her decisions. Besides, if you go blabbing, she'll realize it was Nixie who told us, and then my friend could get in trouble."

"*Yes, but this affects everyone. I mean... She's your aunt, and I trust your judgment, Isabelle; I do. But for the record, I think this is a bad idea.*"

"So do I, but we're not the head of the Order. Please, Janos. Keep it to yourself—just for a little while? For me?"

She could feel him give way to a reluctant smile. "*You know full well I'd capture the moon for you, Miss Bradford.*"

From a hundred miles away, Izzy's cheeks warmed at his flirtation. Ridiculous vampire. He held her heart on a string like a helium balloon. She couldn't stop smiling.

"Go back to bed, you," she chided softly. "It's the middle of the daytime. I won't have you turning to ashes on me."

"*Yes, ma'am.*"

"But wait!" she said playfully, feeling so much better after talking to him.

Janos came back to her awareness, smiling. "*What now, pest?*"

She couldn't help but pout a little. "Why were you quiet for so long? You scared me half to death! Why didn't you let me know last night that you were alive?"

"*I was busy!*" he said. "*Ugly fellows with tusks needed killing, and then your aunt sent me on a spying mission.*" He hesitated. "*Merlin Hall's a wreck, I'm afraid, and I'm sorry to say, the Old Father Yew is dead.*"

Izzy lowered her head, saddened. "We heard. But it's more than that." She hesitated, but she knew what she knew. "I felt you avoiding me. Why?"

He was silent.

"Janos?" she prompted when he was quiet too long.

Empathically, she sensed him struggling to answer, which was strange, glib as he was. "What is it?"

"*I...I didn't think you'd want to talk to me anymore.*"

Baffled, Izzy scanned the opulent bedchamber. "Why?"

He sounded hesitant and unsure, very un-Janos-like. "*I figured you'd probably seen me as I ran off into the battle last night.*"

"No," she said slowly, then furrowed her brow as understanding dawned. "Hold on. You thought I would abandon you as a friend because I might've caught a glimpse of you in your vampire form?"

"*Er, yes.*"

"You cakehead!"

"*Well, it's pretty horrible, darling,*" he drawled. "*More than fangs, you know. Let's just say there are times that I'm* glad *I can't see into a mirror.*" She could feel his shrug. "*I figured you had seen me and that you were revolted, and...I should leave you alone.*"

"Oh, Janos."

"*I certainly wouldn't blame you. Don't deceive yourself about me, Isabelle. One turns into a-a nightmare version of oneself, to be frank.*"

"Well, don't worry, I was too busy having a nosebleed to pay attention to much else," she informed him. "Just being in the presence of so much fury strained my gift so badly that I actually had blood dripping out of my ear."

He fell absolutely silent, but she felt his wild surge of hunger at the mention of her blood.

Abruptly, she remembered she was speaking to a vampire.

"Um, never mind," she said.

"*Right,*" he answered in chagrin. "*Sorry.*"

She winced with sympathy for her friend. "Not your fault."

"*Oh, yes it is,*" he said bitterly, but she felt him wrestle the savage impulse back under control within a few seconds.

By his own choice, Janos never drank human blood. His favored source of blood was from the noble stag, but he made sure that his servants kept the animals alive, not draining them completely, but honoring their life force, leaving them strong enough to bound away into the forest again.

"*Anyway,*" he said, "*I'm sorry I worried you. It's just—I could not bear for you ever to be frightened of me, Izzy. You're my only true friend. If you gave up on me—*"

"That's never going to happen! And it's not true that I'm your only friend," she assured him. "We all care about you—Jake and Dani and all of us. And, for my part, I could never be afraid of you, Janos. I know who you are on the inside. You are good, and I believe in you."

The emotions she sensed from him told her that if he had blood in his veins, he'd be blushing at her earnest words.

"*Are you sure you're not a Light Being, Izzy?*"

She smiled, forgetting all about Aunt Ramona for the moment. "When will I see you? I was so scared you'd died in the battle that I just want to give you a hug."

"*Pah, I rarely die in battles. Best bloody part of being undead.*"

She shook her head at his banter.

"*Stick sends his regards, by the way.*"

Izzy's smile soured. "That's nice."

"*He survived the battle, too. Which is really much more impressive than little ol' me, considering he, for one, actually can die. I'm serious! Our boy Maddox fought like a hero last night. You should've seen him—*"

"Stop trying to foist me off on Stick, Janos Gregorian! You know you're the only one who matters to me."

She instantly sensed how her declaration flustered him, and grinned. It was fun to turn the tables on the expert charmer sometimes.

"*And who's being ridiculous now?*" Janos said gently. "*Goodbye, my sweet.*"

He always went away whenever she told him in so many words that she loved him. She knew full well that he cared for her, too, but he never said it back.

He wouldn't let himself.

"Janos?" she said.

"*What now, Miss Bradford?*" he asked, feigning annoyance.

"How old is old enough?" she whispered boldly.

"*Ugh, go away, you pretty little pain in the neck! It's the middle of the daytime, I killed about fifty Noxu last night, and I'm a bit tired, if you don't mind.*"

She giggled into his mind. "Night-night."

"*Wake me up at once if anything happens with your aunt. Otherwise, perhaps I'll see you soon.*"

Then he was gone.

Still glowing, Isabelle glanced at the clock face. How long until she'd be with him again? She had never known anyone like him.

Time suddenly moved too slow.

CHAPTER TWENTY-SIX
Ice-Breaker

B oris Badgerton's hopes surged and so did his ego after his heroic victory in the bridge room. That foolish reptilian should've paid better attention to his duty, because now the creature was dead.

With a bold leap from the air vent, Badgerton had landed squarely on the control panel. Without a moment's hesitation, he had used his front paws to pull the containment levers, unlocking the massive doors to his co-conspirators' rooms.

The reptilian had roared and reached for him, but the monstrous creature was too late. The lifting of the physical doors had given Fionnula an opening to break Zolond's magical seal. In no time at all, the sea-witch had freed her companions, and the four Dark Druids had come swarming out into the corridors to take back control of the castle-ship.

It had been glorious!

They'd battled Zolond's reptilians throughout the Fortress, while, in the bridge room, the crew leaped on the one stationed there. Clearly, the men had chosen Wyvern's side—and who could blame them, after the Dark Master had robbed the navigator of his mouth? While the reptilian thrashed, outnumbered on the bridge, chaos reigned throughout the onyx hallways.

General Archeron Raige had killed the big one, Druk, striking the crocodile-headed warrior with multiple blasts from one of his fantastical guns. Then he'd spun around and fired repeatedly at the two stone gargoyles Zolond had conjured earlier to guard Wyvern's cell. The pair had come screeching out of the basement and rampaged down the corridors, but the muscle-bound soldier kept firing until he'd turned both into a rain of pebbles.

Fionnula Coralbroom, meanwhile, had flooded one of the hallways and transformed herself into a hideous Kraken to fight another reptilian, who had taken full crocodile form for their clash.

A fourth changed himself into a dragon in the great hall, for all the good it did him. What use were his size, claws, foot-long teeth, or even his thrashing tail when the Red Queen could simply turn into a puff of smoke, whoosh up onto the back of his scaly neck, and plunge her darkling sword into the base of the beast's skull, killing him instantly?

In short, within half an hour, Wyvern's allies had taken back control of the Black Fortress—and it was all because of him!

Boris, Lord Badgerton: Dark Druid.

He was so proud that he could've burst.

And now, with the cooperation of the bridge crew, who kept a record of all past coordinates, the rescue of Wyvern was already underway.

Standing on the edge of a crevasse that ran down the middle of an endless snowfield, the general lit another of his strange grenades off his cigar.

Back in human form, Badgerton watched in alarm and covered his ears like the two ladies, waiting for the boom.

Raige was in his element, sheer glee pouring off him.

Badgerton was not at all sure about his comrade's basic strategy.

The general had said he wanted to stun the ice grendels, slow them down and confuse them, then charge in with a sudden, fierce attack.

It sounded reckless to Badgerton. What if the shock waves from each thunderous blast of Raige's magical bombs cracked the glacier under their feet? They could fall through the ice and end up trapped themselves.

It wouldn't take long to freeze to death out here in subzero temperatures, despite the enchanted winter gear that Fionnula had conjured for them to wear.

The sea-witch, back in diva form, clearly thought she looked fetching in her white fur hat and white velvet gown, waves of long black hair tumbling down her back. She'd said she wanted to "look pretty for Nathan," and, well, the truth was, she did.

Still, he could not get the image of that squidy kraken thing she'd become while fighting the reptilian out of his mind.

Frankly, he did not see why they had forced him to join them on this part of the mission in the first place. He was no warrior. Why could he not stay back in the Fortress with Duradel—where it was warm? Hadn't he done enough for one day?

And what were ice grendels, anyway?

Well, whatever they were, they were clearly in chaos down there, courtesy of the general. Piercing screams, shrill and unearthly, echoed up from the depths of the ice cave.

"Guess they're not used to visitors," Raige said with a grin as he pulled a grappling hook out of his duffel bag. He tested the knot securing the rope, then anchored the hook's metal claws in the ice a few feet from the cliff.

Just then, Viola returned from her spying mission, materializing out of her smoke form across from the general.

"They're humanoid. Small but fast. Gray. I counted ten of them," she reported the moment she stood solid once more. Hundreds of years old, the vampire queen hadn't aged a day since perhaps the age of thirty; she was gorgeous and deadly and clad in a long black coat that hugged her figure, but her face was as white as the snowfield around them.

It was a wonder that she could be out here at all, since it was daytime, Badgerton thought. Indeed, as the lieutenant had warned her when they'd arrived, Antarctica was the land of the midnight sun at this time of year.

Undeterred, Viola had simply downed a vial of some special potion known only to herself, as the leader of the vampires. Whatever was in it, it allowed her to go out for a few hours in the daytime, she'd said.

Even so, it was plain that she was uncomfortable. Behind the dark goggles that covered her eyes, she squinted at the harsh glare of the sun reflecting off the snow. It was already giving Badgerton a headache, as well, and he was used to daylight.

"Ten, you say?" Raige looked disappointed as he tossed his loop of rope into the crevasse. "Pah. Too easy."

"They have weapons. They seem"—she frowned—"oddly advanced. They have a ship hidden down there, as well."

"Really? Hmm. Well, they won't be escaping in it, trust me." The general flashed a half-mad smile.

"Did you see Nathan?" Fionnula asked the vampiress anxiously.

She gave a grim nod. "He's immobilized, tied down on some strange contraption. Looks to me like they're doing experiments on him."

Fionnula winced. "Poor darling! We have to save him."

"That's what we're here for, if you'd quit flappin' your gums. Now, let's go," Raige ordered, "while they're still feeling the effects of my grenades!" With that, the super-soldier leaped backward off the edge of the cliff, the rope fast in his leather-gloved hands. He plummeted without hesitation into the twilight of the crevasse.

Badgerton gulped, watching Raige descend. Then he gestured politely toward the cliff's edge. "Er, ladies first."

Viola sent him a knowing look. "Raige'll kill you if you turn tail."

He frowned. Was he that transparent?

Then the vampire queen ran straight at the canyon. Viola jumped high but slowed in midair, brandishing her darkling blade and baring her fangs; amid a plume of whirling snowflakes, she floated downward with fearsome grace.

Next, Fionnula sent him a dimpled smile of amusement. "Don't worry, Boris. I never forget a favor, and you let us out." Her rosy lips formed a cutesy kiss. "Follow me."

With a twirl of her wand and a soft hum of some enchanted melody, the sea-witch conjured a glistening staircase of ice into being. It grew ahead of her as she marched down the steps in her high-heeled red boots.

Badgerton peered down at it, a bit dismayed to find that it left him no more excuses. He tugged at his waistcoat.

"Right," he said under his breath. Then, with a shrug of his shoulders and a twist of his neck, he changed himself into a badger; though it wasn't the most impressive entrance a super-villain had ever made, it was the best he could do until he got his Proteus Power.

The whole blasted point of all this, he mentally grumbled.

In badger form, he dug his sharp claws into the ice like cleats to keep from sliding all the way down—or worse, off the edge of Fionnula's frigid staircase.

It wasn't easy hopping down the slippery stairs headfirst, but he used his tail for balance and took his time. Unsure what awaited them at the bottom, he saw no need to hurry. If the other three were so eager to fight, let them have at it.

The sounds of their clash had already erupted from the bottom of the narrow crevasse. He heard a burst of the general's maniacal laughter and was rather terrified. *What am I even doing here? These people are mad.*

But he couldn't turn back now. As Viola had warned, Raige would kill him if he did not appear. So Badgerton kept hopping down the steps, one by one, to what he was half certain was his doom.

The sheer cliffs of ice towered on both sides of the gorge like ominous tombstones. He was so cold he could barely feel his face, and the blasts and clamor from the fray that awaited him echoed and rebounded off the ice cavern that widened into a deep blue twilight before them.

At least the vampire queen should feel right at home down there. A low whimper escaped him as he neared the fray. Badgerton strove to gather his courage, but unfortunately, lost his footing about ten steps up from the bottom.

Feeling himself about to fall, he clawed at the ice in desperation, but it was no use. The next thing he knew, he was slipping and sliding, tumbling and bouncing the rest of the way down to the bottom, where he sprawled on his belly and went whizzing across the ice like some awkward baby seal, until he crashed, cheek-first, into something solid.

It turned out to be the heel of the general's boot. Raige kicked him away, and Badgerton ricocheted backward like a hockey puck, only coming to rest when he slammed against the bottom of the staircase.

He sat there panting for a moment, trying to catch his breath.

At least he was out of harm's way here behind the three fighters. Sweet Proteus, he was lucky the general hadn't automatically shot him by mistake.

Well aware he had thoroughly humiliated himself, Badgerton winced. His pride hurt worse than his bruised body, but his first order of business, as always, was self-preservation.

Cowering against the ice staircase, he shook his head to clear it and tried to get his bearings. Thankfully, his eyes adjusted to the half-light in seconds; he was used to making tunnels, being underground.

For a moment, he watched the bizarre battle in progress. The general was having a grand time, blasting away at the little gray freaks.

So, those are ice grendels.

Goodness, they were speedy! Badgerton watched them zip and run around the cave. About four feet tall, with oversized heads and huge, jet-black, almond eyes, they looked like some arctic species of big-eyed goblin to him.

But goblins were stupid. They most assuredly did not set up science laboratories under glaciers, nor travel in sleek silver dirigibles. *What on earth?* Badgerton squinted at the disk-shaped vessel ringed with colored lights.

It looked more advanced than Captain Dread's airship, *The Dream Wraith.* How the deuce had those little creatures maneuvered their vehicle down here?

He watched in wonder as the grendels tried to escape the general's aim.

They could run right up the walls on all fours like goblins did. One tried leaping down on top of Viola, but she grabbed it by its big, bulbous head and snapped its spindly neck with a vicious jerk.

Badgerton shuddered. *Yeeks, she's stronger than she looks.* The vampire queen was fast. Mean, too. Why, she seemed to be enjoying this almost as much as the general.

With her preternatural vampire abilities, the black-clad beauty dove and darted almost too fast for the eye to see, evading the burning beams of red light that shot from the grendels' wondrous little guns.

Badgerton had never seen such weapons before. He could well imagine that Raige wanted to get his hands on them as soon as the creatures were dead.

Their blood, he noticed, grimacing, was green.

Fionnula let out a squeak of pain as one of the shining red beams grazed her arm. Infuriated, she struck back with her wand, turning the grendel into a frog—or rather, its own strange-looking version of one. Frogs weren't normally gray...

With all this playing out before him, Badgerton hung back, feeling redundant. He had come down the stairs, like Viola said. That was enough, he decided. His three vicious comrades clearly had matters in hand. He was done risking his neck today.

As the fight raged on, however, the exchange of magical gunfire and wand blasts and red-beam weapons hammering away at the walls of the ice cave seemed to offend the mighty glacier.

It began to creak and groan around and above them in the most worrisome fashion. Badgerton glanced about, fearing the whole cavern might collapse. *We'd better get out of here soon.*

But first they had to get what they came for. *Where is Wyvern?*

He scanned the farther reaches of the cave, his gaze coming to rest on the sight of the mighty Nephilim warlock hung upside down like an oversized ham in a smokehouse.

When Badgerton saw the son of Shemrazul shackled and powerless like this, he stared in utter shock.

Then he looked blankly at the ice grendels darting all around the cave. *These* little pips had done this to a demon-born wizard twice their size?

Egads, *how?*

On the heels of his astonishment, horror washed through him as he realized the true danger they all were in down here.

Just because the grendels were small did not mean they were weak. Certainly, they possessed very high intelligence. Their light-beam guns and fantastical airship made that plain. Badgerton gulped, staring at Wyvern.

Their leader.

The haughty earl could not even shout for help, gagged, his face flushed red from being hung upside down. What if the rest of them ended up like him?

Fionnula suddenly whirled around and snapped Badgerton out of his daze. "Don't just stand there, furball! Do something useful! Here!" The sea-witch tossed him the keys she had swiped off the belt of an ice grendel she'd immobilized with her wand.

Embarrassed by his cowardice, Badgerton quickly turned himself back into a man and snatched the keys up off the ice floor where they had fallen. As a badger, he couldn't catch them, but at least they had slid right to him.

He was straightening up when motion overhead caught his eye. He tilted his head back and spotted an ice grendel scampering across the cave's rounded ceiling right above him.

Badgerton's eyes widened as it started to drop down onto him, but Viola swept sideways, half woman, half puff of black smoke, and hurled the creature against the distant cave wall. Then she flew after it to slash it with her vampire claws.

Impressive lady. With a gulp, Badgerton gripped the frigid metal keys harder in his cold, sweaty hand. Then he raced across the slippery cave floor until he reached Wyvern, pinned down on his cruel contraption.

When he saw how enraged the Nephilim was, he was almost afraid to go near him. Wyvern was trying to kick and scream, but could not move.

His eyes burned with hate.

Clumsy with fright, Badgerton scrambled to tilt the exam table back to a flat, horizontal position. As fast as he could, he used the key to undo the metal bar across the earl's mouth, then freed him from the collar, slowed only by the trembling of half-frozen hands.

Badgerton unlocked the silver steel bands that pinned Wyvern's arms to his sides. As Badgerton freed the earl's wrists, his gaze was drawn to those six-fingered hands, and he gulped.

As soon as his wrists were free, Wyvern snatched the key from Badgerton and undid his ankles himself. With a baleful look, Wyvern leaped off the table. "Give me a weapon!"

Badgerton remained by the horrid contraption, watching in awe as the warlock took his revenge on his captors. Green blood everywhere.

He had a feeling that Zolond was next.

When all the ice grendels were dead, a silence fell. The only sound was Wyvern, Raige, and Viola panting with exertion.

But Fionnula gave her beau a tender look. "Oh, Nathan, what did they do to you?"

Badgerton saw the earl's eyes go lizard-like at the question; his pupils turned into vertical slits like those of a snake.

"We shall never speak of this again." Then he whooshed away in a cloud of black smoke.

Without so much as a thank-you.

CHAPTER TWENTY-SEVEN
Two Spies

J ake eyed Parliament Square in disgust. *Not this place again.* He could hardly believe that their decision to follow Aunt Ramona had led him and Archie right back to the grassy plaza where they'd nearly been killed by phantom assassins last night.

At least he didn't see any Nightstalkers this time. Of course, they didn't come out in daylight. Still!

Jake doubted he would ever look at this seemingly tranquil lawn of the garden square the same way again. The bronze statues of dead politicians stood on their granite pedestals like silent, knowing witnesses to their ordeal.

Ah well, it was over now.

Nearly an hour ago, Nixie had helped the boys escape Buckingham Palace with what she called a Lesser Vanishing Spell. This was for individuals rather than the big umbrella one she'd used last night to hide the whole group.

Slipping out of the palace, the two transparent boys had spotted Aunt Ramona up ahead on Birdcage Walk, hurried after her, and followed at a safe distance until they'd found themselves at the edge of the square.

Meanwhile, the Elder witch marched right up to the wrought-iron gates that wrapped around the Parliament buildings and presented a note to the guards. The boys theorized on the spot it might be from Queen Victoria; Jake had seen their kinswoman coming from the direction of Her Majesty's office, after all.

Whatever the Queen had written, the guards took one look at that little piece of paper and instantly let Aunt Ramona into the gates. One of them escorted her over to the doorway at the base of Big Ben, whereupon she had gone inside the Clock Tower.

This surprised the boys greatly. They didn't let just *anybody* in there.

"Hmm. You know, I've heard that certain spots are considered neutral ground between the Order and the Dark Druids," Archie had whispered from somewhere nearby. Jake couldn't see him. "Maybe Big Ben is one of them."

"Makes sense," Jake had whispered back.

The boys had been waiting for her in Parliament Square ever since.

Their invisibility spell had worn off in the meantime.

A little girl of five or six belonging to some middle-class family who were just leaving the square after finishing their picnic happened to witness the boys' return to visibility. She had gasped, pointed wildly at them, and told her mother they were ghosts.

Awkward. Thankfully, the mother had chided the tot about her overactive imagination and sent the boys an apologetic smile.

They had smiled back, bowing politely. "Ma'am. Sir," they said to the parents.

"But I *know* they're ghosts, Mama! They weren't there and then they just appeared!"

"Now, now, poppet, there's no such thing as ghosts," the father said with great authority while the mother gently pushed the child's hand back down to her side.

"Don't point at people, darling, it's rude. Now come along, take my hand. We need to cross the street. It's time to go home." As the family ambled off, the boys exchanged a *that was close* sort of look.

"Good thing nobody ever believes little kids," Jake said wryly, then nudged his cousin. "C'mon, we'd better get out of sight, now that we're visible again."

The boys had then retreated to the far end of the sprawling green square across from Big Ben. The lengthening afternoon shadows under the colorful, half-stripped trees would also help them avoid their aunt's notice.

There was a low stone wall to sit on while they waited, and tree trunks as well as a couple of statues to hide behind for when she returned.

The boys had already decided that if Aunt Ramona planned on going somewhere else after this, they'd continue their surveillance, but, visible now, they'd have to follow at a greater distance, for if she spotted them, they'd probably get in trouble. Jake doubted that the new head witch of the Order would take kindly to their snooping, even if they were related.

Getting back *into* Buckingham Palace, well, that was going to be a bit of a trick—and Derek and Miss Helena were probably furious right now to find them gone—but Jake tried not to think about that.

Until Aunt Ramona reappeared, there was nothing much to do but keep an eye on the Clock Tower and wait.

"Maybe Zolond isn't coming," Jake said with a bored sigh after about fifteen minutes. He braced one foot on the wall and leaned a forearm on his knee. "We've seen no one else go in."

Archie sat down restlessly on the wall, leaned forward, and propped his chin on both hands. "Maybe he's late."

"Or maybe we were just wrong."

"Oh, I hope so," Archie murmured with a dire look.

Neither of them fancied the thought of their aunt meeting with the Dark Master. It was upsetting enough to think that the Elder witch would go and meet with the treacherous warlock alone, but fine, so be it. She was the head of the Order, and at some point, a parley with the enemy might be necessary.

But this other thing? The past that she shared with Zolond? Jake could hardly believe she'd kept it hidden from him and his cousins all this time. Not even Isabelle had been privy to her secret.

Fortunately, the Elder witch had confided in her star pupil, Nixie. Back at Buckingham Palace, the rest of them had finally managed to drag it out of *her*.

It had just happened a week and a half ago, on Aunt Ramona's birthday, Nixie had told them. She'd made a magical cupcake for her mentor, and the Elder witch had been so touched by the gesture that Nixie had dared to ask how old she was turning. The answer?

Three hundred and thirty-three!

Everyone had gasped to hear Aunt Ramona's exact age. No lady of mature years liked revealing this information, but the Elder witch, especially—for obvious reasons!

Nixie, naturally, hadn't been able to hide her shock upon hearing it. She had dared to ask the obvious next question: *how* was this possible?

The explanation she received was extremely disturbing.

"I still can't believe Aunt Ramona used to be in love with the Dark Master," Jake said. "Or, for that matter, that Zolond was ever good."

"Pfft, three hundred years ago," Archie said, sounding almost as sarcastic as Nixie. "At least now we know why she's so old. It's all *Geoffrey's* doing, using dark magic to prolong his life. Gosh, I hate magic sometimes."

"So does Aunt Ramona. At least now we know why." Jake paused. "Isn't it kind of weird even to think of her being young?"

"*And* foolish," Archie agreed. "This Montague and Capulet spell they did together? How daft! I mean, as fond as I am of Nixie, I would never make my survival from day to day contingent upon hers. Why, it's downright morbid."

Jake nodded in hearty agreement. "I wouldn't want Dani to die if I got killed, either."

Archie sighed and sat up straight while red and gold leaves rustled overhead in a passing zephyr. "Well, I'm sure she regrets it now."

"Let's just hope *we* don't regret spying on her," Jake said. "After all, we know who'll bear the brunt of it if she sees us: me."

Archie chuckled but didn't disagree. "At least you're used to it, coz."

"Aye," Jake said with a roguish grin. But even if they did get in trouble for this, he did not regret coming.

Both boys just needed to make sure their dear Aunt Ramona stayed safe. Well, they had to do *something*! The likes of Zolond could not to be trusted for a minute.

"I can't believe she agreed to meet with him alone," Jake said, shifting position. "And she says *I'm* reckless!"

"Mm." Archie nodded, lost in thought. "I do hope Nixie doesn't get in too much trouble for spilling her secret, though."

"She had to," Jake replied. "Even Isabelle agreed it was the right thing to do." He caught a falling leaf out of the air and fidgeted with it. "Don't worry, if Aunt Ramona decides to be cross, we'll send Izzy in to talk to her. She can't stay mad at Isabelle."

"No one can," Archie said. "You have no idea how hard it is having a sibling who is generally deemed perfect by our parents and the world."

Jake smiled. "Oh, please! Your parents think you're perfect too, Arch."

"Not anymore," he said wistfully as he straightened his legs out in front of him and crossed his ankles, leaning back on his palms. "Or at least they won't once I have the Extraction Spell to get rid of this dreadful clairvoyance."

Jake raised a brow. "You mean it?"

Archie nodded. "Too much going on in one head." He tapped a

fingertip to his temple. "Father will be offended that I have no interest in inheriting his gift, and Mother will probably be disappointed in me, too. But so be it. I can't work with a cluttered mind. And to be honest, if there's bad stuff happening in the future, I don't want to know about it in advance."

"Really?" Jake said. "Seems like it'd be a pretty useful gift."

Archie shrugged. "Perhaps, but it's not worth it. Believe me, I'd much rather be shocked and horrified along with everybody else when bad things happen. Knowing in advance is just too nerve-racking. Especially when I can't do anything about it."

"But what if you worked with the talent for a while? Maybe you'd get more control. That's how it was with my telekinesis. Maybe then your visions would start coming in clear enough that you actually *could* stop the bad things from happening."

He sighed and looked away. "I dunno."

But now that Archie had broached the subject of his budding psychic gift, Jake studied him intently.

He had not forgotten his cousin's panicked reaction back there in the drawing room. Knowing how touchy the boy genius could be on this topic, however, Jake kept his tone casual. "I take it you had another one."

"I don't want to talk about it."

"If it concerns Aunt Ramona, mate, you have to."

Archie glanced at him, his dark eyes full of anguish behind his tortoiseshell glasses.

That look worried Jake anew. This latest vision must've been bad indeed, because Archie hadn't breathed a word about it, even to him. Usually, Jake was the first person he told.

"Come on, coz. I'm your best friend," Jake said. "I've got eyes. I saw your face back at the palace the minute you heard Izzy describe what Aunt Ramona was feeling."

"I don't want to talk about it, Jake! Besides, it doesn't matter anyway." Archie nodded at the square. "Everything's quiet here."

Now you've done it, Jake thought.

Archie stared broodingly at his feet for a second. "It's not necessarily about Aunt Ramona, anyway," he admitted in a low tone. "I'm just being cautious, following her. For all I know, it's probably just a bad dream."

"You said that the last time; then it came true," Jake replied. Archie had dreamed about the kidnapped Lightriders being kept in a big, cavern-like chamber in the basement of the Black Fortress, and then Tex had confirmed its existence after being captured himself.

"Well, this one isn't going to come true, Jake!" Archie's cheeks flushed with anger, but there was fear in his eyes. "I won't allow it! Now, would you please let it go? You've got bigger things to worry about at the moment, I daresay."

"Like what, the Dark Druids' prophecy?"

"No—him." Archie nodded toward a spot behind Jake.

Still unsettled and confused about what his normally open cousin was hiding, Jake turned around. When he followed Archie's nod and spotted the "him" in question, he dropped his foot off the low wall with a groan and rolled his eyes.

"Oh, you've gotta be joking," he said under his breath.

Jake's former nemesis from his pickpocket days was marching past the row of trees toward the boys.

Truncheon in hand, helmet perched atop his head, sunlight glinting off the shiny brass buttons down his dark blue uniform coat, the copper was already frowning suspiciously at Jake beneath his red handlebar mustache.

It was none other than the bane of his former existence: Constable Arthur Flanagan.

CHAPTER TWENTY-EIGHT
The Rupture

"That *is* the policeman who always used to arrest you, isn't it?" Archie asked, sounding all too amused.

Jake huffed. "Aye. Even when I wasn't doing anything wrong!"

Archie's lips twisted. "Guess he figured it was only a matter of time, coz."

Jake shot the boy genius a scowl. By mere force of habit, a surly mood settled over him as the straight-arrow, ever-meddling do-gooder approached.

"Well, well," came Flanagan's cynical greeting, "look who it is. The boy earl 'imself!"

"Good day to you, constable," Archie offered. Clearly entertained, he rose to his feet and slipped his hands into the pockets of his brown tweed jacket, looking like a miniature professor.

Flanagan harrumphed in reply and eyed the boy genius skeptically. Beneath the brim of his black helmet, his shrewd glance said that any companion of a former pickpocket must be a shady character, too.

"What are ye lads doing, lurkin' around the park on this foine Sunday?" he inquired, his voice tinged with an Irish brogue. Flanagan was rookery-born himself, after all, but he'd made up his mind young to rise above it.

"We're not lurkin'," Jake retorted, barely noticing his own Cockney accent from the old days returning.

Master Henry would be so disappointed.

"We're just standin' here, mindin' our own business—*sir.*"

"Lookin' for trouble, I warrant," Flanagan said. "Eyeing up your next mark, eh, ye young troublemaker?"

Jake let out a large, indignant scoff. "I didn't do nuffin'!" he cried. It had once been a very familiar refrain. Not that Flanagan had ever bought it.

Archie glanced at Jake with barely concealed mirth.

Jake fumed. "I'm rich now, constable. I inherited a goldmine. Haven't you heard?"

"Oh, I 'eard." Flanagan nodded slowly, unimpressed. "But in my wide experience, many thieves consider it more *fun* taking others' property, and you, my lad, you always liked your fun, didn't you, Jakey-boy?"

"Actually, sir," Archie cut in smoothly, "we're just here waiting for our aunt, the Dowager Baroness Bradford. She had a meeting with a gentleman inside Westminster." He nodded toward Parliament. "Her Ladyship should be back at any moment. I'm, er, keeping an eye on my cousin until she returns."

"Well, good luck with that," Flanagan muttered.

But he looked reasonably mollified, reading Archie's honest nature in his face after giving him a good, hard stare with a copper's practiced eye.

Jake shook his head at his cousin's annoying habit of always being nice. (Well, *almost* always.) "It's none of his business, Arch. There's nothing illegal about two people standing in a park. He has no right to interrogate us."

"What! I'm only being polite," said Archie. "Honestly, Jake. You should try it sometime."

"Aye," Flanagan agreed, and his lips twitched beneath his red mustache in something between a smirk and a smile.

"Trust me, Arch, you wouldn't be feelin' so courteous if he'd arrested *you* half a dozen times."

"*Weeeell*, Jake, maybe you had a little something to do with that yourself."

"I like this lad," said Flanagan.

"Judas!" Jake said to his cousin with a half-jesting snort. "Sidin' with the copper against your own kin, eh?"

Archie shrugged. "You've had your moments, coz."

"Thanks a lot."

"I'm just saying..."

Flanagan arched a brow as the two boys began playfully bickering as only best friends can.

"Well, go on, then!" Jake taunted his cousin, tongue in cheek. "Why don't you tell him what we had for breakfast, too? I'm sure he'd like to write down all the fascinating details in his little notebook."

"Can't you ever just cooperate?" Archie exclaimed, his eyes twinkling. "The constable's merely doing his job, Jake. I, for one, am glad we have conscientious officers like him on patrol. They protect us from the rabble."

"Ugh!" Jake said. "Toady."

"Juvenile delinquent!" Archie shot back.

Apparently satisfied the situation was under control, Flanagan began strolling off, chuckling to himself.

They waited until the noble copper was a dozen steps away.

"Do you think he bought it?" Archie whispered.

Jake laughed under his breath and nodded. "You're scarily good at charming adults."

Archie grinned.

At that moment, without the slightest warning, a deafening thunderclap split the clear blue sky directly above Parliament Square.

BOOM!

Its reverberating blast shook the ground and nearly knocked the boys off their feet.

They both yelped, startled; Flanagan whirled around and looked straight at Jake.

"What did you do?" the copper bellowed at him.

"I'm just standing here!" Jake cried as the deep rumbling continued.

Then all three covered their ears as the thunder turned into a giant, ear-splitting screech like the brakes on a train trying to make an emergency halt. It made his very teeth hurt.

The horrendous sound traveled off in both directions, then a rush of wind poured out of nowhere, blowing Jake's forelock back wildly from his forehead, and dust into his eyes.

He quickly raised his hand to shield his face from the stinging bits of debris gusting at him, while fallen leaves went whipping past him down the street.

"Saints preserve us!" said the constable, holding on to his helmet.

There weren't many people around, but most of them ran away, screaming. Others ducked or hit the deck.

Top hats and parasols flew by end over end. Petticoats flashed, exposing the ankles of mortified ladies. Passing carriage horses reared up. The pigeons atop Westminster Abbey were blown from their roosts;

they squawked and fluttered anxiously, trying to right themselves.

Across the square, the guards posted outside the gates of Parliament scanned the building, as though they feared a huge boiler had exploded somewhere in the basement.

Good Lord.

"Was this your vision?" Jake shouted over the din.

"No, it was worse!" Archie yelled back.

"Worse?"

"Never mind that—look!" Archie's face was stamped with terror as he pointed at the sky.

Squinting against swirls of wind-blown debris, Jake managed to lift his gaze.

What he saw filled him with horror.

A dark, massive cloud formation had formed directly overhead—like an earthquake in the sky. Its epicenter was directly over Parliament Square, but it was widening fast, racing off in both directions like a giant sewing stitch unraveling, swathed in churning clouds.

The violent wind they were experiencing was pouring out of this tear in the otherwise-blue sky, along with a new, distant noise—a deep, ominous pounding.

Aghast, Jake turned to his cousin while Flanagan held on to a lamppost to avoid blowing away.

"What the blazes *is* that?" Jake shouted.

"Not sure," said the scholar, the tails of his tweed coat flapping behind him. "I-I-I know of no weather event that matches its description, a-and, well, this is just a hypothesis, but I-I daresay... No! It can't be." Archie shook his head vehemently as he studied the sky-quake. "It's not possible."

"What?" Jake roared.

"I-I fear it's a rupture in the Veil!"

Jake stared at him for a second without comprehension.

"Nixie would know for sure," Archie added with a gulp. "It's a-a magical thing, n-not scientific."

"Hold on," Jake said. "*The* Veil? The one separating the magical world from the human one? *That* Veil?"

"Yes, coz. That Veil." Archie nodded, ashen. "I pray I'm wrong," he added halfheartedly.

But, as usual, the boy genius was right.

And all across the planet, the shock wave of the rupture barreled on, breaking the boundary between the human world and the magical one with unstoppable concussive force.

In minutes, it roared past over an already-battered Merlin Hall. Sir Peter looked up at the sky through a hole in the palace roof, saw those legendary clouds, and turned white. Finnderool winced and raised his fingers to his temples, bowing his head. Dr. Plantagenet reached for the nearest tree trunk to steady himself, while the magical zoo animals rebelled in their cages.

Standing sentry on the palace grounds, Maddox and Ravyn glanced at each other in dread. The rupture even woke Janos in his coffin inside his private mausoleum in the Merlin Hall burial grounds.

Out in the forest, Prue (in skunk form) peeked out of a hollow log where she'd been lounging, while at Shadowedge Manor, Victor looked up from his endless homework, scanned the sky, and arched a brow.

"Well, that's new," he murmured. Then he glanced toward Magpen, who had dived under his bed with a shriek.

Farther afield, Izzy's unicorns whinnied and reared up, breaking into a frightened stampede, as did the wilder herd in the woods around Jake's rambling forest cottage in Wales. The gold goblins there screeched in the trees, while in the town, the crystals in Madame Sylvia's mystical shop hummed with alarm, and the dried herbs hanging from the ceiling swung back and forth.

Even in the depths of Jake's goldmine, the old graybeard dwarf, Ufuud, enjoying his after-lunch pipe in the miners' dining hall, sensed a profound change somewhere on the surface world above.

The wild dragons who lived in the forests surrounding the Order dungeon where Uncle Waldrick had been held began roaring and flew up into the sky, breathing fireballs at the frightening phenomenon.

And although Snorri and his giants up in Jugenheim heard nothing, deep in the sea, the merfolk of Poseidonia felt the rupture travel through the water like a tidal wave washing over their world. It swayed the sea trees of the kelp forest, sent schools of fish scattering in a panic, and scared every crab and sea turtle into its shell. Even the giant octopus dozing in the Calypso Deep awoke.

Deeper still, Shemrazul laughed and laughed, while his minions danced and cheered around him. Even Baphomet was impressed, nodding his congratulations from the Tenth Pit.

Eyeball ran around in circles, waving his hands. "It worked, master, it worked!"

"Of course it worked," Shem drawled, gloating on his throne.

"Well done, my boy." Wyvern heard his demon father's praise in his twisted mind and smiled in his dark glasses, the jump almost complete.

The whole catastrophe, however, was felt hardest in London, for that was where the Veil had initially burst.

Queen Victoria, cool-nerved as she was, splotched the note she was writing to the prime minister when her hand jerked at the boom. She looked up warily as the crystal chandelier above her desk tinkled.

A few rooms away, Guardian Derek Stone quit listening to the kids' flimsy excuses about why Jake and the normally sensible Archie had absconded from the palace.

"Oh, what have they gotten themselves into now?" the warrior whispered. He quickly strode over to the window, Miss Helena a step behind him.

"What *was* that?" Dani cried over Teddy's barking.

Brian shrugged, his face blank, but Izzy doubled over in pain.

"Isabelle!" The governess ran to her.

Nixie took her place at the window, stared up at the ominous line of clouds for a moment, and then murmured, "Oh no."

Derek turned to her at once. "What is it?"

Nixie told them, but across the city, Red already knew.

Standing on the roof of Beacon House, the Gryphon crouched like a lion briefly, startled by the boom. Then he stared at the sky in shock.

In all his nine hundred years of life, not even Claw the Courageous had ever seen a rupture before, but he felt it down to the tips of his magical feathers.

He reared up with a mighty war cry, then launched skyward, flapping hard against the great wind, no longer caring who saw him. It didn't matter anymore.

Magic was out of the box.

He swooped lower, shooting down the Strand just above the roofs. He scanned angrily with his eagle eyes to find whoever had done this terrible thing. People stopped and stared at him as he passed, pointing and shouting. Filled with urgency, Red ignored them. Only one certainty beat in his heart.

Evil was coming.

His boy needed him.

He had to find Jake.

With a beat of his wings, he climbed higher into the sky and scanned the city's horizon for Buckingham Palace.

Inside the great Clock Tower, meanwhile, Ramona and Zolond stared at each other in dread.

The Elder witch pressed her hand to her middle, feeling the tear in the Veil like a physical blow to her solar plexus. The sorcerer-king looked equally pained, wincing with a hand to his temple.

"Oh, Nathan," Zolond whispered, his gnarled grip tightening on his walking-stick wand, "what have you done?" He lifted his gaze to one of Big Ben's huge clock faces, but it was difficult to see much of anything through the white-frosted glass.

Ramona stared at the shadow of the huge minute hand.

Alas, when her darling Geoffrey sent her a pained glance, in that moment, it seemed they both knew that after some three hundred-odd years, their time was up.

PART IV

CHAPTER TWENTY-NINE
They're Here

Back at Parliament Square, the wind had eased and the scar-like line of roiling clouds was already starting to dissipate.

Dazed Londoners began climbing to their feet, looking shaken. What *they* made of all this, Jake could not imagine. He barely knew what to think himself.

Although the thunder and the awful screeching noise had receded into the distance with the weird cloud front racing off in both directions, a new sound could now be heard throbbing out of the rupture. It was fainter and farther away, but getting louder.

Jake turned to the boy genius, his heart still thumping. "I don't understand. Why is this happening?"

Archie shook his head, at a loss. "I doubt even Nixie would know why."

"Well, think! Let's try to reason it out. Why now?" Jake said impatiently. "Maybe because the Old Father Yew died? Could the loss of his magic—and the damage to the dome over Merlin Hall—somehow cause the Veil to tear?"

Finally starting to recover, Archie righted his crooked spectacles, picked a stray leaf out of his hair, and gathered his thoughts. "Well... I don't think something this drastic could happen all by itself."

Jake's brows shot up. "You think someone did it on *purpose*?"

"Don't you?"

He narrowed his eyes. "Could they?"

Archie shrugged. "Depends on who it is, I suppose."

The two boys stared at each other.

"Zolond," they said in unison.

About ten feet away, meanwhile, Constable Flanagan was muttering and gathering himself up, as if he hadn't been scared out of his wits along with everybody else.

He adjusted his helmet, planted his hands on his hips, and looked around indignantly. "What in the blippity blazes is that God-awful pounding?" he demanded.

Jake had no idea. But the deep, vibrating rhythm coming from inside the rupture grew louder by the second.

As the constable tilted his head back and peered at the sky, the boys did the same.

Jake's eyes widened as he spotted bluish lightning bolts flickering inside the line of the swirling clouds.

"Oh, no," Archie murmured, seeing them too.

"Take cover!" Flanagan suddenly roared. "This way, boys!" Racing back over to them, the constable grabbed an arm of each and dragged them toward the nearest statue. "Quick! Get behind Mr. Peel!"

He shoved them to supposed safety behind the big granite plinth supporting the bronze statue of the London bobbies' famous founder.

Keeping the boys behind him, Flanagan crouched down and peered around the wide granite block. "Don't worry," he said absently, scanning the square, "I won't let anything happen to you youngsters."

Behind his back, Jake and Archie exchanged a quizzical look. Jake could not deny he was impressed. Even a bit touched. Flanagan was a father, after all, with many children.

Still, the poor copper hadn't the foggiest notion what he was up against here.

"What do you make of it, sir?" Archie asked, as if he couldn't resist.

Flanagan kept his sights firmly on the square. "Freak storm of some kind, I warrant. Or possibly, a Congreve rocket that went off accidentally," he answered, all business. "Must be a Navy ship docked on the river...or a merchant vessel that's armed against pirates. Mishap with one of the cannons, I wager."

"Ah," said Archie, and looked at Jake.

Jake gave his cousin a wince that said he only wished it were that simple.

For his part, he had a rather strong feeling that he knew exactly what was coming through the rupture. He hoped he was wrong, but in the next moment, his worst fears proved all too true.

The Black Fortress suddenly slammed into view in the middle of Parliament Square, smashing trees, crushing lampposts, arcs of lightning still flickering on its spiky black towers.

And there it sat, dead center of the wide, sprawling green.

The stronghold of the Dark Druids, looming in broad daylight, right in the heart of London.

The lightning winked out, the deafening pulsations stopped, and, for a moment, there was utter, stunned silence.

Flanagan was motionless, as if he barely dared breathe. "Mother Mary. What witchery is this?" he whispered, then blessed himself.

Jake stared grimly at the warlocks' traveling castle. "I'd say it's an invasion."

Then a wave of screams erupted on all sides as hysteria broke out, fanning down the streets in all directions.

"This isn't possible," Flanagan whispered. "I'm havin' a dream."

"More like a nightmare," Jake mumbled. "It's real, sir. Trust me. It's real."

Then the massive drawbridge banged down.

"Oh, this is bad, Jake. Very bad!" Archie squeaked, his stare glued to the castle.

Jake nodded, doing his best to keep his dread in check. "I'd say Zolond's arrived. He's late."

The boys had never seen the Dark Master; they didn't know what he looked like, only that he was an old man.

Well, Aunt Ramona had entered the Clock Tower about twenty minutes ago, but no old man had gone in—nor had anybody else.

"Talk about making an entrance," Archie said in a steadier tone.

But if people were shocked by what they'd seen so far, that was nothing, for in the next moment, out came the detestable Lord Wyvern.

Riding a dragon.

The boys' jaws dropped. They exchanged a stunned glance. Flanagan rubbed his eyes to make sure they weren't deceiving him. Then the constable stared around one corner of the statue's base, while the boys peeked around the other, several feet away.

The orange-red dragon prowled down the open drawbridge of the Black Fortress, the afternoon sunlight glimmering on its scales. It carried its head high, sporting small, backward-facing horns; it stood about nine feet tall. But as the body went on and on, slowly emerging from the castle, a few seconds passed before Jake could determine its full length of some twenty feet, snout to tail.

Its front legs were slightly shorter than its powerful hind ones, but all four were tipped with vicious claws. Wings folded against its sides, it did not seem to mind its leather tack.

Wyvern sat proudly in the saddle, controlling the beast by reins that ran through a loop on the cuff-like metal collar around the dragon's throat. He swayed back and forth with the creature's leisurely walk.

Crowds of people had begun to gather at safe distances around the edges of the square and in the surrounding streets to see what was happening. The entire mass of humanity now gawped at the pair in dumbfounded silence.

In the hush, Jake could hear the snarling breaths that escaped the dragon with every exhalation.

Wyvern rode sedately toward the middle of the green, his mount sinking a trail of three-toed footprints deep into the turf.

The dragon swung its head from side to side, sniffing the crowd with a hungry gleam in its eyes.

It must've looked at some lady wrong, for at that moment, somewhere in the crowd, a woman started screaming.

"Silence!" Wyvern thundered.

The dragon lord pulled out his wand and hurled a bolt of magic at her at once, freezing her before the hysteria could spread.

"Remain calm, ladies and gentlemen!" he bellowed. "Do not interfere, and you will not be harmed."

The dragon snorted and tossed its head angrily, hissing at the crowd. It flicked its forked tongue and whipped its tail threateningly from side to side.

"Easy, Tazaroc! Whoa." Wyvern pulled the beast to a halt near the center of the square.

Archie shook his head dazedly. "I don't think there's an oubliette spell strong enough to make all these people forget this."

Jake nodded but wasn't sure it even mattered anymore, if the Veil concealing the magical world from the human one had been torn. He assumed Zolond was responsible, but why would the old warlock do such a thing?

There was still no sign of the Dark Master himself, in any case. Jake concluded that Zolond must be sending his henchmen out first to put down any resistance.

And his henchwomen.

For who should come strutting down the drawbridge next but Fionnula Coralbroom arrayed in her latest fluffy dress, one hand on her hip, the other clutching her wand?

Jake couldn't help but sneer slightly at the sight of his would-be mother.

Bizarre as it was, knowing that Wyvern wanted to adopt him as his son and heir, the prospect of having Fionnula Coralbroom as his stand-in mother was even more revolting, but that was what the demon-spawn earl had in mind. Wyvern had flat-out told Jake so the day the couple had tried to abduct him.

Strangest family ever.

Jake shook his head in disgust as the siren-born sea-witch came marching down the drawbridge in her high-heeled shoes.

He glanced around at the onlookers and wryly wondered if any of Fionnula's fans from her opera days as Uncle Waldrick's ladybird would recognize her.

Humph! They should see her in her Kraken form.

A giant squid with lipstick.

The former diva used to rule the London stage, enchanting audiences with her singing—literally. Little did her admirers know they were being put under spells. Well, maybe now the truth about Fionnula would finally come out.

Unfortunately, London had bigger problems than the sea-witch, for next came General Archeron Raige.

Jake tensed, recalling how the big, musclebound soldier had slain poor Balinor, the Order's head wizard. Warriors were supposed to show honor—Guardians did—but that brute had murdered an old man by throwing a knife into his back.

Raige carried an arsenal of weapons on him: knives, pistols, a bandolier across his chest lined with large bullets and odd-shaped grenades. Walking down the platform with a cigar dangling out of his mouth, he held a strange long gun in his grasp that looked like something Archie could've invented.

It had the flared muzzle of a blunderbuss, and an array of complicated brass attachments whose purpose Jake could not guess. He scanned the square constantly as he followed Fionnula, as though waiting for anyone or anything to make one false move.

Wyvern's disgusting pet manticore followed Raige out. It was a nasty creature—a kingly lion with a scorpion's stinger for a tail.

Archie frowned at Jake. "I thought Maddox killed that monster last night."

Jake shrugged. "Wyvern must've healed it."

Nearby, Constable Flanagan let out a low oath at the sight of the manticore. No doubt convinced he was having a bad dream, he paid the boys little mind.

All three focused intensely on the square as a second Dark Druid villainess emerged from the castle, gliding down the drawbridge with preternatural grace.

Jake didn't recognize her, but despite the eccentric dark goggles she was wearing, he could tell she was quite beautiful, with jet-black hair and milk-white skin.

Instead of a gown, the woman wore a long black coat with a high-standing collar. The coat was open, revealing her masculine-style riding garb beneath—a loose black shirt, black riding breeches, and tall black knee boots like a pirate.

She had no wand, and the only weapon she carried was a big, nasty knife on her hip. Her lack of a wand made Jake wonder uneasily what her power was. He wasn't sure he wanted to find out, for she carried herself with the confidence of a seasoned destroyer.

Archie nudged him. "I'm pretty sure that's the Red Queen," he whispered.

Jake glanced at his cousin in surprise. "She's a vampire?"

"She's *the* vampire," Archie murmured. "I think she even made Janos. Her name is Viola Sangrey. She started out as a Hungarian countess centuries ago, from what I've heard."

"Huh." Jake looked at Viola again. "How is she out in the daytime?"

Archie shrugged. "Who knows? Dark magic? Maybe the rules other vampires have to follow don't apply to her."

Jake nodded. Then both boys growled as none other than the traitor himself emerged from the warlocks' castle: Boris, Lord Badgerton—disgraced Elder of the Order.

The portly shapeshifter, with his double chins and bushy sideburns, looked nervous as he ventured down the drawbridge, and he should be.

Jake wondered if the skunkies knew about their traitorous uncle.

Finally, an eerie-looking trio came out, dressed all in black.

Tall and slim, with graceful movements, the three men had long, pale hair and complexions whiter than the vampire queen's. But the borders of their long, narrow faces were adorned with serpentine swirls or dotted designs that might've been tattoos or warpaint.

As they walked out three abreast, the two on the ends seemed like warriors; they wore a sort of supple, close-fitting armor of black leather. The one in the middle, by contrast, was draped in flowing velvet robes. Arcane symbols in silver thread were embroidered around the hem and sleeves of his priestly garb.

The two warriors—bodyguards?—were watching out for him as he felt his way down the drawbridge, tapping ahead of each step with the tall, richly carved staff he was carrying.

When Jake saw his milk-white eyes, he realized the man was blind.

Chills instantly skittered down his body as he realized this must be Duradel, the infamous Drow seer who had given the Dark Druids that prophecy about Jake.

Duradel was the one who had claimed that Jake would either become the greatest leader the Dark Druids would ever have or destroy them for once and for all. That was the whole reason Wyvern was so desperate to get control of him.

Archie gave him a sober look but said nothing.

Stomach churning at this reminder of the prophecy, Jake tried not to let the sight of Shemrazul's high priest unnerve him. Instead, he focused his attention on the fact that he'd never seen one of the Drowfolk before.

They certainly bore a strong resemblance to their cousins, the wood elves, like Finnderool, but the Drow were the dark fey. The two branches of elves had split long, long ago. Unlike their forest-dwelling cousins, the Drow lived in underground caverns with the spiders and bats—and usually went bad.

Archie shuddered. "He's a creepy one, in'nt he? By Jove, I don't fancy the thought of having anything in common with that weirdo."

"Well, coz, you might see the future, but at least you're not evil," Jake said quietly.

The moment he spoke, Duradel suddenly turned and looked straight at the Robert Peel statue, as if he'd heard his whisper.

Unnerved, Jake shrank back behind the granite block. It was then that he noticed Constable Flanagan making hand gestures across the square to his fellow policemen guarding the Parliament buildings. When Jake peeked out again around the boys' side of the plinth, he saw the other bobbies gesturing back, as though planning to interfere.

Which would be a terrible idea.

Jake doubted a whole regiment of Guardians would have much luck going up against this many Dark Druids at once.

Absently, he remembered that Derek had arrived at Buckingham Palace. No doubt the warrior was already on his way, along with any other Guardian who might've found himself in London at the moment, drawn by their protective instincts.

But brave as they were, what could the Order's fighters really do against this lot, with all their dark magic?

Besides, as far as Jake knew, there were probably a hundred Noxu barbarians waiting inside the Black Fortress for Wyvern's call—the same shock troops who'd overrun Merlin Hall last night. He shuddered to ponder the sort of mayhem that scores of wild half-trolls could wreak on the unsuspecting city...

Then Wyvern addressed the crowds of cowering civilians.

"Ladies and gentlemen!" he boomed in a deep, cold voice full of authority. "A new day has come. The world as you know it is about to change. As promised, you will not be harmed as long as you stay out of our way. All will be explained in the near future. For now, stay back...and enjoy the show."

With Zolond's top henchmen arrayed across Parliament Square (except for Badgerton and the three Drow, who remained on the drawbridge), Jake fully expected that Wyvern would now present the Dark Master to the world.

But that was not at all what happened.

CHAPTER THIRTY

Insurrection

D erek Stone was fast.
Dani, Nixie, Isabelle, and Brian could hardly keep up as the towering Guardian shoved through the terrified crowds flowing by in the opposite direction.

Dani did her best to keep the big, rugged Guardian in sight as she ran, her gaze glued to his dark hair and the brown jacket hugging his clifflike shoulders.

The streets of London were in chaos, even in this stately part of Town. Ordinary folk careened down Birdcage Walk, so scared that they didn't even notice Miss Helena galloping behind the warrior in leopard form.

Derek had ordered the kids to stay behind at Buckingham Palace, but there was no chance of them doing that if Jake and Archie—or Lady Bradford—were in danger. Of course, their first attempt to follow Derek had earned them a glimpse of his full Guardian wrath. When he'd bellowed at them to stay behind, Teddy had run under the couch with a whine. Dani had nearly done the same.

The master Guardian had then stalked out to the hallway and yelled for a few palace guards to keep them detained, then he was out the door—racing toward the danger, of course. Miss Helena had transformed into her elegant black leopard and followed her fiancé.

Brian and the girls, meanwhile, found themselves locked in the same fancy drawing room as before. Even the earnest Yank agreed they had to break out.

Dani was beside herself, knowing down to the marrow of her bones that she'd find Jake at the center of the tumult. Isabelle and Nixie were likewise desperate over Archie. And everyone was anxious for the Elder witch.

Their minds made up, the kids wasted no time escaping their gilded prison.

While Nixie got ready to use a spell, Brian went to the window and used his keen Guardian eyesight to find Derek and Helena outside so they'd know which way to go once they broke out. Dani had ordered Teddy to stay in the palace, where he'd be safe, while Izzy brought everyone their outdoor coats.

Resolved, they were ready in moments.

Then Nixie zinged the lock on the door with her wand—and zapped the two Foot Guards who tried to get in their way.

She'd knocked the big soldiers over like bowling pins, and they'd quickly escaped.

The next thing Dani knew, she was running up Birdcage Walk, keeping her eyes on Derek Stone, who stood head and shoulders above most in the throng.

The whole road was clogged with people fleeing in the opposite direction. The carriages that had been passing through had come to a standstill, their drivers barely managing to keep their horses calm in the mayhem.

"Don't go that way, children!" a lady in a feathered hat shouted frantically as she tore past, but she didn't say why.

The kids exchanged worried glances, but pressed on.

At Dani's height, it was difficult to see what was happening in the crush.

Isabelle was the tallest of the kids, and even she was only to the shoulders of most of the fleeing adults. Poor Nixie—Brian had to grab the petite witch by the wrist to keep her from getting trampled altogether.

Suddenly, Dani heard a mighty eagle's screech somewhere overhead and behind them. Struggling to keep moving forward, she glanced over her shoulder and spotted Red in the distance.

She halted her friends and pointed. "Look!"

Rocketing toward Buckingham Palace, the Gryphon was fully visible above the treetops lining the broad avenue of the Mall.

The kids stared with astonishment—and they weren't the only ones who saw him.

Half of London did.

To be sure, the sight of a lion-bodied, eagle-headed beast who looked like he'd just leaped out of some knightly coat of arms would tend to get people's attention.

The already panicked citizens and tourists shrieked, pointed, and stared as the Gryphon winged his way by.

"What's he doing, showing himself in public like that?" Dani cried.

Wide-eyed, Izzy stood panting. "He's searching for Jake."

"Red!" Dani yelled, waving her arms, but she was too far away, and her shout was swallowed up in the mayhem.

The Gryphon circled Buckingham Palace a few times, then dipped out of sight.

"Where'd he go?" Brian asked.

"I don't know," Dani said.

"Don't worry, he'll find us!" Nixie said. "We've got to keep moving! Archie and Jake might need us. Let's go!"

The others nodded, then they continued pressing forward. But all of them were grim-faced, knowing they were probably heading straight to the spot that everybody else was running *away* from.

* * *

Jake and Archie, meanwhile, were still crouched down behind the statue with Constable Flanagan, waiting to get their first glimpse of the infamous Dark Master.

But instead of introducing him, Wyvern threw back his head and shouted so loudly that they could almost see his double rows of teeth.

"Zoloooond!" the Nephilim bellowed. "I challenge you! Come down here and fight me!"

"Fight me?" Archie echoed.

The boys looked at each other in astonishment.

"It's a coup," Jake breathed, narrowing his eyes.

Suddenly, everything clicked into place.

"Of course..." Archie said in amazement. "The attack last night, the rupture—it was all Wyvern's doing, not Zolond's!"

"Which means"—Jake's gaze climbed up the Clock Tower—"he's already up there with..."

He didn't finish the sentence. He didn't have to. For in the next heartbeat, Aunt Ramona and a snowy-haired old gent whooshed into view on the lawn in a puff of gray smoke. They both had their wands at the ready.

"Oh no," Archie whispered, but Jake was taken aback at the sight of the Dark Master.

Why, he wasn't scary at all.

He looked like somebody's old grandpa—stately and strict, perhaps. But he certainly didn't look like the evilest person on the planet.

Wyvern, on the other hand, did.

The earl jumped down deftly from the saddle and ordered his dragon to stay. Then he swaggered forward, loosening up his wrist as though warming up for a serious magical duel.

Zolond appeared unperturbed. Slowly and calmly, the old gent walked forward, leaving Aunt Ramona behind where they'd landed.

He showed not the slightest fear of Wyvern or his dragon, though he was small and frail compared to the towering Nephilim.

Ah, but when the sorcerer-king spoke, the tone of power emanating from this understated figure revealed who was really in charge.

"Nathan: your actions are completely out of line." His deep, elegant voice boomed across the square. "You attacked the Order unprovoked, and now you have ruptured the Veil. It is the unforgivable sin."

"No, old man!" Wyvern flung back while the other Dark Druids kept a wary distance.

Badgerton slipped back inside, the coward.

"The unforgivable sin is how you betrayed the Horned One. For her," Wyvern said with a sneer at Aunt Ramona. "Your rule is over. Not even your foul ice grendels could contain *me*!"

"You are rash, Nathan. Let us take our quarrel elsewhere, away from prying eyes." With a twirl of his black wand, Zolond started to whoosh off in smoke form.

Aunt Ramona must've persuaded Zolond to draw Wyvern away from the city before the two had come down from the Clock Tower.

Unfortunately, all Zolond succeeded in doing was enraging the half-demon earl.

"Do not attempt to transport out of here, you traitor!" Wyvern yelled. "If you attempt to flee, I will unleash a blaze worse than the Great Fire of 1666. You have my word that I'll burn this city to the ground!"

People screamed. Flanagan tensed. The manticore roared, agitated by the clamor.

Jake swallowed hard.

"Settle down, Thanatos! Calm these cattle, Fionnula," Wyvern said curtly.

Fionnula's eyes gleamed as she stepped forward, all too happy to sing.

"Quick, cover your ears, sir!" Jake told the constable. "She casts spells with her singing. You'll see!"

Archie nodded earnestly at Flanagan and pressed his palms over his ears. Jake did likewise. Flanagan frowned but followed suit, and signaled to his fellow coppers across the way to do the same. The other policemen looked confused, but did it anyway as Fionnula started to sing.

The siren enchantress lifted her hands and proceeded to soothe the frightened crowds with a gentle lullaby.

Aunt Ramona glared at her, but at least Fionnula kept the people from stampeding in a panic. Within a few bars, they'd settled down.

Jake wished they would all go home.

When Fionnula ended her song, the boys cautiously uncovered their ears. Flanagan did the same, then furrowed his brow at the tranquil mood that had settled over the throng.

Across the green, Zolond had returned from a puff of black smoke to stand beside Aunt Ramona. The Dark Master and Elder witch exchanged a grim glance.

When Jake saw Aunt Ramona touch her knuckles fondly against "Geoffrey's" equally bony hand, the rest of the story became clear.

"I'll bet she's been working on him in secret to try and turn him good," Jake whispered to his cousin. "And she *must've* succeeded to some extent, because Wyvern hates him now."

"But Jake..." Archie turned to him and paled. "If they fight, Wyvern and he—if Zolond dies—then we lose Aunt Ramona. Because of that accursed Montague and Capulet spell!"

Jake's mouth went dry. "You're right." He looked back out across the square. "I have to help her."

"Sorry to say it, coz, but I'm afraid you have to help them both."

"What, help Zolond? Are you joking? That miserable old man was the one who probably gave the order to kidnap my parents! Everything I've suffered is his fault!"

"But he must've changed his ways, at least somewhat, if Wyvern wants to kill him!"

"So? It's too late. I don't care. Let him die."

"Jake!" Archie gripped his shoulder. "If Zolond dies, then so does Aunt Ramona."

Drawn up short by the reminder, Jake frowned toward Parliament Square, where the two warlocks were glaring at each other and starting to circle like swordsmen.

"Listen to me," his cousin said while Jake seethed. "Normally, I would never ask you to risk your neck for anyone, let alone your worst enemy. But this is different. And I'm not just talking about the Montague and Capulet spell." Archie gulped. "I *have* had another vision, Jake. And it's awful."

Jake went very still. "What?"

Archie spoke with difficulty. "That someone I care about...is going to die."

He froze. "Who?"

"That's just it—I don't know! The dreams wouldn't say," Archie exclaimed. "That's why I didn't share it. I didn't want to upset everyone. At the battle last night, I thought it could even be you. But when you survived *The Dream Wraith*, I was worried sick it'd be my parents.

"That's why I panicked when they insisted on staying behind at Merlin Hall. But now, Jake, now I...I think it might be Aunt Ramona." Archie's face was ashen. "That's why I insisted on following her here. Please, coz. You've got to save her. Even if it means saving Zolond."

It was at that moment that Constable Arthur Flanagan rose to the occasion. Adjusting his helmet, he gripped his truncheon, gestured with it to the other policemen, then marched out and began blowing his whistle before Jake could stop him.

Archie gasped. "What is he doing?"

"Oi! You there!" Flanagan hollered at the Dark Druids as the bobbies who'd been guarding Parliament hurried out to join him. Meeting up on the green, they filed after Flanagan toward the demon-spawn earl, a nervous troop.

Jake shook his head in shock. "He's insane."

"That's right, I'm talking to you, mister!" the stalwart copper yelled at the Nephilim. "You can't park that castle 'ere!"

Wyvern turned with a smirk, barely hiding his surprise.

"I don't know who you think you are, or what you're on about, but this is a public area! You're going to have to move along. Go on! Off with you, now!"

Even Zolond arched a brow.

"Oh, this is bad," Jake whispered, shaking his head.

His mind was still reeling over Archie's latest vision—and now Flanagan was going to get himself killed.

"You 'eard me!" the constable shouted. "Off you go!"

Wyvern sent the vampire queen a sardonic look. "Care to do the honors?"

"With pleasure," Viola purred with a wicked smile. Then she moved languidly toward the bobbies, intercepting them before they reached the two warlocks. "Officers, what seems to be the problem?"

Neither Jake nor Archie had ever seen a vampire turn on that magnetic charm peculiar to their kind before. Her goggles were odd, true—like something an evil Archie would invent—but her intriguing smile cast a spell over most of the males in the crowd.

The bobbies shifted uncomfortably.

"How gallant you are, putting yourselves between Lord Wyvern and these poor, frightened people..." The treacherous beauty continued sweetly praising them like they were the greatest heroes in the world, and the men couldn't help but smile and glance at each other as though they agreed.

Only Flanagan seemed immune to her persuasion. Her vampire charms fell flat with the scowling constable.

When she trailed her hand over his shoulder, drifting past him, Flanagan pulled away in disgust. "That will do, madam! I am a married man, thank you very much."

The Red Queen unleashed a graceful laugh but was obviously annoyed by the brush-off—as evidenced by the emergence of her pearly fangs.

Aunt Ramona stepped forward, having had enough. "Don't touch him again, you filth!"

"Stay out of this, you old hag! We'll deal with you later," Viola replied.

"Hag? You're older than me!" Aunt Ramona retorted.

It was then that a fierce caw overhead heralded the arrival of the Gryphon. The crowd gasped at the sight of a third mythical beast in plain view, flying overhead.

The Dark Druids looked up, and so did Jake.

Relief filled him as his fierce protector's eagle-eyed stare homed in on him and Archie crouched behind the Mr. Peel statue. Red dipped as if to join him, but Jake waved him off, anxiously signaling to him not to give away the boys' location.

Fortunately, after all their adventures together, the Gryphon got the message and climbed higher into the sky, well above the treetops.

As he began gliding like a hawk in wide circles over Parliament

Square, ready to swoop in at any moment to defend them, Jake noticed that, much higher, the weird line of clouds from the rupture had nearly faded away.

"He's a welcome sight," Archie murmured.

"Aye," Jake said. But although he was glad to have Red nearby for reinforcements, Jake was not at all happy about the public seeing his Gryphon.

Many were pointing and staring, agog. People liked gold, and gryphons knew how to find it in the earth. It wasn't safe for Red's existence to become common knowledge.

Ah, well. Erasing the onlookers' memories was a problem for tomorrow—one the Elders would have to try to fix.

For now, Jake supposed Derek probably wasn't far behind. The man had a talent for showing up just when he was needed.

Jake quickly scanned the square but didn't see the warrior yet. The clogged streets probably explained his delay. Knowing Derek, he might well have taken to the rooftops as a clearer route of running here.

Expecting him at any minute, Jake glanced around at the Dark Druids, making sure they did not intend to try and hurt his Gryphon.

The dragon hissed and the manticore roared. Red retorted with a war cry. Wyvern ordered his animals to settle down.

Dread had filled Fionnula's face, meanwhile. The sea-witch was particularly frightened of the Gryphon—with good reason. She had helped Uncle Waldrick capture and cage the beast on the day of Jake's parents' supposed murder.

Waldrick and Fionnula had kept the poor Gryphon prisoner for eleven long years.

All that time, the sea-witch had used the magic in Red's feathers to transform from her true, hideous appearance as a squid lady into the glamorous opera star. The star of the stage, whom Uncle Waldrick had been so proud of squiring around Town.

Then Jake tensed as General Raige pointed his big, strange gun at Red as he circled overhead.

Fortunately, the Gryphon saw the threat at once and zoomed higher, out of range.

"Hold your fire, Raige!" Wyvern barked, scanning the square. "If the Gryphon's here, it means my son, Jake, is somewhere close."

"Son?" Aunt Ramona scoffed. "What a ridiculous presumption! You will never sink your claws into my nephew."

The Nephilim smirked at her. "We'll see."

Meanwhile, Zolond had been staring at Wyvern with a look that could've drilled holes into him.

The tension at that moment was excruciating.

The vampire queen resumed toying with the policemen like a cat with a mouse, but Fionnula lost patience, casting a nervous glance at the sky.

"Quit dawdling, Viola! Let's get this over with!" The diva turned impatiently to her new beau. "Nathan?"

Wyvern nodded at the vampire queen. "Quit fooling around."

"Aww. Very well. Sorry, boys." Viola's red lips curved into a sneer, robbing her of all beauty. "You should've left when you had the chance. Now I'm going to start *drinking your blood!*"

Chaos broke out at her words. Screams. When she lashed out at Flanagan, raking her claws across his chest, Jake instantly drew Risker and shot to his feet behind the statue.

The crowd began stampeding off in all directions while the bobbies pulled back, yelling to each other.

As Viola sought her next victim with a twisted smile, the Elder witch lifted her wand to protect the lawmen, but Fionnula quickly blocked her bolt of magic with a counter-spell.

Some good, stout-hearted men in the crowd tried to rush to the bobbies' aid, but Thanatos leaped in front of them and roared in their faces. They stopped cold, while Raige held the crowd back on the other side of the square.

All the while, the dragon watched Red wheeling overhead, its head swiveling on its long, sinuous neck. Jake shuddered. Surely this was all just a nightmare.

He felt hollow with fear and anger at the whole situation. His heart thudded at the prospect of going out there, and his grip turned clammy on his magical dagger. One little knife didn't seem like nearly enough to bring against that many Dark Druids.

But when he glanced skyward, he saw Red watching him alertly, waiting for his signal. The Gryphon's presence bolstered his courage.

He braced himself to enter the fray. "Right. Stay hidden, Arch."

"Will do, believe me," Archie mumbled, also rising to his feet. "Be careful."

"Don't worry. Wyvern won't let them hurt me. I'm the Black Prince, remember?"

"What are you going to do?"

"I'm not sure yet. I'll figure something out."

"Good luck." Archie patted him on the shoulder. "And don't forget, you need to help Zolond."

"Do my best," Jake promised grimly. "But first, I've got to save Flanagan." With that, Jake left the shelter of the granite pillar and jogged out cautiously onto the square.

"Oi! Vampire! Hey, you rancid cow!" he yelled in his loudest, rudest voice. "Why don't you come try that on me?"

CHAPTER THIRTY-ONE
The Battle of Parliament Square

E *gads,* thought Archie, staring after Jake with a mix of pride and dread. *My cousin might be an ex-juvenile delinquent, but by Jove, he is the bravest chap I've ever seen.*

As Jake ran toward the policemen, the Drow prophet came to attention on the drawbridge.

"The chosen one!" Duradel cried, his white eyes staring in Jake's direction.

Archie grimaced. Honestly, if being clairvoyant meant he was going to end up as uncanny as that fellow, he might as well schedule the Extraction Spell for tomorrow.

Well—provided the world still existed by then.

If it did, he and his cousin were probably going to be grounded for a very long time, judging by Aunt Ramona's blanch when the doubler entered the fray.

The dragon sniffed curiously in Jake's direction, and Thanatos snarled. Red still glided overhead, waiting for his cue.

"Why, look who it is." Viola left off tormenting the bobbies and pivoted to face Jake, her long black coat swirling out around her as she turned. Her nails dripped with blood, but so far, she hadn't bitten anyone.

(Archie, admittedly, liked her goggles.)

Poor Flanagan still held his ground, trying to calm his men and restore order, but the red-mustachioed bobby was starting to look like he'd run afoul of a tiger. Several of the shiny brass buttons down his chest had popped off when she'd clawed him. His smart blue uniform had four long rips in the front, showing the white shirt underneath.

Only...that shirt was turning red from the cuts on his chest where

Viola had slashed him with her long vampire nails.

"Get away from him!"

As Jake marched over and planted himself between Viola and the bobbies, Archie glanced across the lawn to gauge Wyvern's reaction.

A cold smile had curled the Nephilim warlock's creepy mouth.

Jake raised his knife like a warning finger in the Red Queen's face. "You leave these men alone, ye mark me?"

The bobbies looked astounded at his arrival. Constable Flanagan in particular appeared shocked at this interference from the former street urchin. Viola scoffed and started to retort, but Jake interrupted.

"I gave you an order, lady! You know the prophecy! I am destined to become the future Black Prince, and the greatest leader the Dark Druids will ever have, and if you don't *back off* right now and do *exactly* as I say, I will remember this against you and *all* vampires when I'm the one in charge. Savvy?"

Wyvern burst out laughing in delight. He looked around at his henchmen with fatherly pride.

Aunt Ramona frowned. Zolond looked astonished, but Fionnula giggled, and even Raige grinned.

"What are you sorry lot laughing at?" Jake demanded, glaring at the smilers.

Good heavens, he might actually make a rather good Black Prince, at that, Archie thought, half impressed. In truth, his cousin could be a very nasty lad if you got on his bad side.

(Archie didn't really have a bad side.)

Viola pressed her lips together as though holding back a chuckle. Planting her hand on her waist, she turned and looked at Wyvern with a shrug.

Duradel was beaming. "He is magnificent! Oh, Shemrazul, you are wise..."

"Ugh!" Jake rolled his eyes and turned to the policemen. "Go, sirs! This isn't your fight. Get Flanagan out of here. He's hurt."

"Now, now, you're just a boy," the constable said. "I'll not be leavin' ye to fend—"

"Go, sir! Please!" Jake cried. "Before she drinks your blood, or the sea-witch turns you and your men into toads—or something worse. I've seen her do it!"

The bobbies stared at him and realized he wasn't joking. There was a castle on the lawn, after all, where there ought not to be one. Archie watched it dawn on the group of officers that there were things happening here beyond their ken, magical matters well outside their jurisdiction.

"Go!" Jake said again, shooing them away with his free hand.

After exchanging uncertain glances, the bobbies decided to take his advice and began retreating, to Archie's relief, bringing Flanagan with them.

At first, the constable balked, but Jake insisted. "Go, sir. You're losing a lot of blood. Your kids need you; don't tempt her. Can't you see what she is?"

Flanagan looked again at Viola, who smiled sweetly, flashing her fangs.

"Mother Mary." The lawman finally glanced down at himself, saw the cuts, and paled. He staggered slightly, feeling the wound at last, Archie presumed.

He had learned in his medical studies that people didn't always realize they were injured in the thick of battle.

Thankfully, the bleeding constable allowed the others to assist him off the field; Jake let out a visible sigh of relief.

"I told you my son is a natural leader," Wyvern boasted to his friends. "Even these trifling human authorities obey him."

Jake spun to face the Dark Druids, his cheeks reddening with fury. "You think I care one jot for your approval—you monsters?"

"Oh, calm down, princeling," Viola started.

"*Don't* tell me to calm down!" With a sudden, angry flick of his hand, Jake used his telekinesis to knock the goggles right off her face.

They went flying and the Red Queen screamed. Archie's jaw dropped. Viola Sangray flung her arm across her eyes, blinded by the brilliance of daylight.

"Quickly! Take her inside," Wyvern ordered Duradel's two Drow assistants. "We can't risk her turning to ashes."

The mysterious, black-clad warriors hurried out to assist Viola back into the Black Fortress with Duradel.

Archie smiled from ear to ear. *Well done, coz!* One down, three to go.

Somehow he stifled the urge to clap and cheer his cousin on. This wasn't a cricket match, after all. Besides, Jake had ordered him to stay hidden. Archie was quite happy to comply. He kept silent, leaning against the granite block.

"Fionnula, go and fetch our son," Wyvern ordered the sea-witch.

"Bring him inside. Where he'll be safe. The Horned One is eager to meet him."

Fionnula nodded uneasily, then headed toward the doubler.

As she approached, Jake gave a loud whistle. Red landed on the grass beside him, spread his wings, reared up, and roared in her face.

The sea-witch shrieked, raising her wand to keep the angry beast at bay.

"Rein him in, Jake!" she said in a shaky voice. "Make him behave, a-and you'll be allowed to bring him with you. Lord Wyvern says every b-boy deserves a pet."

"I'm not going anywhere with you lot, and neither is Red." Jake nodded toward the Gryphon. "He doesn't like you very much, you know."

Red stalked toward her, snarling; he crouched like a lion, then sprang at the sea-witch. She fended him off with a blast of magic, but stumbled in her high-heeled shoes and landed on her bottom with a girly screech.

Jake laughed heartily, pointing at her and hamming it up, while Red shook off the wand blast, looking slightly stunned.

Before the Gryphon could recover, Archie spotted Raige across the square twisting one of the brass attachments on his blunderbuss. Archie drew in his breath as the general took aim at Red.

"Look out!" Archie yelled, pointing, but as Jake and his pet both turned and scowled at him for revealing his presence, Raige's strange gun sent a hunter's net flying out over the Gryphon.

Red instantly thrashed, caught in the rope netting. Fionnula jumped to her feet and blasted the beast again.

"Leave him alone!" Jake yelled. He rushed to free his pet as the warrior stalked toward them.

The infuriated Gryphon had already tangled two of his paws and one wingtip in the net, so Jake had to calm him down before he could cut him free.

Then Archie's eyes widened as Raige glanced over at *him* on his way to help Fionnula capture Jake. Raige sent Archie a look of pure evil.

He melted back behind the Peel statue, but stayed there only for a moment. He could not resist looking out again from around the granite block.

"*Yes!*" Archie whispered as Jake pulled the shredded net off the Gryphon, then managed to whip a piece of it around Fionnula's ankles.

Jake gave the rope a hard yank and sent the sea-witch sprawling on the ground once more. "Don't ever attack my Gryphon again!"

Archie's eyes widened as Jake then used his telekinesis to send Fionnula tumbling and rolling across the lawn, screeching in protest, like she was being blown away by a mighty wind.

Red roared as if to tell her she deserved it, and even Aunt Ramona gave way to a chuckle.

Archie grinned. *Jolly well done, coz!*

Alas, Jake's triumph was short-lived.

When Archeron Raige began stalking toward him, Jake quickly sheathed Risker and lifted both magical hands, ready to block nets, bullets, or whatever else might fly out of the general's gun at him or his Gryphon.

"Get behind me, Red. I'll see to this mumper," he said.

Raige snorted. "Wyvern might spoil you, but I won't, princeling." He twisted the attachment on his gun again with an ominous click. "You either follow orders and get inside the Black Fortress, or I'll blow up that stone block where your little friend is hiding. It'd be a shame if the whole thing fell down on him, wouldn't it?"

"Archie, run!" Jake yelled.

"I'm going to count to five, then I shoot. One. Two..." Raige set his sights on the bronze Sir Robert Peel and began stalking toward it. "Three."

Archie backed away, cursing himself for stupidly revealing his location. But he refused to leave his best friend to his fate.

"Four."

Across the square, a look of fury darkened Aunt Ramona's face.

Before Raige's count reached five, however, Derek Stone rushed out of nowhere, nearly knocking Archie off his feet as he brushed past him, barreling out onto the green and tackling the general just a few yards away.

The blunderbuss flew out of Raige's hands; Archie ducked, afraid the gun might go off when it landed. It didn't.

A split-second later, Miss Helena galloped by, shadowing Derek in her elegant black leopard form, ready to assist.

As the warriors started brawling, the leopardess quickly nudged the weapon farther from Raige's grasp with her flat feline nose.

Unfortunately, the moment Thanatos spotted the other big cat, he roared and bolted after her in full attack mode.

"Helena!" Derek yelled in horror as the manticore charged.

Leopard-Helena ran for her life. Derek tried to go to her aid, but Raige caught him in a headlock, his bulging biceps flexed against the Guardian's throat.

Wyvern laughed at all the mayhem—until Zolond whacked him with a massive crackle of magic.

Aunt Ramona flung a lightning bolt at the manticore, but missed. The two big cats ran too fast around the square.

"Get him, Red!" Jake said.

Red let out a war cry, diverting the manticore's attention.

The monster skidded to a halt, scoring the grass with claw marks. Thanatos quit chasing Helena and turned as the Gryphon launched toward him.

The crowd screamed and Archie held his breath as they clashed: half-lion against half-lion.

The barbed, venomous scorpion tail of the manticore whipped to and fro as he tried to stab Red. The Gryphon flapped a few feet off the ground, attacking the tail from above. Red locked on to the armored appendage with his vicious beak and razor-sharp claws.

Strong as he was, Thanatos waved Red around as the two struggled. The Gryphon beat his wings with great determination and slowly began lifting higher off the ground.

Just then, Dani, Brian, Nixie, and Isabelle nearly gave Archie a heart attack as they all came bumping up behind him.

"There you are!"

"Where's Jake?"

"Thank goodness we—"

"Look!" Archie interrupted, pointing toward the square.

His friends followed his finger, then their jaws dropped as they saw Red lifting Thanatos off the ground by his horrid tail.

"That's it! Get him, boy!" Jake cheered. "Throw him in the river!"

"Lions can't swim," Izzy murmured, staring.

Of course. That was the reason Red had been afraid for so long to fly over water, until Jake had trained him better.

Roaring furiously, Thanatos used his front claws to try to hold on to the turf, to no avail. The Gryphon carried him higher and higher, dangling his enemy from his beak and slowly moving toward the river.

"Sweet Hecate," Nixie mumbled, glancing around at the various battles in progress.

Derek and the general were trading punches like battering rams.

Fionnula had sorted herself out and headed back to try to get control of Jake after Raige had also failed, but Aunt Ramona blocked her, while Zolond and the Nephilim walloped each other with orbs of magical energy.

"Is that a real, live dragon standing on the lawn or did they slip us something funny in our food?" Brian asked, staring wide-eyed at the creature.

"He's real," Archie said.

Then Miss Helena loped over to the kids. Even in her leopard form, Archie could see she looked shaken.

"Reer!" Golden-green cat eyes gleaming, their shapeshifting governess nudged them back toward the trees with her fuzzy, feline head. She hissed at them to stay back, but her attention was divided between minding them and keeping an eye on her beau in case he needed help.

Derek and the general were surprisingly well matched.

"Jake! Get over here!" Dani insisted. Her face was frantic as she beckoned to him.

She should've known better.

Still standing out on the green, he scowled to see her and the others. "Go back to the palace!"

"No!" Dani retorted.

He waved her off and kept watching Red, who had managed to carry Thanatos up, up, and southward, moving steadily toward the river.

Unfortunately, somewhere over the Houses of Parliament, the Gryphon lost his hold on the monster. The manticore dropped onto a flat section of roof, where their fight continued out of view.

The bloodcurdling sounds of it were awful enough.

Hearing the two half-lions' battle made the kids exchange stunned glances.

"And I thought hearing two housecats fighting was bad," Archie said.

Helena hissed, as though offended.

The strangest of all the battles by far, however, was the one raging between the half-demon earl and the sorcerer-king.

Things were escalating between the Dark Master and the would-be usurper. The spells they were using on each other were growing scary and downright weird, Archie thought. The kids started clumping together instinctively, much like they'd done last night under Nixie's invisible umbrella.

None of them had ever seen anything like the warlocks' duel. Indeed, in all its two-thousand-year history dating back to the Roman occupation, London itself had never witnessed such a contest.

Zolond uttered a spell that created nine copies of himself, then they shuffled around in a sort of human shell game.

Archie lost track of which Zolond was the real one. But all ten copies of the old man moved in unison, lifting their right hands, in which a glowing orb of energy now appeared, swirling with orange and blue flame. Then all of the Zolonds launched their fiery spheres at Wyvern at once.

Most of them hit, and Wyvern roared, but his rugged Nephilim constitution kept him on his feet beyond what any normal man could have withstood.

Wyvern quickly conjured a long metal shield, like knights used to carry into battle, and fought back with his wand from behind it. The Zolonds merely laughed as Wyvern kept zapping the different copies of him with jagged bolts of magic from his wand.

The ones the earl destroyed merely vanished; none of them turned out to be the real sorcerer-king.

The whole firing-squad of Zolonds kept striking Wyvern again and again with more energy spheres until, finally, the glowing balls all converged into one huge sphere that slammed into the earl. The direct hit knocked the usurper off his feet.

"Nathan!" Fionnula cried as Wyvern went rolling across the grass, leaving a smoking tear through the smooth green turf.

He landed flat on his stomach, arms splayed out before him, while all the extra Zolonds reconvened into one. Wyvern looked across the dueling field at the real Dark Master in volcanic wrath.

"All of you, stay out of this!" he yelled to his allies. "This is between the old man and me!" Then he lifted his right hand toward his mouth and whispered something into his sleeve.

From out of his starchy white shirt sleeve crawled a large insect. A centipede, as it turned out, for Wyvern then spoke some foul enchantment to the creature that made it grow and swell into a massive beast—a gigantic version of itself, some ten feet long, bristling with disgusting hairs.

The people all around the square screamed at the sight, and Archie shuddered. He was not squeamish about insects—or, rather, arthropods in this case—but that thing was big enough to eat a man. He happened to know, also, that centipedes were frightfully fast...and carnivorous.

Dani and Isabelle made noises of utter revulsion and stepped backward, grimacing.

"That thing better not come over here," his sister mumbled.

Dani tugged on the witch's sleeve. "Nixie, can you fend it off if it does?"

"I don't know! Shh!" Nixie exclaimed. "This is fascinating."

Archie raised a brow at his sweetheart. No doubt she was taking mental notes, he mused as she stood riveted, marveling at each volley the warlocks exchanged.

Wyvern pointed at Zolond, uttering some command. At once, the monstrous centipede began scuttling toward the Dark Master, jaws snapping.

An arctic smile curved Wyvern's lips as he waited to see what the old sorcerer would do.

Zolond smiled back with a look that sent gooseflesh down Archie's arms.

Then the Dark Master cracked open his mouth and stuck out his tongue—which turned into a large, black, writhing king cobra.

The whole crowd gasped at this nauseating feat; the kids jolted with low cries of disgust. Even Aunt Ramona grimaced.

"Oh, blech!" said Dani. "Dark magic is gross."

Nixie nodded with a wince.

The black snake coming out of Zolond's mouth waved about in midair, its hood unfurled, as though it were dancing for a snake charmer. But as the giant centipede sped toward it, the cobra began spitting what must've been a fiery and painful poison at the hundred-legged monster, for it squealed and changed course, confused.

It zoomed around and tried another angle of attack, but the snake kept spitting its venom, splattering the centipede until the hideous thing reared up with a piercing screech.

The poison clearly affected the arthropod's nervous system, Archie thought, because the centipede went wonky after it had been hit enough times. It curved its long, segmented body into a ring and raced around in tight circles about a dozen times, then died. Whereupon it shriveled back down to normal size and disappeared.

Zolond duly ended his distasteful snake spell.

Aunt Ramona shook her head at him with chiding amusement as he drew his tongue back into his mouth, a normal human organ once more.

"Yuck," Izzy muttered.

With Zolond distracted by the centipede, Wyvern had had a chance to gather his strength. He now struck back, shouting a curse over his wand.

At once, the Dark Master dropped his walking stick.

The kids gasped as his left arm began to wither, becoming thin and bony, with discolored skin, until that, too, disappeared, and he was left with no more than the bare bones of his arm and hand.

"What's happening to him?" Brian asked.

"He's turning into a skeleton!" Dani said.

"Sort of," Nixie said, staring. "Wyvern hit him with a wasting curse."

The ring Zolond was wearing dropped off his fleshless phalanges and bounced across the grass.

Wyvern extended his hand and summoned the ring toward himself.

It began rolling in the direction of the Nephilim, as if with a mind of its own.

Archie could see that Zolond was in trouble. The wasting curse was taking hold of him, the skeleton effect spreading across his chest and creeping up his neck.

"Geoffrey!" Aunt Ramona yelled. "Use a healing spell!"

But Zolond had dropped his walking stick/wand.

"Oh, botheration," the Elder witch muttered, then whooshed over to her old friend's side in a puff of white, sparkling smoke.

"I didn't know she could do that!" Isabelle and Nixie said in unison, then exchanged a glance of surprise.

In the twinkling of an eye, the dowager baroness arrived by Zolond's side.

Wyvern smiled and strode toward the ring still rolling across the grass. Archie tensed, worried that it might somehow give the earl the power to finish them both off.

"Hey, Wyvern!" Jake suddenly yelled. True to his promise to help the Dark Master for their aunt's sake, he used his telekinesis to knock the warlock off balance.

Wyvern tripped and stumbled sideways a step before quickly regaining his balance. "How dare you?"

The shove must've broken his focus, because Zolond's ring stopped rolling toward him as he turned angrily to his chosen son.

Jake was ready, already striding toward him.

Archie's heart pounded.

The moment the earl presented a wider target, pivoting to scowl at him, Jake drew Risker and, in one swift motion, hurled his blade at the Nephilim.

The kids gasped in unison; time seemed to slow.

Archie watched the magical dagger fly across the empty space between his cousin and the warlock, and then pierce Wyvern's chest.

Aunt Ramona paused in her hurried effort to heal Zolond, looking over in shock. Even Derek and Raige paused in their brawl. The dragon came to attention, seeing its master struck.

"Oof!" The knife plunged into Wyvern's chest up to the hilt.

"Nathan!" shrieked Fionnula.

Even Jake looked shocked that his knife had found its mark. He took a step backward as the sea-witch rushed to help her beau.

Wyvern brushed her off angrily, glaring at Jake. The crowd stared in silence. Archie held his breath.

With a wince, Wyvern slowly drew the bloody knife out from between his ribs.

From the corner of his eye, Archie saw Dani watching Jake with her hand over her mouth.

"That was...very naughty of you—son." He sounded pained. But, still holding on to Jake's dagger, Wyvern touched the bleeding hole in his chest with the tip of his wand.

The wound started closing.

Then the magical Norse weapon wriggled free from Wyvern's grasp and started flying back, as usual, to its master.

What happened next, not even Archie's visions could have predicted.

"That's curious." Wyvern looked intrigued as the bloody knife started gliding back toward Jake, handle-first.

"Halt!" he suddenly bellowed. Lifting his arm, Wyvern slowed Risker with a summoning wave of his freakish fingers.

The knife trembled in midair; it seemed to struggle to inch back toward Jake. But the half-demon lord somehow overpowered it.

Instead of continuing back to its rightful owner, Risker stopped, hovered halfway between the two opponents for a moment, and then slowly turned, compelled by a force greater than whatever magic the old Norse gods had forged into it.

Archie's jaw dropped. So did his cousin's.

Wyvern flicked his fingers, summoning the weapon.

"Hey!" Jake looked on, thunderstruck, as Risker glided back obediently toward the warlock. "You can't do that!"

"Oh?" When the knife stopped, floating before him, Wyvern reached up, plucked it out of the air, wiped his blood off the blade on the side of his trousers, and then...

The kids gasped with horror as Wyvern tilted his head back, opened his mouth so wide that they glimpsed his infamous, sharklike double rows of teeth, and pushed Risker slowly down his throat like the sword swallower that used to entertain crowds at Elysian Springs.

But instead of simply gulping it down, Wyvern chewed the metal, staring at Jake matter-of-factly all the while, his horrid teeth crunching and grinding the blade into bits.

Archie barely breathed.

Pausing then, as if he'd got a bone, Wyvern reached into his mouth with his finger and thumb and pulled out the blue gemstone from Risker's handle.

He wiped the stone off, then rolled it back to Jake across the grass like somebody's lost eyeball. "Here you are; this part you can have."

Jake stopped the rock with his toe, then looked up slowly at his would-be father in shock.

Wyvern swallowed his mouthful, daintily wiped the corners of his lips, then turned to the dragon and pointed at Jake.

"Tazaroc: *fetch.*"

The dragon roared, as though it had been waiting eagerly for any invitation to participate. Everyone screamed as the beast bounded across the lawn toward Jake.

He stumbled backward, but the nine-foot monster was nearly in arm's reach within seconds. There was no time to run.

Jake used his telekinesis to try to fling Tazaroc back. Knocked sideways, the startled dragon caught its balance with its front feet. But as Jake turned and started to bolt, the orange beast flicked its long tail and swept his feet out from under him.

Jake went sprawling on the grass, and the dragon was upon him with an almost playful leap.

It thinks this is a game, Archie thought, aghast.

Pandemonium broke out. Everyone reacted at once. Derek roared and fought to go to Jake's aid, but Raige nearly knocked him out cold. Aunt Ramona left Zolond to his half-skeletal state to whack the dragon with a bolt of magic, but Fionnula blocked it.

Wyvern was laughing. "Good boy! Take him inside, Taz. He's our guest of honor!"

Dani let out a deafening scream and tried to run out onto the square, but Brian grabbed her and held her back. Not even Nixie had a solution. Archie and Isabelle exchanged a resolute glance and started to run out, but Leopard-Helena leaped in front of them and roared.

"Red! Red!" Dani shrieked. But the Gryphon was still on the roof of Westminster Palace, fending off poisonous stabs from the manticore's tail.

Jake was out there alone, doing his best to get away, but fear made him unusually clumsy. Jake had only just scrambled to his feet when the dragon captured him.

Tazaroc grasped him by the arms, wrapping its talons beneath Jake's armpits. In a heartbeat, the dragon shoved off the ground on its back feet, launching into the air with a flap of its leathery wings.

It did not fly high, but it was fast, swirling around with its prize and banking toward the open drawbridge.

Jake kicked and thrashed to no avail as he dangled helplessly from Tazaroc's claws.

"Jake!" Archie screamed as the dragon sailed gracefully into the Black Fortress and disappeared.

CHAPTER THIRTY-TWO
Belly of the Beast

"**P**ut me *down!*" Jake fought the dragon's grip for all he was worth. It was useless.

The massive beast was unbelievably strong, its hold on him like wearing a pair of steel suspenders. Its hooked claws pinched the backs of his shoulders. The sound of its wingbeats filled the air, and the feel of its reptilian skin was tough, cool, and leathery as Jake strove to pry its talons off him, to no avail.

Though he tried at all times to make light of calamity, Jake was pretty well horrified. He'd been captured!

This can't be happening.

Still in shock at seeing Wyvern *eat* his magical Norse dagger like a pretzel stick, he could not believe he'd now been kidnapped by a bloody dragon.

In truth, he could hardly believe the warlock even *had* a pet dragon. But he supposed it was no more bizarre than *him* having a pet Gryphon.

Wherever that thankless beast had gone!

Jake gave a mental harrumph. Claw the Courageous was off having a grand time battling the manticore—right when Jake needed him most.

Figures.

Once more, Jake was on his own, but so be it. Anything was better than bringing the whole gang with him into the stronghold of the Dark Druids.

His friends' screams faded behind him as Tazaroc banked toward the spiky-towered castle. When the dragon flapped its wings and spun its body sideways, Jake's legs swung out helplessly to one side. Then the beast dipped, swooping beneath the pointed arch of the huge Gothic doorway. The next thing he knew, Tazaroc released him.

Flung across the black stone floor, Jake crashed to earth—a hard fall onto his left hip and shoulder. He cursed with pain and kept rolling onward across the cold flagstones.

His head was reeling when he finally managed to stop himself and looked up, dizzied, to see where the monster had gone.

The dragon landed a few yards ahead of him, but it now turned around eagerly to examine him, all winding tail, rust-colored hide, and claws.

Jake's heart pounded as he faced the towering creature. He didn't move, praying it didn't eat him.

Tazaroc crouched, watching him with an almost frisky air, as though ready to chase. Its golden eyes gleamed with intelligence. Its long tail snaked weightlessly behind it.

Jake was no expert in dragons, but it seemed to be waiting to see what he would do.

Since it did not look inclined to attack, he let his gaze dart about for a second to figure out where he was.

The world was still spinning after all that rolling, but he beheld a vast, dim great hall with a vaulted ceiling and plain, round iron chandeliers.

Blimey. Everything was black. There wasn't a window in the place. The only light came through the open drawbridge, or from wall sconces enclosing weird, low blue flames.

Corridors, tall and wide, opened off the great hall in three directions—right and left and center, with the last directly across from the drawbridge.

The vast chamber itself was more or less empty. Despite the gloom, Jake could make out an elevated dais on one end; on the other, a second-floor gallery with an iron banister looked down upon the vast, bare space.

What little furniture there was had been pushed up against the walls. Maybe ten long medieval-style tables, twice as many benches, and a few throne-like chairs of dark wood.

The dragon hissed at him impatiently, but Jake only spared the beast an uneasy glance before his gaze flicked back to those three dark hallways.

He had no idea where they might lead, but the thought skimmed through his mind that if reports were correct, his parents were lying unconscious somewhere in the building even now.

Maybe, just maybe, he could find them. Save them...

Temptation gripped him.

"May I be of assistance, Lord Griffon?" someone politely asked in an accent he'd never heard before.

It had a dark, lyrical quality, edged with a slight hiss.

He looked up sharply, ready to defend himself.

One of Duradel's eerie, white-haired bodyguards bent to offer him a hand up from the floor.

Wary of these strangers, and certainly unwilling to let anyone touch him, Jake stalled for time as he sat on the floor, still panting. He had every intention of making a run for it, and his thieving days had taught him the usefulness of keeping his center of gravity low to the ground.

The only question was whether to head for the open drawbridge and escape or chance his luck down one of those dark hallways and make a play to find his parents.

Tex had said that all the captive Lightriders were being held somewhere in the bowels of the castle...

The Drow warrior waited, his black-gauntleted hand outstretched.

Jake waved him off. "Give me a minute," he mumbled. "The room's still spinning after all that."

"Of course, sir." The warrior retreated half a step, bowing.

It seemed the dark elves had retained their woodland cousins' obsession with courteous manners. *Humph.* Jake still didn't trust 'em.

Then he covered his nose vaguely, noticing the smell of death that hung in the air. "Ugh, what is that stench?"

The tall, stately Drow looked embarrassed. "Er, apologies, Your Highness..."

Your Highness? Ugh. Apparently, they were in on this whole Black Prince delusion too.

No wonder. The prophecy itself had come from Duradel, inspired by none other than Shemrazul, the Dark Druids' demon-god. So Jake had heard.

Charming.

"We are still finding dead Noxu here and there throughout the Fortress," the Drow chap said in chagrin. "They, er—how you say?—took ill recently and perished."

"What, all of them?" Jake asked, startled. "How?"

"Zolond killed them," the other pale bodyguard replied with a no-nonsense stare.

"Really?" Jake's eyebrows shot up. *Guess that's what they get for siding with Wyvern against the Dark Master.*

But those big half-trolls were vicious!

"Aw, c'mon! You're tellin' me that decrepit old codger killed *all* of Wyvern's Noxu?"

"Correct."

"Blimey. And how'd he do that?"

"Dark magic," the second warrior said sternly.

He had the same dark, singsong accent as the first, but different face markings.

All three Drow sported various dots, bars, and flourishes around the hairline and cheekbones, but while the first chap, the polite one, had a crescent moon above one eye, the second, unsmiling fellow, had an upside down triangle in the center of his chin.

Duradel, for his part, had impressive winglike tattoos fanning out from his eyes.

Their face markings probably had a meaning, but Jake had no idea what it was. Interestingly, though, the ink used in their designs had a shimmering quality. It was blue-black, probably made of indigo, but it twinkled as if it had been mixed with crushed diamonds or pearls.

Maybe it made their face paint easier to see in the darkness of their underground cities, especially against their stark white faces.

At any rate, this second warrior—Triangle Chin, Jake dubbed him— seemed like more of a hard case. Planted by Duradel's side, he cast a few wary glances at the restless dragon, but mainly stared at Jake, as though he fully expected him to run.

Well, he was right about that. But, biding his time and waiting for the perfect moment, Jake still had not decided which way to go. Back down the drawbridge and out into the fray? Or deeper into the Fortress to try to find his missing parents?

There was really no question. It was risky to the point of madness, perhaps, but the temptation to get his family back was too strong.

All he needed was a chance to escape the great hall without getting eaten by a dragon or captured by these formidable Drow.

Duradel had been listening to their exchange, smiling to himself the whole time. "Do not be afraid, Your Highness," the oracle spoke up.

Same accent: courteous, slightly evil.

The Dark Druids' high priest wore a necklace with a large jeweled spider for a pendant, secured by bats with outspread wings. "You are in no danger here, but, as Lord Wyvern said, our honored guest."

"Uh, thanks."

Duradel gestured vaguely with his carved wizard's staff. "Allow my servants to show you to your chamber. I am sure you will find our accommodations to your liking." Then the blind seer listened intently, waiting for Jake's reply.

Jake stifled a cynical snort. If Duradel were any good as a prophet, he should've predicted his next move.

Gathering himself to escape, ready to draw on all his old thieving skills at eluding the bobbies, Jake eyed the distance between himself and the three dark hallways.

The center one was out. It would require him to run straight at the dragon, and he wasn't that dumb.

The corridor to the right might work—taking him underneath the overhanging gallery.

But for some reason, the left-hand corridor intrigued him. True, he'd have to cross much of the great hall and not get caught by the dragon, then exit down by the dais.

From there, well, he'd just have to see. But something inside—instinct, maybe—told him that was the route he should go.

Now: how to get past these warriors?

Jake hid his smile. The trick, as he'd long since learned in escaping Constable Flanagan, was faking your pursuers out—making them expect you to head another way.

"May I assist you, Your Highness?" The polite one with the crescent moon above his eyebrow returned and bent to offer Jake a hand once more.

This time, however, his arctic-blue eyes were steely. "Come." It was more an order than a request as he stretched out his hand again.

"I don't need any help," Jake grumbled, brushing him off. He rose slowly to his feet, only pretending to cooperate.

His pulse pounded, flooding him with newfound energy to bolt. His fingers tingled with readiness to slam these pasty-faced blokes with his telekinesis.

Duradel seemed harmless, but his bodyguards were armed with some serious weapons. Each wore an elvish bow and a slim quiver of arrows on his back, as well as a long sword sheathed at one hip with a dagger on the other. But considering they deemed him some sort of royal personage, Jake already knew the imposing pair wouldn't hurt him.

Tazaroc, however, was another story.

The dragon hissed, as though it could hear Jake's heart pumping faster, smell the blood rushing into his muscles to fuel his sprint.

It would not be easy outrunning this thing.

But maybe, just maybe, there was a way he could slow the beast down. Jake eyed the iron chandelier hanging several feet over Tazaroc's head.

Crescent Moon looked pleased that Jake had decided to come along peacefully. The Drow took a step back and gestured toward the center hallway. "If you'll follow me, sir, the guest chambers are this way."

Jake nodded and turned slowly, pretending to obey...

Then he struck without warning—hurled Crescent Moon backward ten feet with a blast of telekinetic force from his right hand, then pivoted, flung Triangle Chin to the ground with his left—and sprinted off across the great hall.

Jake ran as fast as his legs would carry him; behind him, Duradel shouted with startled confusion.

But Tazaroc was his main concern.

Jake heard the dragon coming: a snarl and a rasp of claws on flagstone zooming up behind him, bounding strides propelled by that sinister luffing of leathery wings.

Jake glanced over his shoulder and saw the dragon bearing down on him like a runaway train. He paused while he still had enough of a lead on the beast to stay out of the reach of those teeth. Lifting both hands with great concentration, Jake walloped the dragon with all of the focused energy he could summon.

Tazaroc collided with an invisible wall and went tumbling sideways with an undignified yelp.

Unsure what just happened, the confused dragon sprang to its feet again and shook its head, dazed.

Jake did not give Wyvern's oversized pet time to recover, levitating one of the tables leaning by the wall off the ground.

With a wave of his hand, he sent it flying through the air, crashing into the beast. Jake immediately followed up with several benches and chairs, battering the dragon from a safe distance. Tazaroc roared, befuddled by the attacking furniture.

The Drow warriors were not so easily dislodged. They, too, had regained their feet and now prowled toward him from both sides.

Heart pounding, Jake cursed under his breath to see other men, in gray uniforms, hurrying into the great hall to see what was going on.

Taking stock of the situation, they quickly arrayed themselves across the open drawbridge to keep Jake from getting out of the Black Fortress.

That wasn't his intent.

The dragon shook off the splintered furniture with an angry grunt and glared at Jake, as if it sensed he had something to do with all this.

Jake realized he had better act fast, or that thing would be upon him in a heartbeat. Lifting his right hand, he poured forth a fierce stream of telekinetic energy and pulled the massive chandelier out of the ceiling.

Standing right beneath it, Tazaroc looked up just as the iron ring plunged straight down over its horned head, pinning its wings against its shoulders. The dragon went mad. Jake grinned as the orange beast thrashed, trying to free itself.

When the Drow rushed back to move Duradel out of the angry dragon's way, Jake took that as his cue to go.

He raced the rest of the way across the great hall, flashing past the dais on his left in a few more strides. As the dark maw of the hallway he'd chosen yawned before him, he entered without hesitation.

Leaving the great hall in chaos behind him.

CHAPTER THIRTY-THREE
Labyrinth

Jake soon found himself in a dark labyrinth of black granite corridors. The walls and floors alike were slick and glossy.

What little light there was came from the same type of sleek wall sconces he'd seen in the great hall. Low flames flickered behind grayish glass, casting arrows of blue light upward onto the walls every fifteen feet or so.

As his eyes adjusted to the interior twilight of the warlocks' stronghold, his other senses grew keener—unfortunately for his nose. He couldn't help gagging on the stench of dead half-trolls wafting on the hallway's chilly draft.

His ears, meanwhile, began playing tricks on him. The stone surfaces all around him created strange echoing effects.

It was disorienting.

He could hear the dragon roaring with frustration back in the great hall, as well as the shouts of the crewmen and the dark elves, but it was hard to gauge the distance or even the direction it was coming from.

The hallway itself was eerily quiet. His boot heels hammered down the empty corridor as he ran, but Jake did not waste time on stealth just yet.

The dragon and the Drow would come hunting him soon. At the moment, speed was everything.

Just keep moving, he urged himself—like in the old days, when he'd used the rookery's intricate web of crooked alleys to escape the bobbies.

He flung around turns at random when he found them, scanning constantly for a stairwell to the basement. That was where he needed to go.

Jake vividly remembered that day at Merlin Hall a few weeks ago, when he had spied on a private session of the magical parliament. With his own two ears, he'd heard Lightrider Tex's report on what he had experienced during his capture.

The cowboy agent had told the audience of magical representatives that all the kidnapped Lightriders were being held in some sort of strange laboratory somewhere in the basement of the Black Fortress.

That *should* include Jake's parents, if indeed Lord and Lady Griffon were still alive after twelve long years in this horrid prison.

Jake believed in his heart of hearts that they were. He had to. Aye, they were here somewhere, he could feel it, and everything in him needed to find them, save them...

Unfortunately, Tazaroc and his master had other plans.

Jake clenched his jaw at the thought of Wyvern as he pressed on. *You're not my father.*

There! Suddenly, Jake spotted the opening to a dark stairwell. He ran to it and peered in, but the steps only went up. He raced on with a scowl.

It was odd, though. The deeper he went into the Black Fortress, the more he felt cut off from daylight and the world of the living.

The darkness was tangible in this place. It seemed to slide over his skin with an oily chill. The layout made no sense to his logical brain.

Its blue-black passageways twisted and turned, zigged and zagged, stopped at inexplicable dead ends, or forked unexpectedly, only to circle back.

The whole place must've been designed by a madman, he thought. The lack of windows, moreover, was making him claustrophobic.

Forget the rookery—this black maze took him right back to his brief stint as a coal-mine boy. All those twisting underground tunnels...

Jake shuddered at the memory.

The orphanage director had had a policy of sending all his charges off to various forms of child labor once they reached the age of nine.

"Boys and girls, you have to earn your keep."

Jake had sampled half a dozen unpleasant careers under apprentice masters with no qualms about beating their future employees into submission with a whip, a paddle, or a backhand across the face.

Even so, he had been more frightened of the choking darkness in those blind underground passages than he had been of any apprentice master.

Cruel older boys who had been there longer than he had made his terror all the worse, abandoning him in the depths of the mine so he had to find his own way out. He'd got revenge, of course, before it was all said and done. He'd made them pay.

Then he ran away and became a thief.

He did his best to route the dark memories of those days as he sprinted on, but his chest had already tightened with half-forgotten fears.

At least he knew something now that he hadn't known back then: that it was all the Dark Druids' fault.

If the evil brotherhood had not set out to kidnap any Lightriders they could get their hands on, he never would've been subjected to that grim world. The world of orphanages, cruel masters, heartless bullies. The world of hunger, poverty, loneliness, and shame. Why, he had been born an aristocrat.

His father was an earl, his mother a countess. By all rights, he should've grown up with a shiny silver spoon in his mouth. *Aye,* came the bitter thought, his family was so rich that his father could've bought each of his former masters' shops and thrown the blackguards out on the street for ever daring to lay a hand on him.

Instead, because of the Dark Druids, his parents had vanished, and he'd had to fend for himself, always.

Well, except for a certain redhead, who had at least given him a reason to keep on surviving even when he'd wanted nothing more than to give up, lie down, and die.

Jake had always known that he had to keep going because, without him, Dani would have no one to protect her from the violence and squalor of their harsh rookery world. He was a fairly bad kid, he knew, but Dani was good.

She deserved better.

Suddenly, Jake spotted another intersection ahead. He dashed toward it and barreled around the corner, only to collide with a pair of uniformed crewmen.

"Hey! Watch where you're going!" one said as he shoved his way between them.

"Who was that?" the other asked.

Behind him, both men turned and stared in confusion, but Jake was already halfway down the corridor.

Blimey. How anyone found their way in this place, Jake had no idea. The only variation he could see in anything was a slight difference in the width of the hallways. The widest were ten or twelve feet across, the narrowest maybe four.

Just then, in the distance, Jake heard a sharp metallic clatter and skidded to a halt, pausing to listen.

Uh-oh. It sounded like Tazaroc had managed to wriggle free of the chandelier.

Despite the danger, a smile twitched at Jake's lips. That had been quite a game of ring toss, but he supposed the fun could only last for so long.

Unfortunately, now all he'd probably managed to do was make the creature angry.

Still, it shouldn't be a problem, as long as he stayed out of Tazaroc's way.

Alas, that proved easier said than done.

Jake was already in motion as the dragon came hunting him. He could hear it somewhere in the labyrinth, snuffling along, growling to itself. It probably had a predator's keen sense of smell, but Jake hoped the stink of rotting Noxu corpses in the air would help disguise his scent.

Those stealthy Drow, though, could be anywhere. And considering they lived underground, they probably could see just fine in the dark.

Jake glanced around uneasily as he jogged along at a rapid clip, taking more care now to keep his footsteps quiet. But when the two crewmen he'd shoved aside moments ago shrieked somewhere in the maze behind him—followed by a long, throaty snarl—he stopped with a gasp, looking over his shoulder.

Tazaroc didn't bother the pair, by the sound of it. Otherwise, there'd have been much more screaming. Jake's heart sank as he realized the dragon had ignored the two men because it had fixed on *him* as its quarry.

Blast. Perhaps the beast had caught his scent, for it began running now, its footsteps pounding closer.

Jake bolted, his heart in his throat. With every step, he cursed the Dark Druids for making these hallways wide enough for Tazaroc to fit through. He winced at the sound of the big lizard's tail slapping the walls as the creature prowled the corridors.

Fairly tiptoeing along at top speed, Jake fumed that he didn't even have a weapon with which to defend himself from that thing, aside from his telekinesis.

He still couldn't *believe* Wyvern had eaten Risker!

Jake hated to admit it, but it showed that the half-demon earl was more powerful than Jake had given him credit for. Aye, the fact that even dragons obeyed Wyvern rather drove that point home. *Humph.* Jake hoped his poor, dead dagger gave the earl the worst stomachache of his life.

Then the sounds of Tazaroc's movements in the labyrinth stopped. Somehow, the beast's silence was even more terrifying than the echo of its stomping strides.

Jake stopped too, melting against the wall. He held his breath, hating this nasty game of cat-and-mouse.

His heart thumped in the hush. He got the feeling Tazaroc was listening.

Jake trembled with a slight gulp. He certainly hoped that beast remembered Wyvern's instructions to *fetch* and not eat him. Black Prince and all that.

Blast. If only he could find a decent hiding place! He could duck out of sight, let the dragon pass, and *then* move on. It always used to work on Flanagan.

There was just one problem.

The rookery was full of helpful nooks and crannies—everything from broken walls to hanging laundry to stacks of crates or barrels to hide behind. But the onyx corridors of this cursed castle were downright stark.

Motionless against the cold wall, Jake racked his brains for what to do next. He didn't dare move, unsure where the dragon was. The monster was close; that much he sensed. But which direction?

At the same time, he knew from experience that it was dangerous to stay in one place for too long. *Keep moving,* his thief instincts warned him.

The dragon, however, was only waiting for him to make one mistake. It probably also had keen hearing.

Briefly, Jake considered taking off his boots for the sake of stealth. He could even throw them to distract the dragon, but he discarded the idea.

The floors were too slippery. He'd slide all over the place in his socks, and it would cost him speed.

Self-doubt crept in as he floundered. *Hang it all, maybe I should've escaped out the drawbridge while I had the chance.*

His parents wouldn't want him getting killed, now, would they? Or forced to become the Black Prince, heir of all evil.

A bead of cold sweat trickled down his face. He brushed it away impatiently, suddenly wondering about the wisdom of all this. *What am I doing here? I'm an idiot. I should've stayed back at Buckingham Palace.*

"Overconfidence, Jake," Aunt Ramona always warned him.

Again? Had he bitten off more than he could chew? Would it be his bloody downfall?

Better too cocky than a coward! Jake vowed, routing his self-doubt with an angry scowl. Besides, it was too late to turn back now. In truth, he wasn't even sure where the great hall *was* at this point.

In short, he was pretty well lost.

So much for his rookery instincts. Every corridor looked the same.

Well, you've got to do something. *Don't just stand here waiting for the dashed thing to find you.*

Right, Jake said firmly to himself.

Steeling his courage and drawing on his old pickpocket stealth, Jake crept up to the next corner and slowly, ever so carefully, peeked around the edge.

To his surprise, there was no dragon in sight. Just another long, fairly narrow hallway with several intersections at uneven intervals.

Jake's jaw tightened when he heard the faint puffing of the beast's nostrils and wondered, briefly, why this particular dragon didn't breathe fire. Not that he was complaining.

Based on the direction of the sound, he'd wager that Tazaroc was lurking down the closest corridor on the right.

Jake needed a distraction to send the beast in the wrong direction. He lifted a trembling hand and focused with all his might on a distant wall sconce, way down at the other end of the long hallway.

He fired and missed his target entirely.

Steady on. His powers went wonky when he let his emotions overtake him, and the human fear of dragons was ancient and instinctual. Pulse pounding, Jake inhaled through his nostrils, determined to calm down. He closed his eyes for a second and concentrated. *Focus.*

He could feel the energy gathering all down his arm. His fingertips began to tingle...

Jake flicked his eyes open fiercely and shot a beam of telekinetic force all the way down the long hallway, exploding several wall sconces in rapid succession.

The dragon roared and whipped around the corner from the very hallway Jake had suspected. He ducked back but couldn't resist a furtive peek out as Tazaroc's long, sinuous body molded around the corner and bolted in the opposite direction from Jake.

Jake watched, studying the creature.

From here, he had a good view of its back, wings, and tail as it chased after the sound. Jake noted that although Tazaroc could fit in the hallways, the beast would have a hard time turning around in them, due to its size.

Best to keep behind him, then.

Emboldened by the realization, Jake slipped around the corner and glided after the creature for a few stealthy paces, then dashed down a side corridor that he hadn't been down before.

He hadn't gone far, however, when a door in the hallway suddenly cracked open a few feet ahead of him.

Jake froze, sure that he'd be spotted.

Someone muttered, "What on earth is going on out here?" Then a familiar face peeked out the crack.

"You!" Jake exclaimed. He could just make out Lord Badgerton's puffy cheeks and bushy sideburns.

"Ack!" The portly shapeshifter saw him and instantly tried to slam the door, but Jake blocked it with his telekinesis.

"Traitor." Infuriated at the sight of Badgerton, Jake strode over to the door and braced it open with his foot and shoulder.

Badgerton huffed but held his ground. "What are you doing here?"

"Maybe I'm here for you," Jake said in a menacing tone. "You betrayed the Order."

"Stay back!" Badgerton's nose twitched with the start of his namesake animal's famous tenacity. Behind the disgraced Elder, Jake saw a room that made no sense: a cozy underground den with quaint cottage furniture.

He shook his head. *Magic.*

"What was that noise?" Badgerton demanded, keeping his voice low.

"A dragon. Would you like to meet him? C'mon, I'd be happy to introduce you. He's just around the corner. Here!" Jake seized the baron's fleshy arm and tried to pull him out of his den, but could not dislodge the man.

Badgerton dug in his heels and wedged himself in the doorway, then finally managed to shake off Jake's hold. "Keep your hands off me!"

Jake glared at him. "You deserve to hang."

"Brave talk for a mere lad."

"Why did you do it, eh?"

"You really want to know?" Badgerton tilted his head angrily. "Because of people like you, Jake. You and that uppity Elder witch."

"She's worth a hundred of you—" Jake felt seriously close to losing his temper. "Ach, never mind. You're not worth it."

Just then, the dragon yowled somewhere in the maze, apparently realizing it had been tricked.

Jake glanced in the direction of the ruckus, then gave the traitor his most menacing glower. "How do I get to the basement?"

The shapeshifter eyed him warily, as though weighing his threat. "You don't want to go down there, Jake. Trust me."

"Trust *you*?" Jake whispered. "You must be joking!"

"I speak in earnest." Badgerton's gaze darted down the hallway, left and right. "Believe me, there are worse things in this castle than dragons, my boy."

"Aye, and I'm one of them," Jake said with great bravado, ignoring the chill that the ominous warning sent down his spine. "Now, tell me what I want to know and I'll be on my way. Otherwise..."

With a quick flick of the wrist, Jake began levitating the chubby ex-Elder off his feet, out of his doorway, and into the black hallway.

"Hmm, which direction did that naughty dragon go?"

"Ack! Stop this, you rotten—" Badgerton sputtered, making a feeble attempt to grab hold of the doorframe, but missed as Jake floated him toward the ceiling of the corridor. "How dare you? Put me down this instant, you ill-mannered little heathen!"

"I'll bash your brains out against the ceiling, I will!" Jake taunted with a hearty grin, starting to feel the dark influence that filled the walls of the warlocks' castle. "Start talking, you coward! Which way to the basement?"

"Egads, you're as bad as he is—Wyvern!" Badgerton choked out. "Like father, like son."

Jake growled at the insult and hefted him higher, within inches of the ceiling. "*Don't* make me hurt you. I could let you fall. Probably break a leg. Then you wouldn't be able to run away from—"

"All right, all right!" Badgerton whispered frantically. "You don't have to be ugly about it! I-I'll make a bargain with you."

"Oh, a bargain? Really?" Jake pressed Badgerton hard against the ceiling, his left hand held high.

"That's right," Badgerton said, his face covered in sweat. "Give a message to the skunkies for me, and I'll tell you what you want to know."

Just then, a shriek from somewhere in the maze suggested that another unsuspecting soul had crossed paths with Tazaroc. A loud clatter followed, like the sound of dropped trays. Then a door slammed.

Maybe the person had escaped.

Then a long, brooding growl rumbled through the labyrinth; Jake and Badgerton looked at each other uneasily.

"Fine." Jake lowered the shapeshifter lord to the ground. "What's the message?"

Badgerton dropped his gaze. "Tell Prue and the boys that I...I haven't abandoned them. That I'll find them as soon as I can. Then they and their mama can come and live with me. Tell them I love them a-and that everything will be all right."

Jake shook his head in disgust. First of all, everything would not be *all right*. There was a rupture in the Veil, for starters.

Secondly, there was no way Jake would ever mention the word *love* to Prue Badgerton. The stuck-up shapeshifter girl already had the most annoying infatuation with him. It made her act like a widgeon—and meaner than ever to Dani O'Dell.

And yet it struck Jake as curious that even the likes of Badgerton cared about *someone*.

"The basement," Jake reminded him.

"You'll tell them? You'll remember?"

"I'm not an idiot. Yes! Next time I see them."

"Good." Badgerton adjusted his waistcoat with his usual pompous indignation, then nodded toward the right. "Go that way until you reach the outer ring—the widest hallway that wraps all the way around this floor and connects to the four corner towers. The main stairwell to the basement lies in the middle of the castle's back wall. There may be others," he added, "but that's the only one I know."

"You'd better not be lying to me."

"And *you'd* better not go back on your word." With that, Badgerton huffed back into his den and slammed the door shut.

Humph. Jake did not like that man. *If I had known you'd turn traitor, I'd have thrown those mashed potatoes at you on purpose.*

Then Jake left Badgerton's door and began cautiously following the route the ex-Elder had described.

He soon found the "outer ring" hallway that Badgerton had told him to look for. Finally, it helped him start to get his bearings in this place.

All right, then, he thought. *So only the inner passages are loony.* The outer ring seemed at least somewhat sane. His hopes mounted as he followed it stealthily to the back corner of the Fortress.

There, he came upon a rounded section of wall that jutted out into the wide hallway. *Aha.* Jake realized it was the base of one of those spiky corner towers.

A closed wooden door gave entrance to the tower beneath a stone-carved archway. Jake tested it out of curiosity; it might make a handy exit.

Locked.

No matter. It was the stairwell he wanted, anyway. It shouldn't be much farther...and it wasn't.

In short order, Jake spotted the opening to another black stairwell ahead. He glanced up and down the hallway as he dashed toward it, making sure that none of his pursuers were in sight.

To his relief, Badgerton proved true to his word. The stairs here only led down.

Without hesitation, Jake slipped into the shadowed entrance of the stairwell and started speeding down the steps. Ever deeper into the Black Fortress he went. The stairs were extremely dark. His sense of evil grew with every step.

He came to a landing where the staircase turned and hurried down the next flight.

As he neared the bottom, he slowed his pace and softened his footfalls. Creeping down to the edge of the stairwell's exit, he furtively peeked out.

To the left, a rounded hallway unfurled before him: empty.

But when he looked to the right, Jake had to stifle a gasp at what he saw.

Lying dead on either side of a pair of fancy black double doors were two Noxu warriors.

At least, they looked dead to him.

They were just lying there, motionless, and the smell was unbearable. When Jake heard flies buzzing around, he grimaced and lifted his hand to cover his nose.

Disgusting. Their kind were ugly to begin with, and death hadn't done them any favors.

They were armed, however. With a quick glance, Jake made sure there was no one else around but him and the dead half-trolls. *All clear.* He stepped cautiously out of the stairwell and sneaked over to the corpses.

Ah! His gaze alighted on the seven-foot spears the pair carried. One of those could come in handy for keeping that dragon at bay.

Jake bent down and silently pried the spear out of the Noxu's stiff gray hands.

He straightened up and hefted the weapon for a moment to get the feel of it. The spear was light enough to wield with one hand, but the shaft was strong, with a ten-inch spike on the end. *Perfect.*

"Thanks, boys," he said under his breath. Then he noticed the glossy black doors the two warriors had apparently been guarding. "Hmm."

I wonder what's in there.

Maybe this was where they were keeping the captive Lightriders. Jake's pulse quickened.

After glancing over his shoulder to make sure his pursuers had not yet picked up his trail, he grasped the handle of one of the big black doors and pulled it open a crack.

But when he peered inside, an ominous wave of awe made him go very still.

What is *this place?*

Everything in him said to get out of there immediately, but Jake could tell that the room was important, so he took a step over the threshold in order to have a look around.

The heavy door swung shut slowly behind him with a desolate moan. Jake stared into the chamber, mystified.

It looked like some sort of arcane temple. A black granite walkway flanked by low blue flames stretched ahead, leading into a dark, soaring chamber.

Towering black columns carved as hideous devils held up the ceiling. The huge sculptures were grotesque, from their twisted horns and leering eyes down to their cloven hoofs.

Dread knotted in Jake's stomach as he tilted his head back to look up at them. The statues reminded him of the demon whose shadow he had seen on the wall last night.

Shemrazul—the warlocks' evil god.

Jake snorted.

You ain't nothin', he told the so-called Horned One with all of his rookery bravado, then dared another step into the Dark Druids' inner sanctum.

Ignoring the giant devil statues, Jake turned his gaze toward the center of the chamber, where thirteen grand chairs were arranged in an inward-facing triangle, the tallest at the apex.

Jake realized he was looking at the throne of the sorcerer-king. The very seat of the warlocks' dark magic.

A chill ran down his spine.

I should definitely not be in here.

He started backing away, but he feared he was too late, for he suddenly got the sense of overwhelming evil approaching. Then came a thunderous voice from somewhere in the room: *"Who's there?"*

Jake gasped and recoiled. Then a burst of orange flames rose from the center of the triangle where the thrones were arrayed.

"Nathan? Is it you? Come. How goes the war?"

A cloud of black smoke and sulfurous fumes joined the flames. An earsplitting clank of chains rasped from the center of the room like the screech of a thousand banshees.

Then Jake glimpsed the tips of two red horns beginning to rise from the center of the inferno, a terror overcame him, the likes of which he had never experienced before—not even in the coal mine.

He spun around and fled the temple so fast that he tripped over one of the dead Noxu just outside the doorway and went sprawling on the corpse.

Horrified, he scrambled upright but managed to drop the spear in his terror. It clattered loudly on the floor. Jake cursed. On his feet again, knees shaking, he turned around and pushed the heavy black door shut.

His pulse beating a panicked staccato, he bent and grabbed the spear, then ran back down the hallway to the relative safety of the stairwell.

There, he paused out of sight, chest heaving with lingering panic. He was trembling from head to toe, his grip clammy on the spear.

Jake leaned his back against the wall and strove to shake it off and get a hold of himself. Ugh, he was glad his friends weren't here to see him like this.

Blimey. Badgerton wasn't kidding, he thought. *I don't know what that thing was, but it's definitely worse than a dragon.*

"Don't be silly, Jake," a quiet inner voice responded in his head. It sounded rather like Celestus. *"You know exactly what that is—or, rather,*

whom. You've met before."

Jake gulped.

"But don't worry. This is not your battle. Yet."

"Yet?" Jake whispered, jolting away from the wall. His heart started pounding anew. "No. No way."

Let Derek do it. Or Aunt Ramona.

Anyone but me.

I'm not going in there ever *again. I only came to find my parents.*

For heaven's sake, he already had enough problems of his own. Jake hung his head, suddenly overwhelmed by all he had to face.

But when a low, bloodcurdling singsong echoed from the direction of the Dark Druids' temple, calling to him, Jake jerked his head up.

"Jaaaaake?" it taunted him.

He held motionless. The voice was deep and dark, soft and deadly— a voice from the pit of Hell.

Then a low, horrifying chuckle resounded through the passageway.

"Why, grandson, is that you? Come back, m'boy. I've been waiting to meet you face to face, and we have so much to talk about. Come, let's have a little chat."

Jake felt the blood drain from his face, but this time, he did not let panic overtake him. With a dry-mouthed gulp, he thought, *Right.* So...the Dark Druids had a demon living in the basement. *Very well.*

That was not his business.

He'd only come to find his parents, and not even Shemrazul would scare him away.

Determined to resume his quest, he stepped out of the stairwell, refusing even to look at those black doors. Instead, he hurried on, jogging up the wide, rounded corridor in the other direction.

"You can't run from destiny, Jake! You'll join us one way or the other, just like Badgerton did. You belong with us! Don't you remember how you trapped those bullies in the coal mine? Such splendid revenge! How good it felt! Remember the people you stole from? The lies you told? And got away with it all, because you're cleverer than other people, Jake. You know you're better than them. That's why you deserve to be the Black Prince. Join us, and together we shall rule the world!"

Sinister laughter filled the hallway.

Jake ran for his life.

CHAPTER THIRTY-FOUR
Visions of Darkness

S till spooked, Jake ran down the curved hallway until he had put a good distance between him and the black doors. Finally, he started feeling more like his old self.

At least now that he knew what resided in the center of the Black Fortress—or could somehow enter the castle there. He also now realized who had sent those imps, lesser devils, and weird little monsters after him and his friends.

Even the imps' cautious treatment of him now made sense. Of course they hadn't attacked him. He was the bloody chosen one.

Shaking his head in disgust, Jake trudged on, spear in hand. Still, there was no point in denying that he was officially out of his depth.

This place needs an exorcism. No—a whole team of exorcists.

But on a more practical level, it dawned on him that he'd better find the captive Lightriders and get out of here before the Fortress jumped. If he wasn't careful, he could end up stranded on the far side of the world with these mumpers.

Suddenly, he heard off-tune whistling somewhere in the corridor behind him. *Someone's coming!*

Jake looked around anxiously for a hiding place and spotted a bench by the wall. He raced over and dove under it, molding himself out of sight as best he could. But, hang it, the blasted spear didn't fit. It was too long to hide fully underneath the bench.

Jake held his breath, watching in silence as a bespectacled man in a white lab coat strolled toward him, head down, studying some papers on his clipboard.

As the doctor or scientist or whatever he was approached, Jake carefully shifted the spear's position to keep it out of sight, first pulling it under one end of the bench, then shifting it to the other as the fellow ambled by.

Once he'd passed, Jake realized he had to follow the man.

Tex had said that the Dark Druids were holding the Lightriders in some sort of large laboratory. The man's white coat made it reasonable to assume he'd be headed that way.

As soon as the scientist moved on around the bend, Jake climbed out from under the bench and lifted the spear, taking care not to bump anything. He couldn't risk making noise.

On his feet once more, he prowled after the fellow with growing eagerness to find his parents.

Admittedly, it had been tempting to abandon his mission after what had just happened in the Dark Druids' temple. But he'd come too far to turn back now.

They're counting on me.

Keeping his footsteps light, Jake followed the whistling scientist around the curve of the hallway.

The dim lighting grew a little stronger as they approached some yet-unseen destination. At the same time, he started hearing a most unsettling sound.

A low *lub-dub, lub-dub* reverberated through the basement like a giant heartbeat. It got louder, stronger, as he trailed the scientist up the corridor. It made him uneasy.

Hadn't Archie mentioned something about this from his vision of the captive Lightriders? If Jake recalled correctly, Tex also had described some huge machine keeping the Lightriders alive but unconscious...

Abruptly, the whistling from up ahead stopped. Jake heard a door creak open. The heartbeat sound grew louder, then slowly softer again.

He waited out of sight with his back pressed against the wall as the door squeaked shut somewhere around the bend.

Jake listened intently for any new sounds—footsteps, or worse, dragon growls—but heard none. His pulse quickened as he decided to investigate.

Step by stealthy step, he crept around the bend and saw that the hallway opened up into a sparse, kidney-shaped lobby. On the left was a pair of brown wooden doors. *He must've gone in there.* Then his gaze traveled on, and he noted that across from the doors lay another stairwell, offering a second way up to the black labyrinth upstairs—and the waiting dragon.

No thanks. Jake was in no hurry to face Tazaroc again.

In any case, between the doors and the stairwell entrance, the curved hallway ended at a room straight ahead. A sign over the open doorway read, *Cloakroom.*

Inside, Jake could see tidy rows of white lab coats hung on pegs. *All right.* He nodded to himself, quickly concluding that the cloakroom held nothing of interest.

Through those doors was probably where he needed to go—and fast, Jake realized as he heard three pairs of feet coming down the staircase.

Voices echoed down to him, a language he didn't know, but he recognized the accent.

The Drow. As the wooden thump of a wizard's staff echoed down the stairwell, he realized Duradel was with them. *Great.*

Jake got moving. He had no choice. The Drow warriors would see him the moment they turned at the landing. Spear in hand, he stalked over to the doors. He hesitated, but blimey, whatever was in there couldn't be as bad as the room he'd just left.

Bracing himself, he pulled the door open, stepped inside, and beheld the strangest room he'd ever seen.

If you could call it a room.

It looked like a huge limestone cavern, but the rounded rock walls were riddled with recessed niches—like the catacombs Aunt Ramona had taken them to see on their Grand Tour.

Fortunately, it was very dim in the vast chamber, so none of the busy white-coated scientists here and there noticed him.

Jake quickly stepped sideways into the shadows and glanced around. *Plenty of places to hide in here.* He sneaked along the wall until he came to a trio of upright barrels. Crouching down behind them, Jake scanned the bizarre chamber, flabbergasted.

His gaze was drawn back to the long, low niches carved into the cave walls. He could not believe what he was seeing.

Lengthwise within every alcove sat a glass coffin, and, inside each, a Lightrider lay motionless.

It was just like Archie's dream.

The reality of it hit harder than Jake had expected. For a long moment, all he could do was stare.

It's true. It's all true.

There were rows and rows of captives, even up high, for the cavern was as big as the ballroom back at Merlin Hall. There must've been a hundred of them. Jake was too overwhelmed with emotion to count.

He didn't know whether to rage or to weep. He'd heard about this twice now, first from his clairvoyant cousin and then from Tex.

But seeing it with his own two eyes, and knowing his parents were probably among the victims, brought tears briefly to his eyes. *Mother... Father. What have they done to you?*

He clenched his jaw with growing fury, blinked away the dampness clouding his vision, and forced himself past the grief. He had to figure out what to do.

Just like Archie had described, thin rubber tubes connected each unconscious captive to the towering, cylindrical machine in the center of the chamber.

Lub-dub, lub-dub...

That cursed contraption was the source of the deep, muffled booming. *Must be Zolond's work.* Some unholy blend of science and magic.

About twenty feet tall and ten feet wide, the heartbeat machine had so many thin rubber tubes flowing out in all directions from the top part that it resembled snake-haired Medusa.

Lower down, inside the thick glass container, Jake could see some sort of metal arm pumping and sloshing many gallons of a bright green potion.

What is that stuff?

On second thought, maybe he didn't want to know. Whatever it was, Jake saw that the liquid was running through the tubes to each of the glass coffins. Maybe it was bringing the unconscious victims the nutrition and water everyone needed to stay alive.

At least they didn't seem to be suffering. But Jake's heart broke to know there were far too many people for him to rescue.

Not without an army—and a large team of healers.

He wasn't even sure how to rescue his parents. Aye, he had to find them first. Maybe they had long since died.

That was still a possibility, he admitted as his grim stare traveled over the honeycombed walls of the cave.

There was only one way to find out. He'd have to check each and every glass coffin.

And, hopefully, he would recognize their faces from the family portrait in the great hall at Griffon Castle. Twelve years older now, they'd probably look somewhat different.

Then, absurdly, Jake started getting nervous to meet them for the first time. Butterflies in the belly and all.

Pay attention! he told himself sternly. What he *ought* to be nervous about were the white-coated scientists or doctors scattered throughout the room.

They drifted here and there, seeing to various tasks: monitoring the unconscious people in the glass boxes, inspecting the tubing connected to each, and jotting notes on their clipboards. One pored over paperwork at a lamp-lit table, while another took readings of some sort off the side of the machine.

Most strolled around at floor level, but a couple wheeled tall library ladders around the cavern and climbed up to check on the captives in the higher alcove niches.

Jake shook his head, seething. *Heartless blackguards.* He gripped his spear, tempted to skewer a few.

At that moment, one of the scientists up on the ladder turned and spotted Jake peering over the barrels.

"Hey! You shouldn't be in here!" he yelled, then pointed at him. "We've got an intruder!"

"*What?*" The man checking the machine turned and saw Jake. He narrowed his eyes, hung his clipboard at once on a little hook, and strode toward Jake at a quick clip. "You there! Who are you? How did you get in here?"

The chap doing paperwork abandoned the table and ran toward Jake from the opposite direction. The rest of the scientists quit what they were doing and came to see what was going on.

Heart pounding, Jake rose to his feet. There was no point hiding anymore, but now what?

With the wall at his back and the first two scientists closing in from either side, the rest already on their way, he looked right and left, unsure what to do.

He couldn't just run. His parents were here. He wasn't leaving without them.

His only option was to seize the initiative. *Good.* Jake never minded going on offense.

He marched out angrily from behind the barrels and took a few aggressive paces toward the center of the dim, giant cavern, ignoring the scientists as they approached.

"Mother! Father!" he shouted at the top of his lungs. "Where are you? Stay back!" he added, menacing the scientists with the spear.

The two white-coated men slowed their pace as they saw he had a weapon.

"Show me Lord and Lady Griffon. *Now!*" Jake ordered them. "Or I swear I'll run you through!"

The two nearest fellows halted, lifting their hands in an effort to soothe his fury with a show of surrender.

The others who'd been working in the cavern gathered around. "Did he say Griffon?" one of the new arrivals murmured to his colleagues.

The others nodded. They exchanged meaningful glances, then the paperwork man looked at Jake.

"So, you are...?"

"That's right! The chosen one," Jake said sarcastically. "And I didn't get picked for the Black Prince by bein' a nice boy, so don't make me hurt you." He brandished the spear at all of them. "I want to see my parents. Where are they? What have you done to them? Show them to me!"

They all just stood there, studying him like he was a lab rat from some experiment that had produced highly interesting results.

"*Now!*" Jake roared, his impassioned order reverberating under the cavern's hollow dome.

"He is hysterical," one of the scientists remarked.

Jake's temper snapped. "Hysterical? I'll show you hysterical!" He strode over to the machine, changed his hold on the spear to use it like a bat, and took aim at the big glass container at its base. "Show me my parents or I'll smash this thing to smithereens!"

The scientists panicked.

"No! Wait, stop!"

"Don't do it!"

"You'll kill them all!"

"What?" Jake paused, still poised to swing.

"The machine is keeping them alive!" said the man who'd been taking readings off the contraption.

"What if I don't believe you?"

"That's a chance you're willing to take?" the man asked.

Jake faltered, then straightened up, at a loss, and lowered his weapon. He hadn't come this far to save his parents only to kill them himself by making some hotheaded blunder.

"Why are you doing this?" He gestured around the cavern at the scientists' unholy work. "How *could* you?"

They looked grimly at each other.

Unfortunately, the Drow must've heard the commotion, for the double doors burst open at that moment, and the black-clad warriors stepped into the cavern with Duradel between them.

The high priest's bodyguards drew their bows in unison, and Jake cursed. *Not these blokes again.*

Good old Crescent Moon, the polite one, and angry Triangle Chin.

Still standing uncertainly by the machine, Jake tensed for a fight. As the tall, graceful warriors prowled toward him, the scientists parted to let them pass.

The high priest hung back near the entrance but looked fully at home in the twilight of the cavern, his pale hair gleaming.

"Do not be alarmed, Jake," Duradel called in his creepy, singsong accent. "As I said, we mean you no harm."

"It would be best if you came along peaceably, Your Highness," Crescent Moon said. "We will show you to a guest chamber you can transform to your liking with nothing but a thought. The rooms here have magic in the walls."

Humph. At least that explained Badgerton's den.

"Illusions don't impress me," Jake replied. But for the sake of the captives, he took a few wary steps away from the machine, then stood planted.

Beyond that point, he refused to budge. His parents were somewhere in this cave, and he wasn't leaving without them.

The Drow crept closer.

"You'd better back off!" Jake angled the spear at them.

"Now, now, boy, don't make a fuss," Triangle Chin taunted him through gritted teeth. "We don't want things to get...messy."

"You won't shoot!" Jake retorted. "Wyvern said you're not allowed to kill me."

"No, but we can shoot you in the legs," Triangle Chin replied. "We're very good with these things, you know." The dark elf indicated his bow. "Our kind begin archery training at the age of five. Do you suppose we'll miss?"

Jake swallowed hard. Quickly shifting the spear into his right hand, he raised his left, palm open, to deflect any arrows they might let loose with his telekinesis.

"Come, Jake, there is no need for any unpleasantness," Duradel said. "Better us then the dragon, surely."

"I don't know about that."

"Let us talk privately for a moment, my lad." Duradel walked over, finding his way with ease, thanks to his carved wooden staff. As he approached, the priest's two stone-faced bodyguards moved closer to protect him.

A pair of bookends, those two.

"Perhaps I can help you understand why you are so important to us, Jake," Duradel said smoothly. Though his milky eyes stared into space, he gave a vague smile, revealing incisors filed into slight fangs. "I can show you the magnificent destiny the Brotherhood is offering you. Will you let me?"

"Will you let me see my parents?" Jake countered, a little put off by the fangs.

"That is not my decision to make. It's up to Lord Wyvern." The prophet inched closer. He smelled like incense. "Put the weapon down."

"Not bloody likely. Where are they? Which of these alcoves—"

"Hush." Duradel reached out without warning and lightly grasped the top of Jake's forehead.

"Let go o' me!" Jake pulled back, but Duradel's grip only clamped down harder.

"Just...*look*," the priest ordered him.

Jake resisted. He still had the spear, but he was not about to stab a blind man. The moment he glanced at Duradel's eyes, though, the seer projected a vision into Jake's mind.

Images started flashing.

Jake rebelled at the invasion into his head, trying to jerk his face away. Duradel's long-nailed fingers dug in insistently at his temples and hairline.

In the next heartbeat, the oracle's psychic power overwhelmed him.

The cavern faded away. Jake stood immobilized. His eyes were still open, but an inner darkness dropped over his mind like a black screen. Then all he could see was the vision Duradel was sending.

Jake saw a family...

The thing he wanted most in all the world.

Not just any family. He stared.

A royal family.

With untold power.

He was the son, of course: the Black Prince. He stood in the center and just ahead of his parents.

Behind his left shoulder towered Wyvern arrayed in the black robes and the tall, viciously spiked onyx crown of the sorcerer-king.

Beside him, just behind Jake's right shoulder, stood Fionnula, glittering in black diamonds and black pearls, her chin lifted proudly.

She held a wand in one hand but rested the other on Jake's shoulder in a motherly pose. Her red nails dug into him, but Jake didn't feel it.

He was staring at himself in the vision.

He, too, wore a crown, a simple iron circlet. He looked *good*.

The three of them stood on a balcony somewhere looking down upon a wide, barren plain, where a throng had gathered to pay them homage.

Jake's gaze traveled over hordes of ogres, trolls, Drowfolk, vampires, wraiths.

Even Nightstalkers bowed in submission. And there were dragons arrayed at Wyvern's command.

Then Jake could not help but thrill as he realized that he, too, had his own private army...of gryphons. He looked up at the night sky and saw them circling under the moon, screeching with battle-readiness to do as he said.

Duradel had his full attention as the meaning of the vision sank in.

Blimey, Wyvern had taken over the world. Half demon, infused with the power of Shemrazul, his dark magic had become unstoppable.

Then Jake's own role in the picture came clear.

Why, he had the power to command anyone he wished to do anything he pleased.

Total control...

This was something that all the wealth in the gold mine he had inherited could not buy.

He could make laws—and enforce them.

Wyvern didn't care if Jake used his power for good, within reason. No, his doting Nephilim papa thought Jake had hung the moon and stars. He was allowed to do anything he liked at any time.

That meant he could do...oh, marvels.

Things that would impress even Dani O'Dell. He could make the world good enough for her. For all his friends. For every kid who'd ever gone hungry or taken a harsh blow from an angry parent...or apprentice master.

He could have revenge on those kinds of people.

He could force everyone to act decent, like they should. Like he'd always known that people ought to act when he was starving on the streets of London and nobody cared.

How many times had he vowed he'd get even with people someday, with this unfeeling world? He had known at the time that it was just a pipe dream. You couldn't force people to care, to do the right thing, not even for penniless orphans.

But maybe...he could.

Jake stared, riveted by the possibilities. He could sic his righteous gryphons on any evildoer, aye, and make an example of him or her. No mercy; no regret.

And crime? Injustice?

In his role as the Black Prince, he could use the warlocks' magic to punish the wicked and even predict crimes before they were committed. He could stop bad things from ever happening to innocent people in the first place.

Gooseflesh ran down Jake's limbs as he realized that the Dark Druids were offering him the chance to wield almost godlike power.

Only...that was how Zolond got started, according to what Aunt Ramona had told Nixie.

Geoffrey de Lacey had started out good.

The road to Hell had indeed been paved with good intentions, at least for the Dark Master...

Zolond.

Aunt Ramona! Jake suddenly thought, yanked out of the vision by the thought of the Elder witch. Panic shot through him as his original mission came flooding back.

What am I doing?

He had promised Archie he'd help defend the Dark Master and, thus, Aunt Ramona. If one died, so did the other. Jake's heart leaped into his throat.

What if Zolond's battle against Wyvern was going badly?

He should be out there! Especially now that he'd glimpsed the Nephilim's grandiose intentions.

He had to stop Wyvern from fulfilling his plans!

He jerked free of Duradel's hold—both physical and mental—and took a step backward. "Keep your hands off me!"

Suddenly, two scientists grabbed Jake from behind. One restrained him with a rough bear hug while the other pressed a rag soaked in chloroform over his nose and mouth, trying to knock him out. Jake fought immediately.

He recognized the sickeningly sweet chemical smell from Archie's lab. The boy genius kept a small supply on hand, as chloroform was the chief anesthetic used before many medical procedures.

First the stuff made you silly, then it knocked you out cold.

Around here, they probably used it on any Lightriders who started waking up.

More scientists piled on to hold him still. The Drow stood back and watched. Fingers tried to pry Jake's grip off the shaft of the spear. He didn't dare let it go.

Aware he had only seconds to break their hold before the powerful sedative took effect, Jake elbowed someone hard in the stomach. Then he lunged one foot forward and sent another scientist flying with a back kick, just like Derek had been training him.

He twisted and he wrenched; he ducked and punched and scrabbled in close quarters as the white-coated men hemmed him in on all sides. Jake fought like a wild thing, and suddenly managed to seize the wrist of the hand still trying to hold the rag over his mouth.

"Watch out! His hand's free!"

Jake pulled the rag away from his face and gasped for air, already feeling woozy. He fought to keep his wits about him. As soon as he'd filled his lungs, he clutched the spear in both hands and swept it sideways with all his strength, using it to mow down all of the doctors ringing him in.

The scientists fell back in chaos, but the Drow lifted their bows.

"Should we shoot, sir?" yelled Crescent Moon.

"Stand down!" Duradel thundered.

Jake didn't wait to see if the bodyguards would obey. He didn't much like it when people threatened to shoot arrows in his legs. He tore the bows out of the warriors' hands with his telekinesis and hurled them off to the farthest reaches of the cavern.

The next thing he knew, Jake was sprinting toward the doors. Clutching his spear, he burst out into the lobby, where at least it was brighter.

For all of three seconds, Jake stood there, panting and trying to clear his head from the slight numbing tingle of the chloroform.

But although he'd escaped the cavern, he realized in the next heartbeat that he was hardly in the clear.

A long, low snarl from several yards down the hallway to his right proved to be Tazaroc, slowly prowling toward him.

"Oh, I really hate this place," Jake whispered, chest heaving.

Then he dashed across the lobby and ran for his life into the stairwell, bounding up the steps two at a time.

A roar shook the basement behind him.

The dragon was on its way.

CHAPTER THIRTY-FIVE
Tazaroc

Stumbling slightly in his haste, and starting to feel a wee bit addled from the chloroform (he must be loopy, for he found the prospect of being eaten by a dragon oddly funny at the moment), Jake raced up the dark stairs and flung himself around the landing.

Perhaps he'd inhaled a bit more of that stuff than he'd realized, for the staircase zigzagged like a ship's passageway at sea. His face felt numb, his feet tingly, and his hands all floaty.

Now that he'd escaped the clutches of the white-coated horde, the effects of the drug they had forced on him became more noticeable. Jake wasn't sleepy, but felt a bit giddy and lightheaded—and knew that he was nowhere near alarmed enough about the dragon chasing him.

Well, that's not good, he thought with amused detachment from it all. His mind seemed to be working slowly. The usually fast-flowing current of his thoughts had turned as lazy as the charming little brook that wrapped around the wooded grounds of Griffon Castle.

Meanwhile, he could hear the dragon pounding down the basement hallway after him. It exploded into the lobby at the bottom of the stairwell with another reverberating roar. Then its footsteps thundered across the big waiting room; its leathery wings snapped like sails in a high wind as it used them to propel itself faster after its quarry—i.e., him.

Jake giggled inappropriately as he stumbled up the wavy second flight of steps.

Shh! he scolded himself. *Be serious! You're about to have your head bit off.*

Fortunately, he sobered up quick when the dragon gained the stairwell, snapping its jaws like it couldn't wait to eat him.

Upon reaching the upper hallway, Jake barely had time to pivot and take a defensive position. Choosing the top of the stairs as the place to make his stand, he clutched the spear tight in his right hand and raised his left to use his telekinesis as a shield. He planted his right leg firmly behind him, shook the wooziness out of his head, and braced for the onslaught.

He didn't have long to wait.

Tazaroc careened around the landing below, molding its serpentine body around the tight turn, and then lunging up the second flight of steps.

Jake vowed that the beast would not pass the threshold of the hallway.

At least confronting the creature here at the top of the stairs gave Jake the advantage of the high ground. *Where am I, anyway?*

A glance around revealed that *this* stairwell emerged not in the wide outer ring, but into a nondescript black hallway somewhere in the middle of the first-floor maze. Jake frowned, having already dealt with this disorienting labyrinth, but quickly looked forward again.

It was then, in those final few seconds before the dragon arrived, that he noticed the sign posted above the stairwell: *No Unauthorized Personnel.*

His lips twitched at the stern warning. Someone ought to tell the dragon.

Then the silly feeling vanished altogether as Tazaroc crept, snarling, to the top of the stairs before him, all hatred and dripping ivory fangs.

"Stay back!" Jake prodded the beast in the nose with his spear and shoved him down a few steps with his telekinesis.

Tazaroc snuffled and shook his head, then tried again.

Again, again, again—and still failed.

Jake was fully focused on the fight now, warily holding his own. This thing was smart, he realized. He could see the intelligence in those gleaming, vertical-slitted eyes.

The orange beast was sizing him up, trying to figure out how to get to him. It rasped out a hiss, flicking its forked tongue.

The dragon clearly understood the concept of weapons and took care to avoid the pointy end of the stick.

But it could not seem to grasp what invisible wall kept blocking it from seizing him.

Jake, for his part, was wondering why it didn't breathe fire at him. *Maybe some species can't?*

Whatever the reason, there was no time to be terrified, as a fierce battle of wills ensued there at the top of the staircase.

The dragon put its head down and kept trying to ram its way through Jake's invisible blockade, while *he* was trapped in position, defending himself. He didn't dare take his eyes off the beast to turn and run. One mistake could cost him his life—or, at the very least, his freedom.

Wyvern had ordered Tazaroc to fetch him, after all. Well, Jake didn't like being fetched.

"I. Am. Not. A. Dog toy!" he said through gritted teeth, jabbing the orange monster in time with each word.

Tazaroc hissed and dodged, whacked the side of the stairwell threateningly with his tail, gouged the top few steps with his grappling-hook claws, and reared up to the top of the hallway, but Jake refused to let him pass.

Lord, this thing is big.

Jake's heart pounded. His thighs burned from holding his defensive stance, and his shoulder muscles screamed from keeping his arms raised. He'd never gripped any weapon harder than that spear.

It seemed like hours had already passed, but it was just a few minutes. The chloroform wasn't helping matters. The silliness was long gone, but now his head throbbed, his stomach churned, and the task of holding back a dragon was quickly sapping his strength.

Much more of this, and he'd be getting a nosebleed. Blimey, he didn't want to think about how the scent and sight of blood might affect the creature.

Now and then, Tazaroc managed to thrust his snout into the upper hallway, but Jake would poke it with the spear, focus harder with his gift, and push the beast back down a few steps.

They were both getting sick of the stalemate, each increasingly frustrated that the other refused to give up.

The haughty dragon tossed its head, bared its razor-sharp teeth, tried slashing at Jake with its claws, to no avail. It could not get through the transparent shield of his telekinesis, and failure was making it furious.

Down in the dark stairwell, Jake heard the wrought-iron banister groan as the metal bent under the force of a particularly angry whack from Tazaroc's tail.

Jake could see the dragon was really starting to hate him.

The feeling was mutual.

With rising desperation, all *he* could think of was the need to get outside and help Aunt Ramona and—like it or not—Zolond.

The Dark Master *had* to stay alive, not just because if he died, then so would Aunt Ramona, but also because the ancient warlock was all that stood between Wyvern and his will to take over the bloody world.

Hold on—what's it doing now? Jake paused, suddenly on alert as Tazaroc gave him an evil look, then withdrew, hunkering backward down to the landing.

Jake did not mistake this for retreat. No, the beast was up to something.

Exhausted, Jake stood there panting, clutching his weapon uneasily in his sweaty grip, and trying to figure out what Tazaroc was plotting.

Then he saw. Having slunk down onto the wider space of the landing, the dragon had enough room to spread its wings.

Oh, I'm in trouble...

Jake's eyes widened as the dragon flapped his wings a few times, rising vertically from the landing.

Suddenly, shoving off the back wall with his back feet, combined with one powerful flap of its wings, Tazaroc zoomed straight at him like a giant orange rocket with a mouthful of serrated teeth.

What happened next came without forethought.

Jake let out a war cry, dropped the spear, and hammered the charging dragon with the most brutal, two-handed blast of telekinetic power he could summon.

It was enough to burst a blood vessel in his eye; he felt it pop.

Hit by an invisible blast of energy, the creature slammed against the back wall, then fell like an avalanche. Letting out an earsplitting scream, it raked its claws down the granite wall as it scrabbled for purchase, to no avail. It toppled to the landing, then crashed down the stairs, all the way down to the lobby floor.

Whereupon Jake heard an odd metallic clank.

Silence.

Is it...dead?

Chest heaving, Jake waited at the top of the stairs, eyes wide, heart pounding. He quickly bent and grabbed the spear again, just in case.

But Tazaroc wasn't moving. Jake heard the scientists rush out of the Lightrider cavern below and start marveling amongst themselves at what they saw.

Ha! A smile of disbelief slowly spread across Jake's face.

Spear in hand, he was already in motion, turning away and starting to jog off down the corridor on shaky legs.

I just slew a dragon!

He couldn't wait to tell the carrot-head. Knight in shining armor and all. *Wonder if this'll get me a kiss?*

No such luck.

Tazaroc wasn't dead yet.

A one-ton creature makes a lot of noise when it moves about, and Jake hadn't gone more than five paces when he heard the sickening sounds of the dragon waking up, shaking it off.

Jake froze mid-stride and then slowly turned back toward the stairwell. *No.*

But it was true.

Tazaroc was still alive. Jake realized he must've only knocked the wind out of the beast, stunned it for a few seconds.

Standing there in shock, he heard the menacing click of the dragon's nails scrape the floor as it rolled upright, shook itself like a dog, and then snorted.

The scientists reacted with alarm.

The dragon coughed a few times as if to clear its throat.

A faint *"Oh, no"* reached Jake from the downstairs lobby.

"The fire collar's off!" one of the scientists yelled.

Fire collar?

"Ruuun!"

At that moment, a roar louder than any Jake had heard so far reverberated through the lobby and up the stairwell—a wild bellow so forceful that it shook the very castle.

A ferocious explosion of reptilian freedom.

Leather snapped and buckles jangled as the dragon, Jake assumed, freed itself from its saddle and harness.

A worrisome guttural hiss filled the space below, followed by a soft, vibratory rumble, like a factory-sized bellows getting ready to fire up a furnace.

Then came the fire blast.

The scientists screamed.

Jake's eyes widened. *Ohh—!* "Fire collar." So that's why—

Before he could finish that thought, Tazaroc went on a rampage.

Rooted in place, Jake listened to every detail in morbid fascination.

He couldn't help it.

He knew he should run—and he would, shortly—but he hearkened to the fray below for a moment longer like his life depended on it.

Maybe it did.

Panic took hold below. Footfalls scattered and shrieks erupted as the beast wrought mayhem on the scientists. Considering what they'd done to the Lightriders, though, including his parents, Jake did not feel especially sorry for them.

Well, maybe a little. It sounded like a gruesome way to go.

Hmm. Being a boy of thirteen, he could not resist sneaking back to the stairwell entrance, slipping down a few steps, and peering around the bend, almost daring himself to see some blood and guts. Just to confirm the situation, of course.

Blimey. There was a trousered leg lying near the bottom of the stairwell. So much for that chap's efforts to escape.

At least, from here, it was easier to make out what they were saying.

"Lock down the lab!"

"Get out of here! This thing's out of control!"

"No, no, please— *Aaaah!*"

Tazaroc struck the fear of God into all those heartless, white-coated know-it-alls whose innate curiosity had drawn them out to investigate— and whose arrogance had kept them there, watching, when they should have fled.

It was too late now. Heart pounding, Jake listened to all the cool, logical men turning...how had they put it?

Hysterical.

Bodies thumped against walls as the dragon tossed men like toys. The screaming was horrible as various limbs were separated from their respective owners.

All the while, hungry hisses and snarls of delight rose from Tazaroc.

"Somebody get Lord *Wyyyy*—" The words broke into a bloodcurdling scream.

Only the Drow kept their cool, by the sound of it.

"Omric, you stay with me. Zumeth, find the boy. Protect him!" Jake heard Duradel order his bodyguards in their particular accent.

Aw, how sweet, Jake thought with a smirk. Well, being the chosen one did have its advantages. *Thanks, but no thanks.*

He didn't need their help. He was getting out of here.

Deep down, Jake knew that terrorizing the scientists was only a temporary game for the dragon. *He* was the prey Tazaroc had fixed on, and any minute now, the beast would come looking for him. He'd already wasted valuable time.

With that, Jake dodged back up the stairs and ran.

Not a moment too soon, as it turned out. He had barely sprinted ten yards down the corridor when a huge fireball rolled up out of the stairwell, right where he had been standing seconds ago.

He ducked instinctively, glanced back, and squinted in the fire's blinding flare. Then he swallowed hard.

Tazaroc was coming. And this time, Jake knew, the scaly beast wasn't playing fetch.

Time seemed to slow as Jake whirled around and started running down the corridor.

His heart slammed behind his ribcage. All his thoughts were fixed on finding his way back to the outer ring. Then he could enter one of the corner towers, as he'd plotted earlier, run up onto the ramparts, and flag Red down to come and pick him up.

Unless the dragon got him first.

All of his old rookery instincts warned him that he had to get out of sight. Where the deuce was a side hallway when he needed one? He couldn't afford to let the dragon see him.

There! Up ahead. An intersection in the labyrinth. *Finally.* Jake pounded toward it.

Now the big question. *Do I go right or left?*

The wrong choice could be fatal. It seemed so hard to decide.

Counting the seconds until he reached the crossroads, Jake kept looking over his shoulder as he ran. His frantic panting filled the hallway, making far too much noise. His whole body felt hot and cold, flooded with unnatural, wild strength and jittery weakness.

But even his top speed was not enough.

Tazaroc climbed out of the stairwell, spotted him at once, and started galloping after him.

Jake cursed. The intersection zoomed up. He decided on a right-hand turn at the last second, diving around the corner just in time to take cover from another lad-sized fire blast that ripped through the intersection like an out-of-control freight train set ablaze. The heat was intense as it gusted by.

Then the chase was on.

Through the twisting, turning pathways of the blue-black labyrinth,

Jake followed hard-won survival instincts honed in the roughest sections of the rookery. Aye, the whole pack of wild O'Dell brothers couldn't have caught him now, ducking right, dashing left, whipping through forks in the road as though driven by some higher consciousness than his own.

Tazaroc refused to be shaken.

The dragon had seen where Jake had entered the maze and would not let him out of its sight for more than a moment or two.

Sometimes the beast was right behind him; others, Jake managed to trick it into a brief separation, veering off unpredictably to put a few hallways between them. But Tazaroc kept pace and always reappeared, glaring at him from some parallel hallway—a terrifying sight—lobbing fireballs or snapping its deadly jaws.

Jake dryly decided that perhaps he would not mind the Drow chap's assistance, after all. He wondered if Zumeth was here in the labyrinth somewhere.

Oh, come on! He's not going to risk his neck getting in this thing's way to rescue me, no matter what Duradel says.

A curious crewman with very poor timing poked his head out of a room in some random hallway to see what the fuss was, only to become a human candle. The man barely had time to scream.

Sorry! Jake thought with a wince. *Too bad. I could've asked him for directions.*

The blasted outer ring had to be here somewhere.

Jake ignored the fact that he was completely exhausted. Ignored the slight trickle of blood from his nose. He wiped it away with his sleeve and kept running.

When I grow up, he thought, I *shall petition Parliament to outlaw fox hunts.* He now knew exactly how the poor foxes must feel with a pack of hounds on their trail.

Then Jake nearly made the mistake of turning down a dead end. He stopped himself from going that way with a small gasp.

He turned, took three steps the other way, and found himself facing a weird little circular section of the labyrinth that branched off in five different directions.

Five hallways, all different shapes and sizes.

Now what? Jake stood in the middle, considering his choices in a state of misery. He had no idea which way to go and was too tired to think his way through any more life-or-death decisions. In that moment, a part of him simply wanted to surrender.

He could hear Tazaroc snuffling in a corridor somewhere close. Could feel the evil influence that filled the warlocks' stronghold oppressing his soul, telling him he wasn't getting out of here alive. That it would've been better to cooperate and agree to become the Black Prince while he still had the chance.

Now he was destined merely to become dragon food.

Lost, out of breath, and at his wits' end, Jake closed his eyes in despair. *Please, God, a little help?*

Jake waited, hearing the dragon's footsteps pound closer and closer...

But then—

His eyes shot open with astonishment as the answer came at once. Why, he must've paid better attention in church than he'd realized, for a fragment of a Bible verse popped right into his head.

Narrow is the way which leadeth unto life, and few there be that find it.

Narrow? Jake scanned the five choices of hallways before him.

The middle one was as skinny as a catwalk. Too thin for a dragon, to be sure.

Go! Jake ran, plunging straight ahead into the oddly thin hallway. It was the blackest he had seen, hardly any of those weird blue-glowing wall sconces.

He hadn't gone three paces before doubt crept in. This seemed all wrong. Narrower and narrower with every step he took, this passage was even creepier than the others and probably led out right into Tazaroc's mouth. Jake half expected to be incinerated at any moment.

But having made his choice, he pressed on in faith, determined to get free of this castle, ignoring his fears and the dragon and everything that told him he was doomed.

The passage grew tighter and tighter until it became too narrow for his shoulders. He had to angle his body slightly sideways to fit through. *What loonbat designed this?*

Probably Zolond. Again, urgency filled Jake to get outside and go to the Dark Master's aid, and Aunt Ramona's.

If only he could reach the outer ring!

The skinny passage narrowed even more, and Jake had to hold his breath to squeeze himself out the other end.

The next thing he knew, he stumbled into a wide corridor, caught his balance, and looked around. A broad smile broke across his sweaty face. *It worked!* He was standing in the outer ring. He could tell by the hallway's width.

Better still, no dragon.

Blimey. I think I lost him.

Jake dared to hope that his luck must finally be turning, for he spotted the round base of one of the towers not far ahead. The thick wooden door was propped open under the archway, just waiting for him. It was a beautiful sight.

Already in motion, he folded his hands for a second. *Thank you!*

Then he sprinted toward the exit with all he had left. If he could just get to that tower, he might actually make it out of here alive.

But the Black Fortress had...other plans for Jake.

Just as he was closing in on the open doorway, freedom almost in his grasp, Tazaroc skidded out of an intersecting hallway a few yards ahead and blocked his path. The foul beast turned toward Jake and let out a triumphant yowl, then blasted fire at the ceiling.

Aghast, Jake stumbled to a halt.

The dragon roared at him and gathered itself to attack. Jake glanced toward the nearest hallway opening—but then, as Tazaroc started to bound toward him, he heard a yell from somewhere behind the dragon.

An arrow suddenly struck the beast in the rump.

The Drow! Jake realized, amazed.

Tazaroc bellowed at the injury just as Zumeth neatly shot a second arrow into the dragon's flank, then a third into its shoulder. Clearly the dark elves shared expert archery skills with their forest-dwelling cousins.

Jake ducked into the nearest side hallway but, still determined to reach the tower, did not run away. Instead, he watched from around the corner as Tazaroc easily wriggled his body around in the large hallway to face the other direction, then growled with utter menace and went after the archer.

Eyeing the back half of the dragon and the distance to the tower door—maybe fifty feet—Jake considered making a run for it while the monster was distracted. But he quickly discarded the notion.

He was pretty good at sneaking, but not that good. Not good enough to tiptoe past a dragon while it dealt with an enemy.

And lucky he hadn't tried it, for the battle didn't last long.

Tazaroc, with shocking speed and surprising agility—nimbly dodging arrows on the way—bounded up to the corner of the outer ring where Zumeth was hiding. The two clashed, but then the dragon forcefully swatted the Drow with its front leg. Zumeth went flying.

Judging by the two thuds Jake heard, the blow sent the warrior crashing against the granite wall and then down to the floor. Before the dark elf could pick himself up, the dragon roasted him.

No! Jake thought, stricken.

For a second, he just stared at the back of the dragon in shock. He didn't want anyone sacrificing themselves for him, not even a Drow! He didn't even know which one "Zumeth" was—Triangle Chin or Crescent Moon.

Angry now, Jake was done hiding.

He stepped boldly out of the side corridor and watched as Tazaroc yanked the Drow arrows out with his teeth, spat them onto the floor, and then curled his big, slithery body around, ready to deal with him.

"You didn't have to kill him," Jake said in a hard tone. "We both know it's me you want."

Tazaroc hissed. The lizard's golden eyes gleamed in the dim, bluish light of the hallway with cruel anticipation.

Jake stood uncertainly in the middle of the corridor, spear in hand, not quite sure what he intended. But he couldn't run anymore. He wanted out.

The dragon looked different now that they stood on equal footing. It looked gigantic and impossible to beat.

It towered over him, its horned head as high as the ceiling of his bedroom back home at Griffon Castle. The apex of its muscular, rust-colored legs was as high as Jake's shoulders, and from this angle, each of its claws, as long as his forearm, reminded Jake of meat hooks.

When it snarled at him again, he noticed the blood on its fangs. He grimaced. "Haven't you had your fill yet, ye glutton?"

"Rrrrrrr," said Tazaroc, twitching its tail.

"Easy," Jake said as the growling dragon bristled before him.

Now that its fire collar was gone, Jake could see how the metal cuff had chafed the skin all around its neck. There were small, round wounds, as though the collar had been riveted into the beast's flesh.

He almost felt sorry for the creature, but the feeling wasn't mutual. Tazaroc's snakelike eyes were wicked, assessing him. The dragon fully intended to savor killing him.

Then it snarled, its upper lip curling over its gums like a dog baring its teeth.

Jake took a step backward. "Can we talk about this?" he mumbled, weighing his chances of running past the dragon.

Not very good.

"I'm, ah, the chosen one, remember?"

He tried a quick feint to the left, but Tazaroc stepped right to block his path with ease. Far down the hallway, its tail flicked, showing the sort of pleasure a cat took in toying with a mouse it knew it had cornered.

Jake dodged to the right; the dragon mirrored his motions. He could've sworn the thing was laughing at him.

"Now look here! I am the Black Prince!" It was worth a shot, anyway.

Tazaroc was not impressed. The rumble in its throat grew louder as it tired of the game.

Suddenly, it tilted its head, leaned down, and bellowed at top volume in his face.

Jake's hair blew back, but he stared in astonishment as decorative flaps of skin that had been held down by the fire collar fanned out around the dragon's neck. They fluttered menacingly as Tazaroc roared.

Well, that's new. Jake was pretty sure this showy, warlike display meant the beast had had its sport and was ready to eat him now.

Jake took a step back, unnerved by the newfound depths of the dragon's ferocity. *Blimey.* He thought this thing was mean before, but this was a whole new level of vicious.

Then Jake blanched as the dragon's chest began to glow.

Just in time, he flung up his left hand and let out a cry as Tazaroc blasted him with fire. Jake had never attempted to use his telekinesis to hold back flames before and didn't even know if it would work.

It did. But he could feel the barreling inferno warm his palm and fingers, growing hotter and hotter.

The fire blast seemed to go on and on. *How is this possible?*

Finally, the dragon stopped to take a breath. Jake shook his hand, trying to cool it. He noticed the ground was smoking and charred all around him. He glanced at his palm and saw the flesh was reddened. But he was alive.

Tazaroc glowered, looking angry and confused that the fire blast had failed to fry him.

Then the battle was on.

Jake used his telekinesis to ram the dragon's head hard against the ceiling. Bits of masonry rained down, pelting the floor below. A cloud of brick dust filled the air.

Tazaroc howled.

Jake stabbed it in the foreleg with his spear, but the creature barely seemed to feel it. Then the dragon fought back, attacking him again like in the stairwell. It snapped and lashed with stunning speed. Jake held it off, though it towered over him. It even tried to stomp him, rearing up on its hind legs and then pouncing down at him.

Jake managed to dance out from underneath its feet, but the dragon's scaly head darted to and fro on its long neck as it tried to bite him. He walloped it in the face with his telekinesis then, as the creature charged again, nearly poked it in the eye with his spear, ducking and diving out of the way.

All the while, Tazaroc slapped his tail back and forth from one side of the hallway to the other. Apparently, this was something the dragon did to show its displeasure.

It felt like an earthquake hit the corridor. Jake's eyes stung from all the debris in the air.

This thing isn't going to be happy until it eats me.

Jake gulped when he saw the dragon's chest begin to glow bright orange. *Here we go again.* Then it drew itself up tall and let loose another fire blast.

"Aaargh!" Jake shielded himself again with his telekinesis, sweating in the heat.

I guess it likes its food cooked, he thought with gallows humor as he waited.

Dying would be bad enough; he at least wanted there to be something left for his friends to bury.

When its fire failed to kill him for the second time, Tazaroc snapped at Jake in disgust.

Jake thrust the spear upward hard, aiming for the roof of the mouth in hopes of piercing through to the beast's brain.

Tazaroc thwarted him unexpectedly, grabbing the spear between its teeth.

Unfortunately, as Tazaroc whipped his head back, Jake released his grip on his weapon a few seconds too late. He went flying over the dragon's wing, hit the ground hard with a solid *oomph*, and tumbled down the hallway, rolling to a halt a few feet away from the charred Drow.

Ugh!

Jake felt surging pain all over. The back of his head had hit the ground hard when he landed, and he touched it, dazed. His hand came back bloody.

He scowled, then looked up just in time to see Tazaroc crunching down on the spear, splintering it, rendering it useless. The dragon dropped the pieces to the ground, then looked at him as if to say, *Now I've got you.*

Tazaroc took a massive inhale. Jake saw the dragon's chest shining with an angry orange light.

He realized he was about to die.

Before setting him ablaze, Tazaroc roared once again in Jake's face, spraying dragon spit instead of fire this time, its orange ruff flittering with triumph.

Overwhelmed by the creature's ferocity, Jake was out of fight.

He tried once, feebly, to get up, but the dragon smacked him back down and held him pinned in place with an icy stare.

Jake was exhausted, in pain, probably concussed, and, at that moment, everything in him wanted to quit. He rolled onto his back, looked up into the beast's terrifying snake eyes, and felt utter despair.

"Just get it over with," he mumbled.

But then, from the corner of his eye, he noticed the dead Drow, maybe six feet away, and the dagger sheathed at his side.

In the last instant before Tazaroc engulfed him in fire, Jake stretched out his right hand and used his telekinesis to draw the blade to himself. The fine elvish weapon slid out of its scabbard and whisked across the floor straight into his grasp. It was warm to the touch, but not overly so.

Jake wrapped his fingers around the hilt, drawing strength from its balanced weight and barbarous feel.

Then, raising his left arm, he warded off the fire blast that was meant to be Tazaroc's finishing blow. The tempest of white-hot flame bent all around him. The circle of ground surrounding his body started to glow red with the intensity of the dragon's wrath.

Over and over, the fire blasts kept coming.

Jake struggled up onto one knee, shielding himself from the fiery onslaught all the while.

The dragon raged at Jake's refusal to die, working harder to unleash an inferno upon him.

Heart pounding, chest heaving, sweating profusely in the heat, blood trickling down the back of his neck from the blow to his head, Jake tightened his grip around the short handle of his dagger and waited.

Would it never end? A pained whimper might've escaped him as he used all of his remaining strength to outlast the beast.

With the next, furious blast, the dragon thrashed its head from side to side, as though to make sure he'd be evenly toasted.

Jake counted the seconds...

Now!

When the dragon ran out of breath, Jake surged up onto his feet, leaped into the air, thrusting his whole body forward, and, in one quick motion, hurled the Drow blade straight at the dragon's fiery heart. Still soaring toward the beast, he used his telekinesis to drive the dagger in with incredible force.

The blade plunged deep, fully disappearing in the dragon's chest, handle and all, while Jake landed squarely in a crouch.

Tazaroc reared back and screamed.

Shaking from exertion, Jake retreated a few yards down the corridor for fear of being stepped on as the dragon began clomping around in its death throes, screeching with rage.

Its razor-sharp claws gashed the walls, giving off sparks. The wild flapping of its wings broke several sconces, plunging the hallway into even blacker darkness. The monster unleashed one last fireball that rolled along the ceiling.

Jake ducked as it blazed by overhead.

Although he was trembling from head to toe, bloodied and still dizzy from the blow to the head, there was no time to recover. Distant shouts rose from behind him. He had to get out of here.

Jake turned and saw some of the gray-clad crewmen cautiously entering the far end of the corridor. They only held back because Tazaroc was still on his feet, thrashing about. He clenched his jaw. Apparently they were evil, not stupid.

For his part, Jake was completely spent. Blood oozed from his nose. He wiped it away on his sleeve. At this point, he could not have lifted a feather with his telekinesis. He just wanted to go home and collapse into bed.

Unfortunately, if he did not get out of here right now, he was going to be captured, and this all would be for naught.

Go. Glaring at the still-distant crewmen, he turned to face Tazaroc.

The dragon was still bellowing with fury and writhing around violently in the hallway, blocking his path to the tower door.

Jake had no choice but to chance it. He had to get past the dying beast before he was captured. For a moment, he watched the creature anxiously, but trying to predict its fitful movements was impossible. *Here goes nothing.*

Jake launched into a full-out sprint.

As he charged toward the dying monster with all he had left, disaster nearly struck. *Bad timing!*

The towering beast started falling toward him.

Jake reacted automatically, dropping backward and sliding under the angle of the dragon's wing. He felt the breeze from the leathery sail whoosh past his face as he glided by under it.

The second he was clear, he sprang to his feet on the other side of the beast, jumped over its whipping tail, and raced to the tower, darting through the doorway.

Behind him, Tazaroc let out a last rage-filled roar and crashed to the ground, dead.

CHAPTER THIRTY-SIX
The Reaper

Jake ran up the spiral stairs that coiled up and up the tight, narrow tower. He could not wait to escape this cursed castle.

He held on to the railing as he ascended, dizzy from the aftermath of his ordeal, not to mention the nasty blow to the head. His whole body felt full of aches and pains. He'd been through a lot in his thirteen years, but blimey, fighting a dragon might well leave him with considerable mental trauma, he thought wryly. He could still smell the thing's smoky breath.

Unfortunately, his ordeal wasn't over yet. He would not feel safe until he was back down on the ground—and there was still the matter of what might've happened in his absence. Were Zolond and Aunt Ramona still alive? Were his friends safe? Or had Wyvern destroyed London? Was Jake already too late?

The questions made him woozy, and a wave of exhaustion caught up to him. Halfway up the spiral stairs, Jake paused to rest his burning leg muscles and brace himself as best he could for whatever awaited him outside.

It was then, as he stood catching his breath, that he heard wild singing outside. Frustration filled him.

Fionnula.

Oh, what is she up to now? Gathering his strength, Jake forced himself onward, wiping the sweat from his brow and the trickle of blood from his nostrils. He *hoped* the nosebleed was only due to overusing his gift, and not an aftereffect of smashing his head against the floor.

Still, all things considered, he'd take it. He didn't even want to think about what Tazaroc *could've* done to him. Jake pushed belated terror out of his mind with a shudder and kept on climbing the stairs.

'Round and 'round the dark tower went. The spiral staircase was making him so dizzy that he feared if he let go of the banister, he could tumble right back down into the clutches of Wyvern's henchmen.

They had not yet started after him up the tower. Perhaps they were afraid he'd fling them down the stairs with his telekinesis.

As if he could right now. No, he was out of steam. Good thing *they* didn't know that.

Jake just hoped Red could pick him up quickly, before the crewmen worked up their nerve to try to capture him now that the dragon had failed.

In any case, Fionnula's singing grew louder as Jake reached the top of the tower. He braced himself before bursting out through the door, knowing he might have to cover his ears to protect himself from her magic.

When he stepped out onto the rampart wall around the top of the Black Fortress, Jake discovered the sea-witch had summoned a gale that was ripping any remaining dead leaves off the trees around Parliament Square.

To Jake, the wind felt good on his face. It helped revive him after the head smash, the chloroform, the demon...

He did not even want to think about the Lightrider cavern. It was too painful knowing he had failed to get his parents out of there or do anything useful for all the other captives.

There was nothing he *could* do now but swallow his anger and focus on the situation at hand. Glancing around from high atop the ramparts, Jake saw he had emerged from the back tower on the side closest to where he'd left his friends.

A wave of missing them washed through him after all he'd just gone through. They were always so kind to him. Jake sighed. He would be with them soon.

He decided *not* to try to get the gang's attention, for fear they might react in a way that revealed his presence to Wyvern. Jake could not resist sneaking over to the crenelated battlements, however, and peeking down to make sure they were all right.

Oh, no. Sir Robert Peel stood all alone. To Jake's alarm, his friends were no longer hiding behind the statue.

A sick feeling twisted in his stomach. He hoped with all his heart that they had left, gone back to Buckingham Palace. Maybe Leopard-Helena had forced them to retreat to safety.

Somehow, though, he doubted it.

Crouch-running to the front of the castle, Jake spotted Red still engaged in a vicious battle with Thanatos atop the roof of Westminster Palace. *Blimey.* Lion roars and eagle screeches punctuated Fionnula's singing. (Jake had not covered his ears, but did not feel affected.) He could see the creatures' duel, since he, too, was up high.

Jake knew he had to get Red's attention to come and pick him up, but the Gryphon was fully engaged in his duel against the manticore. He dared not break Red's concentration by trying to signal him yet.

What he saw of their fight was disconcerting. Mighty as he was, the Gryphon could not seem to defeat Wyvern's pet monster. Indeed, as Jake looked on, Thanatos leaped off an angled part of the roof onto Red's back and started biting the scruff of his neck.

Jake stared; Red thrashed, but it seemed like his magical healing feathers gave him some sort of protection. The Gryphon flapped a few feet up from the roof, and Thanatos fell off him—but then suddenly captured one of Red's wingtips in his jaws. The manticore pulled the Gryphon back down onto the roof, as though insisting that he stay there and fight him. Red seemed happy to comply, roaring in his enemy's face.

Both lion-bodied beasts continued rearing up and slashing at each other with their front paws, trying to gouge each other—Red with his sharp, hooked beak, Thanatos with his hideous scorpion tail.

Uneasily, Jake looked down into the square to see how the other battles were proceeding. Fionnula had summoned two isolated hurricanes into being around Derek and Aunt Ramona.

Hurricane winds, driving rains, and wild tornadoes whirled around each of them. As either one tried to walk forward or fight their way out of the storm, their own personal tornadoes moved with them, buffeting them with hail and rain.

Jake gasped when he saw that Aunt Ramona's wand had blown out of her hand. Derek also was vulnerable, barely able to take a step forward despite all of his Guardian strength. His jacket and his dark hair whipped wildly in the winds assaulting him.

Fionnula sang and laughed, pleased with herself.

Over to the left of the square, though, things weren't going so well for General Raige.

Jake's jaw dropped when he saw that his friends had rushed the deadly warrior en masse, tackled Raige to the ground, and proceeded to beat the tar out of him.

A grin broke across Jake's face as he stared, incredulous.

Raige's fantastical blunderbuss lay a few yards away from him on the ground with its barrel all bent at right angles. Jake could only figure that Nixie must've whomped it with some sort of spell. The thing was mangled.

Having charged the general, slammed him flat on his back, and disarmed him, the kids were attacking him with great gusto—even dainty Isabelle.

The bobbies had rushed in to help, but it didn't look to Jake like his friends needed their assistance. With the five of them working together, they had managed to take away Raige's knives and even strip him of his ammunition belt. And now they were giving the oversized bully what could only be described as a proper thrashing.

It was glorious to see. Jake laughed quietly. He had never been prouder.

Brian held Raige in a wrestling chokehold. Isabelle had torn one of the bobbies' truncheons out of his grasp and was beating Raige about the shoulders, while Dani kept punching him in the stomach like a little rookery savage; Archie went for the eyes. Nixie was on her feet, kicking Raige repeatedly in the thigh.

The general roared, but if he shoved off one, the others fought harder.

Meanwhile, Miss Helena was doing her best to end Fionnula's attack on Derek and Aunt Ramona.

The snarling black leopard-governess crept up from the side, then sprang at the sea-witch, chomping down on her right forearm.

Fionnula yelped but managed to keep singing, though she sounded in serious pain. Somehow she kept the two hurricanes going and quickly shifted her wand into her left hand, aiming it at Helena.

The leopardess had to release her grip and dart from side to side as she ran to avoid being turned into heaven-knew-what.

Jake watched Fionnula cast a quick healing spell on her chewed-up arm, then a furious lion's roar sounded in the distance.

He looked across the square to find Red flying slowly and with great effort toward the river; the manticore's horrid scorpion tail was clamped fast in the Gryphon's beak.

Jake's eyes widened. Thanatos dangled upside down, unable to do anything but slash at the air with his paws.

Then Red dropped him.

"Whoa," Jake whispered. From his vantage point on the ramparts, he saw the huge splash as the manticore plummeted into the cold gray Thames. "Yes." *Good boy, Red!*

The Gryphon screeched in ferocious victory, rising a few feet higher now that he was free of his burden.

Jake waved his arms eagerly, trying to get his pet's attention without Wyvern seeing him.

But for all his eagle vision, good old Claw the Courageous was still so full of righteous fury at his enemy that he missed Jake's signal. The Gryphon swooped off down the river.

Aw, no! Jake watched in alarm. *Where's he going?*

Red! he yelled mentally. *Come back! Don't leave me stranded here!*

But the Gryphon glided off over the Thames, following the manticore down the current. Apparently, he wanted to confirm that the beast had drowned and would not climb out of the river downstream to start terrorizing London again.

Jake scowled. *Well, be quick about it.* He glanced over his shoulder at the tower door. There was no sign of the crewmen. He wondered why they had not come after him.

Unless...

An alarming thought struck.

Maybe the Fortress was preparing to jump and the crewmen had to see to their duties. It made sense that they'd be in charge of that process, whatever was involved. Jake cursed silently, then eyed his distant Gryphon.

You better get back here soon, you big birdbrain.

All the while, Zolond and Wyvern were exchanging lightning-bolt wand blasts of nigh-cosmic intensity.

The Dark Master was still very much alive, but beneath the brim of his black bowler hat, his wrinkled face was stamped with icy wrath.

Thankfully, he was no longer part skeleton. Jake could tell Zolond had reclaimed his magical ring from Wyvern, too, because a lime-green glow radiated around the Dark Master's left hand.

As Jake looked on, Zolond started an ominous incantation that made Wyvern step back.

The sorcerer-king angled his walking-stick wand toward the earl as he spoke words in some arcane language; then the ring on his finger sprayed forth a cloud of green gas.

The cloud floated forward at once, turning dark and soupy as it descended toward the stretch of grass between the two warlocks. When it hit the ground, it turned into a large puddle of gooey black liquid resembling tar.

The inky black goo slithered across the grass toward Wyvern. He took another step backward, as though unsure what this was.

When the black puddle neared him, it stopped.

Wyvern eyed Zolond with suspicion, gripping his wand.

Suddenly, the cloaked figure of a Grim Reaper exploded up out of the substance. It was either made of the black goo or covered in it—Jake couldn't tell. Immediately, the reaper swung its famous sickle of death at the Nephilim.

Fionnula's song broke off. "Be careful, Nathan! Those things don't stop until they kill the person they've been sent for!"

Wyvern glanced uneasily at her, then ducked the reaper's blade as it swung by, inches from his chest.

Jake watched and couldn't help cheering inside for the gooey black figure.

Then a flash of action from another section of the field caught his eye. Nixie had noticed that Aunt Ramona's wand had blown away, and left off kicking General Raige to fetch it for her.

Dangerous. Archie looked over in alarm.

As that was happening, Red left the river and began circling back toward the square, apparently satisfied that Thanatos was good and dead.

Jake retreated from the edge of the battlements so Wyvern wouldn't see him and stood tall in the middle of the ramparts walkway, waving his arms to get his pet's attention.

He persisted anxiously until Red cawed to acknowledge he'd spotted Jake. He began flying faster toward the Fortress, but Jake did not want the Gryphon's arrival to alert Wyvern that he was there. So he signaled Red with urgent gestures to fly around and approach the castle from the back.

To Jake's relief, Red understood, banking away and flying lower to avoid notice.

Good boy. Knowing it would take the Gryphon a few moments to arrive, Jake sneaked back to the battlements to continue watching the proceedings.

While Wyvern dodged deadly whacks from the reaper that Zolond appeared focused on controlling, Nixie grabbed Aunt Ramona's wand from where it had blown onto the grass. The Elder witch had been unable to retrieve it herself, fighting the whirlwind around her.

Bravely, Nixie ran toward her mentor.

"Girl! You there! What do you think you're doing?" Fionnula demanded, pausing her song, though she kept the storms whirling with her wand.

Nixie ignored her. "Lady Bradford—here!" Holding on to the wand with both hands, the brave little mage slowly poked it in through the side of the tornado.

Aunt Ramona seized it; Fionnula cried out with anger.

"You meddlesome little brat!"

Nixie raised her own wand but backed away as the sea-witch homed in on her.

There was too much going on at once! Jake didn't know where to look. Fionnula zinged magic at Nixie; Nixie leaped clear.

With her wand back in her grasp, Aunt Ramona started overcoming the tornado that imprisoned her. Meanwhile, the reaper stalked forward, determined to slice Wyvern in half. Jake glanced briefly over his shoulder and saw Red beginning his descent. The Gryphon was gliding toward the back of the castle to come and get him.

Jake looked forward again, not wanting to miss a thing. Big Ben started tolling the hour of four, its booming voice filling the square from atop the nearby Clock Tower.

At that moment, Raige suddenly threw the kids off him with a roar. Jake's friends toppled aside; Raige dove for his ammunition belt and unclipped a red metallic ball.

"*Shield!*" he bellowed across the square at Wyvern and Fionnula, then yanked the pin out with his teeth. Instantly, a red transparent dome of energy covered Raige as he hurled the mysterious object toward the middle of Parliament Square.

It had rings around it like the planet Saturn. They whirled 'round and 'round as it rolled.

Wait. Jake narrowed his eyes. *Is that some sort of...grenade?*

Wyvern saw the weapon and instantly conjured a solid metal capsule around himself. Fionnula encircled herself behind a thick wall of water.

Then came a boom and a flash as Raige's weapon exploded.

But this was no ordinary bomb.

A great ring of magic rushed out in all directions. Everyone in its swiftly widening radius suddenly went motionless, as though Time itself stopped.

A time bomb?

The Grim Reaper froze mid-swing.

Derek and Aunt Ramona looked like mannequins. Even the tornadoes around them quit whirling.

Jake's friends were stuck in their various poses, starting to get up after Raige had scattered them like bowling pins.

Then the wave of magic swept over Jake, and he found he couldn't move.

A few yards behind him, Red was frozen in midair.

Time slowed to a trickle.

Big Ben stopped mid-bong.

Jake felt even the mere blink of his eyes decelerate, as though each...blink...took...

Forever.

Then he saw that Zolond was frozen, too.

Oh no...

The only ones unaffected were Wyvern, the sea-witch, and Raige.

As for the rest of them, they were fully conscious—able to see, hear, and think—but they could not move.

As soon as the blast wave passed, Wyvern's metal capsule disappeared, then he simply ducked beneath the Grim Reaper's motionless sickle and stepped around the frozen phantom.

Raige's red dome dissolved. He climbed to his feet, and Fionnula came out from behind her wall of water.

Jake watched in dread, unable to move, as Wyvern sauntered toward Zolond, who was all but paralyzed.

"Thanks for your help, Raige," the Nephilim said in a casual tone. "I won't forget this."

The general grunted. "Just get it over with. This is taking too long. We don't need Deathhand showing up."

Deathhand? Jake could only hear what they were saying because the rest of the square had gone absolutely silent.

Wyvern strolled right up to the Dark Master, who could only stare balefully at him.

He looked at him for a long moment, hands on hips. "Didn't expect to see me again, did you? Here's what I say to your ice grendels." Wyvern reached for the old man's hand and pried the ring off his finger. "I'll take that." Then he put it on his own.

Extending his freakish Nephilim hand, he looked at it admiringly. "It suits me better than you." He lifted it and showed the ring to Zolond, wiggling his fingers with a mocking smile.

"Hurry up, Wyvern! The effect only lasts three minutes," Raige said. His battlefield commander's voice carried across the square.

Wyvern snorted. "You must forgive me if I can't help but savor the moment. I've been waiting a long time for this."

Jake strained uselessly to move, an icy feeling in his gut. *Please, don't...*

He was powerless to stop what he knew was about to happen.

Wyvern bent down to Zolond's eye level and gave him a terrifying smile. "First, I'm going to kill you; then I'm going to kill your grandson." He straightened up again. "Goodbye, Zolond. Give my regards to Shemrazul."

Wyvern clenched his hand into a fist and whispered a dark spell into the ring he had taken from the Dark Master. The stone began to glow with an angry reddish hue.

Jake watched, horrified, as Wyvern aimed the ring at Zolond. He strained uselessly against the paralysis that had imprisoned him and everyone there. *No, please, no...*

Aunt Ramona!

A smoky black arrow flew out of the sorcerer's ring with a sound like the concentrated scream of a thousand banshees.

The arrow struck Zolond in the heart at point-blank range, dissolving into his chest as it entered.

The walking stick fell out of Zolond's hand. When it hit the ground, it changed into a tall rod with a horned shape on top, like the sleek, pointy ears of jackal-headed Anubis, Egyptian god of the dead.

Wyvern reached down and picked it up, admiring it with a smile of proud fascination. "The scepter of the sorcerer-king..."

"And don't forget *this*, my lord," Fionnula said. She had joined him and now presented Wyvern with Zolond's bowler hat. "Or should I say, Your Majesty?"

Wyvern laughed while Jake strained in helpless rage. Then Wyvern tapped the bowler with the scepter he had claimed. "Reveal!"

At once, the plain round hat transformed into a sinister black crown, polished to a midnight gloss, and ornately sculpted with tall, twisting spires. Jake recognized it from the vision Duradel had projected into his mind.

"Magnificent," Wyvern said, touching it reverently. But he did not take it. "This must be entrusted to Duradel until the night of my coronation."

"Yes, my lord." Fionnula gave him a formal curtsy, then carried the crown solemnly into the Fortress.

Wyvern scanned the square, openly gloating, then strode after her with Raige covering his exit.

Jake could barely see the evil trio anymore for the tears in his eyes. His gaze swung to Aunt Ramona.

He did not know how long she had or if there was any way to fix this. As for Zolond, Jake could not tell if the Dark Master was already dead on his feet or still breathing.

Then Wyvern paused on the drawbridge and turned to face the crowd.

Standing right beneath Jake, he lifted his hand as his deep voice rang out in a gleeful shout: "Farewell for now, London! Expect to hear from me again soon!"

Then he stalked into the Black Fortress and disappeared.

As soon as Raige entered the castle, the drawbridge slammed shut.

At once, a deafening sound erupted behind Jake, nearly scaring the daylights out of him. Machinery creaked and rumbled to life from somewhere down in the courtyard at the center of the castle. That same awful pulsation he'd heard after the rupture filled the air again—a deep, vibrating rhythm that meant the Black Fortress was about to jump.

Jake cried out in terror as movement returned. He quickly spun around to find a huge, bluish-white ball of electrical energy dancing atop a whirling metal contraption that looked like something an evil Archie would've invented.

Red stumbled to a landing near Jake just as the blinding orb shot lightning out to the castle's four pointy spires. Jake swung onto Red's back and prayed they'd be fast enough. The Gryphon leaped off the ramparts; Jake ducked low over Red's neck to keep his head beneath the lightning arcs crackling above him.

The warlocks' castle had already started flashing.

In the few short seconds it took Jake and Red to reach the ground, the Black Fortress was gone.

CHAPTER THIRTY-SEVEN
The Strongest Magic

The Gryphon pounced to earth. Jake swung off his back and started barreling toward Zolond and Aunt Ramona.

The moment she could move again, the Elder witch had whooshed over to her beloved Geoffrey's side in a cloud of white sparkles.

Zolond was on the ground, and she knelt beside him, shouting, "No!"

Exhausted as he thought he was, Jake's legs pumped with wild speed, carrying him faster toward the Elder witch than he had run from the dragon.

And yet he was too late.

He'd never seen such panic on his aunt's face, and it terrified him as he realized what it meant. Death was on its way.

No. Not you.

Jake felt his throat constrict with emotion. He ran faster, cursing himself for not being strong enough, smart enough, powerful enough, to stop this.

But now Jake's other gift came into play.

He could already see Aunt Ramona's spirit flickering in and out of her body as he approached—much like that sinister castle had done a moment ago, preparing to leave its current location.

Physically, the dowager baroness was on her knees, clutching the old man by the shoulders, trying to wake him, her voice sounding weaker by the second as she repeated his name. "Geoffrey!"

Zolond didn't stir.

There was no blood on the Dark Master that Jake could see as he skidded to a halt before them, just a strange burn mark on the front of his black coat.

"What can I do? Red!" Jake shouted. "A feather! Here—Aunt

Ramona—your wand!"

Red bounded over to his side while Jake scrambled to pick up her wand from where she'd dropped it nearby. His hands were shaking and he tripped over his own feet in his haste to bring it to her.

But Aunt Ramona didn't take it.

She just looked at him with three centuries of weariness in her eyes.

The color was ebbing from her face. Her skin looked papery thin, and all of a sudden, a woman he knew as a tower of strength seemed impossibly frail.

But there was no wound on her! He refused to believe she wouldn't be all right. He shoved the wand at her again.

"Take it! Do something!" Then Jake cried out as he saw a transparent copy of the Elder witch rise from her body and stand behind the old woman kneeling on the ground.

"No—Aunt Ramona, please." He spun to face the Gryphon. "Red!"

The Gryphon had already plucked one of his best golden feathers from his otherwise scarlet plumage and now offered it to him. Jake didn't even know yet what the gold ones did; they'd only just grown in since Red's recent molting.

The physical Aunt Ramona's eyes crinkled with fondness at the corners as Jake dropped to his knees beside Zolond, prepared to use the Gryphon's best magic feather on the Dark Master.

If he could heal him, then Aunt Ramona ought to be all right...

Wouldn't she?

"Save it, you darling boy," the flesh-and-blood Ramona whispered sadly. "I'm afraid it will not work." She looked down at Geoffrey again.

"We can at least try!"

"He's already dead, Jacob. In a few seconds, I will be too. At least I was able to be with him at the end. Now, listen—"

"No! You can't leave us. Don't go."

She shook her head with a wince. "I have no choice. I know you don't understand but...our lives were inextricably bound."

She didn't know Nixie had told them her secret. Jake didn't see any point in telling her now.

Too weak to remain upright any longer, Ramona lowered herself slowly to rest her head on her old beau's chest. She closed her eyes and sighed with exhaustion. But even as her life force ebbed, the spirit copy of her shone all the brighter.

Jake looked at it, at a loss, then Archie arrived, screaming her name.

The girls were a step behind. Jake had just come back from fighting a dragon, but right now, of course, they didn't even look at him.

He gazed at his friends, bewildered. *How can this be happening?* All the sounds and sights around him seemed cloaked behind a fog of disbelief.

He just stood there, lost, while the others shoved in front of him to gather 'round the Elder witch in panic.

It was then that he spotted Zolond's ghost nearby, removed from the knot of children around the motionless pair.

The Dark Master was dressed in the same plain black clothes he had been wearing in life, except for the bowler hat. He was just standing there, looking forsaken and as shocked as the rest of them at what had just occurred.

At that, Zolond's gray specter turned slowly and saw Aunt Ramona's shining spirit.

"Ramona," he said.

It was the saddest three syllables Jake had ever heard in his life, filled with mournful regret.

"Dani, use the feather—she's dying!" Isabelle screamed.

"Give it to me!" Dani yelled through her tears.

"I-I can do a spell..." Even Nixie was sobbing, her hand shaking so badly as she lifted her wand that it wobbled all over the place. "Archie, get out of the way!"

"No! Magic is what caused all of this rubbish. Stay back!" Archie sounded ferocious. "I can save her! There are methods of resuscitation. Just—give me some room! She's still breathing, but just barely."

Archie gently rolled Aunt Ramona onto her back and then proceeded to blow air into her mouth and pump the center of her chest with his hands. He kept checking her pulse in between these strange attempts to revive her, but gave no indication it was working. He'd whipped off his glasses, and his cheeks were wet with tears.

"Jacob," the spirit Ramona said gently, "tell them to stop this nonsense. I love them for trying, but this is what I want. I am ready."

"But *we're* not ready!" Jake yelled at her.

His friends all paused and looked at him.

"No, no, no," Isabelle whimpered, the first to realize Jake was speaking to Ramona's ghost. The empath pressed her fingers to her lips.

"Tell her to come back right now, Jake," Archie said in a shaky voice. "I can make this all right. I know I can."

Jake shook his head, tears rolling down his cheeks. "She doesn't want to."

"Well, too bad! We need her!" Nixie wrenched out. "The Order needs her! This isn't fair!"

Aunt Ramona's spirit winced with sorrow. "Jake, tell the girls they are stronger than they know."

Jake flinched but nodded. "Everyone, be quiet so I can hear her." He swallowed past the lump in his throat. "Zolond's here as well."

"Well, you can tell him to go straight to Hades, where he belongs! This is all his fault!" Archie said with utter hatred.

As though reminded of his destination, the Dark Master let out a groan of despair that grew into a shout. He lifted his hands out to his sides, looked at the sky, and unleashed a deafening, ghostly *"Noooo!"*

Suddenly, Celestus appeared near Aunt Ramona in his most radiant angel form.

Inhaling sharply at the arrival, Jake stared in wonder at the angel's white wings and ethereal robes.

Though his light shone on the kids—and on Derek and Leopard-Helena, who now joined them—none of the others acknowledged him. Jake realized that he was the only one who could see Celestus this time.

His heart sank, for he knew why. He had seen Celestus in this role before—as the sort of angel who escorted the departed to heaven.

Celestus smiled warmly at Aunt Ramona, and alarm filled Jake anew.

He stepped forward. "You're not really going to take her from us, are you?"

The angel gave him a faraway smile, aware that Jake could see him. His manner was so gentle that he seemed like a different being than their fierce, black-clad rescuer from last night.

"That is not up to me," he said softly. Then he offered Aunt Ramona his hand, as if to assist a lady into a carriage.

"But..." Before Jake could gather words for his protest at all of this, two more otherworldly visitors arrived.

A pair of hideous, red-skinned devils climbed out of the ground in a puff of sulfurous smoke. Larger and uglier than the pitchfork crew who had harassed Jake and his friends the previous night, they climbed out of the ground and approached Zolond, cackling and leering at him.

"Well, look who it is!" The first turned around and pulled his colleague the rest of the way up out of the dirt.

Scrambling to ground level, the second picked a clod of grassy turf off one of his horns, where it had become impaled.

Jake stared at the sneering, ugly creatures in dismay.

Warily, they approached the ghost of the sorcerer-king. Zolond backed away, then tried to flee.

One leaped ahead of him while the other blocked his escape, laughing gleefully. "Come with us, Master Zolond!"

"Why do I smell sulfur again?" Brian mumbled.

Isabelle and all his friends were watching Jake.

"What's happening, coz? Tell us!" Archie said.

"Two devils have come for Zolond," Jake reported, watching the creatures chase the Dark Master. "Celestus is here for Aunt Ramona."

"What?" Isabelle whispered.

Aunt Ramona's spirit watched in distress as the two devils chased Zolond about. "Make them stop!" she said to Celestus.

He did not respond, looking on with inscrutable serenity, as though he had gazed upon this scene a million times before.

"Come, come, that's enough of that!" the taller devil said. "Don't be a baby! Shemrazul is eager to welcome you home to the Ninth Pit!"

"You're gonna love it there, *Your Majesty*," the other one said with a sneer.

"Leave him be!" Aunt Ramona cried, but the creatures ignored her.

Celestus' dispassionate gaze slid toward her, but still, the angel did nothing. "He chose this, Ramona."

Even Jake started to feel a bit sorry for Zolond as the pair of devils seized him by the arms.

"You hear that, deadie? You're doomed. We have your signature, in your own blood! I have the contract right here." The taller devil cracked one of his horns open sideways and pulled a scroll out of a hidden compartment inside.

He snapped his horn upright into place again, then unfurled the parchment, while his snickering partner gripped Zolond's arm to stop him from fleeing.

"See this?" He held up the paper and tapped the bottom with his claw. "That's your name right there, inn't it? Geoffrey de Lacey. Your *real* name. Not your stupid fake identity—Zolond! You can't fool us, mate. Nobody cheats the devil."

Aunt Ramona moaned while the shorter devil waved his forked tail eagerly. "I suppose you thought the Horned One would let you off the hook, eh? Not hardly!" he said. "Our master kept *his* end of the bargain, Geoff. Can I call you Geoff? You should've kept *yours*."

The taller one snapped the scroll shut, then tossed it carelessly over his shoulder into the gaping black hole they'd left in the turf of Parliament Square. "You got everything you wanted, stupid human. Now it's time to pay the price. Fair is fair."

Glancing from one to the other, Zolond looked far more terrified of these creatures than he had been of Wyvern.

"This was almost too easy, wasn't it, Ronny?" the short one said to his chum.

"Aye!" said Ronny. "Not much of a Dark Master, are you? The ones before you were at least worth our time. Well, enough dawdling. Come on, you!" Roughly, they grabbed Zolond and started dragging him off toward the hole.

Zolond looked back at Aunt Ramona's shining spirit. "Forgive me."

"Oh, Geoffrey—I never stopped loving you!" she said.

"I love you too, my dearest Ramona. Farewell."

"Wait!" she said. Jake looked on as Aunt Ramona turned desperately to face Celestus. "Is there nothing you can do? Please!"

His glowing blue eyes remained impassive.

"But there must be!" she insisted. "I beg you, if I have done any good at all for these children, o-or the Order or the world, then let him receive mercy! He was lied to, deceived! He held the truce for centuries, prevented wars— There is good in him! I've seen it!"

It nigh broke Jake's heart to hear the strong, stoic Elder witch pleading like this.

"Listen to her! Please, Dr. Celestus!" Jake interjected, ignoring the fact that Zolond was the one who'd sent his parents into that terrible cavern.

Celestus turned to Jake intently, studying him for a moment, then again at Aunt Ramona, as though weighing her request.

For Zolond himself, the angel spared only a brief, contemptuous glance.

It didn't look promising.

"Hmm," he finally said. "Considering how much losing him at this late date would enrage my old friend, Shemrazul, perhaps I can call in a favor. Let me check. Hold!" he ordered the two devils.

They whined and protested, but it seemed they had no authority to resist a Light Being's command. They stopped dragging Zolond toward the hole and waited, muttering.

Celestus closed his eyes for a long moment. "Yes... Yes, sir. I understand..."

Jake held his breath and tried not to listen to the heartbreaking sound of the girls sobbing as he waited. He still could not believe any of this was happening.

Aunt Ramona couldn't possibly leave them now. She had only just started mentoring Nixie—and now there was a rupture to deal with. How was the Order supposed to fix *that* without the Elder witch?

It wasn't as though they still had Balinor. She was their leader now. And what was he, Jake, going to do without her?

Celestus opened his eyes. "Your prayer has been heard," he informed her. "The prisoner shall be shown mercy."

"Oh, thank you, Lord!" Aunt Ramona lifted her eyes to the sky.

"Seventh Circle," Celestus informed them. "Thirty thousand years."

"What? Hey! Now just hold on!" the devils protested. "What about the Ninth Pit? We've got a contract!"

"Thank you," Zolond uttered, gazing at the angel.

"Don't thank us yet," Celestus said crisply. "Your new home is not exactly cozy. Unhand him. Now!" he ordered the two devils, who whined.

"What are we supposed to tell Shemrazul?"

Celestus chuckled. "That's your problem."

The pair began raging at this last-minute stay of execution, roaring and cursing, stomping their cloven hoofs, and thrashing their tails.

Jake was glad no one else could see this. Their temper tantrum was ugly and slightly terrifying.

"This is a travesty! Your side claims to care about justice? What a bunch of hypocrites! *We have a contract!*" the taller one howled.

But when a transparent rectangular door opened out of thin air nearby and another angel stepped out, the nasty pair fell back and instantly cowered.

"Yea, what is it?" the new arrival asked Celestus, looking rather bored with it all.

Even Jake was intimidated by his appearance. He stole a glance at his friends, but they couldn't see this Light Being either. He was kind of scary.

"Jake," Celestus said pleasantly, "allow me to present my old friend, Azrael. Angel of Death."

Jake's eyes widened.

The death angel smiled with grim amusement at his reaction. He was taller than Celestus, with high cheekbones and long, dark hair. He wore a silver tunic that was cinched around his lean waist and just grazed his knees; on his feet, he wore Roman centurion sandals that laced up his muscular legs.

In his hand, he carried a silver spear. This Azrael was such a formidable fellow that his brief gaze sent a shudder down Jake's spine.

When he glanced at Zolond, his eyes flashed briefly with white flame. Then he turned to Celestus. "Change of plans, eh?"

Celestus sighed. "Upstairs agreed he doesn't deserve the Ninth Pit after all. A speck of love has been found in his heart. Two specks, actually."

"Aww!" The devils started complaining again until Azrael gave them another sharp look.

"And he did keep the truce," Celestus added, "thus preventing a war and sparing countless lives. So, there's that. However." Celestus' cobalt eyes narrowed as he stared at Zolond. "He murdered seventy-three souls in his lifetime, and violated Creation by fashioning numerous unnatural creatures."

"I-I was going to destroy them as soon as I'd finished here! It's the truth!" Zolond cried.

"Well, you ran out of time, didn't you?" Azrael drawled, then snorted. His grumpy air reminded Jake of Maddox. "Seventh Circle is more than fair, you murderer. You'll fit right in."

Celestus nodded. "It would've been the Ninth Pit, but Upstairs says he qualifies for Seven, since there's real love for this woman in his shriveled old heart."

Azrael nodded. "I checked his file on my way here. It says he does not leave the Earth unloved, despite all he's done. That's usually a good sign. Her love for him is genuine enough. And the boy cares for him as well."

"Uh—no, I don't," Jake blurted out.

Azrael glanced cynically at Jake. "I wasn't talking about you, kid. The other boy. The real Black Prince."

"What?" Jake forgot all about the Dark Master's body count at this revelation. "Real Black Prince?" He hadn't known there was one! But there would be, wouldn't there? "Who is it? Oh! His grandson?" He'd heard Wyvern say something about that.

"Never mind!" Celestus said, scowling at the Angel of Death. "That will do, Azrael. Pay him no mind, Jake. Azrael was just leaving. *Weren't you?*"

"Sorry!" Azrael muttered to Celestus. "I didn't know it was a secret. Nobody ever tells me anything. You all just call on me whenever you need some human dragged off to one place or another."

"Well, start dragging," Celestus said in annoyance, gesturing at Zolond. "Get him out of here. I'm sick of his face."

"At least let us take *part* of him back to Shemrazul, please?" Ronny pleaded. "You have no idea what our master will do to us if we go back there empty-handed!"

Azrael cracked a grim smile. "I can imagine."

"Aw, c'mon, either half will do! An arm?"

"No."

"Just the head, then!"

"Get back!" The death angel prodded his red-skinned foes away from Zolond with his spear. Then he took the old warlock by the arm with a no-nonsense grip. "This way, Mr. De Lacey."

"Goodbye, Geoffrey." Newfound relief had filled Aunt Ramona's face. "We will see each other again one day."

"I will always love you," Zolond said earnestly, unable to tear his gaze off her.

Azrael rolled his eyes. "Please. I just had my lunch." Looking disgusted, he led Zolond toward the weird, out-of-nowhere door while the devils' tantrum continued.

"Wait!" Zolond cried.

Azrael's grip tightened. "No, *now.*"

He started pulling Zolond through the doorway into a foggy realm, but the Dark Master's ghost resisted, struggling to shout one last thing to Aunt Ramona. "Warn the Order of my creatures in the desert!"

"What creatures, Geoffrey?" she exclaimed.

Then the door slammed—and in the twinkling of an eye, it vanished altogether.

Jake stood there, stunned.

What creatures? And what of the real Black Prince?

But there were no more answers to be had. Zolond was gone; Azrael did not return.

Suddenly, without warning, the red devils were sucked backward, tumbling toward their hole as a terrifying roar echoed up from deep underground.

Jake jumped, nervously looking around. That voice was all too familiar.

It seemed Shemrazul had just heard about the lighter sentence handed down to his longtime servant.

He'd want someone to take his fury out on, and Jake had a feeling he knew who it was going to be. The two red devils scrabbled with their claws along the turf, trying to cling above ground, but they could not avoid their fate any more than the Dark Master.

They were dragged back under, and as soon as the tips of their horns ducked beneath the soil, the hole in the lawn disappeared.

The grass was green and perfect again. The ground looked undisturbed.

"What's happening, Jake?" Dani whispered.

He swallowed hard. "The Angel of Death has just taken Zolond away."

"What about Aunt Ramona?" Isabelle asked, teary-eyed.

"She's still here. I'm looking at her right now. Why, she looks...different. Young! She's smiling. She looks beautiful."

And she did. Even as her ancient body struggled for its final breaths, her spirit shone brighter. She seemed to be getting younger by the moment.

"You do look really pretty, ma'am."

"Thank you," Aunt Ramona whispered, staring in awe at the back of her hand as the wrinkles smoothed out.

"No," Jake said, "I'm the one who has to thank you."

When she looked at him in surprise, Jake could no longer hold back his tears. He could not bear to lose her too—the first, maybe second adult he'd ever trusted in his life, after Derek.

Yet he knew she had to go. She deserved to. It would be good up there. And, heaven knew, she'd waited long enough.

He just needed to tell her how much he cared. "I never would've made it without you," he forced out, tears spilling down his cheeks. He couldn't stop them despite his embarrassment that his friends saw. "You were always there for me. For all of us. Rock-solid. I mean it. I love you, Aunt Ramona." Jake broke down. "I never even got to hug you."

Through their sobs, his friends also told her they loved her, and Aunt Ramona turned to Celestus in distress.

"Please. Give me one more moment with them. I was always so stern." She sounded like she could cry.

"Very well."

The angel took her hand, and then the golden-white light from heaven shone down from behind the pair. Jake's friends gasped and paused in their crying.

Jake looked over and realized that now, everyone could see them.

"My dearest children." Aunt Ramona's ever-younger face glowed all the brighter as she gazed at them. "I love you all so much. I know I was strict and frequently unapproachable, but the lot of you mean the world to me." She brushed away a tear. Celestus gave her a reassuring look. "All of you have given me such joy in my long journey—despite occasionally driving me mad," she admitted with a sniffle and a short laugh.

They smiled and sobbed, each staring at her with the light rays from beyond illuminating their faces.

"I will miss you all so much. My pure-hearted Isabelle. Noble Archie. Steadfast Daniela. Nixie, my fierce little lioness. And brave, unselfish Jake."

"Unselfish?" Jake whispered.

"I'll be watching over all of you, I promise. Just know that I love you."

The crying kids answered in kind and told her they would miss her so much.

"It's time," Celestus said softly.

"Right," she whispered, gathering herself with a businesslike nod. "Righty-ho, then. I'm off on a grand journey! Derek, Helena, dear, take care of them, and as for yourselves, do aught in your power to live happily ever after together, hm?"

"We will, ma'am," Derek said, while the leopardess sat down sadly by the dowager's motionless body.

"Red, old friend, I know you'll be looking after these rascals, too."

Red let out a mournful "becaw" and gave the baroness a formal bow.

"Well, then!" Spirit-Aunt Ramona wiped her eyes and straightened her shoulders back to her usual firm posture. "It's bon voyage, my darlings. I can hardly wait to see the blessed isles!"

Jake shut his eyes to squeeze away the tears. When he opened them again, her spirit was radiant, almost sparkling. The peace of the realm she was headed to had smoothed all the wrinkles from her face and the sorrow from her eyes.

To his wonder, the years had fallen away from the Elder witch until she stood before them, tall and proud, a woman in her prime. Her eyes were blue, her long, wavy hair a rich walnut brown.

"You're a brunette!" Dani blurted out.

"Am I?" Ramona pulled one of her dark tresses forward, saw her long, youthful hair, and laughed. "Ha! So I am again! Goodness me, I am going to like being dead. What fun! Strange, though. I feel more alive than ever. Now, listen, you all. Don't you worry about me. I shall be in fine company—and so will you all, as long as you stick together."

"Will you come back and visit me sometime—as a ghost?" Jake asked in a leaden voice, but his question was halfhearted. He already knew the answer.

"She won't be able to," Celestus chided. "Once she crosses over, you will have to wait until it's your time to join her."

"Ah, don't cry, dear boy," Aunt Ramona said, wincing, as a small sob escaped Jake. It had been worth a shot to ask.

Aunt Ramona held them in a loving gaze. "I'm so proud of you all. Such extraordinary children. Remember: stay brave. Stay true. And above all, stay together." She glanced sorrowfully toward the spot where Zolond had been standing.

Then Celestus laid his hand on her shoulder. His light touch visibly comforted her. "We must go."

The new, young Aunt Ramona gave the shining blond angel a grateful nod, then looked at them for the last time. "Love is the strongest magic, my dears. It lasts forever. Goodbye." She blew them all a kiss, then her frail, ancient body, still lying on the ground, rasped out a long, last, painful exhalation.

"No," Nixie moaned. Dropping her wand, she hung her head and cried.

Archie fell to his knees and stared at Aunt Ramona's body in stupefied silence. Dani and Isabelle clung to each other and wept.

Jake had never felt such terrible pain in his whole life.

The now vibrant and glowing Ramona Bradford turned away, hand-in-hand with the angel. Celestus led her off into the light, then it, too, disappeared. Jake could not have seen more, anyway, for the tears blinding him.

The next thing he knew, Derek was standing there, pulling him into a fatherly hug. "It's all right, lad," he said gruffly. "You still got me."

Red let out a mournful caw.

All the kids were crying. Derek gathered the others to him as well, and hugged them all together, as far as his strong arms could reach. The leopard-governess meowed sadly and pressed in, too, comforting them as best she could.

"It's going to be all right," he whispered, but Jake didn't see how.

Overwhelmed, he stepped back from Derek's brawny embrace with a resolute sniffle after a moment. Brushing the tears roughly off his face, he noticed in surprise that they were the only people left in Parliament Square.

Everyone else must've been scared away. No wonder.

Brian stood apart from them, since he hadn't known Aunt Ramona personally. The young Guardian squinted down the road toward the river, then turned to them with an awkward look, somber but dry-eyed.

"Um, Mrs. Appleton and Mr. Mayweather just pulled up to the river's edge in a barge over there," he said, hooking a thumb toward the Thames. "They're waving at us. I think they're here to pick us up."

Derek nodded. "Good lad," he said. "Will you go tell them we're on our way?"

"Yes, sir." Brian darted off like he was glad to remove himself from all this raw emotion and wished to give his new friends privacy at such a time.

"Come on, kids," Derek murmured. "Let's get you all to Beacon House. We need to figure out what we're goin' to do."

As they all stepped back, nodded, and attempted to collect themselves, the girls' tear-stained faces wrenched Jake to the core.

Dani, at least, had dealt with death before when her mother passed away. But Isabelle was shattered, and Nixie looked like the rug had been yanked out from under her world.

Archie stood there, desolate, as though this was a puzzle not even he could solve. He wasn't crying anymore. One hand resting atop his head, he just looked lost. He turned to Jake, dropped his hand to his side, and shook his head. "I know she's happy, but..."

"Aye." Jake stared bleakly at him. "I'm sorry, Arch. I promised you I'd save them, and I-I let you down."

"Coz, there was nothing you could do. You got carried off by a dragon. We nearly lost you too." Archie suddenly hugged him.

Jake hugged him back, but he still felt terrible for somehow letting this happen.

Archie had no sooner released him than Dani came crashing into Jake's arms. He nearly started crying again as they clung to each other.

There they were again—two orphans hanging on to each other for dear life, like shipwreck victims who had found one boulder in the midst of an angry sea. Dani didn't even talk, just sobbed, and Jake's heart broke anew at the sound.

He knew she was thinking of her mother.

"Come on, everyone," Derek mumbled, bending to retrieve Archie's glasses from the lawn for him. All his years of Guardian training had probably not prepared the warrior for how to deal with a bunch of grieving kids. "I'll stay here and see to their bodies, but it's time for you all to go and get on the boat. Come on. Let's go. That's enough for one day."

He was right. There was nothing they could do here anymore.

So they went.

CHAPTER THIRTY-EIGHT
Dark Victory

Wyvern could not understand why every joy he managed to eke out of life came tainted with a dose of bitterness, disappointment, sorrow. He had gained the Black Crown, yes, but he'd lost the only two creatures on the planet he considered actual friends.

He hadn't planned on that.

What made his loss especially poignant was that it was his son who'd done it—Jake and his thrice-cursed Gryphon.

Yes, Wyvern had seen the Gryphon drop Thanatos into the Thames and knew at once that his pet would not survive. The river was too deep, the current too strong, and lions couldn't swim.

But engaged in his duel with Zolond at the time, there was nothing he could do but let his pet be sacrificed. Instead, he'd focused all the harder on his fight, telling himself that this one casualty, hard as it was, would be worth it in his quest to seize the Black Crown.

But once Wyvern had entered the Black Fortress, prize in hand, and landed on the other side of the jump in the desert of Karakum, only then had the crew found the courage to inform him that Jake had murdered Tazaroc and escaped.

Wyvern had run to see the body, staring at it with a wave of sickening shock. The ground-up dagger in his belly wasn't helping matters. He'd enjoyed seeing the horror on Jake's face when he'd eaten the thing, but it sure as Hades had given him a stomachache.

And so, on the very eve of his victory, Wyvern sat alone, brooding with anger. Let the others have their celebration. He was somewhere between anguish and volcanic rage.

He hadn't even had time yet to recover from the ice grendels' torture. First that humiliation, and now this gut punch when he should've been on top of the world. He didn't know how to feel. He wasn't much for feelings in the first place.

But perhaps the thing that gnawed at him the most was the rare whiff of self-doubt he found himself experiencing. He was not terribly pleased with his performance in the duel. He cursed quietly, glanced down at the Master's Ring, and reminded himself that he'd won. That was all that mattered.

And yet, deep down, Wyvern didn't like *how* he'd won.

In truth, it wasn't much of a victory, was it? Considering that if Raige had not assisted with his time bomb, Zolond's reaper would've killed Wyvern.

Acknowledging that put him in an even darker mood.

Wyvern stared into space, loath to admit that the old man had spanked him like an amateur with that ghastly conjuration.

Then again, nothing Wyvern did ever quite lived up to his own cruel, unforgiving standards. Just like nothing he did was ever truly good enough for his infernal father.

Shemrazul was also in a bad mood, for that matter. Around the edges of his mind, Wyvern could hear the demon raging. Something about a last-minute change of plans concerning Zolond's fate.

Wyvern shrugged it off. He was not in the mood for the Horned One's constant whining and never-ending demands. He had enough problems of his own.

He could not route the image of his beloved dragon slumped, lifeless, in the corridor with a blade thrust deep into its heart. *How could this have happened?*

At least Wyvern had had the magical blood of the dragon collected before levitating poor Tazaroc's body into the burning crater outside for cremation.

Already missing both of his pets, he got up from the chair and prowled restlessly across his chamber, increasingly angry.

To think that his own, soon-to-be son could have done this, well, it felt like a very personal betrayal.

The boy had to be punished.

Wyvern was not surprised that Jake had survived the beast's attack, of course. A lad destined to be the Black Prince ought to be able to handle himself against one of the smaller species of dragons, like the Ruffed Orange Darter. Begrudgingly, Wyvern admitted that perhaps Jake *was* rather young for how well he'd done.

Still, this changed things between them.

As Wyvern gazed at himself in the mirrored walls of his chamber, he realized that his pets were not the only thing that had died today. So had his hopes for some form of an affectionate father-son relationship with Jake.

He shook his head at his own foolishness. What had he thought— that they'd go to the park together and toss a ball around? *Idiot.* He shook his head at these daft longings.

Such weakness could only be ascribed to his pitiful human side. No more of that. The boy would obey henceforth because Wyvern would *make* him.

No more of this indulgence. He'd beat Jake into submission if he had to. It was not what he had hoped for, but this was Jake's own choice. So be it. Wyvern would raise him the same way he himself had been molded for greatness.

Through punishment and fear.

In fact...

He rose from his chair and left his chamber, the cruel, petty side of him churning with spite. Wyvern had been hurt; he wanted to hurt something in return. He couldn't hurt Jake. He wasn't here. But Wyvern could hurt the boy's parents.

He found his way easily through the black maze, well familiar with it, then went downstairs and entered the dim recesses of the Lightrider cavern.

Only one scientist was on duty tonight. The others were either dead or too traumatized by the afternoon's events to do their jobs.

The lone white-coated man monitoring the patients and the machine jumped like a startled hare when Wyvern walked up behind him.

"Sir!" He clutched his chest and strove to calm down. "Can I help you?"

"Roll out Lord and Lady Griffon."

The doctor stared at him uncertainly for a second. "Y-yes, sir." Then he hurried to fetch the hydraulic platform used to lower the various glass coffins to the floor as needed.

While he waited, Wyvern watched the magical potion slosh in the big glass base of the machine. It was a pulpy and disgusting green brew that nourished as it sedated. The doctors knew the right ratios and all the boring details.

As for the machine itself, Wyvern had no idea how the thing worked, nor did he care. It was one of Zolond's top inventions, and without the old man here, they'd be in trouble if it broke.

No matter. It only had to last long enough for Wyvern to bring his father's grand design to fruition.

Probably by the spring.

Knowing that the final conquest of mankind would take place under *his* rule, and that he, not Zolond, would get all the credit, cheered Wyvern up considerably—enough to lift one corner of his mouth, at least.

Then the scientist finished lowering the Griffons. "They're ready, sir."

Wyvern stalked over to where the two glass coffins sat at waist level, side by side. Inside slept the captive Lightriders.

He studied them in cold, ominous silence.

The mother was beautiful, he could admit. She'd given Jake his blue eyes as well as the ghost sight. Staring at her, Wyvern felt vengefully glad that Jake had been deprived of a mother's love, the heartless little thief.

The father, though...

Wyvern walked around to the Earl of Griffon's glass case and stared at the man, hard.

Hatred filled him. He opened the glass lid. The urge to destroy throbbed through him. *You and your golden hair and your perfect wife and strapping son...*

He pressed the end of his wand against Lord Griffon's temple as though it were a pistol. In his hands, it might as well be.

"Sir?" the scientist said in alarm.

Wyvern sent him a look dark with evil intent.

"W-we'll need every subject we have in order to get the portals open wh-when the time comes."

"Oh, really?"

The white-coated man nodded anxiously.

Wyvern debated, lowering his gaze to Jacob Everton's peaceful face. *It would be so easy...*

That would hurt Jake, all right. *You take two of mine, I take two of yours. How does that sound, brat?*

I'll put you in your place. And if that doesn't teach you to behave, then I start killing your friends.

Just then, the door to the cavern opened and a voluptuous silhouette appeared.

"Nathan? There you are!"

Wyvern lifted his gaze as Fionnula invited herself in and bustled toward him, the click-click of her high-heeled shoes resounding beneath the quiet dome of the cavern.

"Come and join the celebration, darling. You've earned it! This is your big night."

Wyvern said nothing but straightened up, withdrawing his wand.

The future queen of the Dark Druids slowed her approach, and her face turned grim when she saw what he was doing.

She nodded the scientist's dismissal; the nervous little man retreated, discreetly sending her an imploring look.

Wyvern regarded his bride warily from across the glass coffins. He figured she had come to manage or manipulate him somehow. He wasn't blind to what she was, after all; he wasn't Waldrick.

Her wiles didn't work on him quite as well as she thought.

"Was there something you wanted?" Wyvern prompted.

"Um, Raige wants to know if he should give the order now for your Drow hirelings to move in on Shadowedge Manor. You wanted to wait until it was dark for the attack, and it is now, so...?"

"Right. Yes." Wyvern nodded and sighed, remembering his duties. "Tell him to candle-call their leader. I want to know once it's done."

Fionnula toyed with a ribbon on her skirt, avoiding his gaze. "So, you're sure you still want Prince Victor dead, then?" She peeked up at him from beneath her lashes.

"Of course I do. Why wouldn't I?"

She shrugged. "Well, we just thought perhaps you'd change your mind about the Black Prince, since Jake..."

"No," Wyvern said firmly. "Zolond's heir has to die. I don't want factions rallying around him. Tell Raige to make the call. It's time. Anything else?"

"Well..." She tilted her head prettily and clasped her hands behind her, twisting to make her skirts swish back and forth.

I think I make her nervous.

"What?" Wyvern demanded.

"Dear, I realize this might not be the best time—I know you're upset—but some of us feel it would be prudent to discuss the *other* members of the Council without delay. Those whose positions on your rise to power are not yet clear."

"Like Deathhand."

"Yes, and the swamp witch," Fionnula said. "Both are old friends of

Zolond's. Word of his death is bound to travel fast."

"Hmm. Well, I haven't been able to track down the necromancer. He's always been elusive. But Mother Octavia told me she wouldn't interfere."

"And no Dark Druid would ever lie," Fionnula teased.

He smiled faintly in spite of himself. "I suppose you are right to be concerned. They are both formidable foes and must be treated with respect. The rest will fall in line, but those two... It would be best to have them on our side."

"It would look better," she agreed.

"Well then, we need Prince Victor dead—now. We can't afford to have them organize around Zolond's heir as a symbol."

Fionnula nodded. "I don't like the notion of them getting control of that boy, either, if what I've heard about him is true."

"It's all true," Wyvern said grimly. "He is impressive. Highly trained, multiple gifts. Shame to have to kill him, frankly. He'd have been useful. But...Father knows best." A twinge of bitterness crept into his voice. "I have my orders. Jake's to be the one. Like it or not." His gaze dropped back to the unconscious Griffons.

"Hmm." Fionnula nodded, studied him, and bit her lip.

"What?" he demanded.

She forced a cautious smile. "I know you're angry, my love, but...what exactly are you planning here?" She flicked a glance down at the Lightriders. "I mean, is this a good idea?"

"Why shouldn't I be rid of them? Duradel said this is the first place he ran to. He could've tried to escape, but no! Instead, he came here to try to save them. How do you think that makes me feel? All I wanted was to be the boy's father."

"I know. Still. You might need them."

"I can catch more," he growled. "I'll hire an army of Drow mercenaries if I have to."

"I don't know," she said. "I'm sure the Order's very much on guard now after you trounced them so thoroughly."

Her unfailing flattery left him cynically amused, transparent as it was. She'd probably say anything to make him do what she wanted.

"Nathan, I'm no expert on children, but if you do this, you might just drive Jake to fulfill the *reverse* side of Duradel's prophecy. Instead of becoming our future, this could be the thing that turns him into our nemesis. At best, you'll never get him to cooperate."

"Cooperate?" Wyvern scoffed. "He lost his chance to do that when he killed my Darter. No, my lady. I'm done trying to win him over. Now I mean simply to break his will." He looked at the parents. "Just like you do with a wild young dragon."

"Aha." Fionnula nodded, pursed her lips, then drummed her nails briefly on the mother's coffin. "I wonder..."

"What?" Wyvern prompted as she coyly let her words trail off. He knew she was up to something, but the mischievous gleam in her eyes intrigued him.

"Well, I was just thinking," Fionnula said with an innocent air, leaving her post and rounding Elizabeth's coffin. "If you *really* want to punish our son, use these two for the project first, and *then*, once you have Jake under your thumb..." She sauntered up behind Wyvern, draped her arms around his shoulders, and whispered, "Make *him* do it."

Wyvern glanced at her in surprise. "You mean...?"

She gave him a peck on the cheek. "Mm-hmm."

"Make the boy kill his own parents, eh?" A dark laugh escaped him. "My lady, I like how you think."

Fionnula giggled then turned Wyvern away from Lord and Lady Griffon, clinging to him with her arms around his waist. "Now come back to the party!" she said playfully, wielding all of her siren's charm. "We're having champagne in the bridge room, and Raige has saved you a cigar."

Wyvern grimaced. "Those things are disgusting."

"I agree." She laughed. "Oh, come, don't be sad, my love. We'll get you a new dragon, I promise."

"I don't want a new dragon," he answered sulkily.

"You will, in due time. It'll make you feel better. Now, come along, dear. I'm not going to let you do something that could jeopardize your master plan just because you're grumpy. Put them away," she ordered the doctor, nodding at the inert Lightriders.

He hurried to obey the future queen with a look of relief.

Wyvern harrumphed, well aware she was up to something, but maybe she was right. He had just won the bloody Black Crown and would soon become the new sorcerer-king.

"We have to plan your coronation! Oh, darling, we're going to make it the most awe-inspiring night the dark realms have ever seen! And you, my dreadful Nathan, you are going to be the most terrifying Dark Master who ever lived..."

She prattled on about his greatness as they stepped out of the Lightrider cavern and passed through the lobby, where burn marks still marred the ceiling and walls. The area had been blood-soaked when they had first returned to the Black Fortress, but Fionnula must've cleaned it up with a spell. His future wife knew he could not abide a mess.

"Oh, try to smile, Nathan. It's your big night, and you're so handsome when you smile. Don't worry, there'll be other dragons, all in good time."

She patted his arm as she led him up the stairwell, past the mangled banister. Wyvern looked at it morosely as they passed. It bore a dent shaped like Tazaroc's tail.

How he'd miss him.

Then she continued raving about the coronation.

"We'll have a long red carpet and torches lining the way. Black flags everywhere, and scarlet banners! There'll be fearsome songs, and then fireworks—right after the sacrifices! Won't that be nice? And just think of it, Nathan, everyone will bow down to you, as far as the eye can see..."

She continued petting him and heaping praise on him as she led him back to the party, and even though Wyvern didn't trust her for a second, somehow it helped.

* * *

The swamp creatures were restless that night.

All day, Mother Octavia Fouldon had felt unsettled. Clear across the Atlantic in the wilds of the Atchafalaya Swamp, she had seen the rupture tear across the sky and couldn't believe Shem's son had gone so far.

"Aw, this ain't good," the old Cajun witch mumbled to herself, then spat tobacco juice into a big, rusty can and stared up at the ominous line of clouds across the Louisiana sky. "This ain't good a'tall."

Nothing much had come of it—yet. The dark clouds eventually faded, and that seemed to be that for the day.

But something in the air had shifted. The whole swamp sensed it.

All the critters were tense.

Oh, the flies buzzed, same as always, and the humid air sat heavy among the tupelo trees. But the gators was restless, and the frogs had gone quiet.

Hardly any catfish was bitin'. The water bugs skated over the algae-covered surface of the blackwater below her front porch, and the old

Cajun witch read portents in the trails they made.

Yup. She lifted a weather eye to the overcast sky. *Trouble comin' like a hurricane.*

And then, just a little later that afternoon, about half past three, the anxious cry of a loon warned her for certain that something *else* had happened.

That was a bad sign. The loon's cry meant death.

She needed to find out what was going on. So, naturally, she took out her meat cleaver and gutted one of the chickens she kept in the coop behind her shack.

Near the goats.

The entrails ought to have somethin' to say.

She had a mighty bad feeling it had to do with ol' Z, as she affectionately called the Dark Master. They went way back.

Wyvern, that young upstart, had come here a few days ago, tellin' her his big plans to take his place, asking her if she was in.

Under normal circumstances, Tavey would've told him where to go and warned her friend about the threat, but this was different.

This was coming from Shemrazul's own little boy.

The will-o-wisps, them pretty blue glowin' balls of swamp gas, well, they served the chief witch of the Americas as signals from the Horned One himself. They had told her before Wyvern arrived that the wind, it was a-changin'.

So old Tavey kept her mouth shut when the Nephilim came calling and told that devil's son to go do what he had to do. She wouldn't get in his way.

"Just leave me out of it," she'd grumbled. "But do me one favor. Make it quick 'n' painless on the man. It's the least he deserves."

The truth was, Tavey had taken a shine to ol' Z when she was just a girl, but that dang highfalutin' miss priss, Ramona Bradford, well, any other filly might as well not even exist, as far as Zolond was concerned.

Anyway, the strange day passed.

Ultimately, Mother Octavia received the confirmation of Zolond's death that evening from her familiar, the swamp hawk she had named Bandit.

Like any osprey, the big, pretty falcon was strong, smart, and fast. He had a snowy-white chest and brownish-gray feathers on his back and his wings, but the handsome black stripe around his eyes made him look like he was wearing a highwayman's mask.

Bandit was a good bird, sensible, and he always found out the gossip before the rest of the critters in these parts.

Tavey sat down hard when he told her the news.

She might've even shed a tear or two for Zolond. Nah, not really. She was a Dark Druid, after all, hardhearted, and her mind was already churning on the next thing.

Still, the death of her old friend left the swamp witch a little low.

Wandering out to the porch around her cottage, built on stilts over the water, Tavey leaned her elbows on the wooden railing for a while.

She listened to the bats screeching as they flapped by, snatching moths out of the air, and gazed at the will-o-wisps dancing in the dark.

All of a sudden, Mother Octavia narrowed her eyes. *What about the grandkid?*

What was his name again? She searched her memory. *Victor. That's it.* That boy had meant a lot to Zolond. Tavey frowned at the gators. Surely Wyvern wouldn't stoop to killin' the young'un, too.

Would he?

CHAPTER THIRTY-NINE
Farewell

Victor was determined to find out what in Hades had happened to the sky this afternoon. The bizarre cloud formation. The boom of thunder ripping past overhead, as though the atmosphere itself had exploded.

Master Nagai suspected it was something called a rupture, but Victor had never heard of that, and the rugged samurai had no idea yet what it was all going to mean. The wizened warrior tried contacting Grandfather to ask, but there had been no reply.

Humph, thought Victor. *I'm always the last one to know.* He was the bloody Black Prince, but they loved treating him like a child. Getting his elders to share information with him could be like pulling the eyeteeth out of a troll.

Whatever it was, the rupture made Nagai step up security around Shadowedge Manor even higher.

While his sensei was preoccupied piping still more lethal traps into being around the grounds with his traditional Japanese flute, Victor went out to ask the two dragons on the lawn if they knew anything.

Not really. The transformed reptilians were as shocked as everyone else, but they told him not to worry; His Majesty would soon have everything under control.

Well, Victor wanted answers.

As darkness fell, bringing the early twilight of autumn, Nagai refused (of course) to let him pick up a weapon and help in his own defense. Told him to do his homework.

Fine, thought Victor, gritting his teeth. He'd see to his studies, but tomorrow's assignments could wait.

Instead, he strode into the manor's sprawling library and took out every supernatural reference book he could find. Shadowedge Manor housed a splendid collection of grimoires and spell books, occult histories, bestiaries, and arcane scrolls, potion recipe cookbooks, astral traveler's guides, illustrated instruction manuals on the use of different magical weapons—in short, fantastical tomes of all kinds had been curated over the centuries for the education of each Black Prince in succession.

Victor was certain there had to be something in one of these texts about what ruptures *were* and what they meant.

He loaded Magpen up with a pile of research books that weighed as much as the imp did, failing to notice that the little fellow could no longer see over the stack.

Satisfied, Victor nodded and pivoted. "Let's go," he ordered.

The imp zigzagged back and forth under his burden, but Victor had already marched back out into the hallway, his determined gaze fixed on the staircase ahead.

As he swung around the newel post, heading back to his bedchamber, he suddenly saw that his servant wasn't behind him. "Magpen, quit dawdling! I need those!"

"Yes, master!" The imp staggered out of the library. "Beggin' your pardon, sir. Perhaps Your Greatness wouldn't mind levitating a few of these—in the interests of time?"

Victor looked back, then his lips twisted. He could not deny that it was funny watching his little pointy-eared footman struggle under the tower of books.

But this was no time to amuse himself. Impatient to get to work, Victor waved his hand and used his telekinesis to lift the huge stack of books out of Magpen's arms and send them gently up the side of the staircase.

As the heavy tomes began floating up the stairs and then down the hallway toward Victor's room, Magpen leaned forward, bracing his hands on his knees and panting. "Oh, thank you, noble master!"

"Sure," Victor drawled, then bounded up the steps after the floating stream of books.

Magpen scrambled to catch up.

Soon, Victor had laid out all of his research materials on his large canopied bed. He stood back and surveyed them, hands on hips. "Doesn't look like I'm going to be getting much sleep tonight."

"At least eat your dinner, Highness." Magpen carried in a tray with his meal.

Victor had refused to go down to the dining room. He could eat while he worked, as he often did. It was depressing sitting at that long, formal table by himself, anyway, with the servitor footmen standing silently by the walls. They were always ready to pass the salt, refill his goblet, or whisk his empty plate away, but were not designed to sustain a conversation. Nagai rarely ate with him; it was not proper. There was no one to talk to. Victor hated it. Might as well work.

Thrusting aside the constant, haunting presence of his loneliness, Victor picked up the next book from his selection and skimmed the table of contents.

"Victor," came a raspy whisper into the room.

He didn't look up from the grimoire. "What is it, Magpen?"

"Huh?"

Victor frowned and looked over at the imp.

It was then, to his astonishment, that he noticed the Dark Master standing on the far end of his chamber, by the wall.

"Grandfather!" A startled smile broke across his face, and he snapped the book shut. "Just the man I was hoping to see!" he said brightly.

Magpen looked around in confusion. "Er, who are you talking to, sire?"

"Where are your manners, slave?" Victor gave his servant a look, casting a meaningful nod toward the projected image of the sorcerer-king. "Bow to His Majesty." Victor did so himself, but Magpen looked around the room, then turned to him in confusion.

"Where?"

"There!" Victor gestured toward Zolond, rather intrigued to see that Grandfather had appeared to him in full-body form instead of just his head. *I didn't know calling candles could do that.* Must be some new kind.

Whoever had made it must still be working out the kinks, though, because Zolond's grayish, semi-transparent image looked all floaty and unfocused. *No wonder I barely heard him.*

"Sir, I don't think your calling candle is working very well. You're a bit blurry, and your feet missed the floor."

The sorcerer-king was floating about eight inches over the carpet. Then Victor's voice faded to nothing when he looked down at his grandfather's feet and saw the shackles around his ankles, with great gray chains floating out behind them...

His gaze climbed back up to Zolond's face as shock slammed him like an icy fist to the stomach.

"Grandfather?" His heart started to pound.

"Run," the ghost moaned.

Victor just stood there in disbelief. "You're *dead*?"

Magpen looked at him in alarm.

"Go," the warlock moaned. Zolond's deep, distinctive voice sounded bizarre—like a reverse echo. It was thin, as though coming from a vast distance.

Victor felt nauseated. This was no drill.

"I-I don't understand. How could this happen?"

"No...time."

"What is it, master?" Magpen cried.

"Grandfather's dead, Magpen." Victor stared at the apparition, his mind still refusing to grasp it. "Wyvern—killed him."

The imp's jaw dropped and tears welled up in his bulgy eyes, but for Victor, dread turned to fury.

Finally breaking the paralysis of shock, he ran around to the other side of his bed, closer to the ghost. "Where is he, sire? I'll kill him!"

"Noooo. You...must...go." It seemed to take a mighty effort for the Dark Master to project himself here from wherever he was.

Victor feared he *knew* where Zolond was. But he swallowed down his frenzied emotions.

The Dark Master wouldn't have gone to this much trouble without a good reason. "Very well, sire. Speak. I am listening."

Victor shushed the horrified Magpen and listened, using all of his inborn ability to communicate with the dead to hear what the sorcerer-king had to say.

The ghost gathered his strength, taking one slow, painful word at a time. *"Get...out of the...house. Quickly. They are... coming."*

"Who?" Worried, Victor stalked over to the window, but, by the light of the torches burning around the property, he saw nothing out of place.

Beneath the waxing gibbous moon, the dragons stood guard on the front lawn, the Noxu kept watch from their posts all over the property, and the horned silhouette of the armored samurai waited, statue-still, with his katana in the darkness.

"Hurry!" Grandfather urged.

When Victor turned around again, Zolond had vanished, but then reappeared over by the bedroom door.

"What's he saying, sir?" Magpen ventured.

Victor gave his servant a grim look. "Basically, that Lord Wyvern and his followers are on their way here to kill me."

Magpen didn't panic, to Victor's surprise. Instead, his ugly little face filled with resolve.

Beneath his pointy nose, the imp's dark blue lips flattened into a thin line. "Master Nagai told me this might happen. That we should be prepared. I've already packed our things, just in case, sire."

The imp trotted over to the massive wardrobe by the wall and pulled the doors open.

Victor scowled. "I'm not afraid of Wyvern, and I'm certainly not going to just run away and abandon Master Nag—"

"If the sorcerer-king says go, we go!" his servant cried with sudden defiance. "Come, Your Highness! With all due respect, if they can kill Master Zolond, they can easily kill you!"

Victor found he had no argument for this. He suddenly realized that Magpen was right.

With that, countless drills and a lifetime of training kicked in. Victor still couldn't quite bring himself to believe that this was really happening, nor did he *actually* intend to run away like a coward, but the pull of long-practiced habit took over.

Baal's beard, he'd been going through the motions of emergency evacuation procedures since he was a wee princeling. He could do it blindfolded and half-asleep.

Indeed, he often had. People trying to destroy him came with the crown.

"Must I go, Grandfather? It feels wrong," Victor said to the waiting ghost as he pulled the heavy leather satchels out of the wardrobe when he saw the imp struggling under their weight. "Why can't I just stay here and fight beside Nagai?"

"Too...many," Zolond intoned.

"But we have your dragons—"

"Too many!"

Victor stopped, chilled. "If Nagai is going to be that badly outnumbered, then he'll need my help all the—"

"Go! Doomed." Then the ghost looked mournfully toward the window. *"Too late. They are here."*

At that moment, one of the dragons roared, explosives boomed, and all Hades broke loose out on the front lawn.

Magpen shrieked and flew behind him, but Victor froze as fear finally found him.

Reality slammed him in the face. This was real. This was happening.

His royal grandfather had been murdered—overthrown—and the son of Shemrazul was outside, come to kill him.

"You...go...now." Zolond glared balefully at Victor. *"Preserve...my...bloodline!"*

At the reminder of his royal duty, Victor could only manage a nod. He was terrified for his noble sensei, but he clicked into motion.

Swiftly and efficiently moving around the room, he grabbed a few essentials: his beloved box of crystals, his runes, his dragon's-blood candle, along with a few others. Who knew if he would ever be back? He threw them all into his smaller satchel, along with his little black spell book and the most promising of the rare reference texts he'd taken from the library.

Then he buckled on his weapons belt, making sure he had his alderwood wand securely sheathed, as well as his razor-sharp katana. Finally, he shrugged on his black leather coat, pulled a satchel up over each shoulder, and strode toward his chamber door.

Magpen pattered, barefooted, ahead of him. "We'd better go out the back, master."

"No," said Zolond. Urgency lent the ghost newfound strength—at least enough to speak in full sentences now. *"The manor...is surrounded. Use...the tunnels."*

"But Grandfather, I don't know how to find the entrance." The secret tunnels under Shadowedge Manor shifted and moved as an added security feature. "Plus, Nagai put a cloaking spell on it so I wouldn't try sneaking out."

"Come." The ghost floated through Victor's closed bedroom door.

"C'mon, Mags," Victor said. "He wants us to leave through the royal escape tunnels. He's going to show us the way."

Zolond was waiting in the hallway, drifting toward the stairs with his chains waving slowly behind him. His eyes were fierce, and his white hair blew in an otherworldly breeze.

Gazing at him, Victor was heartsick that his only family member had been murdered, but there'd be time for grief later.

"Follow," the Dark Master ordered him, then turned and glided down the staircase, but his feet never touched the ground.

As Victor neared the bottom of the stairs, the entrance hall itself was dark and still, but through the mullioned windows around the front door, he saw the orange glow of flames outside and the brilliant flashes of bluish-white light that usually meant a wand duel.

He heard dragons roaring, Noxu screaming, Nagai yelling orders. Victor swallowed hard.

The windowpanes rattled as another boom sounded. Then he heard glass break as a window upstairs somewhere shattered. One of the dragons unleashed a bellyful of fire; the other screeched with what sounded like pain. Clearly, it was chaos out there.

Then a thunk hit the front door; it sounded like an arrow. Several more followed in quick succession.

"Drow," Grandfather said. *"Hurry."*

"Yes, sir," Victor said, trying to sound brave, but he gulped. The Drow were among the stealthiest of Dark-kind. They were known to make great bounty hunters and assassins—and terrifying archers.

Starting to feel a bit jumpy, Victor focused on his mission and followed the ghost. Zolond led him down the hallway toward the back of the house, and then through the manor's sprawling kitchens, where they took a narrow servant staircase down to the wine cellar.

It was dark, cool, and clammy down there. Magpen grabbed a lantern from the kitchen, then stepped through the door, pulled it shut behind him, and followed Victor down the creaky wooden steps.

The cellar had stone floors and brick-lined, barrel-vaulted ceilings. The air was stale and smelled of oak barrels. Victor's nose soon itched, for everything was coated in a thick layer of dust.

At least the frightening sounds from outside were muffled here under the house. There was just the nervous patter of their footfalls as they followed the ghost.

Glowing an ethereal white in the darkness ahead, Zolond swept confidently through the maze of honeycombed aisles, past rounded niches housing huge casks and countless wine racks draped in cobwebs.

Zolond made a sharp right, zoomed down another stark passage, and stopped at the end of it. Victor hurried after him.

"Come, boy. You must...do the spell. I cannot in this form."

"What do I do?"

Zolond told him, and Victor carried it out. Raising his arms before the solid brick wall, he gave it the command Grandfather had said: *"Aperi ianuam!"*

The magic flowed forth from him, and the brick pattern of the wall before him shimmered and dissolved. A half-smile tilted Victor's lips as the cloaking spell revealed the heavy metal door behind it.

Aperi ianuam. Victor committed the phrase to memory. *I'll have to remember that. If I ever see this place again.*

He grasped the cool metal handle and pulled the door open. Surprisingly, for its size, it swung without a sound on well-oiled hinges. Victor peered into the black tunnel again.

"Go."

He turned to the ghost. "Where does it lead?"

"Out. Away. Hurry. You will see. Survive," Zolond rasped, gazing at him wistfully. *"Live."*

"I'll do my best, sir."

The ghost nodded slowly. Magpen scampered past Victor into the tunnel, lifting his lantern high.

Victor paused, at a loss for what to say to his dead grandfather. It wasn't as though they had been close, but this was probably the last time he'd ever see him. "I'm sorry they did this to you, sire. Thank you for warning me. You saved my life. I...I'll miss you." Growing tongue-tied, he sketched a respectful bow and turned to go.

"Grandson?"

"Yes?" Two steps into the tunnel, Victor paused and turned back hopefully.

Zolond's reverse-echo words wafted into the darkness as he offered one last piece of advice: *"Look for...Griffon."*

Victor was taken aback. "Huh? Look for a gryphon?" What an odd command. "Whatever for?"

Suddenly, Zolond lifted his gaze to the ceiling. *"They are in the house. Run!"*

With that, the ghost slammed the metal door shut in Victor's face.

On their own now, Magpen and Victor looked at each other in shock.

The imp wore a grimace of terror by the dim glow of the lantern. The Black Prince hoped he didn't look as scared as Magpen, but at least he kept his wits about him. That light in the imp's hand could get them killed.

"Give me that." He snatched the lantern from Magpen's grasp and blew it out. They were instantly plunged into darkness.

"But master—"

"Don't be afraid," he whispered. "They might notice the light. We don't know how far this tunnel goes or where we might come out. We can't risk them seeing us. Here." Victor slid his wand out of its sheath and uttered a lesser illumination spell.

At once, small baubles of pale orange light lifted from the tip of his wand and floated weightlessly a few feet ahead of him and his servant. *Still too bright.* He dimmed them with a low-toned command, adjusting the hue to a subtle blue glow, like will-o-wisps.

"That should do it. C'mon, before they make it to the cellar."

As he and Magpen set off into the dark subterranean passage, the imp looked askance at him.

"What was that you said about a gryphon back there, Highness?"

Victor shrugged. "Grandfather told me to look for one."

"Why?"

"No idea. Far as I know, all they're good for is finding gold. Perhaps it was another warning of some kind? With my luck, probably just another enemy that wants to kill me."

Magpen furrowed his brow. "Well, did he say *look for* a gryphon or look *out* for one, sir? Like, find one, or make sure this gryphon doesn't find *you*?"

"Now that you mention it...I'm not sure." Victor frowned, questioning himself now. "Ghosts are not the best communicators, Magpen!"

The imp ducked at his exasperated whisper. "Well, don't worry, sire, it's all right. We'll worry about that later. For now, let's just get out of here. We'll keep our eyes peeled for any gryphons either way."

Victor nodded, still annoyed at himself, and not just for mixing up the message in his panic, but for escaping like a coward through the tunnel in the first place. It seemed all wrong.

He walked on in silence for only a few more paces, then stopped and turned to Magpen, overwhelmed. "I can't do this! I can't leave Master Nagai to die. He's like family. And those dragons came here to protect me! I'm going back—"

"Master, no!" His little servant seized his wrist in a viselike grip with his long blue fingers. "Magpen won't let you!"

"But he's my sensei!" Victor's anguished cry echoed down the tunnel, and tears rose briefly in his eyes. "He's going to die out there, like the stinking Noxu!"

"He pledged to Zolond he would protect you with his life, master, if the time ever came! And so did them stinky Noxus. So did I, for that matter!"

Victor shuddered. "Oh, Magpen, I don't want you to die for my sake, ever!"

The imp's bulgy eyes grew even wider with wonder. "Master...cares for Magpen?"

Victor remembered abruptly that he was the scion of all evil and only cared about himself. "Of course not. Don't be absurd."

The imp nodded, looking almost relieved. "Listen to your humble servant, Highness. Great Master Nagai trained you how to survive if calamity ever came. Do not disobey all he told you, now that it's here. And you can't ignore His Majesty's orders, even if mighty Zolond is just a ghost. You are Prince Victor—the heir to the Black Crown! If you go out there to help Nagai and get killed, Wyvern wins, don't you see? For now, we must go. But later, when you are all grown up, then you can come back and take revenge. Make the crown stealer pay for this night."

Victor gazed up angrily at the rough rock of the tunnel's low ceiling. "You really think they're going to give me the chance to do that, Magpen? To grow up?" He looked grimly at his servant again.

"Well, don't make it easy on them to kill you!" Magpen tugged insistently on Victor's sleeve. "Come, my prince, we must go! Look on the bright side. At least you're finally getting out of Shadowedge Manor."

"Not quite the way I envisioned it," Victor mumbled.

"But you'll get to see the world, sir, finally. And *girls*."

That got his attention.

Victor looked at him intently. "Well, I suppose there's that."

And the small fact that, if he was free, he would no longer have to endure Professor Labyrinth's ghastly hypnosis treatments to keep him in line.

Indeed, if he vanished right now, maybe he wouldn't have to become a Dark Druid at all.

He could be anything, go anywhere he pleased...

Then a muffled blast reached them from somewhere in the manor house above. Magpen glanced up fearfully at the tunnel's roof. "They are close," the imp whispered, "I can feel it."

So could Victor. And with that realization, his hopes of becoming some sort of free-wheeling grand tourist began fading fast.

Fugitive is more like it. Hunted by traitorous Dark Druids and their Drow assassins, he was probably going to have to lie low for the next decade.

But by then, if he lived that long, he'd be old enough to come back and destroy them all.

"Come, master, we must go!"

Resigned to his royal duty, Victor gave no further argument, but commanded the feebly glowing orbs to lead the way.

Then he followed them into the darkness with his servant, headed he had no idea where.

CHAPTER FORTY
Beacon House

That evening, Jake stared down at the black, swirling current of the river gliding by below the terrace at Beacon House. Alone and brooding, lost in his thoughts, he leaned against the stone-carved balustrade between two lanterns affixed to higher square pillars at regular intervals around the border of the terrace.

The lamps shone out feebly against the early-arriving darkness of October. It was barely seven but it looked like midnight.

Felt like it, too. With his unseeing gaze fixed on the lonely river view before him, Jake fingered the conch shell necklace he always wore around his neck. The one his mother had been wearing and quickly draped around him as a baby on the fateful day when Uncle Waldrick's betrayal had separated them.

Jake could not believe that today, some twelve years later, he had stood in the same dark cavern where the Dark Druids had been keeping his parents all this time. Aye, and most of all, he could not believe that he had left without them.

He shook his head as his painful thoughts moved on, gliding restlessly over the past, Time flowing by like the water beneath him.

The little conch that he rolled back and forth between his fingers gave him the ability to call on the water nymphs if ever he needed their help. (His mother had done them a favor back in her Lightrider days.) Derek had had Jake blow into it on the night the mysterious warrior had first brought him and Dani here, to Beacon House. The same night Derek had shown the two of them that magic was indeed real, and they were surrounded by a whole world that most humans had no idea existed.

The Guardian had proven his claims when Jake's unwitting puff through the seashell summoned Captain Lydia Brackwater of the

Thames water nymphs.

The green-haired guardian of the river had grabbed Jake off this very terrace and plunged him—literally—into a world of wonder he would not have believed possible. They'd traveled at top speed underwater as the fierce freshwater mermaid dragged him off to show him the home he'd come from: Griffon Castle.

That night, Jake had learned who he was, and his whole life had changed.

It had changed again today, to be sure, but once again, he had no idea where it all would end.

He only knew that his soul ached worse than his body did tonight, and that was saying something, after being beaten up by a dragon.

Why, he had barely recovered from his aerial battle against the dirigible before being carried off by Nightstalkers and then nearly eaten by a dragon.

But none of that had prepared him for the agony of today.

He could not believe Aunt Ramona was dead. A layer of shock still overlaid his churning loss and grief and pain, like a sheet of ice that formed on top of a lake in the winter.

It made no sense.

He could not stop thinking about her, her prim, pursed lips, the way she'd arch her eyebrow, her efforts not to smile when he and his friends amused her. He thought of her embroidery needle that sewed by itself because the Elder witch did not have time for such idle hobbies. He thought of her beehives at Bradford Park and that stupid mechanical monkey Jake had given her for her birthday. He wished now he would've given her a better gift...

When tears started to sting his eyelids again, Jake squeezed them back and reminded himself how young and happy she had looked with Celestus.

Still, he did not know how life went on without the ol' girl. After both Derek and Red had been captured by the Dark Druids, the indomitable curmudgeon had remained the one sure pillar in his life. Well, he was on his own.

And so was the Order, for that matter.

Without the Elder witch or Balinor, Jake could not see how this rupture thing was going to be fixed.

Straightening up from leaning on his elbows, Jake sighed and wondered if perhaps the damaged state of the Veil explained why the ghosts of London were so restless tonight.

Maybe they were the first supernatural creatures to feel the weakening of the usual barrier that separated the human and magical worlds, since they, too, straddled two realms—those of life and death.

True, he mused as he listened to the rattling of the dead leaves above him still clinging to the trees, ghosts came out more at night in general, and especially loved haunting in October.

But Jake could see several translucent spirits on and around the river right from where he stood. A ghostly drowned girl sat on a moored fishing trawler with her feet dangling over the side. A few minutes ago, a whole party barge of Renaissance aristocrats had floated by, entertaining themselves with jugglers and spectral music from their time.

Not long before that, a half-blown-up frigate from Admiral Lord Nelson's era had come limping slowly upriver from some Napoleonic sea battle, seeking its home port.

But it wasn't just the ghosts who'd begun to react to the Rupture. Jake had caught a snatch of some water nymphs' song as well. He gathered that the naiads were offering up a moonlit dirge for the fallen Elder witch.

Still, they knew full well they should not be weaving their alluring melodies this close to human populations. It was dangerous. People could become enchanted, wander into the river in a trance, and drown.

Jake marveled they'd even come this far downriver anyway, polluted as it was near the city. They must be really upset.

Still, they could not be as crushed as Jake's friends were. His heart hurt at the thought of them. They were inside Beacon House at the moment.

Each had retreated to separate bedchambers to weep and mourn privately. Isabelle was inconsolable; Nixie was furious with grief; Archie sat in the dark in a guilt-stricken daze.

Dani had cried so hard that the royal garden fairies (who loved her, and often congregated at Beacon House when they were off duty) had gathered around the carrot-head anxiously, trying to console her with kind words and flittering antics.

It didn't work.

Though Dani had found "Her Ladyship" intimidating, the Elder witch was the first adult who'd ever taken real notice of Dani O'Dell since her mother died. The dowager baroness had given the penniless Irish lass a chance—first, merely making her Isabelle's hired companion, but eventually, putting Dani forward for the Lightrider program, for the dauntless redhead had won no lesser prize by her deeds than Aunt Ramona's genuine respect.

So Dani kept crying, and not even Jake could comfort her.

Alarmed, Gladwin had finally sent her fairy friends to go fetch Teddy from Buckingham Palace. They had done so at once, bringing the wee dog to Dani so swiftly in their worry for their favorite that they didn't even care who saw.

But perhaps this was the new normal state of affairs in the world, now that the Veil had been torn: for ordinary folk to look out their windows at night and see a dog floating over the roofs of London, gently carried along by a tiny troop of fluttering fairies leaving sparkle trails behind them.

Humph. In any case, Jake knew that having Teddy back in her arms would help his poor carrot-head tremendously. What to do about the Bradfords and Nixie, though, he had no idea.

He wasn't even sure what to do with his own grief. There didn't seem to be much time for it. Wyvern had just seized power as the new Dark Master and had real plans—however insane they might sound—to take over the world.

Jake wouldn't put it past him, to be honest. But where *he* fit into Wyvern's dark fantasy at this point was difficult to say.

Wyvern had tried three times now to kidnap him. First, at Griffon Castle, then through the Nightstalkers, and finally, through Tazaroc. The Nephilim warlock could not be happy that Jake had slipped through his fingers *again.*

Maybe the sight of his dead dragon would finally help the madman get the message that Jake was never going to become the Black Prince.

And yet Jake's very victory today gave him fresh cause for fear. *He had better not take it out on my parents. He had better not take it out on my friends. Or the Order.*

You really think he's just going to give up?

No, Jake admitted as he watched a leaf swirl by on the current. If anything, Wyvern was only going to fight harder from here on out.

Perhaps, like the dragon after Jake had thrown it down the steps, the warlock's goal also would change from *capture* to *kill* when it came to him.

Anything was possible—especially now, with the rupture.

How Jake longed for life to go back to normal, but deep down, he knew it probably never would.

Just then, a voice spoke up behind him and nearly startled Jake out of his skin.

"There are you," came the deep, familiar baritone.

It was Derek—hardly a threat—but Jake clutched at his thumping heart, ridiculously startled. *Blimey.* Ah well, perhaps his jumpiness was understandable after the last few days he'd had.

The big, rugged Guardian prowled out through the double doors that opened off the enchanted library and joined Jake on the terrace with a frown.

"You shouldn't be out here alone. They could still be looking for you," Derek said.

Jake shrugged. "It's been quiet." *I can take care of myself.* Hadn't he proven that today? "Was there something you wanted?"

He just wanted to be alone.

Derek stopped across from him, rested his hands on his hips, and gave Jake an assessing stare. "It's time to go. I've been summoned back to Merlin Hall for an emergency meeting of the Elders, and I'm taking you lot with me."

Jake heaved a sigh, exhausted. "Can't we just sleep here? Mrs. Appleton—"

"No. I'm needed, and I'm not letting any of you out of my sight. Besides that, your aunt Claire and uncle Richard want their children brought back to them, posthaste."

"I can imagine," Jake mumbled. His cousins' diplomat parents might be a bit lackadaisical, but at least the glamorous pair attended *occasionally* to their children, instead of being locked up somewhere in a warlocks' castle.

Jake shook off a twinge of self-pity and glanced at his mentor. "Congratulations, by the way. I heard about your big promotion this morning."

Derek snorted in reply, as though taken off guard. His stern face relaxed a bit. Then he drifted over to sit on the wide stone balustrade near Jake. He shook his head wryly and folded his arms across his chest. "I hope Her Ladyship knew what she was doing."

"She usually does—did," Jake corrected himself with a wince. Then he turned his back to the river and slumped onto the balustrade beside Derek.

"By the way," said the warrior, "after my meeting with the Elders, they're probably going to want to interview you about everything you saw and experienced inside the Black Fortress."

"Tonight?"

"They might let it go until tomorrow, under the circumstances, but they'll probably say the sooner the better, before you have a chance to forget any details." Derek eyed him. "Think you can handle it?"

Jake let out a weary exhalation. "Why not? Won't be getting much sleep tonight anyway."

Derek studied him intently, his craggy face illumined in the golden glow from the nearby lanterns. "How are you, lad?"

Jake snorted. "Been better." Then he shrugged. "I dunno. I'm all right, I guess. It's the others I'm worried about. I was thinking, maybe Uncle Richard and Aunt Claire should take my cousins home to Bradford Park for a few days. Izzy would feel much better, I think, if she could see her unicorns, and Archie always manages to sort himself out after a few hours in his lab."

"Not a bad idea," Derek agreed, staring harder at him. "What about you? And don't give me that 'I'm fine' rubbish. I invented that. I know it when I see it."

Jake gave a wan smile and considered the question. "I just want this to be over. Whatever we have to do." He paused, recalling the Lightrider cavern. "I only wish..."

"What?" Derek asked while the river babbled by and the autumn leaves shivered on the branches above them.

"Derek—I was in there today!" Jake finally blurted out in frustration. "The very same cavern room Tex described, in the basement of the Fortress. I got away from the dragon and searched until I found the chamber where the Lightriders are being held. I was in the *same room* with my mother and father for the first time since I was a baby. I was so close! But I never even got to see them. I was so sure I could save them if I tried—"

"No, you couldn't," Derek said matter-of-factly.

Jake scowled.

"Jake, listen to me." Derek laid a hand on his shoulder. "Janos and Ravyn barely made it out alive the night they rescued Tex. They're both battle-hardened warriors, and there were two of them. You were just one kid. Don't do this to yourself. You did brilliantly today."

"You don't understand! I risked my neck to find them, but after all that, I'm no better off now than I was when these rumors first started and I found their empty caskets." Jake shook his head in dismay. "Just because what Tex said is true and that the cavern is real, that doesn't mean that my parents are still in there. I didn't have time to look for them, and that means I still can't be sure if they're dead or alive. This hope is what's killing me," he said, quite pouring his heart out for once. "Maybe I should just give up and tell myself they're dead, because this hope, not knowing...this is torture."

Derek fell silent.

Jake suddenly realized his mistake. "Oh—I'm sorry! I shouldn't use that word around you, after what you went thr—"

"It's all right. Jake..." Derek took a deep breath. "There's something I have to tell you."

The uncertainty in his voice nearly stopped Jake's heart. He pulled away. "No, please don't, if it's bad. I can't take one more thing—"

"It's not," Derek said quickly. "It's a good thing. I just wasn't sure...if you were ready to hear it. But I think now's the right time."

Jake relaxed slightly, but something in Derek's eyes worried him. "Very well."

The warrior stared hard at him. "Jake: your parents *are* alive. We've just had confirmation of it. Enough to convince even me."

Jake's mouth dropped open slowly. "You're joking."

Derek shook his head.

Jake's heart started pounding. He leaped to his feet. "What kind of confirmation? How? From who?"

"Waldrick."

"What?" Jake cried angrily. "He's a liar!"

"Just hear me out," Derek said.

Jake folded his arms across his chest and scowled, but waited to hear his wicked uncle's latest cock-and-bull tale.

"After you battled the airship and left through the portal with Dani, Waldrick defected from the Dark Druids. He came racing out of the Black Fortress and threw himself on the mercy of the Order. He surrendered to me personally."

Jake shook his head in disgust. "It's some kind of trick. Obviously."

"I don't think so, because I saw both Wyvern and Fionnula try to kill him before he reached us."

Jake mulled it. "Why would he do this? He must be up to something."

"He says it's because he *did* see your parents in that cavern with his own two eyes, and it shocked him back to his senses."

Jake narrowed his eyes, but his heart pounded with the yearning to believe. "He'd say anything to save his skin."

"Perhaps. But Waldrick says he wants to clear his name and try to get his life back. He swears he didn't murder them, and the fact that his supposed victims are still alive is his proof."

"Proof..."

"Aye," Derek said. "Waldrick wants them rescued now almost as much as you do—only for more selfish reasons." Derek shrugged. "That's what he says, and I believe him."

Jake pondered the news with guarded fascination. Derek Stone was no fool.

"You see," the warrior continued, "after the Black Fortress left Merlin Hall and things there started calming down, I went in and interrogated Waldrick myself. I thought he might know where the Dark Druids were headed next. He didn't. He claims he does have *other* information to barter, but seeing your parents was ultimately what drove him to change sides."

"Again," Jake pointed out sarcastically.

Derek did not argue that point. "Apparently, Waldrick also did some sneaking around while he was in the Black Fortress. He found the same underground cavern room that you did today. But, unlike you, with no one chasing him, Waldrick had more time to look and managed to locate your parents. Seeing Jacob's face again shocked him back to his senses."

Jake thought of the blond man in the family portrait back at Griffon Castle and swallowed hard. "He's sure my dad was still alive? Not just preserved somehow?"

"Your father opened his eyes and looked right at him."

Jake drew in his breath.

"Your mother was in the alcove right above your father. Waldrick *did* look to confirm it was she, but then he had to get out of there because one of the scientists noticed him."

Jake sat down hard on the balustrade.

"How's that for your reward after slaying a dragon today?" Derek asked.

Still struggling to absorb the news, Jake looked again at his mentor. "You really believe him?"

"Aye. I know a lie when I see one. He was tellin' the truth."

Jake blew out a quiet breath and sat dazed for another moment, his pulse fluttering.

A ghostly ferryman rowed by on the Thames, whistling a sea shanty.

Jake ignored the specter and glanced again at Derek. "Do you really think we'll ever get them back?"

"I think we just might, lad. We just might." The warrior gave Jake's shoulder an encouraging squeeze, but Jake flinched and could not hide his grimace. Derek quickly lifted his hand. "What is it? Blast it, boy, you're hurt all this time and you didn't say anything?"

"It's not serious!" Jake assured him. "That's just, um, the shoulder I landed on when the dragon threw me like a dog toy. Ow."

"Sorry." Derek shook his head with a chiding look. "You gave us quite a scare today."

"That makes two of us," Jake muttered.

"Well, you came back. That's all that matters." Then Derek slapped his hands down onto his thighs and pressed up from the balustrade. "Right! That's enough jawing. We need to get going." He headed for the double doors. "Let's have one o' the healers take a look at you when we get to Merlin Hall."

"I'm fine!" Jake gathered his strength and heaved himself up from his cold perch on the balustrade.

"Just do it," Derek replied, then eyed him strangely as Jake went toward him.

"What?"

The warrior shook his head again with a rueful laugh. "I can't believe you slew a dragon today, you little scamp!" As soon as Jake was in arm's length, Derek rumpled his hair affectionately.

"Hey!" Jake swatted the callused hand away. "You know I hate that!"

"Why do you think I do it?" Derek flashed a roguish grin while Jake scowled and quickly fixed his hair again.

Then the big man opened the library doors and gestured Jake in with a flourish. "Your Lordship."

Jake snorted and tried to look disapproving as he stepped into the enchanted library.

Derek pulled the terrace doors shut and locked them. The Inkbug watched them pass as they strolled across the room.

Then the warrior slung his arm around Jake's shoulders, taking care not to hurt him. "So," he said. "You killed a dragon, eh? Clearly, I am an excellent trainer."

"Oh, I see, so you're gonna take the credit for my heroics?"

Derek laughed and rumpled his hair again, much to Jake's annoyance. "I'm bloody proud of you, lad."

Warmed by his words, Jake smiled up at the towering knight. "And here, I was worried you'd be annoyed. You like dragons."

"Yeah, but I like you better, I suppose. C'mon, then." Derek released Jake and walked ahead of him into the narrow passage at the entrance of the library. "They'll be waiting for us in the foyer," he said over his shoulder. "Helena already rounded up your mates. You were the last straggler."

"How are you taking us, anyway? I hope you don't expect poor Dani to open another portal."

"Nah. Got something else in mind." A mysterious smile played at Derek's lips as he looked askance at Jake.

"What, the train?" Jake hoped so. He liked train rides. "Did you get us a private car?"

"Nope."

"Oh." Puzzled, Jake followed Derek through the passage. "So, we're just taking a carriage, then?"

"You'll see." With that, Derek opened the door and walked out into the stately foyer, where Jake had recently given Mrs. Appleton such a dreadful scare.

As Jake's eyes adjusted from the dark terrace and dim library to the brightly lit foyer, he beheld the rumpled, ragtag sight of all his dispirited friends.

Already wearing their coats, they leaned, stood, or slumped around the room, dazed, red-nosed, puffy-eyed, lost.

Except for Brian, who sat patiently on the ornate wooden staircase, they hardly looked like the same bunch who'd thrashed Archeron Raige this afternoon. At the sight of their heartbroken faces, Jake felt his improved mood from Derek's praise start sinking back down again.

About two dozen fairies hovered anxiously around the kids or perched on the banister to watch the proceedings.

Derek went over to Miss Helena, who was back in human form and smartly dressed once more in a chic little hat and an elegant bustle gown, the cord of her satin handbag draped over her wrist.

The fashionable French governess was leaning her shoulder against the wall and conversing in low tones with Mrs. Appleton.

"Pardon, ladies," Jake heard the Guardian say. "Is everyone ready to go?"

The governess nodded, but her golden-green eyes flicked a worried glance over at the kids.

Derek followed her gaze, skimming the group protectively. Then he gave his fiancée a stoic look. "I'll go make sure we're all set to travel."

"Mayweather should have the carriage ready by now," Mrs. Appleton said as Derek started walking away.

"Good. I'll go see if he needs anything." Derek headed off down the hallway to the kitchens and exited by the same back door where the kids had entered Beacon House last night.

The coach-house was out that way, behind the manor. *Wonder why he was acting so mysterious. Nothing special about a carriage ride.* Jake would've rather taken the train. It was faster, anyway.

"Where did you go?" Dani asked as she shuffled over to Jake, holding Teddy in her arms.

The sight of her gave him a pang. Her eyes reminded him of Christmas decorations, all green and red.

"Outside." Jake gave Teddy a scratch under his fuzzy chin. "How's he doing?"

"He's all right." Dani's lips trembled the way they always did when she was trying not to cry. "I'm sending him back to Buckingham Palace."

"You are? Why?" Jake asked.

"Things are too chaotic at Merlin Hall for a little dog now. And the Queen's house is sure to be the safest place in London. Besides, the Dark Druids are after the Order, not so much the human world."

Jake gazed at her with compassion as Gladwin swooped over from atop the newel post to hover beside the two of them at shoulder height.

"Don't worry, Dani," the five-inch fairy courier said solemnly in her little, tinkling voice. "I give you my word: I will take care of Teddy personally." She pressed her tiny hand to her chest. "It would be an honor after all you and Jake have done for me."

"Thanks, Gladwin." Dani sniffled, fresh tears glistening in her eyes.

Some of the other fairies flitted over and chimed in with promises that they'd help look after Teddy too, but Dani was sad to leave her dog behind anyway, even though it was safest for him.

Moved by her misery, Jake gathered his dear redhead and her dog both in a hug for a long moment. While he held them, his gaze wandered to the others. Isabelle just stared into space. Nixie and Archie stood side by side, but both seemed to be in their own worlds.

Not good, Jake thought. He had never seen them like this before.

All of a sudden, an announcement rose from behind him.

"Ladies and gentlemen," Mayweather intoned, "your carriage awaits."

Jake hadn't even heard the old butler come in. He released Dani and the dog, turning to find Mayweather standing at the edge of the hallway down which Derek had vanished a couple of minutes ago.

The old man's cheeks were pink with exertion, his thin white hair windblown around his balding head. Jake was just glad he wasn't holding a shotgun.

"It's time to go, everyone!" Miss Helena said primly.

"Then I guess this is goodbye." Dani kissed her dog's fuzzy head. "Be a good boy, Teddy. Listen to the fairies, and don't embarrass us in front of the Queen."

Gladwin gestured to her colleagues, and about half of the fairies zoomed around Dani and her dog, leaving sparkle trails behind in all directions. Jake got out of the way as Dani carefully handed Teddy over to the troop of fairies.

As they floated him in midair amongst themselves, Teddy looked quite safe and perfectly content.

The odd sight of the wee brown terrier borne aloft by a dozen always-confident royal garden fairies roused a faint smile from Dani, from Nixie, even from Isabelle.

Then the redhead nodded to let the fairies know she was ready; Gladwin and Rosebud got the front door, then the group of fairies carrying the dog flew out, up, and away at a smooth, steady pace.

Dani waved goodbye through the open door until Jake caught her hand and gently pulled her away, determined to distract her before she started crying again.

He didn't think he could take any more tears tonight from anyone, himself included. He shut the front door, gave her a reassuring smile, and then tugged her along by her hand after their friends. The others were already shuffling down the hallway toward the back door.

"Bye, Mrs. Appleton," Jake and Dani said.

"Goodbye, dears." The portly housekeeper waved. "Stay safe, now, you hear?"

"Let's go, ladies!" Gladwin called, and the *other* half of the royal garden fairies who'd remained behind buzzed down the hallway after the kids.

Some zoomed ahead out the door, which Archie was holding open for everyone, ever the English gentleman, even in a daze of grief.

All of a sudden, Jake stopped. "Where's Red? Blimey, I almost forgot him!" He turned around and strode back into the foyer while Dani continued outside.

"Red!" Jake shouted toward the top of the stairs. "Here, boy! We're leaving!"

"Um, Jake, he's already out here!" Isabelle called from outside.

"Oh," Jake said to himself. Then he turned around and joined the others outside in the black, chilly night.

But he had no sooner stepped through the back door than he grinned at the unexpected sight awaiting him.

Hitched to the large black carriage waiting for them out back was...the Gryphon.

"What's this?" Jake asked, laughing, as he closed the door behind him.

Even his friends had come out of their deep gloom enough to look amused.

"I thought we'd travel in style tonight." Derek opened the coach door, which was emblazoned with the yew-tree insignia of the Order. He gestured to the roomy interior. "Well, don't just stand there! Ladies first."

Miss Helena led the way, letting her beau hand her up into the coach. Izzy shrugged and climbed up next, followed by Nixie, Archie, and Brian.

Dani hesitated, frowning at Red with concern.

Inside the luxurious vehicle, which apparently belonged to Beacon House, the others started fluffing out carriage blankets and draping them over their laps for the long, cold journey through the night.

"Becaw!" Despite his fierce battle today against the manticore, Red seemed eager to play carriage horse, flicking his wings and pawing the ground.

"Uh, Derek," Jake drawled, "I'd never dream of questioning an *Elder*, but don't you think we're going to be just a bit conspicuous, riding down the road with a Gryphon pulling our coach?"

"And this is a lot of people for Red to have to pull!" Dani agreed.

Derek wagged a finger playfully at her. "Not if we're flying, my dear. Gladwin?"

"Coming!"

"Flying?" Dani echoed as Gladwin zoomed over to the Guardian.

Derek sent Dani a wily smile. "I'd get in if I were you,"

To Jake's relief, the redhead actually giggled and sprang up at once into the coach, nudging in beside Izzy.

"One second," Jake said, passing Derek to go and check on Red at the front of the carriage.

He scratched the Gryphon on the side of his feathery head. "You're sure you don't mind, boy?" Jake asked softly. "You got pretty beat up today."

Red snuffled, as though happy to ignore his own aches and pains to put smiles back on the kids' faces.

Jake gazed fondly at him. "You're a kind creature, Red."

The Gryphon nuzzled him, and Jake hugged the beast. He'd come awfully close today to never seeing him again, after all.

"Thank you for doing this, boy."

Red nudged him away, as if to say, *Go get in the coach!* Then he reared up in the traces, eager to go. With a chuckle, Jake went.

"Mind you lock the carriage door behind you," Derek said, strapping himself in on the driver's box and gathering up the reins as Jake walked by. "It'll be a long way down."

Jake gave him a casual salute, then heaved himself up into the coach and locked the door safely. But he moved to the middle of the padded leather bench to let the others sit by the windows—Dani on one side of him, Izzy on the other, Miss Helena squeezed in on the end. Nixie sat directly across from Jake, with Archie and Brian on either side of her.

"Everyone all right back there?" Derek called, releasing the brake.

"All set!" Miss Helena replied in a tone of amusement while Jake and his friends smiled at each other in the darkness.

"Red?" Derek said.

"Becaw!"

"Good! Ready when you are, ladies!" the warrior said to Gladwin and her fairy troop.

Jake leaned forward to watch out the window as Gladwin and her friends all took out their tiny pouches of sparkling fairy dust and started sprinkling it all over the carriage.

Sparkly plumes of gold, blue, pink, orange, green, and silver dust trailed past the coach windows like a meteor shower.

Everyone let out eager exclamations as the coach began lifting off the ground. Red flapped his wings, ascending with it.

Higher and higher they rose.

The second floor of Beacon House floated by, then the coach-house roof. Mrs. Appleton and Mr. Mayweather waved up at them from the ground, getting smaller and smaller.

"Don't drive too fast now, Guardian Stone!" the housekeeper called up to Derek.

Jake laughed. The next thing he knew, they were floating higher even than the ornate roofs of Beacon House, past the shining cupola.

"Ugh, I think I'm gonna be queasy," Brian said, pressing his back flat against his seat.

The fairies flew up with them, surrounding the vehicle; the tiny winged creatures steadied the coach whenever it tilted too much in any direction. (They were very strong for their size.)

The coach gave them some trouble when it passed through a windy stretch of the lower skies, not far above the treetops.

"Let's fly a little higher!" Gladwin yelled as the vehicle pitched and tossed a bit from side to side.

"That's all right," Brian mumbled.

Isabelle smiled ruefully at him, but the fairies doled out more of their shimmering dust and the carriage continued floating upward like a hot air balloon.

Soon, they'd cleared the windy layer and the coach leveled out, reaching a comfortable elevation somewhere between the low-hanging clouds beneath the spoked carriage wheels and the bright gibbous moon out the window.

"This looks like a fine cruising altitude, Red!" Gladwin called, her wings whirring just outside the coach window. She cupped her hand around her mouth. "To Merlin Hall, girls!"

The fairies cheered. "Let's go!"

Then Red flapped his wings and the airborne coach zoomed forward. The carriage shot through the dark sky while the lights of London glittered below. Jake caught a parting glimpse of Big Ben, but its glowing face did not make him as happy as it normally did.

It reminded him of all that had happened today—and Aunt Ramona. Their wondrous jaunt through the night sky helped soothe their heartache, but Jake knew that this day had left scars on all of them.

The kids looked around at one other in silence.

Then Jake took Dani's hand in one of his, Isabelle's in the other. Across from him, a soulful-eyed Nixie linked arms with Archie and Brian.

Nobody spoke.

Nobody had to.

This had been the worst day of their entire lives, but at least they were together.

Jake couldn't help thinking the ol' girl would have approved.

EPILOGUE

Angels

"Fine work today, Celestus."

"Why, thank you, Azrael. Your help was instrumental and very much appreciated. Cheers."

"Not a problem. Cheers."

The two angels clinked their icy-cold celebratory drinks together as they sat on the sweltering edge of the Ninth Pit, dangling their feet over the side of the canyon and enjoying the great fool that Shemrazul was making of himself with his temper tantrum over losing Zolond.

Meanwhile, a condemned soul continued inching toward them on hands and knees across the desert landscape of the plateau. He reached his hand out toward them, just a few feet away now. "Water!" he croaked. "Just one sip, I beg you!"

"Shove off!" Frowning with annoyance, Azrael aimed his Brightwield at the dead man and hurled him back into the flames with a white-hot zap of divine power, then took another carefree sip of the heavenly beverage.

Celestus eyed his friend in mild disapproval. "I think you enjoy doing that a little too much."

"Who, me?" The Angel of Death snickered.

Sentimental, he was not.

But the water of heaven was admittedly worth coveting, especially down here—clear, frosty bottles of health, life, rejuvenation. After all, this was no ordinary water. The exquisite libation full of fizzy bubbles flowed from the crystalline springs of the tranquil realm the two called home.

They were far from there now, of course. But even Celestus (who was known as a high stickler) could not stop his lips from twitching with amusement at how the lesser devils and lost souls wept and gnashed their teeth, watching the smallest droplets of condensation roll slowly down the sides of the sparkling bottles.

Azrael chuckled and took another swig. "Eh, I see no harm in tormenting them a little. I figure they brought it on themselves."

"True, true."

"Ugh." Azrael shook his head, staring down into the canyon. "Look at him down there. So dramatic!" They had a good laugh at their former colleague's ill temper.

The grotesque fallen angel, the would-be god, was throwing quite a tantrum, punching the sides of his pit and stomping his cloven feet, thrashing his tail and roaring, as if anybody cared.

"Zolond! I'll get you, you traitor!"

"You're not going to get anybody down there!" Celestus yelled.

"Hey, Shem! Want a drink?" Azrael heckled the Horned One. "Just kidding."

"Honestly," said Celestus, frowning at the beast's lack of self-control, "I don't know how he keeps his minions with these churlish displays. You'd think they'd have run away by now, considering how he's always blowing them up."

"There goes another one." Azrael pointed as an imp exploded with a cry, then Shem kicked a weird little eyeball monster into the lava. "They probably figure none of the other major devils would be any easier to serve."

"Probably right about that." In a philosophical mood, Celestus took another icy sip.

One of the nicest features of the heavenly beverage was that the bottle never ran out. You could drink all you liked and it always replenished itself. Which was good, as the hot breeze never stopped blowing through Hades.

"So." Azrael paused, held the cold bottle against his face, and swung his feet idly. "What do you think he'll do now?"

"Who, Shem?" Celestus snorted. "Go after the boy again, probably."

Azrael scowled. "Don't tell me you set any store by that mad Drow prophet's fevered hallucinations?"

"I don't know! I just do as I'm told."

"Wait—I thought your charge was Dani O'Dell," Azrael said, looking confused.

"Technically, yes, but nothing is more important to Dani than Jake."

"Ah, how cute," Azrael drawled.

Celestus ignored his friend's cynicism. "Still," he continued, "Jake is important in his own right."

"Even I know that," the death angel grumbled.

Celestus nodded grimly, then they both sat thinking while Shemrazul splatted the unfortunate Blobby against the canyon wall again.

After a moment, Azrael cocked a shrewd glance his way. "I should think the boy now sees the shape of the battle."

"Yes. He's not enthused."

"I wonder why!" Azrael laughed, then paused. "Think you can talk him into it?"

Celestus shrugged. "Jake has to choose for himself. They all do."

"Bloody free will." Shaking his head, Azrael leaned back and propped his hands behind him, then set his drink aside to flick some ash off his wing. The air was thick with it down here. "You have my sympathies, Celestus. Dealing with the living. I don't know how you put up with them all. The dead are hard enough to tolerate, always whining, 'Oh, I'm dead, I'm dead!' Why are they always so surprised? I mean, they *know* it's going to happen eventually, but then they're always so shocked when it does."

"They don't like thinking about it."

"They don't like a lot of things that are good for them. Like broccoli. Have you ever tried it, by the way?"

Both angels grimaced.

They sat for another thoughtful moment while the howls from below echoed up the canyon wall and the heated updraft blew their shining hair.

"So," Azrael finally said, "what are you going to do about Jake?"

He shrugged. "There's nothing I *can* do."

Azrael sent him a piercing stare. "Are you *sure* about that?"

Celestus furrowed his brow. "What do you mean?"

"The kid doesn't even have a weapon," he said.

Celestus gave his friend a searching look, then peered back down into the canyon. "Hmm... Perhaps there *is* something I could contribute. Even the odds a bit?"

Azrael flashed a knowing smile. "That's the spirit. Cheers." His silver eyes glowed as the Angel of Death clinked bottles again with Celestus. "To Jake."

"To Jake," Celestus mumbled, his mind churning. Then they drank.

The End

Dear Reader,

Whew! That was close. If you made it to the end of this book without getting eaten by the dragon, we congratulate you. Hope you enjoyed the story. For many of you, you thought this was going to be the last installment of The Gryphon Chronicles—*and we did too!* But that rascal, Jake, had different plans for us, his humble authors. Read on to find out how this BIG NEWS all unfolded...

We're Adding More Books to the Series!

From Eric: As many of you know, Book 7, *The Dragon Lord*, was originally going to be the end of The Gryphon Chronicles. But a funny thing happened on the way through the first draft...

You may have heard us share about our working method as a writing duo—how we plan and outline our stories together on big ol' white boards, then Gael writes the first draft and hands off each new chapter to me, then I go through it and find ways to make it even better. Sometimes *I* rewrite it, sometimes *Gael* rewrites it, and sometimes *we both* rewrite it many, many times (like Chapter 35, Tazaroc, which we must have passed back and forth 8 times, lol, until we LOVED it).

Now, even though Gael usually writes the scenes in linear order as they unfold, sometimes she gets inspired to jump ahead and work on one out of order. Being the right-brained type, she just flows with it.

Well, one day, the end of the book called to her—the actual final scene of the whole shebang. So, she started jotting down the dialogue between the two characters having a heart-tugging conversation, as often happens at the end of a book. (She cried, by the way. She does that sometimes when she's writing, lol. Or I'll hear mischievous giggling coming from her office at the funny parts.)

Anyway, she quickly drafted all the way to the end of this poignant little conversation—supposedly the final scene in the final Gryphon Chronicles book—when, suddenly, a strange thing happened...

Gaeley-girl, take it from here...

The True Story of How Jake Chewed Me Out

From Gael: First of all, I'm not crazy, lol. Okay, maybe a little. All writers are, they say, but I'm perfectly harmless, I assure you.

So I'm sitting there at my desk crying like a sap over this scene, and wondering how The Gryphon Chronicles could possibly be over. (These guys have been with us since 2010 when we first started brainstorming the series!)

But then something happened which has NEVER happened to me before in my twenty-plus years as a full-time author. They say some characters really come alive, and let me tell you, apparently, that's true, because...Jake burst into my office, banging the door open with his telekinesis, marched right over and planted his hands on the other edge of my desk, then glared at me over my computer.

"Lady!" he said angrily. "If you think I'm leaving any time soon, you're barmy. I'm not going anywhere!"

Me: looking around. *What is happening?*

Suddenly, a vivid image filled my mind of exactly what could happen NEXT in the series. Answer: a *whole* bunch of stuff. Important stuff!

And a huge smile broke across my face.

Jake sort of harrumphed, then faded back into Gryphon-world, satisfied he'd made his point, and I immediately shot up out of my chair and raced out of my office, yelling, "Honey, honey, you'll never believe this! The Gryphon Chronicles isn't over!"

And that, my friends, is the true story of how Jake got his way. (Heck, I wasn't about to mess with a doubler. Did you see what he did to those rock golems in *Secrets of the Deep*?)

So, hooray! We've got more fun to look forward to with our Gryphon friends. Several additional books beyond *The Dragon Lord* await and we are so excited to write them.

The adventure continues...

And to you, dear reader, thank you for reading our books! We so appreciate you!

The easiest way to be notified when these upcoming novels are released is to sign up for our Mailing List. (As a thank-you for subscribing, you'll receive a prequel short story entitled, *When Dani Met Jake*. Find out what happened in pre-magic days when these two rookery ragamuffins—and Teddy!—first crossed paths.)

Another bit of business that you may not know about and find useful, especially you parents and grands previewing books for the kids in your lives: Did you know we have our own little online store on our website, where you can order autographed paperbacks of our books (personalized either to you or your special someone if it's a gift)? We are also able to give our readers big discounts on the non-autographed paperbacks and hardcovers (audiobooks soon, too!) because we have the books shipped directly to you from the printer, so there's no middleman. You can really save some money, and who doesn't like that. Just a friendly FYI.

Final bit of business! If you love, love, love middle grade/younger YA fantasy books and would like to join a fun, friendly group of readers who share your interests, come join E.G. Foley's Magical Adventure Bookclub on Facebook!

It's a laidback meeting place for everyone who loves All-Ages Fantasy Novels. If you loved Harry Potter, devoured the Fablehaven series, whipped through all of Rick Riordan's fantastic Heroes of Olympus books, and so many other great fantasy series with wholesome content, this is the Facebook Group for you! All ages welcome.

If you're too cool for Facebook, lol, we can understand that, so we're also on Instagram. Hope to see you on either one.

Thanks again for reading our books. It's such a privilege to entertain you. And on that note, we had better get back to writing! *The Devil's Lair* waits *(mua-ha-ha)*...

Until then, much love!
Eric & Gael of
E.G. Foley
egfoley.com

Don't miss Jake's next exciting adventure...

Coming Soon!

THE DEVIL'S LAIR

The Gryphon Chronicles: Book 8

* * *

The Gryphon Chronicles

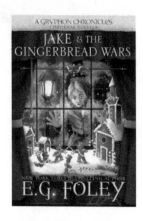

In case you missed it…

It's Jake's first Christmas with a family, but nothing's ever quite what you'd expect. Celebrate a Victorian Christmas with a Gryphon Chronicles holiday novella.

JAKE &
THE GINGERBREAD WARS

Peace on Earth, Goodwill to Men…And Gingerbread Men?!

Santa's Horrid Little Helper

Wanted! Humbug, the disgruntled Christmas elf.
Reward: One Christmas wish granted, courtesy of Santa.

Humbug hates being a Christmas elf. Instead of making toys, he'd rather make mischief. Angling for a new job in Halloween Town, he sets out to prove he's frightful enough for the task by ruining Christmas for as many people as possible—until Jake and his friends capture him. The kids set out on a rip-roaring adventure to the North Pole to hand the troublemaker over to Santa and collect the reward. But the way is fraught with danger, leaving them to wonder if they'll make it back in time for Christmas…or if they'll even make it back alive!

Turn the page for a Sneak Peek…

CHAPTER ONE
A Very Merry Mishap

"I know the Christmas pageant in the village means a lot to Aunt Ramona. I just don't see why I should have to be in it," Jake grumbled, only half in jest, as they wandered out of yet another shop. "Honestly—did you see the fake beard I have to wear?"

His three companions laughed, for they had.

It was dreadful.

"But you have to be our St. Joseph, Jake. You're the tallest," said Isabelle.

Jake looked askance at her.

Of course, his golden-haired cousin was quite content with her (very fitting) pageant role as the angel who would go and call the shepherds.

"Ah, well." He let out a longsuffering sigh, but deep down, he supposed he didn't *really* mind being made a fool of for his elderly aunt's sake at Christmas. It was just that, as a tough ex-street kid, he had a certain reputation to keep up. Especially now that it turned out he was an earl. "All I know is I'm going to feel completely stupid in that getup, standing out there in front. Everybody staring at me. Why can't I just hide in the back with Archie as one of the Three Wise Men?"

"You? A wise man? Sorry, Jake, you're not that good an actor," Dani O'Dell (their pageant Mary) teased. "I know!" The freckled redhead turned to him with a mischievous grin. "You could be the donkey!"

"Ha, *ha*." Though he gave her a sardonic look, even Jake could not help laughing any more than he could hide the holiday twinkle in his eyes.

It was all a little bewildering, in truth. He had never felt this ridiculously happy two days before Christmas.

For the first time ever, the holidays had put a kind of spell on him beyond anything that even a good witch as powerful as Aunt Ramona could've conjured. There was magic in the air.

Christmas magic.

He could feel it in the afternoon's light snowfall wafting over London. It dusted the cobbled streets around them like sugar and trimmed the bonnets and top hats of passing ladies and gents with its delicate, frozen lace.

This year he thought it very beautiful, but last year at this time he would have hated it, mainly because he would've been sleeping out in the cold most nights. Last year, instead of smiling at his fellow man with general goodwill, he would have been eyeing up the passersby with the goal of picking their pockets, watching for packages and coin purses he could steal.

Everything was different now, including Christmas.

The odd, merry mood had taken hold of him a few days ago, stamping his face with a slightly dazed smile, as if he had eaten a whole roly-poly pudding by himself. He felt so strange.

In the past, all the Christmases he could remember had been ordeals of torture, more or less. It was a day that made most of the kids back at the orphanage wish they were dead.

Ah, but this year, for the first time, Jake had something of a family. Not parents, they were dead, but two cousins and a few random adults who did not bother him too badly. (Very well, he quite adored them—not that he would ever admit to any such mushy sentiments out loud.)

He also had Dani O'Dell, his little Irish sidekick from the rookery. The carrot-head had taken charge of their Christmas shopping excursion, as she was wont to do in most matters.

"Indefatigable," Archie remarked, sauntering along, hands in pockets, as he watched the redhead march ahead of them, her mittened hands balled up at her sides.

Jake nodded vaguely, though he only understood about half the words that ever came out of the boy genius's mouth.

Dani stopped at the corner and glanced around, choosing which row of shops they'd tackle next. "Hurry up, you lot!" She beckoned to them when there was a break in the steady flow of carriages and stagecoaches, hansom cabs and delivery wagons rumbling by in both directions.

All the world was hurrying to finish up their yuletide preparations.

As for Jake and the others, their mission this day was almost complete.

Possibly the best thing about his new life as the rightful Earl of Griffon was that he now had the means to make Christmas a little less miserable for the orphans and assorted street urchins he had left behind in his old life.

If Father Christmas or St. Nick or Santa Claus or whatever the useless lout wanted to call himself could not be bothered to visit the orphans—which he never did—well then, Jake had decided, he would jolly well do it himself.

At all the different toymakers and linen drapers and food stalls they had visited today on their quest to gather presents, they had ordered everything sent to Beacon House, awaiting Christmas Eve delivery.

The trick was how to make the gifts appear magically, so the orphans would think that Santa had done it. They were still working on that. Maybe one of Great-Great Aunt Ramona's magic spells would do the trick...

Jake wished he could see their faces when they woke up on Christmas morning to find that Santa had finally remembered them, especially the little ones, like Petey, a six-year-old who used to follow him around everywhere and tried to be just like him. *Poor kid.*

"Isabelle." When they joined Dani on the corner, she gave the older girl a probing stare. "How are you holding up? Do you need a break?"

"Hullo? What about us?" Jake asked, nodding at Archie.

The other boy nodded eagerly. "We could use a break, too. Christmas shopping is *exhausting.*"

"We're hungry," Jake agreed.

Dani looked at him. "What a shock."

Isabelle laughed. "I'm doing fine, thanks. Better than expected, actually."

They all knew that being in the crowded city was difficult on Isabelle as an empath, picking up on the emotions of everyone around her.

She shrugged, reading the doubt on their faces—or, more likely, sensing it in their hearts. "Maybe I'm getting stronger or finally learning how to shield myself. But I think somehow it's just easier to be out and about this time of year." She glanced around at the busy street. "Most people just seem to be in a...kinder mood."

The four of them exchanged wry, knowing smiles, then paused to appreciate the holiday spirit that warmed the frosty air.

Carolers nearby sang "God Rest Ye, Merry Gentlemen." All the wrought-iron lampposts wore garlands of evergreen boughs tied with red ribbons. Sleigh bells jangled on the harnesses of the carriage horses trotting past.

But as to the question of whether to take a break from shopping, the mouth-watering smell of sweet cinnamon somethings baking somewhere nearby decided the matter for them.

"Maybe a snack *is* in order." Isabelle inhaled the enticing odor with a dreamy smile. "Is that gingerbread?"

Jake flashed a grin. "Let's go find out!"

They ran. Well, the boys did.

Isabelle was much too well bred to go pounding down an elegant London street like a wild heathen, thanks to strict training from her governess, Miss Helena.

Dani managed (just barely) to restrain herself to a sedate walk alongside the older girl, determined to be as ladylike as the older girl someday.

In any case, the boys were the first to reach what turned out to be not one, but two pastry shops crammed into one tall, narrow brick building.

On the left, a few steps led upward into a glittering, pastel jewel box of a bakery, whose sign read in flowing calligraphy: *Chez Marie Pâtisserie Parissiene.*

On the right, a few steps led downward into a snug, rustic, cozy space rather like a hunting lodge, its doorway proudly hung with the Union Jack and announcing in plain block letters: *Bob's British Bakery.*

The boys had difficulty choosing which way to go first.

If they had waited for Isabelle, the empath soon could have told them that the two renowned pastry chefs—Marie and Bob—had once been partners, but now were sworn foes. They did everything in their power to antagonize each other.

Especially Bob, who had got his heart broken.

But, being boys, Jake and Archie were oblivious to romantic matters for the most part. They went whooping down the stairs, past the pinecone garland and the life-sized toy soldier just inside the door.

"Welcome, gents," the mustachioed owner drawled. Bob himself was leaning idly against the counter talking about the latest sporting news with a few of his male customers: the London prizefights and the winter foxhunts going on out in the countryside.

The boys nodded back to him, then suddenly stopped in their tracks. "Ho! Look at that!"

They immediately rushed over to gawk at the gingerbread display: a towering castle with candy banners flying from the turrets. All around it, little gingerbread knights and soldiers were arranged as though tending to their duties.

There were even gingerbread horses with white-frosted manes, and gingerbread cannons loaded with peppermint cannonballs.

Meanwhile, the girls had been unable to resist the glowing chandeliers and silk-hung walls of the French-style pâtisserie upstairs. As they entered, Isabelle told Dani that "pâtisserie" was simply the French word for a pastry shop; Dani thought it a fun word to say and kept repeating it.

As it turned out, the owner, Mademoiselle Marie, had no intention of being outdone by her ex-beau, Bob, during this most important shopping season. She *also* had made a dazzling gingerbread display to lure in customers. But—she being French—hers was of course the height of elegance and whimsy, and in every way superior. One only had to ask her to confirm that this was so.

Marie had made a gingerbread Versailles with candy swans in the fountain and meringue shepherdesses tending marshmallow sheep. Wee cookie courtiers in service to the Sun King strolled through the candy formal gardens; gentlemanly ginger-men, fashionably frosted; noble cavaliers, prepared to fight for the honor of their crispy kingdom.

While the boys bought chocolate-dipped pretzel lances below, the girls gazed in rapturous wonder at Marie's marvel of baking artistry.

"What a lot of frou-frou," Archie said, glancing around, brow furrowed, when the boys joined them upstairs a few minutes later.

"Yes...isn't it wonderful?" Isabelle said breathlessly.

"Where have you two been?" Dani asked.

The boys told them about Bob's British Bakery downstairs, and the girls hurried down to the lower level to explore it, too.

The boys followed, and while Jake went to show the girls the castle, Archie was drawn to an old photograph on the wall of a cavalry regiment. Apparently Bob used to be a soldier.

"Looks like they're having a contest of some kind." Jake nodded at the sign beside the gingerbread castle inviting customers to vote on which display they thought was better.

"Aha, clever way of getting more shoppers in the door," Archie said as he rejoined them.

"I don't think that's entirely the reason these two have made a contest of it," Isabelle said under her breath.

They all glanced curiously at her, but she was too discreet to gossip about the ongoing lovers' quarrel she sensed between the two bakers.

Jake shrugged off her mysterious remark with a decisive nod. "We should vote, too."

"Let's!" Dani said. "I need to look at both of them again."

Bob glanced over in amusement as the kids barreled back up the stairs into Marie's dainty boutique to consider their choices.

Having already determined he liked the castle better, for it reminded him of the one he had inherited from his father, Jake wandered off hungrily to look around Marie's fanciful shop and choose another snack.

He had never tried French pastries before, but looking around, it was impossible not to be impressed. He had to admit those French knew their food, despite the centuries-old love-hate relationship between England and France. Thankfully, there had not been bloodshed for many years between the two countries, but most good loyal Englishmen, like most French folk, could give you a list off the top of their heads why their country was better than the one across the channel. And yet, at the same time, they secretly admired certain traits about each other.

Clothes, for example.

Every London lady simply had to fill her wardrobe with fine French gowns, while men's English tailoring ruled the streets of Paris.

As for food, well, most of the world had long since concluded that the French beat everyone in that category, except for maybe the Italians. Ah, but the British were better at sports and bred better horses, and, at least in their own opinion, told funnier jokes.

It was true the French were traditionally better at dealing out a witty insult with devastating style. But when it came down to a fight, Jake thought, ha! His country was better at war, as evidenced by the fact that they had trounced the French in the last one.

Ah, but of course all that was long before he was born, those bloody days of Napoleon versus England's Iron Duke. And as an avid fan of all things edible, Jake was quite prepared to let bygones be bygones. He drifted through the cramped, crowded aisles of Marie's shop, marveling at the exotic French sweets on offer.

He read the dainty placards with all the unfamiliar foreign names. The pastries were all such exquisite little artworks it almost seemed a shame to eat them.

There were rows of *Mont Blancs*, small whipped cream mountains with a candy perched atop each crest. There were *Opéras* with many thin layers of sponge cake held together by coffee syrup and topped with shiny chocolate ganache.

There was *Strawberry Savarin* dusted with powdered sugar and *Tarte Tatin*, a glossy puff pastry cradling caramelized apples. There were individual lemon soufflés and something called *Canelé*: tiny golden-brown bundt cakes. There were *éclairs* and *Napoleons*, *Fondant au Chocolat* and *Forêt Noire*. There were macaroons and *Lunette aux Abricots*, danishes that looked like pastry blankets wrapped around sleeping golden apricot babies.

But what stood out in glory, second only to the gingerbread Versailles, were the magnificent edible "Christmas trees" capping the ends of each aisle.

Jake heard a lady explaining to her husband that these were called *Croquembouche*, though she had never seen them made so large before. Creampuffs had been stacked up into pyramids like edible pine trees, held together by long ribbons of caramel.

His mouth watering at the splendid sight, Jake was wondering if his stomach had enough capacity for him to eat one all by himself. Probably yes, he mused, when suddenly, he noticed a whiz of motion from the corner of his eye.

The barest hint of a sparkle-trail followed as something went speeding along the top shelves of the shop, flush against the walls.

Startled, he looked twice, turning to catch a better glimpse, but he was too slow. It was already gone, the red-and-green sparkle-trail fading so fast that he wondered if he had imagined it.

Intrigued, he took a few steps out of the aisle and scanned the upper shelves, brow furrowed. Whatever it was, it had disappeared, but he was sure he had seen something.

Indeed, now that he noticed it, he could feel the slight tingling sensation at his nape that usually alerted him when something supernatural was close by.

Obviously, his first thought was to wonder if the shop was haunted. To be sure, there were ghosts all over London. It wouldn't have surprised him.

But as far as he knew, only fairies left sparkle-trails. Not even their nearest cousins, the pixies, had that particular trait. He knew because he had just met some in Wales.

Hold on—! An astonishing question suddenly filled his mind. *Is that how she's doing this—baking such amazing things? Has this French pastry lady got fairies helping her?*

Unfair advantage! Jake huffed in surprise, instantly indignant on British Bob's behalf. Well, typical, he thought. Leave it to a Frenchwoman to make her own rules.

His instant suspicion of Mademoiselle Marie would have to be forgiven.

Though he was only twelve, all British males were warned from an early age to resist as best they could those magnificent, impossible French ladies, who were famous worldwide for doing whatever they pleased.

Humph. Nobody liked a cheater.

He shook his head in disapproval, determined to even the odds in British Bob's favor—and to learn the secret of Marie's exquisite skill. He started prowling around the small, crowded shop, on the hunt for the fairy or whatever it was that had made that sparkle-trail.

Small as fairies were—five inches tall or so—it could be hiding anywhere. Jake searched the high shelves, the back of his neck tingling away, but he never saw anything—and yet he got the feeling after a few minutes that the fairy had definitely noticed *him* hunting for it.

Aye, he could feel it watching him. The creature must've realized he was on to its trickery. *I am going to find you...*

He searched the shop for several minutes more while his companions bought a few goodies to eat. Stalking down the middle aisle, he sensed that he was closing in. It was close, very close...

Determined to take it by surprise, he suddenly jumped out of the middle aisle and spun in midair like a startled cat, facing down the next aisle. "Ha!"

The other customers looked at him strangely.

Alas, the fairy was already gone.

Once again, he saw nothing but the green-and-red sparkles already fading. *No worries. You're a fast little devil, but you're mine.*

Hmm. As he continued his hunt, collecting a couple of treats to buy along the way, he mused on the fact that although he had met his share of fairies, he had never seen a sparkle-trail in those strong colors before.

The royal garden fairies he knew usually had gold or silver or pastel-colored sparkles.

Was there some specific kind of Christmas fairy? he wondered. Burning with curiosity, he crept down the aisle, and then stood on his toes to peer warily behind one shelf's display of cherry-laced *Clafoutis*.

The creature he was hunting must've started getting nervous about the danger of being caught, for suddenly, without Jake even noticing, it struck back.

Apparently, it hoped to get rid of him by causing a distraction.

"Timberrrr!" a small voice taunted.

And with that, the *Croquembouche* Christmas tree behind Jake started tipping over. He whirled around as the unseen speaker sped off with a snicker, red-and-green sparkles in its wake.

Jake gasped when he saw the *Croquembouche* toppling, sending a snowstorm of sugar-dusted cream puffs and macaroons flying through the air.

He started forward automatically, lifting his hands to use his telekinesis to try to save it—but thankfully, he stopped himself in time. It would have been a disaster for him to use his magical powers in public.

And so, there was nothing he could do but stand there and watch the beautiful, edible Christmas tree go crashing to the ground, destroyed.

It then occurred to him that, as the person standing closest to it, he was about to take the blame.

Aw, crud. Jake let out a sigh. *Story of my life.*

CHAPTER TWO
The Way the Cookie Crumbles

J ake hated being blamed for things he didn't do, but for some reason, that always happened to him.

Customers shouted and everyone leaped out of the way of the falling pastry tree. There were cries of dismay, then everybody in the shop turned in shock and glared at him.

He stepped back, wondering if there was any point in telling them it wasn't his fault. It was the fairy.

Right.

They'd haul him off to Bedlam.

A woman with dark eyes, a sharp nose, and a smudge of flour on her cheek came rushing out of the back with a look of horror on her face. "What have you done?" Her accent promptly informed him that this must be Marie, the *artiste* herself. "You will pay for zis!"

"Excuse me, it wasn't my fault," Jake said sternly.

He couldn't help it. Perhaps it was ungallant of him to refute her, but facts were facts. Besides, she was a cheater anyway, with her secret fairy helper. Unfair advantage over poor British Bob.

"*Mon Dieu!* Do you have any idea how many hours my staff and I have slaved over zat?"

"Aha, your staff, right," he drawled.

"What?" she spat. "Where is your mozeur?"

"My what?"

"Your mamma!"

He stiffened. "I don't think that's any of your business, madam."

"*Garçon horrible!* Not even an *apologie*? Give me back those boxes. You are not worzy to eat my creations!" She snatched the treats he'd chosen out of his hands.

"Ma'am, I did not knock over your...thing."

(He was not sure how to pronounce it.)

"Ha!" She snapped her floury fingers in his face. "Get out of my shop, and don't come back until you learn how to walk upright like a *personne*, not a shimpanzee!"

"Now, look here," he started in lordly high dudgeon. "I will pay for this mishap, even though it wasn't my fault." He took out his small coin purse with a look of reproach. "But I *don't* appreciate your calling me a liar."

Mademoiselle ignored him, suddenly glaring past Jake toward the doorway of her shop. *"You."*

Jake turned and saw British Bob leaning against the doorframe, looking amused by all the commotion.

"You put him up to zis!"

"My dear, I have no idea what you are talking about," Bob said with a mild smirk under his mustache.

"You sent this little *monstre* in here to wreck my shop!"

He folded his arms across his chest and said calmly, "Nonsense, you daft harpy. I told you the *Croquembouche* was a bridge too far, but no, you had to best me. Well, there you have it. Right again."

Marie unleashed a stream of angry French verbiage on him; Bob replied with maddeningly cool British sarcasm, and the two rival pastry chefs proceeded to spread the Christmas cheer by hollering at each other in the middle of the shop, ignoring all their customers—and unbeknownst to them, attracting the attention of a passing constable.

Jake's friends ran to him.

"What did you do now?" Dani exclaimed.

"Oh, thanks a lot," he retorted.

"I say! What is going on in here?" a deep voice boomed from the doorway behind British Bob.

Everyone looked over; Jake blanched. *Blimey.*

Of all the bobbies to respond, Jake saw it was none other than his old mustachioed nemesis from his pickpocket days, Constable Arthur Flanagan.

The policeman's stare homed right in on Jake; recognition flashed in his eyes, then he brushed his way past the angry bakers. "Well, well. I should've known I'd find this one smack in the midst of all the trouble."

"Good afternoon, Constable Flanagan," Jake said courteously through gritted teeth. Ah, the memories.

"Why, look at you, all dressed up like a gentl'man. Never thought I'd see the day!" Flanagan declared as he stepped in. "Got a whole new life these days, from what I read in the papers, don't ye? But I see you're still the same young rascal I remember. Up to your old tricks, eh, Jakey boy?"

"It wasn't me!"

The bobby laughed heartily. "Ah, how I've missed hearin' you say that." Then he quit laughing and resumed his usual warning glower. "What did you steal from this lady's shop?"

"Wot?" Jake cried, sounding like his old pickpocket self once more. "Nuffin'!"

"*Non,* Constable," Marie snapped. "He did not steal from my shop; he only half destroyed it."

"Tempest in a teapot as usual, constable," Bob said. "But that's the French for you, innit? Look, the lad already got out his coin to pay for the trouble—"

"He'd better pay," she retorted.

"Ah, leave him alone, Marie. He's just a kid and it's nearly Christmas," Bob grumbled. "I'm sure 'twas an accident."

"Fine. Just get him out of my shop. And don't come back!" she added, glaring at Jake.

"I said I was sorry!" Jake exclaimed, tossing the coin in her direction as Constable Flanagan took hold of his ear.

"Come on, you." He led him firmly out of the shop and deposited him in the snow outside.

"Ow!"

"You might be quite the fine young lord now, laddie, but I'm on to you," the bobby warned, wagging a finger in his face. "You'd better watch your step. The rest of the world might bow and scrape to ye now, but I don't care in the least if you're the Earl of Griffon or the Prince of Siam, mark me? You'll not be goin' about causin' trouble like you used to."

Dani elbowed Jake hard in the ribs to shut him up before he gave the tart rejoinder on the tip of his tongue.

"Happy Christmas, Constable Flanagan," she offered.

The bobby tipped his dark helmet to her. "Miss O'Dell. You look after 'im. He's not so grand nowadays that I won't still toss him in the Clink if he earns it."

"I will, sir. Er, give our best to your family?"

"Move along, children. *His Lordship* has caused enough mischief for one day." The bobby waved them off, raising a bushy red eyebrow at

Jake, who, scowling, righted his coat and harrumphed.

Dani took his left arm and Archie took his right, and they both steered him away from there before he was tempted to say something he'd regret.

Constable Flanagan kept an eye on them until they had gone off safely down the lane, then he moved along, on patrol once again.

"What just happened in there?" Archie demanded.

"I'll have you know, it wasn't me who knocked over that what-cha-call-it tree thing."

"Then who did?" Dani asked.

He pulled his arms indignantly out of their grasps. "A fairy or something," he muttered.

"What?" they exclaimed in unison.

"There's something weird going on in that shop—and I intend to get to the bottom of it," he declared. "How dare that woman yell at me like that? I do *not* deserve to be publicly humiliated for something I didn't even do!"

"A fairy," Archie repeated.

"Aye! That French lady's using magic as an unfair advantage over Bob, and that's not right! So, you know what I'm going to do?"

"Um, nothing?" Dani suggested.

Jake shook his head. "I'm coming back here tonight when the shop is closed, and I'm going to catch that meddling little creature and remove it. That'll teach Miss Hoity Toity Mademoiselle how we deal with cheaters here in England!"

"That's a terrible idea," Dani said. "She told you never to come back. If you get caught in her shop a second time, she could have you arrested."

"Especially after hours, when it's closed," Archie added.

"Well then. I won't get caught," he said.

"And why do you want to do this?" Isabelle asked.

"Obviously—it's a matter of honor!" Jake declared. "I am the Earl of Griffon and she called me a liar in front of all those people! Intolerable! Then Flanagan insulting me, too, when I didn't even do anything. I am not a pickpocket anymore! I never cause trouble!"

"Wellll," the others said in response.

Jake glowered. "Are you with me or not? Well, do as you like," he said, waving them off impatiently. "I can catch that rotten fairy by myself, if need be. But you're mad if you think I'm just goin' to take this. I will *not* be insulted and unjustly accused. A gentleman has to defend his honor. Right, Archie?"

"Uh, I guess so."

"Besides, Marie's a cheater, anyway. British Bob deserves a fair fight in that contest of theirs. A matter of honor, I say. My own—and England's!"

Isabelle shook her head with a sigh. "You're daft."

Jake ignored his oh-so-mature elder cousin, and held up his fist to rally his two most reliable followers, the younger pair. "For England!"

Well, it was worth a shot, anyway. But Archie and Dani merely exchanged a dubious glance.

ABOUT THE AUTHORS

E.G. FOLEY is the pen name for a husband-and-wife writing team who live in Pennsylvania. They've been finishing each other's sentences since they were teens, so it was only a matter of time till they were writing together, too.

Like his kid readers, "E" (Eric) can't sit still for too long! A bit of a renaissance man, he's picked up hobbies from kenpo to carpentry to classical guitar over the years, and holds multiple degrees in math, science, and education. He treated patients as a chiropractor for nearly a decade, then switched careers to venture into the wild-and-woolly world of teaching middle school, where he was often voted favorite teacher. His students helped inspire him to start dreaming up great stories for kids, until he recently switched gears again and left teaching to become a full-time writer and author entrepreneur.

By contrast, "G" (Gael, aka Gaelen Foley) has had *one* dream all her life and has pursued it with maniacal intensity since the age of seventeen: writing fiction! After earning her Lit degree at SUNY Fredonia, she waited tables at night for nearly six years as a "starving artist" to keep her days free for honing her craft, until she finally got The Call in 1997. Today, with millions of her twenty-plus romances from Ballantine and HarperCollins sold in many languages worldwide, she's been hitting bestseller lists regularly since 2001. Although she loves all her readers, young and old, she admits there's just something magical about writing for children.

You can find the Foleys on Facebook/EGFoleyAuthor or visit their website at www.EGFoley.com. They are hard at work on their next book.

Thanks for Reading!

CPSIA information can be obtained
at www.ICGtesting.com
Printed in the USA
LVHW040900290721
693966LV00001B/111